THE
TENTH
PLANET

What would you think if I were to tell you that there are not just nine planets in our Solar System, but ten? What if I were also to tell you the tenth planet was discovered over three hundred years ago by an Irish nobleman and soldier of fortune? And what if I were to tell you this Irishman visited this tenth planet in the year 1649?

His is a record of one man's harrowing experiences in a strange world fraught with danger and extreme beauty, and it is also the tale of a three-century-old battle and of one man's attempt to change its course and that of history.

On these pages flow a man of great integrity. A man once of national acclaim in his own country. A man who rose to lead a nation, only to be branded a traitor by the very people he endeavored to save! Should this record be true, perhaps this writing might serve to vindicate a name that for centuries has lain in disrepute . . . struck from the very pages of history he helped to write.

This then is his adventure as he set it down over three hundred years ago. While I have no reason to believe that it is true, I neither have reason to believe that it is not. *You must judge for yourself!*

WARLORD

OF

GHANDOR

by
Del DowDell

DAW BOOKS, INC.
DONALD A. WOLLHEIM, PUBLISHER

1301 Avenue of the Americas
New York, N. Y.   10019

FIRST PRINTING, AUGUST 1977

1 2 3 4 5 6 7 8 9

PRINTED IN U.S.A.

Foreword

〰〰〰〰〰〰〰〰

What would you think if I were to tell you that there are not just nine planets in our solar system, but ten? What if I were to also tell you the tenth planet was discovered over three hundred years ago by an Irish nobleman and soldier of fortune? And what if I were to tell you this Irishman visited this tenth planet in the year 1649?

I'm crazy, you'd say? Out of my gourd? Hallucinating? Ask any grammar school student, you'd say, and he will tell me there are nine planets in our solar system. Any high school student, you'd say, can tell me the last planet to be discovered was Pluto, identified in 1930 by the United States astronomer Clyde Tombaugh. The most highly skilled astronomer, you'd say, would tell me that other than the numerous asteroids in our solar system, of which Ceres is by far the biggest in mass, no other heavenly bodies will be found between the sun and the orbit of Pluto! Of this they will be emphatically sure. Of this, they will say, there can be no doubt! But of this, I reply, they will be wrong!

In August, 1649, a soldier of fortune and an Irishman by birth, set foot upon the tenth planet in our solar system. This globe, called Ghandor, meaning "homeland" in the language of its inhabitants, revolves in an orbit 92,950,000 miles away from our own sun. This planet is approximately 4,000 miles in diameter and is visible either by the eye or through telescope from every planet within our system save that of our own Earth! The reason no earthly scientist or astronomer has ever seen this planet is because it occupies the exact same orbit as that of our own world, and is always on the far side of the sun from us!

Giving these figures to a local astronomer friend of mine, Vincent LeCourtiere by name, I asked him if, hypothetically of course, another planet could exist in our own orbit on the far side of the sun, and if so, how would it have come to share our identical path.

"There could be many reasons," he replied one night over a friendly game of chess. "In the early creation of our own planet this other world might have been part of the original mass. Due to diverging gravitational pulls of our own sun and other forces about which we may know nothing, the two masses could have separated. If this other planet is only about half our size, probably it was swept into a faster rotation around the sun than our own world. This would mean, of course, that sometime in the future it would be visible to us and eventually would catch up with our own planet along this identical orbital path. Eventually the two would collide, but first tremendous gravitational pulls would be effected."

He seemed to warm up to his subject. "Of course," he said, "oceans would change, mountains would collapse, and earthquakes and tidal waves would occur all over the planet. Thank goodness your question is only a hypothetical one!" he added emphatically.

I could not at that time bring myself to tell him it was a very real possibility to me. All I had to back up my claim was a manuscript of questionable origin, written perhaps more than three hundred years ago. But then I am getting ahead of my story. Let me start at the beginning.

The science of genealogy, which is a systematic effort of searching for one's ancestors, has always been one of my interests. There have been great fortunes spent by men trying to prove they were a descendant of this or that family—men who were trying to prove they were something that perhaps they were not. There have been others who created their own family tree as it pleased them. And still others so intent upon whom they wanted as their progenitors that they swept records and facts aside in their pursuit of desirable ancestry.

To these and many others like them, genealogy is not a science but a means by which they can "prove" whatever they want to prove. Truth and factual history mean nothing to them.

While the genealogical woods are full of such persons, there are others who have an honest desire to know who their ancestors really were and do not care that some may well have been the proverbial black sheep! It is among this latter group that I have long labored. Since each subsequent generation backward doubles the amount of surnames that belong to one's family tree, there is never an end to the work that could be done. Though I have traced many of my lines back into medieval times, I have never succeeded in learning as much about the DowDells as has been my dream. Nor have the many other family members who have made the attempt been able to come up with the answer, even after more than fifty years of expensive and time-consuming research.

Consequently, it was with great interest and a certain amount of excitement that I received a letter from Ireland from whence, it is said, the DowDells came. The letter contained a lead as to the whereabouts of documents once belonging to a branch of the Dowdall family of County Antrim, later removed to County Armagh.

This information seemed to fit with other research on the suspected ancestral homeland of our Dowdall progenitors, so I sent off a check in the requested amount and asked that they send me all the documents and records in the Dowdall collection. Not long after, a large package was delivered to my door bearing several foreign stamps of that island country.

It was with great interest that I tore into the package. Would records be enclosed showing information that would fill in the many blank spaces of my research? Excitedly, I ripped away the last wrapping only to be sorely disappointed, for rather than documents showing births, deaths and descendants, all the package contained was a mottled manuscript of some antiquity. There were more than two hundred pages of soiled parchment upon which someone had written with a fine, flowing hand. The characters bore out the definite age of the manuscript, and the ink was very faded from age. Each page was covered on both sides. The handwriting was strong, denoting a strength of character and aggressiveness not often found in such ancient records. With mounting curiosity I began reading the barely visible script.

The story that unfolded shook me to the very depths of my being. On the parchment was written a tale so unbelievable that it tested the very limits of reason.

After reading it through twice, it seemed the least I could do was to set this story down so all may read and decide for themselves. Was this man truly a traitor, as history has so carefully inscribed? Or did he really encounter circumstances beyond his control that whisked him off to an adventure so strange, so unbelievable, that it passes the bounds of all reason?

Not only is this a record of one man's harrowing experiences in a strange world fraught with danger and extreme beauty, it is also the tale of a three-centuries-old battle and one man's unsuccessful attempt to change its course and that of history.

On these pages flow a man of great integrity, a man once of national acclaim in his own country. A man who rose to lead a nation only to be later branded a traitor by the very people he endeavored to save! Should this record be true, perhaps this writing might serve to vindicate a name that for centuries has lain in disrepute ... struck from the very pages of history he helped to write.

This, then, is his adventure, as he set it down over three hundred years ago. While I have no reason to believe that it is true, I neither have reason to believe that it is not. You must judge for yourself.

CHAPTER ONE

My name is Robert Dowdall, the Fifth. I was born in the year 1619 in County Antrim. My home was a small village town called Glenarm overlooking the channel between Ireland and Scotland. My father was called James, as was my older brother. I had three other brothers, all younger, named Patrick, Egan, and George. I also had a sister, Elizabeth, named after my mother who was an O'Faolain and right proud of it, too!

I was named after an uncle who was a Member of Parliament until Cromwell's invasion and the subsequent shifting of power to the hated English.

We Dowdalls were always a proud people, having lived upon the Old Sod of Eire for more than five hundred years. The Dowdalls were originally from Scandinavia by way of Normandy. We entered England with the Conqueror in the eleventh century. There had been a Dowdall with Rollo the Dane when he successfully attacked Paris and defeated the French king. As a result, the Dowdalls held large estates in Normandy, but gladly left them to join with William to conquer the English at Hastings two centuries later. It was said that the Dowdalls fought gallantly upon the hill of Hastings, turning the English flank and helping to win the day.

It was while the Dowdalls were in England as Norman Conquerors that they adopted the Christian method of surnames. My ancestors lived in a valley overrun with doves, and they took the surname of dove dale, or DowDell, after the Norman custom. The spelling was changed to Dowdall a century later when they entered Eire.

The Dowdalls were not English implants but conquerors of Old Eire in the twelfth century. Absorbed by the Green, the name became as Irish as O'Fallon throughout Ulster, but the sixteenth-century settlement of Northern Eire by unlawful grants of the English Crown to English and Scottish settlers robbed us of most of our land and wealth.

It was because of this and many other similar injustices that my father, forced to move from our ancestral home, came to Armagh. But being a proud man, he did not take the injustice of it all for long. Finally he rose up in rebellion, and the Clans joined him. The Clans dealt the English a crushing blow in the Ulster battles of the early 1640's that eventually took my father's life. The day he was struck down he had led the Clans in glory, and the English would not soon forget!

Word of his death reached me, but since no new wars seemed imminent, I chose not to return home. I had spent many years in Paris and elsewhere on the Continent under the tutelage of master swordsmen and artisans of the royal courts, and with my father gone and no family left for which to return, I desired to see more of the world. But it wasn't many months later that the Clan called me home. England was rising in anger and was upon my homeland.

My father, James Dowdall, sometimes called The Fair, had been a popular leader and one of the Sod's favorite sons. It had been his magnetic personality more than his fighting ability—though he was gifted in that, too—that had banded the Clans together, overcoming their natural animosity toward one another in the Ulster Wars. With him gone, the Green would be hard-pressed to rally around any single banner, since so much jealousy and fear split the peoples of my homeland.

The messenger that found me at the Danish Court held that I was the Old Sod's only hope. So full of the blarney was he that I sent him packing. Fighting was not my intention, anyway. My father had sent me to the Continent when I was sixteen. His intention was to keep me from becoming entangled by the bloody wars that had racked my island homeland for a hundred years. His vision of the future was a grim one.

"Scotia*" will never be able to hold out against the

---

* I at first thought Robert had referred to Scotland by its ancient name and therefore was confused. However, in looking up the ancient history of Ireland, I found that as late as the eleventh century Ireland was called Scotia and its people called Scots. Supposedly the name was derived from Scota, the daughter of the Pharaoh, one of the ancient female ancestors of the Milesians (Eber or Heber being the first Milesian King in Southern Ireland). The modern name "Ireland" seems to have originated

English," he had told me on my fifteenth birthday. "Alba†
fell to them and eventually so will the Green. The English
are a conquering nation and desire to tell the whole world
how to live. You mark my words, boy, Scotia will someday
fall and the falling will be a terrible thunder felt throughout
the land. There will be a great suffering of our people that
will make the plague, the one that exterminated the Par-
tholanians, insignificant. You mark my words, boy!" He
seemed to have a distant look in his eyes, but then my father
was often given to visions and mystical insights.

The next year he shipped me off to the Continent. There I
wandered for nearly fourteen years under the special supervi-
sion of some of my father's old friends and retainers, always
kept away from battles and wars. At first I was rebellious
about not being allowed to join my father against the English,
but as the years went on and the wars continued with seemingly little effect, I grew less and less interested in them. Finally, when Gault found me at Court in Denmark in May, I
considered myself more of a Continental than from the land
of my birth.

But in June, Gault returned with two Clan chieftains. We
met in Council, and Willard of Wexford talked long into the
night and through the next day trying to persuade me into
coming home. It took three days of his slick tongue to wear
me down, and I think then I only began to believe half of
what he said.

I found it difficult to believe, for example, that some puritan named Cromwell was mounting an invasion force to sail

---

with the Northmen in about the seventh century and was later
solidified by the English. The fact that Robert's father, James,
refers to his country as Scotia would appear to indicate that the
old clansmen still clung to the ancient name as late as the seven-
teenth century. Very possibly the terms "Ireland" and "Irish"
were not totally adopted until after England's domination of
Ireland following Cromwell's devastating defeat of the island.
The fact that the Northmen referred to the island as *Ir* or *Ire*
from the Gaelic term *Eire*, and that it was the English that
anglicized this to Irish and Ireland, may be the reason that Robert
never once refers to his homeland as Ireland or his people as
Irish.—DD

  † Alba was the original name of Scotland, and it was changed to
Scotia and its people to Scots because the Scoti of Hibernia,
having again and again colonized there, built in it a strong kingdom
which gave the Scotic (Irish) people dominance there.—DD

against the Green. We had heard stories of Cromwell ousting King Charles at Court, and many were the voices that laughed at this puritan upstart. But as we traveled home secretly through England, I learned the horror of this man's intentions. His intention was to level every town and kill every man, woman, and child of the Old Sod.

I arrived in Eire to find dissension splitting my island home. O'Neill had been called back from the Continent some time before and had become the national leader to most of the Old Irish Clans after my father's death. General Preston had also been called back from exile on the Continent and placed in charge of the Catholics and Old English, since O'Neill held no sway with them. Between these two leaders and several other fragmented groups with their own leaders they tried to rally the Irish Clans into one fighting army, as my father had done the previous year. As I set foot on the Old Sod, I learned quickly enough that none of these had been able to rally the Clans to one banner.

I found the Clans in bitter argument. No one trusted another. The English threatened, but the several leaders were more concerned about their own petty grievances than the threat of English conquest. No successful force could be marshaled. It was for this reason that some of the farsighted Clan chiefs had called me home and sent Willard to fetch me when Gault had failed.

In a grand council of the Clan chiefs, I rose to reconcile the dissenting forces. There was much I had to say, and all listened. For four hours I spoke, that being one of the Dowdall gifts in life ... to pass along the blarney and keep the girls spellbound. But for a different purpose it was being used that day! All within ear of my voice eventually came to agreement that I would lead the Clans in the repelling of Cromwell's invasion, for the Dowdalls had held sway with all the Clans. My father had always treated everyone and everything fairly. At a time of jealousy and petty Clan grievances, they once again relied on the Dowdalls.

We gathered thirty thousand Clansmen around our banner, a shamrock-green background with a gold harp decorating its middle. Thirty thousand men were marching on Drogheda where Cromwell had sworn to land. I felt mighty proud of the grand old Clans, waving their individual banners to the heavens. It was a fight the English wanted, and it was a fight we were going to give them!

It would have been a glorious day for Old Eire. The English thought they were going to catch us with our kilts down, but they were the ones who were going to be in for a surprise. The English had been desirous of our tiny island for centuries and felt they could implant their people and religion all across Eire. But we were determined to put an end to it. Ulster had been the beginning. Now it was time the Old Sod stood up and said, "Enough!"

Oh, but if only my amazing adventure had started upon another night, history would surely have been different! Cromwell would have suffered defeat, and my beloved Eire would not have had to suffer so much, nor have had so many of her native sons and daughters lost to her forever. But it was not to be. Lady Luck beckoned her fickle finger, and I was spirited away on the very eve of Cromwell's landing.

There is no doubt, of course, that we would have kicked the pants off the English and booted them clear back across the sea had our plans gone the way I laid them out. Since it was only my person, though, that could guarantee all the Clans would fight, the glory was not to be. The other leaders, even O'Neill and Preston, could not have gotten all the laddies together for that great battle. Nor was the Anglican Butler, the exiled King Charles' lord lieutenant, able to mold the thirty thousand fighting men together that had followed me to the hills outside Drogheda. And a proud battle it would have been, too.

But Lady Luck had her way, and on the day of battle that was to have seen Cromwell stopped, I was nearly two hundred million miles away. The Clan chiefs, fighting for leadership of all the Clans, ignored my plans in their petty squabbles and consequently lost the day. Oh, the thirty thousand laddies were ready, make no mistake about that, but an army needs a leader, and with me gone and the other chiefs squabbling, the laddies broke and allowed Cromwell to gain a foothold on the Green with his devastating cannon.

The Clans did well enough after they regrouped, but the spirit wasn't in them. They had lost their leader and didn't quite know what to do until it was too late. The butcher Cromwell decimated Drogheda and Wexford, murdering every man, woman, and child he could lay his hands upon. Of course you know all that, for it is history. What you won't find in history, though, is my extraordinary experiences on the eve of Cromwell's landing.

I was feeling confident that night, though a little restless. I had just concluded a meeting with the several Clan chiefs, and all were in agreement. I felt certain we would toss Cromwell back into the sea and kick the Torries all the way back to England. The hope of peace and continued independence was strong within me.

I left my tent on the banks of the sea sometime after midnight, unable to sleep. It was a bright and beautiful night. The moon was in full bloom, and the grassy slopes upon which I trod were bathed with a luminescence that gave the entire valley before me a rather unreal but beautiful appearance. Life felt great! I was already beginning to taste victory ... a victory the Green sorely needed and one which would cure the hated English of their imperialistic, coveting desires toward our island home.

As I stood on the grassy knoll some thousand yards or more from my tent, looking out over the sparkling sea, it was hard to imagine that this beautiful valley would be running red with blood on the morrow.

Looking up into the heavens, I noticed a swirling mist upon the point of a knoll several yards above me. Now, mists are not uncommon along the shores of Eire, nor all across her boundaries. But this mist was something different. Swirling as though a gusty wind moved the mist, a rectangular doorway seemed to form upon the knoll. Not given to superstition, as are most of my countrymen, I moved up the slope to investigate.

Approaching the swirling mist, I realized that it seemed to be boiling about within the confines of the space it occupied, beginning about eighteen inches above the ground and ending at about a height a little above a tall man. The closer I came to the strange apparition, the less noticeable it became. Had it not been for the full moon, I probably would not have noticed it at all!

One thing was certain, though. This was not an imaginary substance—it was definitely real! Unsheathing my sword, which I always carry with me wherever I go, I swung around slowly, taking in the countryside about me. Perhaps one of Cromwell's spies had landed before him and was even now setting up some type of signal, though from what means such a sight might have been created, I could not guess. However, the hills that fell away before me on all sides were bare of any abnormal sight. Free of tree or shrub, I had an unobstructed view for more than a mile. The only out-of-place object within sight was the swirling mist before me.

Turning back, I tentatively stuck my hand into the swirling mist. As I did so, my hand vanished from sight, only to reappear again as I quickly withdrew it. There had been a slight tugging on my hand as it disappeared into the mist, but otherwise it was as though I had merely stuck my hand out into the air before me. Puzzled, I stuck my entire left arm into the light to see if it would extend beyond the swirling mist, which appeared to be only a few inches thick, like a weird patch of fog held in place by some strange power!

As soon as my arm extended into the mist it disappeared from sight as had my hand before. The tugging sensation was greater this time, and I felt as though something or somebody had given it a jerk. I don't know if I would have been able to stand that awesome pressure had I not immediately jerked my arm back out of the swirling mist.

I can still recall the queer feeling I had that night, standing upon the grassy knoll, looking into that swirling mist that I could not penetrate with eye or limb. Angry, I stepped back and ran my sword into the boiling mist. Perhaps there was someone or something there that my trusty blade could find that I had not been able to see. As the blade entered the mist, it was wrenched from my grasp, and it disappeared from sight.

That particular sword had come down through the Dowdall line for generations. It was said that the first Robert carried it into battle with William when they trampled the English at Hastings. My own grandfather had used it in quelling the last of the Danish raids to the north. My father had carried it in the Ulster uprising. It was a strong blade and had served him well. It was of Norman origin, forged by a metalsmith descended from the Danes who had come south with Rollo hundreds of years before. It was a blade I was proud to own, and I wasn't about to lose it.

Feeling angry and somewhat arrogant, no doubt, for arrogance had seen me through to victory many a time when logic told me all was lost, I stepped into the swirling mist. Reaching out to grasp hold of my missing sword, I stepped into an adventure the likes of which I am still somewhat hesitant to believe myself!

CHAPTER TWO

It was an eerie feeling as I stepped through the swirling mist. I felt my entire body being drawn forward, and I braced myself for a frightful collision, but no sooner had I stepped into the mist than I stepped out on the other side. But I was no longer on the grassy slopes above Drogheda, nor anywhere else in Eire that I could tell. Nothing I had seen in all my travels throughout Eire or the Continent could compare with the sight before me.

I was standing upon a flat carpet of grass in a large meadow surrounded on all sides by a thickly grown forest. Yet the grass was like no other I had ever trod. Instead of the lush green of my native land, it was a riot of colors matching the beautiful autumn hues so familiar upon the Continent. Yet no grass in Europe could compare with this finely manicured carpet. Each blade seemed to be of a different hue and embraced so many colors it was difficult to determine its overall shade. Bright oranges and reds, soft yellows, and even hints of magentas, vermilions, and browns could be found within the grassy carpet.

Looking about me I could see a startling panorama of beautiful colors and hues. In the far distance were tall mountains bathed in several shades of deep purple and crimson. They were sawtooth mountains of extreme beauty, much like those in western Eire. Yet they were not the indistinct colors of the Twelve Bens in Galway, but sharp and clear-appearing. They seemed so close I felt I could reach out and touch them.

Between the mountains and where I stood was a patch of forest that would set a hunting man such as I to drooling. Many a long hour I had spent in the forests of Carnlough in my youth, hunting wild boar, stag, and elk. But this forest was far more lush in color and dense of foliage than any I had ever seen. The trees were so close I could see individual growth, and birds and animals scurrying about. Though it must have been several hundred yards off, I could detect flowering acacia trees and shrubs, bamboo-like stalks, large philodendron leaves, and numerous bushes of unknown origin. Many of the larger leaves appeared to be vernicose in nature, but at that distance it was difficult to tell.

The meadow upon which I stood stretched down into a gorgeous miniature valley that sloped gently toward the forest before me. The forest completely encircled the meadow in which I stood. Automatically I determined the direction in front of me to be north. Perhaps it was because I was standing facing north when I entered the swirling mist above Drogheda, or perhaps it was because I have always possessed an uncanny sense of direction and been able to determine where I am at all times, even in the thickest of battles. In any event, that was north to me, and I later found my sense of direction in this new land to be as correct as I had always known it to be.

To the south and east the valley leveled out in an unbroken run to the forest. So smooth did the grass in these two directions appear that it seemed one could have played a billiards game upon it. To the west lay a series of pools of water. I didn't think of them as lakes, for they were small and perfectly formed, not like the irregular shapes of small patches of water one is wont to find in Eire. It seemed as though man had made these pools and spaced them evenly, not so much for physical use but rather for the beauty they created.

No other object grew within the meadow except for a gigantic tree off to the south, about twenty yards from where I stood. The tree was enormous in its proportions, at least fifty feet thick at its base and taller than I could see, its top branches lost in the clouds above. The thick bole tapered upward but was still some twenty feet thick where it disappeared from view.

Upon the bole of the tree were many inlaid areas of twisted growth, forming what appeared to be almost footholds, or at least indentations that one could use for climbing. The sight of these gave me the idea to climb up the limbs to investigate what might be seen beyond the forest. There must be a city or town somewhere nearby. The grass was too well manicured not to have someone attending it reg-

ularly, and the pools of water had to have been deliberately
formed by the hands of men. Surely no one would go to that
much effort unless they were nearby and intended using these
creations for something, though for what, I had no idea.

The quiet of the peaceful meadow was shattered by the
screeching of thousands of birds that began taking to wing
within the forest off to the west. I had always thought the
bagpipes of the Albans was the most ominous noise on earth,
but this din would have made even my Alban friend,
Holyday, envious!

My eyes were drawn to a distant movement within the
forest as more and more of the screeching birds took flight. A
definite pattern was forming as the birds left the trees, and I
could discern that whoever or whatever was frightening the
fowl was heading directly for me. Whatever it was, I dis-
counted the possibility of animals, for animals are of the
forests and the birds generally take them for granted. This
had to be man, and man as a danger!

The thought immediately struck me that perhaps the man
might be a danger to me, too. I realized in almost the same
instant that I was unarmed, and this gave me some little moment of thought! As I looked at the birds, noting the beautiful colors of their wings and feathers, I could not penetrate
the denseness of the forest to see what possible danger might
be approaching.

Again the tree came to mind. I decided to climb it to see if
I could discern what was approaching from the forest, for as
the birds continued taking wing, a definite path was forming,
and there was no question that whoever it was was coming
directly toward me.

I turned and a very strange thing happened! As I turned,
my feet left the ground, and I spun around two or three
times in midair before losing my balance and tumbling to the
grass.

Despite the possibility of approaching danger, I was
stunned at this rare phenomenon. Could I have merely
slipped on the grass? Certainly not! I am a well-coordinated
man with unusual strength. Many a defeated foe would testify to my agility upon the battlefield, and there were more
than a few fair maidens that have espoused my gracefulness
on the dance floor. What, then, had caused the strange occurrence? Mystified, I pushed to my feet, only to find myself
shooting up into the air, well above the grass carpet. Turning

a half-circle in the air, I landed heavily upon my shoulder and back, angered by whatever power was interfering with my normal movement. How little I understood at that moment how thankful I would later be for that strange power!

After two such encounters with this strange happening, I carefully turned over on my side and pushed to my feet. The ease with which I gained them was surprising, even to me. Suddenly I realized that I felt lighter on my feet than usual. At over two hundred pounds, despite my normal agility and softness of movement, I felt as though my strength had doubled.

Quickly remembering my predicament and the approaching of possible danger, I again sprang for the tree. You would think I would have had enough sense to learn from two earlier unsuccessful efforts at movement, but I can only say that the Green within me gave no thought to such trifles; the possibility of a fight was upon me, and I wanted to know who and what my enemy might be. In any event, as I sprang for the tree, I again left the ground in a leap that would have done me credit at the Clan games in Antrim.

Catching my balance in midair, I hit the grass carpet with a bound and took another step that propelled me toward the tree with fearful force. I struck the bole a mighty blow, momentarily stunned. Quickly shaking off the blackness that threatened to engulf me, I took a foothold on the bole and shoved upward. This movement propelled me beyond the first limb, and I found myself in midair once again, this time thirty feet off the ground without a hand or foothold to break my fall. Flailing, my arms outstretched, I managed to grasp a branch as I started to fall back.

Grasping the branch, I easily pulled myself upon its sturdy arm and there tried to determine that strange new power I had to move with such little effort. I have always been a strong man, being the champion of the Clans at wrestling and most sports, but never in my life had I been able to jump thirty or forty feet at a time! It was puzzling, but I had little time to contemplate the strange phenomenon, for the clamor of birds arrested my thoughts, and I began climbing up into the dizzy heights of the tree. As I did so, I took special precaution to move with great care. It took little time to master control of my increased strength as I climbed higher to see if the cause of the disturbance could be determined.

Under normal circumstances, climbing that tree would

have been a Herculean task. The added strength I mysteriously possessed, however, made the task a simple matter, and I arrived within moments at a position where I could see through the dense foliage.

The birds were still in flight, but I noticed that they did not fly away from the area of the disturbance but continued to climb higher above the exact same spot from which they had taken to wing. By now there seemed to be hundreds of thousands of the birds taking flight. The disturbance that caused their fright was still approaching in my direction, though I could not in any way determine its nature. Yet I still believed it was a man or men, and that meant possible danger to me, since the aggressiveness of movement meant unusual flight or pursuit to my trained, battle-conscious eye.

Again I swept the valley. Through the foliage I could see fairly well at this height. Nowhere could I see any other hiding place except the tree in which I was perched. Though the thought occurred to me that perhaps the reason they were headed in this direction had something to do with this remarkable tree, I decided that this was where I would stay. No doubt they could see the tree through the forest, since its height rivaled the distant mountains in penetrating the sky. Still, it was my only sanctuary, and I was determined to remain hidden until I could ascertain the nature of whoever approached.

Looking around for a better foothold by which I could ascend the tree even higher, my glance caught the flash of sunlight off metal at the base of the tree. This sight intrigued me, because having no weapon I was much interested in anything that might serve a purpose. Moving down the bole of the tree a few feet, I worked myself into a better position by which I could observe the ground.

There below me, staring up, was my old friend. The blade shone in the sunlight, and it surprised me I had not seen the sword earlier. Perhaps it had been the intriguingly beautiful sights of the surrounding countryside that made me miss seeing it before. In any event, I began to descend quickly from the tree to retrieve my sword. Once it was in my hand I would gladly tackle any foe. To be without a sword was akin to being naked at a social gathering.

No sooner than it takes to tell, I was on the ground and reaching for my sword. It was good to feel once again the familiar touch of the hilt in my grasp. Swiftly jumping to the tree, I gained the first branch. Looking off into the distance I still could not tell what it was that was approaching. Determined to stay hidden until I could learn about the impending danger, I braced myself for another leap. As I prepared to do so, I chanced to look back toward the forest and saw the most beautiful sight that has ever assailed my eyes, before or since!

Emerging from the forest edge was a girl. She was not just an ordinary girl but the most beautiful woman I have ever seen. I'm not sure I can describe her appearance in that first moment of discovery, so strikingly beautiful did she seem.

As she ran at breakneck speed across the clearing, her long limbs moved with the velvety smoothness of a cat. Her long, deep yellow hair trailed out in a graceful sweep behind her. I got the impression she was frightened since she was looking behind her, yet she also possessed poise and confidence as she bounded across the clearing. She seemed in complete control of her faculties, and though knowing capture and perhaps death were imminent, she appeared calm in her outward expression.

As she came closer I could see that her skin was smooth as silk. Her eyes were large, but not from fright. High cheekbones and a sculptured chin, strong but small, dominated her features. She had even white teeth, and her lips were faintly reddened as though from some artificial source, but not the deep red that was so prevalent at the courts on the Continent.

She wore a simple garment of a soft animal skin, or perhaps it was cloth—I could not tell from that distance. At her waist hung two long, curved knives, perhaps sixteen to eighteen inches in length. The scabbards of both were beautifully encrusted with bright gold and precious stones. A thick belt surrounded her slim waist, and this, too, was studded with jewels. Another belt extended from the first and connected to a leather collar that loosely surrounded her neck. There were no stones upon the neckpiece, nor the belt that connected it, save a large round disc about the size of a small saucer which was imbued with what appeared to be a beautifully emblazoned coat of arms or symbol.

She covered the distance quickly, unaware of my presence in the tree. She possessed a supple, full figure that flowed in graceful movements as she ran. She appeared to be in her early twenties, but I could not be sure. Her skin was of the most beautiful color I had ever seen upon a human being. Almost bronze, it was far healthier-looking than the coveted whiteness of the girls I had known.

Certainly here was a woman who had spent much of her time outdoors and was very familiar with her environment. Her stamina was evident as was her tremendous strength. She seemed fully six feet in height, if not taller, and was well proportioned. Her agility, though out of place in women of my homeland, seemed to complement her great beauty.

I was so enchanted by her that I failed to notice what was causing her flight. Suddenly a crashing of brush in the distance brought my attention to that matter. As I was swinging my gaze from the girl, I noticed that she slipped on an uneven spot on the carpet and fell. A slight groan escaped my clenched lips, but whether it was from seeing the girl fall or the sight that emanated from the forest I cannot be sure. It was no wonder the girl was running for her life, for there before my very eyes was the most astonishing and hideous sight I had ever seen!

CHAPTER THREE

Coming out of the forest were several beings. They could not be called men, though I later learned to refer to them as such. They were perhaps six feet tall with two arms and two legs, two eyes, and a mouth. But what made them difficult for the mind to accept as men was the way in which the normal parts were distributed across their ugly and hideous countenances.

Even at this great distance I could see that their eyes were extremely wide-set, almost at the extreme edges of their heads. An ugly appendage which I recognized as a nose sprawled across the face from eye to eye, some six inches in width. It was triangular in shape, with the point of the triangle nearly reaching the hairline and the bottom extending to the top lip of the mouth. And what a mouth! Split from one side of the face to the other, it extended outward from the head, giving the appearance of a bulldog, but far more ferocious and much more hideous!

The head tapered up to nearly a point at the top, with appendages on either side near the point that I later learned served as ears. Yet, as hideous as the head appeared, it was not the most menacing part of these ferocious creatures. Their heads were cradled in an indentation of the chest. There was no neck—they merely rested, as it were, upon a space that sloped downward from both shoulders about three or four inches.

Their chests were huge in size, nearly three feet or more across. The arms were likewise large, with rippling muscles that could be seen corded beneath the deep pink skin, even at this great distance.

Their bodies did not taper at the waist as a human's but rather extended straight down into large, muscular thighs that ended in knobby knees. As they drew closer, I could see that the kneecaps had several boney appendages sticking out, which I later learned made these beings terrible antagonists in a rough and tumble brawl.

The lower legs were something unique to medical knowledge. They did not slope to an ankle and foot but rather were broken up into two joints. The first joint was about a foot below the knee. The leg then sloped backward from this second joint about six inches to what I will call an ankle. From the ankle a foot sloped downward and spread wide, ending in what appeared to be several toes.

The arms, too, were triple-jointed. That is, the elbow appeared just below the biceps area, much higher than a human's, and then extended down to another joint halfway between a normal elbow and wrist. This, I later learned, gave the creatures tremendous ability to throw what they call a *thwarpa*. This is a leather pouch attached to wires that is slung much like a slingshot, but with such tremendous force that a stone the size of my fist can travel nearly a mile. And I was soon to learn that these beings could throw their missiles with astonishing accuracy.

The beings wore no clothing. That is, not in the same sense that I was used to. Their simple raiment consisted of a wide leather belt that traveled around the chest widthwise, from which were suspended two straps on either side of the body, connecting with a second wide belt that surrounded the body at where the waist would normally be. From this second, lower belt hung a skirt-like affair of some animal skin which extended just below the crotch. It looked much like a shortened kilt. I could not see at this distance but later learned that another smoother cloth connected between the legs, serving as a loin cloth. Hanging from both belts and straps were several objects I could not make out but which I felt had to be weapons of some sort.

As I watched in fascinated horror as these beings approached, I remembered the girl. She had now regained her feet, but the beings had closed the distance as a result of her fall. As she came on toward the tree, I was once again struck with her uncommon beauty, and, too, with her poised appearance, even in flight. On closer inspection she, too, was well muscled, but in a soft, pleasing fashion. One look had told me that no lass of my experience, certainly among the fairest in the world, could stand a chance against such a creature as this . . . either in beauty or strength.

As she neared the bole of the tree, she once again slipped on the grass carpet and tumbled full-length upon the ground. It was then I noticed how swollen her feet were. Blood streaked her legs and arms and covered her feet, no doubt the reason she had twice slipped and fallen. Her single garment, which covered her from neck to crotch in a well-fitted but modest fashion despite its skimpy size, had also been torn and ripped.

The thought passed through my mind that perhaps the beautiful forest I had been admiring was far more savage in its underbrush than I had at first imagined. But such thoughts I discarded from my mind. Here was a lass in danger, and no true man of the Sod could withhold his aid. The Dowdalls did not spring from the loins of cowards, and I could feel the blood of thousands of warriors coursing through my veins. Despite the fact a dozen of the most hideous beings I had ever chanced to see were descending upon me, I dropped to her side.

I reached down and gently took hold of the girl's elbow to help her to her feet. Immediately she sprang to her feet, a long, curved knife appearing in her hand which was half-raised for a striking blow. As she caught full sight of me, a smile spread across her face and the menacing knife was lowered. Her expression was strong, much like an athlete who is about to engage in a tremendous effort, rather than someone about to die. There was absolutely no fear about her nor could I even tell that she was concerned about the creatures that bounded across the meadow toward us. I was later to learn the people from which she sprang did not know the meaning of fear, nor do they have any such word of its many derivatives in their language.

She realized at once I was not one of her pursuers but ready to help her. For a brief moment she let her eyes fall upon my form. Standing just over six and a half feet tall and weighing well over two hundred pounds, I present a large figure of a man. Too, the clothing I wore was from my native Eire and no doubt caused her some surprise, for I was wearing the red, black, and white plaid of my Clan, both in the fighting kilt that hung to my knees and the long cloak that hung nearly to the ground. I was wearing knee-high boots of soft doeskin, a white blouse with flowing sleeves bound tightly at the wrist, and a tam upon my head. She took it all in, even to the feather upon the tam. To what extent my appearance might have surprised her, I did not know. However, when her eyes traveled up to the sword that I still held grasped in my hand, her eyes lit up. It wasn't until much later, when I saw more of her people, that I realized what a sight I presented to her in my native attire.

Upon seeing the blade in my hand, already drawn, a twinkle came to her eyes. She swung around to face her antagonists who now were nearly upon us. In that same fluid movement, she drew the lefthand dagger and stood poised, each hand armed with one of the thin, curved blades that looked like it would cut its way through a man with little trouble. I was certain she knew how to use them.

Though her antagonists were almost upon us, I couldn't help but notice the girl's beauty. The garment I had first thought was animal skin turned out to be a cloth of the most beautiful workmanship I had ever seen, and I had seen many fine raiment in the royal courts of Europe. This, though, was nothing like what I had seen upon the Continent. It was of a dull sheen, and many beautiful colored threads had been worked through the material to form, as I had supposed at a distance, a colorful animal skin.

Her hair hung down her back, fully six inches below her shoulders. It was a lovely deep, golden yellow. It seemed to sparkle in the sunlight as she moved in a slight swaying motion. She was, as I had suspected, a little over six feet in height. Her eyes were a deep green color, flecked with tiny spots of gold. Her nose was short but strong. Her appearance was very feminine, despite the two long knives she held at her side.

It had been my intention to whisk the girl up into the tree before the creatures spotted me, but such was not to be. It seemed the girl, now with aid at her side, was quite willing to stand and fight where she had been fleeing but a moment before. Such, I was later to learn, was the nature of this strange and beautiful race. Where one would run from small but uneven odds, two would stand against odds they could not hope to defeat, a strange paradox in their nature that I have not been able to figure out even to this day.

Having the blood of knights in my veins and chivalrous to a fault, I stepped in front of the girl and faced the horde pounding down upon us. My blade was in my hand and the blood of warriors flowed through my veins. Despite the odds, I was glad for a chance to defend this beautiful damsel in distress. Perhaps I had been robbed of the chance to fight Cromwell, but nevertheless I had an equal battle before me, one from which none of my Clan would ever shrink!

It had been my father when I was still a wee lad who first brought me in contact with the tactics of battle. Then, as I grew, I learned of the legend of James, my father, a mighty Son of the Green. The English had feared him almost as much as death itself, and wherever he fought the Torries had lost. I had heard the English were jubilant when they learned of his death in Ulster. His name was known throughout England, and Cromwell had placed a thousand pounds upon his head.

When I was old enough to hold a sword, my father sent me off to the Continent to learn from the masters. Under their tutelage I learned the finer points of fencing and swordplay, but it had been from my father that I learned the tactics of fighting.

He was a genius at the game of war, and no slouch when it came to wielding the sword. His had been the skill that had won him countless battles and duels. Some said he had magic in his wrist and ice in his veins. Some also said he could take on old Satan himself and come out best. There were some, even, who said he had already defeated the old devil at his own game. But then, the men of the Green are a superstitious lot and Satan lurks behind every bush, so one can well imagine how the stories had grown. Yet my father had been a brute of a man, standing well over six feet and weighing nearly three hundred pounds, and all muscle. He could lift an ox or pick up two grown men at a time and throw them a far piece. This I had seen him do, and I was able to duplicate his ability myself.

My father was never satisfied with what he felt he could teach me, so he sent me off to Europe to learn from the masters. I had traveled the courts of three nations while still in my teens, learning the rare skills of swordsmanship, the bow, and other weapons of war. It was a life I had much enjoyed, even though I had often thought how much better off I would have been had I stayed at home and stood beside my father in the battle that killed him. But when I received word of his death there seemed little reason for me to return home, and I traveled much of the known world, fighting in Asia and Africa and traveling upon the seas to far-off islands.

And here on this strange land, defending the most beautiful girl I had ever seen, I needed the skills that I had learned on a dozen lands fighting hundreds of battles. For nearly upon us was the most formidable foe I had ever chanced to engage. They brandished four-foot-long broadswords in the air and descended upon us with loud screams that set my skin to crawling.

I had not before noticed the swords they wielded because, as I later learned, they carry them in scabbards at their back, hanging from the top of the two leather belts. And what magnificent swords—fully four feet in length, broader of blade than my own, double-edged, and deadly in appearance. But I was soon to learn that they lacked something my own blade had, and it was this, as well as my skill, that saved our lives.

CHAPTER FOUR

As I shoved the girl behind me, I noticed a surprised look cross her face. But I had no time to dwell upon it, for the beings were upon us and it was time to act.

My father had imparted much wisdom to me that over my lifetime had served me in great stead. "Robbie, my lad," he was wont to point out, "if you ever find yourself greatly outnumbered and unable to disengage, which of course you will, this being the Clan's way, always remember that it is best to start the fight than let them carry it to you. Surprise and aggressiveness will decide more battles than mere strength of numbers."

As I jumped forward to engage the foremost warrior descending upon us, I let out the yell of the Clan. The call boomed from my throat in such volume that it almost startled me. It certainly had that effect upon those who bore down upon me—so much so that my first thrust was not even parried, and I shoved the sword into the breast of my foe to the hilt. Yanking it out, I swung to and fro with mighty slashes that I would never have been able to equal back in my native Eire. My muscles were far superior to those I was used to, and the first few strokes of my blade nearly carried me off balance. Yet they were sufficient to down three of the warriors before the fight had begun.

As another pressed me with slashes of his huge blade, I noticed the weapon was not made of steel, as my own, but some type of alloy that was both luminescent and clear. Its workmanship was astonishingly beautiful but, as I quickly learned, of little use against my own blade. For as the warrior swung his sword at me, I countered by deflecting his thrust with my own blade, and much to my surprise and his chagrin, my blade cut cleanly through his with ease.

Dispatching him quickly, I swung at another blade de-

scending upon me, and the same strange thing happened. My
own sword bit through his blade as if it were made of wood.
Indeed this would not be an even fight, twelve against one,
but with the advantage of a superior weapon and unbelievable power of muscle and movement, I felt certain that I
stood a chance.

Two others were closing in on me, and I decided to test
the expanded muscles I seemed to have. Gathering my legs
beneath me, I jumped my full extent directly at the two before me. To their and my bewilderment, I jumped completely
over them and found myself in a small clearing of bodies
with antagonists on every side. But so surprising had been my
maneuver, they were caught completely off guard. In that
split second, I swung my blade with all my strength, severing
heads and limbs. Another jump took me over another wave
of the horde, and as I crossed over one, I swung down with
my sword, cleaving his skull beneath the sharp steel.

Bounding, weaving, fencing at times, but mostly slashing in
a most barbaric fashion, I dispatched the dozen antagonists so
quickly that I was hard-pressed to believe my own accomplishment. So quickly had it been accomplished that none of
the creatures had gotten past me to the girl.

I stood in the midst of twelve bodies strewn across the
bloody carpet. I was a little dazed, to be sure, for only moments before I was certain I would never walk away from
this battle. But here I was, safe of body and free of soul,
looking about me at the most horrible carnage in which I had
ever participated. The hideousness of the creatures notwith-
standing, I felt somewhat depressed at the havoc my single
blade had wrought! But that feeling was fleeting, for the purpose of the fight was pressing upon me, and I was certain
that had I let up at all, it would be me lying dead upon the
grass, and I was certain they would not have given it a passing thought!

A squeal from the girl brought me back to my situation.
At first I thought it was her belated reaction to the carnage
of my blade, but as I looked up, I saw her looking off in the
distance. Coming over the forest from the southeast was a
strange sight. It was a flying machine skimming the treetops
and bearing down upon us. At first I was filled with apprehension but the girl's smiling face told me these were friends.

The airship was shaped much like an overturned bowl with
the bottom nearly flat and sloping upward at the sides to

form a bulwark for the inhabitants that I could see upon the deck. A long, narrow mast stuck out from the inside of the bowl at a forty-five-degree angle, and as the ship came closer I could see three other masts of equal size and length sticking up from the deck, all at opposite forty-five-degree angles. There were no sails on the masts, and I was hard-pressed to determine their worth. Upon each was a riot of pendants, ornately decorated, but whether they bespoke rank, military unit or national colors I could not guess.

The flying machine appeared to be made of the strange material from which the warriors' swords were made. This alloy was luminescent and seemed to give the appearance that you could see through it, yet at the same time it was very definitely opaque. A beautifully and intricately ornate symbol was painted upon the center of the underneath hull. At this distance it appeared to be two birds, bill to bill, with some kind of foliage underfoot. I was to later learn that the emblem, which also includes a sword and the universal peace sign of this strange land, were representative of an entire race and covered everything that moved within the kingdom, including the loyal subjects. What set this particular emblem off as being different from the others I was to later see in profusion, was the golden crown that settled upon the heads of the two birds. The wings of each bird were fully extended, and a matching pair of wings were on either side of the crown, which also supported a small cross at its top. It was not the cross of the Christian world, but rather resembled an "X" with a small bar through the middle of the crossing arms. It was the exact same emblem that adorned the girl's leather collar which encircled her lovely neck.

I could see nearly twenty warriors peering over the bulwark of the airship, and it wasn't until I could discern their size that I realized just how large the ship was. In fact, I later learned that all objects in this strange land appeared much closer than they really are because of the thinness of the air. Many objects appear as though you can reach out and touch them when, indeed, they are many miles away.

The airship was easily a hundred feet through the middle and some twenty feet high at the gunwales. Strange pieces of metal hung over the gunwales at about ten-foot intervals, and there appeared on closer inspection queer markings along the extension of the barrel. Could they be weapons? I could not tell, but as the ship closed down upon us I got the distinct impression they were some type of weapon that emitted a projectile through the long barrel.

The girl took my arm and started pointing toward the ship. She was talking excitedly, though in a tongue I had never before heard. I was taken with the natural animation of her voice and arms, but I could not decipher a single word. Though I was conversant in English, French, Spanish, Danish, Italian, German and Gaelic, nothing she said made a bit of sense to me.

I tried all of these tongues known to me but none brought any response from her lips other than surprise. In fact, as I uttered my first word her brows lifted up in faint surprise, and as I continued through the six languages, the expression deepened until it was almost comical. When I tried Gaelic in desperation, she almost laughed, and I must admit the sound of that ancient tongue emitting from my lips did seem humorously out of place.

The airship was about a hundred yards away and I was struck with its noiseless approach. Though I have never seen anything like it before in my life, I at least expected some type of noise involved with propelling it. Even a ship at sea makes noise as it cuts through the waves, with the wind bristling in her sails. But this ship emitted no sound whatever. The overall impression it gave was quite eerie, and once again I was reminded of the Death Wagon and ghostly stories of my homeland. I doubt if I would have been at all surprised had I seen the Little People upon the bulwark of the airship rather than the bronze-skinned people like the girl beside me.

I took the girl's arm and started to propel her out of the area of carnage in which we stood, toward the descending airship. But no sooner had I taken my first step than I caught sight of a scene more alarming than these dozen dead warriors had first presented as they charged out of the forest after the girl. Off to the northeast, not far from where the first group had emerged, came a horde of hideous creatures to which I could not place a number. And instead of their being on foot as the first group had been, they rode on animals the like of which I had never seen.

Two-legged and swift, the animals bore their riders across the yellow carpet, rapidly covering the mile that separated us. The beasts resembled some type of bird. They had a large flat beak and tail feathers, but there the resemblance ended. The

eyes were huge, at either side of the head, and long ears pro-
truded up out of tufts of small, white feathers. The legs were
long, fully six feet or more in length, ending in large two-or
three-toed feet.

Stopping in my forward movement the girl chanced to look
back over her shoulder at me and caught sight of the approaching horde. Letting out another one of her strange
squeals, she darted away toward the descending airship. But
she had not taken more than a dozen strides when she looked
back toward me, talking excitedly all the while. I did not realize what she was trying to tell me until it was too late.

Oh, if I had only known the language then, what a difference my life within this strange land might have been. But I
was so taken with the sight before my eyes that I paid little
attention to the girl or her animated chatter.

Misunderstanding my motive for not running to the airship, the girl returned to my side to stand and fight, as she
had determined this was my plan. Since the custom of her
race demands that one stand beside his fellow in danger if he
chooses not to retreat, and despite overwhelming odds, she
could no more leave my side than I could have kept from
coming to her aid earlier.

I am not usually slow of wit or action, but I must admit
that upon seeing that strange horde closing upon us, I was
immobile for a moment or two, and in that time the girl had
returned to my side and determined that we would stand and
fight. Realizing the futility of such an adventure, I took her
arm and started toward the airship. But her determination to
fight was now unshakable.

"Are you mad?" I yelled at her. "There must be five
hundred of them. Come, let us fight another day!" Of course
she couldn't understand my words, but I felt she understood
my meaning, for she gave me a disdainful look and turned
back to face the approaching horde.

Had I known of this strange but admirable custom of
her people, I might have been able to rewrite this strange
tale, but as it was, I was foolishly heading toward an adventure I would have rather avoided!

CHAPTER FIVE

Though I pleaded with the girl in as much sign language as I could muster, my efforts were in vain. I tried to take her arm and propel her toward the approaching airship, for that was our only means of escape, but to my great surprise, she shook her head violently and stood firm, feet planted squarely in the middle of the carnage, looking off at the horde. I couldn't believe the girl could be that stubborn. I implored her to move so we could escape, but she wrenched her arm from my grasp, shot me a startled look of contempt, and bent down to pick up a dead warrior's sword. There was no question she intended to stand and fight, though the effort would surely mean her death. It was also clear that if I stayed here with her, I would just as surely die at her side! While I might be able to dispatch a dozen warriors, it was very doubtful I could overcome five hundred.

"Lady, I certainly can't question your bravery but I must insist that your sanity leaves something to be desired," I said while reaching out and encircling her waist with my arm, making to carry her by force to the airship.

She yelled some words at me which I could not fathom but there seemed little doubt of their meaning.

"You may think me a coward if you wish, beautiful one, but I would rather save you and fight another day than see us both dismembered on the spot!" With that I lifted her from the ground and headed for the airship. As we bounded over the grass carpet, her fists beat at me furiously.

I had never thought much about my father's words on women until that moment. "Laddie," he was wont to say, "you can never understand why a woman acts the way she does. Some say they are a little touched in the head, but about that I am not sure. They do, however, lack consecution!"

My father was certainly right! As beautiful and intelligent as this girl appeared, she lacked good, logical thought. Here I had just risked my life to save her from a dozen hideous creatures, and now she was beating upon me with all her strength because I chose to run from five hundred more of the hideous brutes. What did she want of me, to stand and die that we both might join our ancestors? I do believe I thought she was daft!

Ignoring the repeated beatings of her fists upon my person, I looked over my shoulder to see how far distant were the creatures. It was depressing to see how much of the distance they had closed between us. Barely a hundred yards of yellow carpet separated us, and it was with all my strength that I headed in great leaps for the approaching airship.

The ship was settling toward the ground, but I was surprised that it did not land. Perhaps they were as concerned about the approaching numbers of warriors as I! Or perhaps the airship for some reason could not touch down upon the grass. In any event, I reached the side of the ship with the girl still struggling in my arms, just as the warriors aboard lowered one of their fellows over the side in a rope chair, something like a boatswain's chair of the English navy but without a board upon which to sit. It descended quickly toward us with a warrior crouched within its netting. I could also see another such chair being lowered after the first. This one did not contain a warrior and was plainly for me, while the first was for the girl.

As I went to disengage the girl from me to hand over to the first warrior, she struggled more violently. It seemed plain that she did not want to leave me, though from the beating she had given me coming across the meadow, I would have thought she would be glad to be free of me forever.

"You are a most perplexing woman," I yelled at her, trying to hand her over to the warrior. But at that moment the side of the airship was struck with hundreds of pellets. One struck the warrior beside us, splitting his skull.

The creatures, thinking we were escaping, had slowed their pursuit to fire their *thwarpas* at us! Some of the rocks striking the hull of the ship, though not damaging it, were bigger than my fist. It must have been one of these that the warrior caught full in the forehead.

"Like it or not, my lady fair, up you go!" I said to her, as gathering my strength, I tossed her toward the deck and the waiting arms of a dozen shouting warriors. That they were concerned about her safety there could be no doubt, and as she sailed over the gunwale, two dozen arms reached out to break her fall.

A quick look over my shoulder told me the horde was within twenty-five yards. It was now or never, I decided, and I jumped for the deck myself. In mid-flight, one of the projectiles struck me on the side of the head, and I could feel my strength leaving me. Desperately, I reached out for the gunwale as I felt myself falling. The blow had only been a glancing one, thankfully, but it had struck with such force as to knock me off course in my leap. The gunwale was my only hope of reaching the deck.

Struggling to hold on to the gunwale, I saw the girl running to my aid, as were several of the ship's complement. I caught a fleeting glance of a flat deck strewn with irregular-shaped protruding structures, an overabundance of rope, and some type of mechanism in the center of the four masts. About this latter object were several hands heaving to on wooden handles that were secured to a central round disc. Its purpose or what the warriors were about I could not guess, nor did I have time to dwell upon the mystery. My strength was ebbing, and before anyone could reach me I felt myself slipping from the smooth gunwale.

Falling from the ship as it lifted away from the ground, I saw the girl leaning over the gunwale, reaching out toward me. Her face was marked with anxiety and concern for me. The last thought I had was the paradoxical nature of this girl. One minute she was beating upon me and the next she was clinging to me. One minute she was trying to be rid of me and the next she was trying to save me. Perhaps my father had been right. The fairer sex was impossible to figure out. I wondered if all the women in this strange land were like her.

I must have been out before I struck the ground, for I do not recall anything at all except the beautiful but sad face of the girl peering over the gunwale of the ascending airship.

I regained consciousness in a soft bed of feathers in the darkness of some structure. My hands and feet were bound with a thin twine. I could not move to either side as I was wedged tightly between two solid objects that held me imprisoned as securely as though I were tied to a stake. I'm not sure why I said the substance upon which I lay was feathers, except that was the only thought that came to me as I sank lower into them after the effort I exerted trying to move.

I was a captive of the hideous creatures that had descended upon us, I had no doubt. That they intended to end my life shortly I was also sure, for I had dispatched twelve of their comrades in arms but moments before, and certainly they would not let them die unavenged. The punishment, I felt sure, would be terminal and very painful. My only happiness at the moment was the knowledge the girl had gotten away safely and back in the hands of her own people. Had I known then of the fate that befell her airship only moments after it disappeared from view over the forest to the east, I would not have been so happy.

Several hours after I awakened in my prison, I heard a noise nearby. It was the first sound I had heard in all the time since regaining consciousness. In fact, the absolute silence had been eerie, and I was beginning to wonder if my captors had left me in the forest, perhaps to be devoured by what type of evil predatory animal I could not even imagine.

The noise sounded as if metal was being scraped against wood, and shortly after, a squeaking of old hinges reached my ears. A beam of light appeared on my left, and as it expanded I realized I was not confined in a room, as I had first imagined, but in a small coffin-type of box. And the top was being removed.

One of the hideous faces appeared in the opening, staring down at me. I could almost imagine it slavering at the sight of me, its first appearance so much resembling the bulldog breed. As the top of the coffin prison was removed, I could see several of the creatures standing around the box in which I had been incarcerated. As the lid was completely removed, I could see it was fully two feet thick, and rather than being a box, I was lying in a shallow ditch or grave. The thickness of the lid and the dirt walls of my prison had no doubt been the cause for the complete silence.

Rough hands were laid upon me and I was dragged to a standing position inside the ditch. A quick glance told me several hundred of the creatures stood nearby. My vision was mostly cut off from the rest of the area by the tightly packed bodies before me, but I could see here and there through the milling crowd. A few buildings were scattered about what must have been a central compound in which we stood. By the buildings were what I guessed to be the women and children, though I cannot say why I felt they were women, as they were in no way different from the creatures before me.

The bonds on my feet were quickly removed, and I was roughly hauled out of the ditch and placed upon my feet. I noticed that it took three of the creatures to accomplish this, no doubt my weight being far heavier than my height and appearance would normally note. I could not tell if they were astonished at my weight or that it normally took three of them to accomplish such a task. In fact, I could not discern a single expression upon their countenances. It was a long time before I was to realize that their fixed expressions actually altered to show emotion from time to time, as does a human face. It merely took a practiced eye to notice the difference.

The three creatures that had hoisted me out of the hole stepped back once their task was accomplished. It was almost as though they were afraid of me, and I could well imagine that they might hold me in some awe since my height and size were superior to their own and the feats they had observed on the battlefield no doubt surpassed anything they had ever before seen. I didn't know it at the time, but that was exactly how these strange creatures saw me ... almost like a super-being! My accomplishment of dispatching a dozen of their best warriors had unnerved them, for they had been at the edge of the meadow during the entire fight. I later understood they had held back, out of courtesy at first, since the warriors that had been chasing the girl appeared to have her cornered. Their code prevented them from joining the fracas until it was concluded.

Then, as the awful carnage took place, they sat their mounts in stunned silence, hardly able to believe their eyes, for their fallen comrades were the famed *howogi*, or king's guard, and had been considered invincible. It wasn't until the shock wore off that they emerged from the forest bent on my destruction and the capture of the girl.

As the three stepped back, I could see a tall creature, tall by their standards, approaching. He was by far the most impressive of the brutes. His head was slightly larger, but his impressiveness was not in its size but how he held himself high and straight, which was no mean task when his head was cradled on his chest without a neck! How he managed to give the appearance he did, I could not guess.

His skirt, or *kwai* as they are called, was of a deep purple and not of the animal skins as were the others. He carried two long, curved knives at either side of his lower belt, much as the girl had done, only his were not studded with precious stones as had been hers. The only precious ornament he possessed was a large stone that hung about his neck. It was a highly polished stone and had the appearance of fire as the light danced upon its surface. The beautiful stone was as much out of place upon his person as he would have been standing upon the streets of Dublin.

As he walked toward me I noticed a strange phenomenon. He was able to direct his eyes independently of each other. While one eye held my gaze, his other searched my frame. It was a weird feeling, standing there being ogled in such a fashion. I had not noticed that the others had moved their eyes in such a manner, but later learned that these creatures can operate either eye in any direction they choose and are capable of recording the separate images each eye receives and evaluating its picture.

I supposed him to be the leader of the warriors about me. He approached with a show of casualness which I did not feel he possessed. There was a dignity about him, but the air of arrogance was so noticeable it was hard to place any attributes upon him.

I also noticed that his leatherwork was not the same as the other warriors. His harness was intertwined with feathers and other bits of colorful regalia. Clearly he stood out among his fellows, and they made room for him as they would for a stalking, dangerous animal. Not only was it clear he was the leader, it was also very clear that they greatly feared him.

He came to within a couple of paces of me and spoke in a rather harsh, gutteral tongue which I could not understand. Where the girl's voice had been soft and slightly running along the musical scale, his was harsh and flat. Shrugging my shoulders, I replied first in one language and then in the others but to no avail. All the while he merely looked at me with that expressionless face of his and reached out with his long *thwarpa* and slapped it across my face. I hardly felt the blow and wasn't sure whether he had meant to hurt me, or if that was all the power he could manage. I later learned both had been the case. Though the creatures appeared to be quite strong with noticeable muscles, their strength was next to nothing compared to my own in this strange land. And too, the effect of being hit by a *thwarpa* is of great importance, for the sling is meant to be used at great distances, and when a warrior can get close enough to use it in such a manner, it

is considered a great coup and an affront to the person so
struck.

I cannot say why I acted in the way I did, but it may have
been the only thing that saved my life. The puny effort of his
strength seemed rather ludicrous to me. Here I was, standing
surrounded by hundreds of the most savage-looking creatures
I had ever seen, armed to the teeth with swords and knives,
and their leader merely struck me a puny blow. Yet his fellows reacted as if he had done something of great daring.
The entire scene struck me as quite humorous, and I laughed.
Not a hysterical or nervous laugh, for I am not wont to respond in such a manner, regardless of the circumstances. But
a loud, boisterous laugh that shook the compound.

I cannot say what power I had in this strange land, nor
from whence it came. All I know is that my strength and
prowess seemed to have doubled in volume. Always having
possessed a strong, baritone voice, this additional power gave
it such emphasis that no doubt it penetrated to the very core
of those close around me.

Where many emotions or actions might have been different
in this land from that of Eire, at least this creature was able
to quickly determine that my laugh was an insult to him. He
acted immediately. Moving forward, he struck me a blow
that can only be described as a haymaker. He brought it up
from his toenails, figuratively speaking, of course, since these
creatures do not possess toenails. It landed squarely on my
jaw and no doubt the creature expected me to topple like a
felled ox. However, the blow felt like nothing more than a
slap and budged me not. I had been slapped harder than that
by a wench in old Kelly's tavern not more than a fortnight
ago.

I believe my muscles reacted before common sense caught
up with them, for easily breaking the bonds that held my
hands, I returned the creature's blow with my doubled
strength. The blow landed on the jaw of the creature, lifted
him off the ground, and sent him flying backward ten feet before he crashed to the ground!

The reaction of his fellows was something to behold. Each
had one eye upon their fallen leader and another eye upon
me. None moved to interfere with me. In fact, several of
those close at hand moved back as far as the pressing crowd
would allow. I am sure they didn't know quite what to do
with me. Perhaps no one had ever struck their leader before,

or perhaps I seemed like some apparition from the legends of their superstitions. Whatever the reason, they gave me a wide berth, though not surrendering me my freedom by any means.

It appeared that the throng of creatures did not know what to do. Surely they had the means to run me through many times over. But just as surely they did not seem capable of doing so at that particular moment. I could not tell whether it was out of fear of me or because they had orders not to.

The moment didn't last long, however, for another creature, much like the one I had dispatched, stepped forward and walked over to his fallen comrade. He, too, wore the different markings that bespoke his rank among them. He seemed even taller than the other one, and though I cannot say why, he didn't seem as ferocious to me as the first creature had.

Kneeling down, the second fellow appraised the condition of the first. His hands went to certain places upon the fallen body, much like a doctor; however, the places were not at all in the locations you would expect them to be. First, he felt of the right foot, somewhere near the middle of what might pass as an instep. Then he felt of the left elbow, not on the inside of the joint, but on the point of one of the barbs I now noticed emanating from the knobby joint. Looking much like those sticking out from the knees, the elbow appendages were much shorter in length.

Finally, the hand darted to one of the ears, within which he stuck one of his bony, multiple-jointed fingers. A whishing noise came from between his huge lips, much like the escaping of breath in a human. If it seems that I refer continually to a difference between these creatures and humans, it is only because they can in no way be considered *homo sapiens*. Whether they come from some other class of men or have an entirely different origin back in antiquity, I cannot say, but I do not think of them, even to this day, though I know differently, as human beings.

Taking one of the small, curved knives from his scabbard, the creature reached out and deftly cut off the right ear of his fallen comrade. He then reached for the brightly-colored pendant stone and carefully removed it from the other's body. The care and reverence employed in the handling of this flaming stone bespoke its importance. Placing it carefully within the pocket of a pouch which hung from one of the belts of his harness, the creature unceremoniously removed the belts from the fallen body.

Pulling himself to an upright position, the creature, whom I assumed was now the new ruler of the tribe, turned to stare at me. Both his eyes fastened upon me, and it was the first time I had seen any of the creatures look in the same direction with both their eyes at the same time. Funny, but now that seemed odd and out of place.

He took a few steps toward me and then reached his right arm up and behind him in a sinewy movement that I much admired. Drawing the sword that hung upon his back, he extended it toward me before I could tell quite what he was doing. I had never seen a weapon drawn so fast. It was beautiful to behold. I felt sure that my time had come, and there was no doubt in the face of this new antagonist that he knew exactly what he was going to do. As he moved the tip of the large broadsword up to point at my middle, I could feel the end touching against the belt buckle of my own garment. I could see what I imagined was an intake of breath among his fellow creatures, but except for that slight sound and movement, not a muscle twitched anywhere in the group. It seemed all were merely waiting for the *coup de grâce*.

And without a weapon, there was nothing I could do but await the ignoble end. I couldn't recall at that moment any words of wisdom my father had passed on to me that would help in this situation, unless it was to die like a man when the time came. And surely this looked like the time.

CHAPTER SIX

Evidently the end was not to come immediately, for the creature spoke in his guttural tongue, pointing profusely with his sword and then strode off. His fellows made a wide path for him, but I got the distinct impression that they were not moving back because they feared him, but rather out of respect for his position among them. Perhaps he was their new leader for there seemed no doubt that the creature I had felled was no longer being numbered among the living.

The brute had walked only a few steps when he turned. Perhaps he had motioned for me to follow, but I could not tell. His expression, though not noticeably altered, seemed to tell me he was surprised at my action. Again he spoke in his guttural tongue and pointed his sword at me. Was he telling his fellow creatures to dispense with me when he left? I could not tell.

Again he turned and made to stride away, but after a few steps turned to look over his shoulder and what he saw made him stop short once again. I couldn't tell if he was angry or what, but there seemed little doubt that he was growing impatient, for he pointed the sword at me again and in a swirling motion made it clear that he wanted me to follow him, which, of course, I did. It seemed strange to me that his fellow creatures made no effort to assist him in getting me to follow, but instead stepped farther back for me than they had for him as I crossed the compound to catch up.

I followed him across a large open area I had not noticed before, past buildings to one of the largest structures I saw anywhere in the village. It was clearly twenty feet tall and about one hundred and fifty feet square, with a pointed roof made out of some type of reedy material. It appeared to be much like the thatched roofs of Eire. But the workmanship that was needed to support the reeds in covering that large expanse seemed unbelievable. The walls were of wood and had been covered by some type of gummy material that had hardened in place, effectively caulking every crack. It looked like a sturdy building, much more so than the several others we had passed. Curiously, there were no females nor children surrounding this building as there had been around all the others.

The creature stopped in front of an entrance opening and motioned for me to enter. As I did so, I passed from bright daylight into the darkest of nights. A hand at my back carefully guided me forward and I passed through another, smaller opening, into the interior of a large rectangular room which was bathed in light. Whether it was from my eyes changing from the glare to the darkness that had kept me from seeing anything in the anteroom we had just passed through or because there was some cleverly concealed doorway into the second, larger room I could not tell, but I made a mental note to find out if ever given the chance.

In the center of this large room was an elevated chair of ornate workmanship. It so surpassed anything in its carved beauty that I had seen in the village of these hideous creatures that I at once felt they had stolen it from some other, much more intelligent race—perhaps from the people of the girl I had saved.

With a gentle touch on my arm, my companion guided me toward the chair which appeared to be the royal throne, making it clear that I should sit upon it. I didn't understand if this was some special privilege offered me or his way of saying that I would be given my last meal before my execution.

I decided this must be some barbaric custom of honoring the condemned. Yet, I seemed to have no choice but to comply. But before I could sit upon the magnificently carved chair, my host stopped me, and reaching into one of the many pouches hanging from his harness he poured an oily substance into the palm of his hand. Then reaching over he spread the odorless liquid across my forehead. The ritual completed, he motioned me to be seated.

My perch upon the throne chair, though comfortable with its cushions of feathers, seemed most precarious. Any moment I expected the empty room to explode with these ugly, hideous creatures brandishing their weapons, screaming for my blood. Or for whatever such creatures screamed in this strange land.

"Moga!" the creature said, pointing to himself. Several times he repeated this gesture before I finally decided he was telling me his name. When he pointed his finger at me and spoke something that might have been a question, I replied, "Robert."

He stumbled over the unfamiliar sound, much to my delight. His awkward attempt to pronounce my name would have been humorous had it not been for the circumstances in which I found myself.

It took some coaching, but he finally managed the strange sound. As I nodded and repeated my name once again, then pointed to him and called him by name, his face split in a hideous characterization that could hardly be called a grin.

I tried to get him to pronounce my surname but finally gave it up. Although I did not know it at the time, no one in this strange land possessed a surname, and it was for this reason that I could not get Moga to understand what I was trying to get him to say.

At my companion's becking, a smaller creature appeared. Though I could not discern any difference between the two, I felt that this was one of the females I had observed earlier.

"Toogo," he said, pointing at the other. When I repeated the name he seemed pleased once again. Then he bowed slightly and backed out the door.

The female, Toogo, turned out to be my personal slave and teacher. It didn't take long for me to realize that I was not to be killed, but kept in captivity for some special reason. Perhaps they were cannibals and wanted to fatten me up, I didn't know. But though the reason was obscure to me at the time, the treatment was completely understandable, and I decided to take advantage of it.

The first thing that Toogo accomplished was to teach me the language. Having a working knowledge of Gaelic, perhaps the most difficult language ever devised, and being fluent in six other tongues, I found it surprisingly difficult to learn this strange tongue. We were hampered by having no common ground for communication, and the learning progressed slowly. For several hours each day I learned from Toogo, who always made sure she sat at my feet. She also made sure her head was never higher than mine. If I sat, she sat. If I reclined she reclined lower. If I were to lay flat on the floor, she would do likewise, with her face buried in the floor. At no time was I able to communicate to her that she needn't do so. Even after I mastered enough of the language to talk in broken sentences, she refused to obey my simple wish.

"No, it is not allowed," was all I could get from her.

The first couple of nights in captivity I learned that I was no longer on my own planet. At first I thought this was some strange land upon an island about which the mariners often talked. Their tales had always amused me, so full of disbelieving adventures. But, from my adventures with the girl and among these hideous creatures, I could not doubt the tales I had heard.

However, that illusion was quickly shattered for the first night I became aware of there being two moons in the night sky. Nor were they white as the moon I was accustomed to seeing. Both were of a bluish tint or hue and gave off almost no light at all. Nor were the stars in their right positions. Being a member of a warring clan all my life, I had spent innumerable nights, sometimes in strange places, having only the stars to chart my directions. The funny thing about it was that I recognized the constellations above me, but not the exact positions they were in. Everything seemed rather backward, as though I was looking at them from a different or opposing view than I had seen them from that last night on the soil of my birth.

I was not a mariner and knew not of the names they had given the many stars, but I knew them by my own names. I was as familiar with the different configurations during all seasons as I am with the back of my own hand! But how different they appeared. I puzzled over this for many days. Finally, I felt I had learned enough of the language to venture a question about where I was.

"You are in the land of the Bomunga," was Toogo's simple reply.

"But where is the land of Bomunga?" I persisted.

"It is here!" she answered, pointing all about us.

"But where is here?" I persisted.

"Are your brains disturbed that you do not know where 'here' is?" she retorted, then realized what she had said, and apologized profusely. I waved off her apologies and continued the line of my questioning.

"But 'here' must be somewhere, surely there is something larger than the land of Bomunga?"

"Certainly, but Bomunga land is here where we are!"

"Yes, yes, of course. But what lands are outside the Bomunga?"

"No lands outside the Bomunga of any importance. Bomunga is the only land!" she exclaimed. Her eyes were beginning to eye me from all levels and in different directions, in what I had come to realize was a perplexing state into which the creatures worked themselves.

I gave up for the time being, but a few days later as my vocabulary increased, I tried again, only this time from a different approach. Since Toogo knew exactly where we were, it was ridiculous to her to bother explaining that simple fact.

"I am not familiar with the names you have for all of this area, even beyond the Bomunga boundaries. Would you tell me their names?"

"Of course. To the north is the Togaoa lands. Farther north is the Meoathai country. They are bad. We never go there. To the south are the hated Taajom, they are our bitterest enemies upon all Ghandor."

I asked her about Ghandor and learned that is the name of their planet. Literally translated it means "home," or, as I learned much later from one of the so-called higher races, "homeland."

Though the Bomunga were not great travelers, they had a surprising understanding of the nature of their world. Far to the north were several kingdoms of what Toogo referred to as *umjah,* or higher people. The Bomunga were classified as part of the *nujah,* or lesser people.

There were evidently many northern kingdoms, though many of their names Toogo did not know. She did know the name of the most powerful, however, and referred to them by name as the Thu, meaning "Ancient Ones." Bomunga, the name they called themselves, I learned, translated into "Pretty Ones." It was quite humorous that the Bomunga referred to all of the races such as the Thu, those that were human in appearance, as the Tojoga, or "Ugly Ones."

Far to the east I learned was a no man's land. That is, no one seemed to know anything about it. There was a very large sea in that direction also, but it was not known by any name to Toogo. She called it merely *ku,* for sea, and I was to later learn that was the general name everyone of this hemisphere called it.

I did gather that the sea was extremely large, but since the

Bomunga do not possess knowledge of distance measurements, it was impossible to come to a conclusion of its approximate size or shape. You can tell distances by reckoning how long it takes to travel it in the Bomunga terminology, but as no Bomunga or any *zumtai* to Toogo's knowledge had ever been on the great sea, there was no knowledge as to how long it took to cross or even walk around it.

There were six tribes in all like the Bomunga. There were the *Togaoa* to the north, the *Taajom* to the south and beyond them were the *Uumai*. To the east were the tribes of the *Agoai* and the *Cothai*. Though separated by tribal custom, law and leadership, all belonged from the same ancestry and were referred to collectively as the *Zumtai*, but never by the Bomunga. This is because Toogo's people considered themselves a higher order than the other tribes and refused to acknowledge any kinship with them.

The great forest that surrounded the Bomunga encampment Toogo called the *Blou Tresai*, or Ghost Forest. It extended in all directions for fully a hundred days' walk which would make it several thousand miles in length. This was one of the reasons why the Bomunga had never been out of the forest area and had no firsthand knowledge of other parts of their world. The knowledge they did have they had learned from captives.

One day, during our afternoon language lesson, I felt that I had progressed enough with my servant or bodyguard, I didn't at that time know which she was, to ask a question that had been on my mind since my capture.

"Toogo, do you know of the woman in the valley to the east that I saved and who escaped in a flying ship?"

It took some time to phrase and rephrase my question until she finally understood my meaning, but her answer was not particularly illuminating.

"She is a very important *Tojoga*."

I certainly had to agree that she was a very ugly one by Zumtai standards. The uglier in their eyes the more beautiful in mine, I was sure.

"Tell me more of her."

"There is nothing to tell. She is a *Tojoga*. Not fit for a Bomunga to discuss." And that was that. Try as I did, she would not answer my many questions about her. I decided to give it up and try later when I had a better grasp of the language. Perhaps in some way I had not asked the question correctly.

The Bomunga are great hunters. In fact, that seems to be all the males do. As soon as I had mastered enough of the language to carry on a simple conversation, Moga took me out on the hunt with him. My first adventure in their forest was something of an eye opener for me, as my first hunt had been, when I was a lad and I accompanied my father into the wilds after boar and deer.

During my treks into the forest to hunt, I was always accompanied by Moga and at least a dozen special warriors. It seemed that the purpose of these dozen warriors was not to hunt but rather to guard me from escaping, or so I thought.

The forest was a maze of interconnecting trails. The Bomunga, as do all of the Zumtai, have an uncanny ability to know in which direction they are heading and what trail is where and exactly where it will take them despite there being thousands of such trails from which to choose. I learned much from Moga, for he was bent upon teaching me all he could once he realized that I knew nothing of the great *Blou Tresai,* or the numerous predators that roamed its unruly growth. The bigger animals were forced to stay upon the trails, as we were, since the undergrowth to either side of the trail, though beautiful in appearance, was so thick and tangled that it would be next to impossible to make any headway.

I learned from Moga that the clearing where they had first captured me was far to the southeast. On one of our journeys through the forest looking for *vruumtai,* a succulent and tasty small animal about the size of a large dog, but far more ferocious, Moga told me of the adventure that had ensued that day. They had been chasing the girl through the forest and marveled at her speed and woodmanship, a term used by the Bomunga meaning ability to choose the right path. A rare ability, he told me, among the *Tojoga.*

How the girl got into the forest, or why the Bomunga were chasing her, he did not say, nor did I feel it prudent at the moment to ask. That they were upon her and wanted very much to capture her was evident, for fully the entire encampment was after her and so was a rival tribe called the *Taajom.* It was the combined forces of these two tribes streaming out of the forest as we made for the airship that I had seen.

In chasing the girl they had employed one of their favorite tricks of the hunt, that is, to split forces and divert them into different paths in order to place their forces ahead of their escaping quarry at some future point in the trail. It was this successful maneuver that had forced the girl off the trail and into the underbrush. She was near the clearing and was aware of that fact, no doubt, and wanted to make for it. Looking back on the incident, it also seemed she was headed for the large tree in which I had been stationed. Why she did not seek refuge in one of the smaller trees in the forest through which she was running, I could not guess. It was her travel through the underbrush that had torn her clothing and scratched her badly. The fact that her cuts and wounds were no worse than they were testifies to the fact that she had not been far from the clearing when she left the trail. Moga boasted of how his cunning had cut her off, and how it would have been a real coup had he grabbed her as a result of his maneuver, for she was escaping from Portoona for whom Moga had no love. The fact that she got away did not bother Moga in the slightest, for she had escaped from Portoona, the ex-Bomunga ruler who I had slain with one blow. In fact my dispatching of twelve of the *howogi*, or honor guard, was of much merriment to Moga, for they were thought to be Bomunga's best warriors, at least according to the deposed ruler.

The weather in the great forest and this part of the planet was very muggy and extremely warm. To a native of Eire, the equatorial temperature far exceeded my normal comfort. It was because of this that I decided to bid farewell to my Irish clothing that I had worn on that night which was to have been the eve of the battle with Cromwell. Taking the knee-high boots, I cut them down to ankle length. So pliable was the soft doeskin that it was no mean trick to rework them into well fitting short boots. The blouse I removed and tossed to Toogo, who acted as if I had given her a great prize. In place of the blouse, I donned the two leather belts that had been Portoona's and cut down my own kilt to the shorter length that appeared to be the custom upon Ghandor, for even the Thuian warriors of the airship I had noticed wore a kilt just reaching the crotch. Retrieving my blouse long enough to cut away part of the white cloth, much to Toogo's consternation, I worked out a loincloth to wear under the shortened kilt as was also the Ghandorian custom.

I suspended the scabbard of my sword on its small leather thongs from the lower belt on my left and hung Portoona's long sword at my back, hooked to the upper belt, as all the Bomunga wore their swords due to their great length. To some, no doubt, it would seem a cumbersome weapon and positioned in a most unusual and worthless place, but the Zumtai, as I can testify from my first meeting with Moga, have a surprising ability to bring this blade into action as fast as I can draw mine from the hip.

The tam I kept, complete with its red feather, matching the flaming red hair I inherited from my mother. I wore the hat everywhere I went, much to the amusement of the Bomunga, since headgear is unknown on Ghandor. I also deemed to keep my cloak, also patterned in the red, black and white of the Dowdall plaid. There was no telling when I might need its warmth in my planned travels, should I encounter northern temperatures. And, too, a Clansman doesn't quickly discard his cloak, for it is his connection to his family and its history and that covers about everything that is worthwhile in life. But being as it was so warm I decided to fold it up into a foot-square bundle and tie it to the lower belt at the small of my back. After a while it became quite a comforting feeling, and I carried it everywhere I went.

As we walked along a path in single file on one of these numerous hunts, my mind began wandering back to my native land. I wondered for the thousandth time what had happened the morning after my disappearance in the hills above Drogheda. What had happened? Had the Clans stayed together in my absence? Had Cromwell been defeated or ... I refused to think of the other possibility.

Instead I let my thoughts wander to the girl. She had been in my thoughts and dreams every day since my capture. That look in her eyes as she stood on the deck of the airship, reaching out to me, haunted me continually.

A scream interrupted my reverie. Looking up I caught sight of one of the warriors being hauled upward into the trees above. A strange-appearing sinewy limb encircled him by the waist and was quickly pulling him upward. Before I could reach him he was gone from sight, the foliage converging back into place covering the hole his body had made as it was dragged, struggling through it.

"Moga, what was it?" I yelled. "The feared *Qouri*," he replied in hushed tones.

All the others were huddled closely together, squatting and looking upward. "Get down!" he whispered harshly. "You present a nice target standing there. Your size would make a tasty morsel for the *Qouri*."

But no sooner had he spoken than something slithered about my shoulders and slipped down to my waist, pinning my arms and my sword to my side. I could feel contracting muscles squeezing the very breath from me, and before I could brace myself for a struggle, I was whisked off my feet and upward into the foliage.

Branches and leaves scraped my face and shoulders as I was propelled upward at an astonishing rate. If only I could free my sword arm, but the pressure encircling me made this impossible.

My ascent slowed until I could finally get my bearings. I estimated that I had been pulled several hundred yards into the trees and as I got a better look I could see it was a long tentacle of an animal that surrounded me. Its arm was as thick as a tree, some two feet in diameter. It was of a pinkish color and rippling with muscles under the smooth, slimy skin. It wound off into the foliage above me, and I could imagine I was being pulled upward into gaping jaws.

I struggled, trying to free my arms, but the creature tightened its grip even more. The more desperately I struggled the tighter the muscles contracted about me. Finally I gave up and relaxed, realizing that struggle was useless. As I relaxed my efforts, the muscles contracting about me relaxed, giving me the faintest inkling of a plan. Perhaps the creature sensed my presence through some nerve endings in this limb and reacted to them. If I were to play possum, it would think me dead and perhaps loosen its grip on me.

As I was being pulled toward what I feared was the final foliage hiding fearful gaping jaws, I totally relaxed my entire body, going limp in the creature's slimy grasp. I could perceptively feel its muscles relaxing, too, but not enough. It still held me securely pinned. And then I was through the foliage staring into two flaming eyes atop a set of jaws fully three feet across, ringed with several layers of jagged teeth.

The slavering jaws gaped even wider as a yellow liquid ran down the sides of the head and along the neck that disappeared back behind the bole of a tree it seemed to be encircling.

Flaming eyes, ruby red, swimming in a dull, yellow sea

stared out at me as I was held suspended in midair, four feet from the gaping jaws. A horrid, fetid breath gushed out at me and I forced myself to go totally limp, even though every muscle ached to fight. It was this Herculean effort at limpness, though, that saved my life.

Evidently sensing I was dead from my limp body, the creature dropped me to the limb of the tree and shot what I now realized was its tail back down for more of its quarry. I fell heavily and rolled to a stop against one of my companions ... or, I should say, what was left of him. Evidently he had not been able to play possum, and about half of him had made a tasty meal for the creature.

I assessed my position and determined the only course of action lay in attacking the creature and killing it. Taking no thought to the difficulty of this task, I jumped to my feet and drew my sword. Immediately, the creature sensed my presence and swung his huge head around toward me and from all about me dozens of tails of other creatures dropped from the foliage above.

Being a man born of action and always lusting for a fight, I took no time to assess my present predicament but leaped toward the creature that had captured me and swung my blade. The metal cut through the creature's neck as a knife through butter, and as the head fell to the thickly entwined limbs, it emitted a terrible roar that was almost deafening. It was immediately apparent that I had not killed the thing, only decapitated its head.

Quickly, other creatures reached for me while the severed head kept snapping its jaws in my direction. Perhaps its brain was so small the creature hadn't yet realized it was dead.

In any event, I didn't wait to find out. Taking a firm hold on my sword, I jumped for the creature's body and tail which extended down through the foliage. Had I been able to see from what dizzying heights I jumped, I might not have done so, but all I could see was a pink, slimy body disappearing down through the foliage and it seemed to provide me my only means of escape from this precarious position.

I crashed through the foliage, catching a brief glimpse of great distances downward. Then I was too busy to look, grasping hold of the dead creature's body and sliding crazily down its length.

So fast was my descent the creature's muscles were unable to respond until I neared the ground. Then, at the last minute, the tail began to curve upward in an effort to encircle me. At that moment I spotted my friends and leaped free of the creature, at the same time swinging my blade backward and cutting through soft flesh, severing the last twenty feet of the tail.

I landed with a crash, amid much excitement from my comrades, but our revelry ended abruptly as dozens of tails darted out of the foliage above us, reaching out in our direction, searching for us.

Jumping to my feet I began swinging my sword to left and right, severing one after another of the tails that sought our little group. Finally, after seeing how easily my blade cut through the creature's flesh, my comrades took heart and jumped to their feet, swinging their four-foot broadswords with gusto.

It wasn't long before we had dispatched over a dozen tails amid a din of screeching from the branches above. Soon the other creatures withdrew their tails, and as suddenly as it had all begun, it ended.

The Bomunga shouted at the top of their lungs as they saw the creatures withdrawing into the trees above.

"Never have we ever killed any of the *Qouri* before," Moga shouted above the roar.

"I'm not so sure any are dead, Moga," I answered.

He shot a look into the trees above, each eye taking in a different area, but after a time he seemed satisfied the *Qouri* were all dead, and with great excitement that I had not observed before among my captors, we returned to camp.

"Why is everyone so jubilant?" I asked Moga after a mile's pace.

"Because you have returned from the very mouth of death."

"It was close," I agreed.

"And also," he continued, "we have found the *Qouri* no god at all!"

"You thought those overgrown worms were gods?" I asked in disbelief.

"Never before has one ever died. We always believed them to be indestructible. Is not a god indestructible?"

I couldn't argue with his logic.

The little party began to sing of their prowess and of the battle all the way back to camp. All that night great celebrations took place, and everyone danced and shouted. Everyone, that is, but me. I was fast asleep, dreaming of gaping jaws and slimy pink bodies reaching out for me.

I was still not sure of my station among the Bomunga. They treated me with solemn dignity wherever I went among them. Only Moga and Toogo spoke in my presence. Yet wherever I went, I also had Moga and the twelve guards whom I could never shake, no matter how hard I might try. Moga always laughed at my attempts to do so, thinking it was good practice for the dozen warriors. I thought it was disgusting.

About the third week of my imprisonment, a strange thing occurred that was to open my eyes to my true position among the Bomunga. I wasn't so sure it was better than what I thought had been my status. In fact, it made me feel more of a prisoner than ever.

CHAPTER SEVEN

It was in the early afternoon that Toogo came running into my chambers. I had been given the several smaller rooms inside the large building, where I had first seen the throne of Bomunga, as my private chambers. I never ventured into the large rooms which I took for the Bomunga's council chamber. The rooms I occupied had an entrance to the side of the building, and it was through this door that I journeyed to and fro.

They were appointed nicely enough I suppose, considering the culture and lack of craftsmanship among my captors. I had a pallet of feathers that was quite soft, and extremely comfortable once you got used to it. Three crudely constructed wooden chairs made from the tall, hollow reeds I had seen growing in the forest, and a table built from the same material in the same poor fashion completed the furnishings. Each of the three rooms was similarly appointed except for the pallet. Evidently the Bomunga spent very little time indoors and did not build for comfort but necessity. When they ate it was usually cross-legged, in the Indian style, on a mat woven of a type of bamboo also found in the forest. This weaving, however, was of intricate design and accomplished with loving care by the females of the tribe. Each room also had one of these mats and in each a table contained several of the tribe's eating utensils: a large and small wooden bowl and a tall cup for drinking; all were made from extremely heavy but porous wood which had to be covered inside with pitch or a similar gummy material to keep liquid contents from seeping through.

When Toogo approached me I was having my afternoon meal of *vruumtai* steaks, washed down with a milky white substance they call *dui* which was similar to cow's milk but

56

had a brackish taste to it, though it was palatable once you became accustomed to it.

"The council room is filling and you are needed," said Toogo excitedly as she approached, quickly falling to a position so her head was not higher than mine. "Moga awaits you at the throne." The urgency in her voice was great, and I put aside the remains of my meal and started toward the door.

"Wait, Yatahano, you must wear these," she said, holding up several objects. One was the flaming stone that Moga had taken off the fallen Portoona, which I had come to think of as a talisman of the tribe. Also, Moga had taken the victim's ear and placed it on a leather thong. This, much to my consternation, Toogo said I had to wear hooked to my lower belt. She also insisted I don the long Bomunga sword, so I strapped it on and then slung my own blade to my hip. As I was about to leave, Toogo delayed me once again, and taking a pouch from her simple harness, poured some more of the oily liquid into her palm as Moga had done when he conveyed me to the throne chair. The unction completed, Toogo stood back to survey her work. Nodding imperceptibly, she motioned for me to hurry into the chamber room.

As I entered the throne room, I saw it was filled nearly to capacity. Moga stood beside the throne and motioned for me to be seated upon it, doing so in his own inimitable manner of expansive movement of arms and legs. As I entered and was recognized, a hush fell over the several hundred creatures. They all turned in my direction as if on command and bowed as I passed them on my way to Moga and the throne.

The way they were treating me one would think I was someone of great importance instead of a captive. But strange are the customs of different races, and these seemed the strangest of all.

I sat down as Moga suggested by a sweep of his hand and looked out over the audience. I could not tell any difference between these in the room and those I had seen my first day in the encampment. For all I knew it could have been an entirely different group of creatures or the exact same ones. The only person I recognized in the room was Moga, and it was to him I turned.

"What do you wish of me?" I asked.

"There is a slight problem, *Yatahano*," he replied simply.

I was unfamiliar with the term he used to address me, and

I decided to ask Toogo about it after this session was completed.

"How may I help?"

"These have offended the Bomunga. law," he stated simply,
pointing to two creatures that had just been brought into the
room and roughly escorted to within a few feet of the throne.

One was a warrior, though the other was of somewhat
lesser rank. It seems there are some dozen or so ranks within
the Bomunga social strata. There is the highest level of warrior class, or *bamo* and the lowest level called *bamoto*, or
more literally "lesser ones," wore but one single belt, this
about their waists, and they carried no sword or other
weapons that I could distinguish among the several objects
that always seemed to hang from all Bomunga belts. I had
once asked Toogo how to know to which level an individual
belonged, for just because a Bomunga wore two belts, he was
not necessarily of the *bamo* group. "Oh, silly," she replied,
"one just knows." She hadn't, of course, used the word silly,
but its translation is something akin to that meaning.

"In what way have they offended the tribe?" I asked curiously. I was more interested in why Moga was conferring
with me on this matter than what the two had done.

"This *bamoto*," he began, pointing to the one wearing but
one belt, "has offended the tribal law by attacking his superior
officer."

Bamoto in the Bomunga language refers to all of the ranks
between the *bamo* and the *bamoto*. It could mean this individual was just below the other in one rank or a dozen ranks.
All that seemed certain to me was he was not of the lowest
level. Had he been, he would surely been put to death immediately, for it is the law that should a *bamoto* offend any of
the warriors of the tribe, he is immediately killed. This speaks
somewhat of the importance warriors are held in and the
contempt for the *bamoto*.

And, too, I wasn't sure whether one was a superior of the
other in the true military sense of the word, though I use the
term superior officer for want of a better translation.

"So?" I asked my companion.

"So, how do you wish to decide?" was his simple answer.

A sudden funny feeling began creeping over me and I
wasn't sure that I liked it. Was this some sort of test or was I,
in fact, some type of ruler or judge among these strange
people? Had my death blow wrestled the crown from the

head of the Bomunga leader that day several weeks ago, or was this just another part of the game I was being asked to play before some terrible death was inflicted upon me? The answer was not clear to me, but I made up my mind that before the day was out I would find the answer to this and many other questions that plagued me.

For some reason I didn't feel I could ask what the differences in rank were. Moga seemed to think I should know this, and I didn't want to disillusion him.

"Do you wish him killed, *Yatahano?*"

"How have you handled such occurrences in the past, Moga?"

"All cases have been handled by the will of the *Yatahano*. Sometimes one is killed, another time an arm is cut off, or a leg. Always it is different. What is your desire?"

"Is my desire final?"

"Yes, of course, you are the *Yatahano!*"

That seemed to answer one of my questions; however, what exactly was a *Yatahano*? I know that a Yoto meant slave and *Yotoha* meant warrior, but I had not the understanding to decipher the meaning. This was truly the only tricky part of the language and one that was giving me some problem. For by adding a consonant you could either be adding a more descriptive meaning to a word or changing its meaning entirely. There seemed no rhyme or reason for the method in which words were added to in order to make such changes in the language.

It wasn't until later that I realized the Bomunga language, as all of the languages upon Ghandor, had grown out of necessity instead of logical use. When a new word was needed, a consonant was added to an existing word or a letter added, or maybe two words combined to form the new word. Since the Bomunga have no written language, nor are they interested in any written form of their speech, it is no wonder that their manner of adding to their vocabulary is anything but logical.

All eyes in the room were upon me. I didn't know for sure if they were waiting to see what mistake I would make or willing to do whatever I bid. I was determined to find out.

"All right, all within the hearing of my voice take heed. This is to be the final law of the Bomunga. No more will there be death sentences carried out in such offenses against the tribe. Since all have stations and it is forbidden to aggress a companion not of one's own station, there shall be this simple method of redress when such an offense occurs.

"For every station or rank separating the offending parties, one *shaitai** shall be collected. If the offense is physical, such as the case before me now, the offended party may have the option to return the physical offense as many times as there are stations separating them rather than the payment."

There was a sound of great intake of breath within the room. A sound that I had come to identify with the emotion of great surprise. As I have mentioned earlier, the Bomunga do not have the facial expressions as do humans. They emit emotion as much as anyone, but in more subtle or at least less noticeable ways to the uninitiated. The reaction I received told me I had accomplished the same thing I would have if I could have materialized an entire Alban bagpipe regiment into the room, all blowing their hearts out on those squealing instruments.

Then, almost to a man, the Bomunga raised their right arms and shook their fists at me. It was impossible to read their expressions, but the implication was not difficult to fathom. I had made my first and, evidently, last mistake as their *Yatahano*.

* The *shaitai* is a form of possession among the Bomunga. It is akin to an earning in money, yet not exactly since the Bomunga do not have a medium of monetary exchange. However, every four weeks each warrior receives a sort of possession from the tribe. It may be meat or other food, or it may be an animal or even a female possession or slave captured from another tribe. Each receives according to his station and his accomplishment during the previous period of time. The more the tribe benefits from his activities, the more he receives in return. What he receives is from a common warehouse or holding house where everyone gives one-half of all he receives from his hunting, fighting, conquests or whatever might befall him. And since the Bomunga are honest to a fault, there is never any chance of cheating or being dishonest in their dealings. Thus, all share and share alike in the success or failure of the tribe.—DD

CHAPTER EIGHT

I was to learn over and over again during my many months on Ghandor, my first impression of the Bomunga and many of the less intelligent races of this strange land always seemed to be the wrong one. So conditioned was I to the habits and patterns of the people of Eire and the Continent that unconsciously at least I expected all people to be somewhat of the same temperament. It took many experiences over many months to realize that these people, even the more intelligent races, had a set of habit patterns all their own and in no way can they be compared with those of the peoples of my native world.

As the fists were being shaken high in the air, Moga turned toward me. "It is a good law, *Yatahano*. But what will make it a final law? What will keep the next *Yatahano* from sitting here and saying something different?"

Many in the front ranks of the group about us heard Moga's words, and quickly the question spread around the chamber until all leaned forward to ascertain my answer. For though it was a good law, indeed, what was to keep other chieftains after me from changing it?

"All of you will keep the law final," I replied so that all could hear. "From this day forward, no law will be passed or enacted unless the entire tribe agrees. All laws must be passed in council such as this and all fists must be raised or there is no new law."

Again the great shouts, the arms raised and the fists shaking in what I had just learned was the Bomunga form of agreement. It was like Parliament with their ayes and nays, though somewhat less refined.

When I finally returned to my chambers after the harrowing but somehow exhilarating experience, I cornered Toogo and got some answers. I learned that *Yatahano* means literally "Mightiest One." *Yatahan* is great warrior, and as I already knew, *Yotoha* is warrior and *Yoto* means slave.

I was the ruler or king of the Bomunga. I had been right in that the kingship had transferred to me, even though not of the *Zumtai* race, by right of arms. I had defeated Portoona and by so doing had ascended the Bomunga throne. The flaming stone that I wore was the Bomunga symbol of leadership. It was inviolate and because of that, the ruler was like a god. No one dared talk to him or be anything but overly respectful in his presence. This explained the strange behavior of the warriors to me over the past weeks.

It also became evident to me that the stroke of fortune that had evidently saved my life and given me my freedom as the untouchable ruler of the Bomunga also imprisoned me even more, for now I would not be able to leave my loyal subjects, and the girl seemed lost to me forever.

"Then why," I asked Toogo after the meeting, "if I am your ruler do Moga and his guards follow me around wherever I go?"

"Because they are your *howogi* and Moga is their *yatahan*. They do not follow you around, but rather, are for your protection should you need such. Though from what I have heard about your prowess with the sword I do not believe you need their help."

Her answer brought laughter to my lips and, no doubt, a reproachful look from Toogo, though you could never tell exactly what her expression might be under that mask of domestic servitude she always showed me.

I learned later from Moga that the line of ascension in the Bomunga tribe as in all of the *Zumtai* race is based upon the power of the strongest. Whoever wins among the great chiefs is the tribe's ruler until he is deposed, and then the challenger becomes the king. A most impractical method of choosing leaders, for seldom will a mighty fighter make a good ruler.

It was evident that their present form of government had been responsible for their lack of social advancement. Such tribal laws tend to stymie progress and achievement rather than foster it. The Bomunga had for centuries been halted in their development because of leaders interested only in their own personal glories and the ability to dictate their whims upon others. Of course, theirs was not unlike the land of my birth that had been torn with internal strife from much the same circumstances, to the end result that England had been successful in her devious plans to rule my homeland. Had the Clans welded together into one central government at any time in her history the English would never have been able to gain a foothold on the Green. This was one of the reasons I was glad to accept my father's offer and travel the Continent and see part of the world. I was fed up with the internal dickering of the chieftains as to whom should lead which group into battle. It had always been thus. When there hadn't been foreign enemies the Old Sod was torn with domestic battles. As far as I knew, this had been her history for centuries before my ancestors ever set foot on her soil. There I had not had the chance to change the political picture except for that one effort to fend Cromwell's invasion. But here I was the king! I could set the policies and dictate the laws if I could get my loyal subjects to understand the scope and the meaning of them. I decided as their new leader I would make some additional laws that would have far-ranging effects upon the tribe.

In the next session of the council of the warriors, I presented my plan. It took some talking, and after Moga sided with the idea the other warriors slowly followed suit. Simply, it was that never again would the *Yatahano* be chosen by mere force of arms. Only by the majority of warrior's votes delivered in the council chamber could one be accepted as the new ruler.

If someone among the tribe feel their *Yatahano* was being unfair toward them or not suggesting good laws, they had the right to demand a vote at the time the *shaitai* was delivered. This meant that once every four weeks a special vote could be called to reinstate or discard the present ruler. But if no special vote was called, then at least once every year a vote had to be taken among no less than three prospective rulers. In this way the *Yatahano* would always be on his toes to serve his tribe if he wanted to stay in power.

This was perhaps not the greatest method ever devised by man, but certainly less barbaric than killing political foes in order to decide supremacy.

A few days later as Toogo and I sat cross-legged on a mat of reeds over our afternoon meal, I approached her on the matter most pressing on my mind.

"Toogo," I began hesitantly, "where exactly are the other races of Ghandor that look more like me? Those northern tribes of which you once spoke?"

"The *Tojoga* races are far to the north. They require a cooler climate than do the Bomunga and seldom venture this far south except in their flying birds. Why do you ask, *Yatahano?*"

"I would like to visit them, perhaps," I replied, feeling my way. I could not tell from any movement whether she was interested in my conversation or merely perfunctory.

"It would not be wise, *Yatahano,*" she responded casually, not taking her eyes off a tidy morsel that she was devouring. "I believe they would kill you once they learned you were from the Bomunga!"

"Perhaps. What of these airships of theirs I saw many weeks ago?" I asked, changing the subject.

"Only the Thu have the flying birds. At least among the ones that fall to earth not to rise again, only those of the Thu race have been discovered. They must be a very weak race, for they travel only in the flying birds. They are not like the Bomunga at all. Our people can travel for days on foot and never tire. They are nothing but *taijai,*" she added fervently, which is to say, "they are weaklings!"

"If you dislike the Tojoga so much, do you dislike me also?" I asked, curious for her vehemence was real and had increased as she had warmed up to her subject. To Toogo, nobody but the Bomunga was worth two cents.

"You are not *Tojoga,*" she replied warmly, "you are the *Yatahano!*"

Though I could not see the difference there was a striking difference in the thought to Toogo. So much so, that she felt no further explanation was necessary.

"Toogo. On the day I was captured by the Bomunga, a girl was with me. She got away in one of the Thuian airships. Do you know of her and where she might be?"

"Ah, yes. The day the mighty *Yatahano* slayed twelve Bomunga warriors. Truly a miraculous feat. But of the girl, I told you before she is very important. Not for the Bomunga, except to kill."

"How is she important, Toogo?"

"She is the Princess Marjano of the Tojoga race that call themselves the Thu. They are of the north country and are a very important people! They rule much of Ghandor but are always at war with other *Tojoga* races. Perhaps they will all kill one another and we will have no more of them."

"Why were the Bomunga after her?"

"The Princess' flying bird crashed in the forest and our bitter enemies, the *Taajom*, had captured her and her warriors. However, she effected an escape and Portoona found out about it and set out to recapture her. He wanted to bring the *Taajom* her head and show them that the Bomunga were much superior warriors than the weaklings the *Taajom!*"

"Can you tell me how to get to the kingdom of the Thu?"

She emanated that curiously Bomunga intake of breath, showing her surprise. Then came a slow jerking of the shoulders which was the Bomunga equivalent of displeasure. There was no doubt that had I not been the *Yatahano*, I would not have received an answer.

"No Bomunga would want to go to Thu!"

"But the *Yatahano* wants to know how one would get there should a Bomunga ever decide to travel to the country of the Thu. Perhaps an expedition could be led there to recapture the Princess Marjano and bring her head back to the *Taajom!*"

Instant pleasure emanated from her through an almost imperceptible twitch of the flattened nose. In the several weeks I had been among the Bomunga I had come to recognize all their oddities of emotional reaction.

"That is different, *Yatahano*. I will show you."

She pulled a portion of the mat upon which we were sitting to the side and began sketching out an intricate map upon the flooring of the room with a hardened stick that made barely perceptible impressions. I was greatly surprised to learn she possessed so much knowledge pertaining to the lands of Ghandor. Her map also gave me the first inkling of where I might be, but it was many months later that I fully comprehended exactly where my passage through the swirling mist back on the rolling hills of my native Eire had actually taken me.

After my talk with Toogo, I began devising a plan to leave the Bomunga and try to find the land of the Thu, for the pull was strong to search out these people of my own kind. I wasn't sure what type of reception my plan would receive once I told of it to Moga. That I was the *Yatahano* there was no doubt, but what exact privileges that gave me when it came time for me to leave the tribe, I could not guess. Perhaps to the Bomunga once a *Yatahano*, always a *Yatahano*.

I broached the subject with Moga one day while we were out on the hunt. It was a beautiful day, as nearly all my days upon Ghandor had been. The sun shone down upon us with great intensity, but the dampness in the air cut down on the heat of the sun and it was quite pleasant. I had long ago given up my last link to the land of my birth when I said farewell to the clothes of my Clan and donned the more pliant and useful belts and kwai of the Bomunga. The flaming stone hung always about my neck, and though I still carried my own trusty blade at my side, I also carried one of the Bomunga swords in its scabbard upon my back.

We were making for a small clearing which was completely surrounded on all sides by dense forest. The foliage was a riot of color with acacia, philodendron, giant ferns, and an orchid-like flower that grew in profusion. And, as always, the numerous birds. Their chirping had become such a common sound to me that I hardly noticed the awful din. It was only when they stopped, or the pitch of the racket changed to a screaming clamor as they took to flight, that one noticed their presence.

For the first time I noticed their precocious young running about, many of which were just hatched. Rather than nesting in trees, the birds of the forest built their nests in the dense foliage of the forest floor. When the young hatched, ready to move at once, they wandered about in search of their own food. I never did learn how long it took them to fly, but it was evident that they learned quickly, for so many enemies roamed the underbrush that no doubt only a few made it to maturity—another one of nature's abundant checks and balances of this strange planet.

We were standing within one of the many clearings that dot the forest. None of the Bomunga seemed to know why these clearings were spaced as they were, but they knew them all within their imaginary boundaries and could make for one from any point within the forest should the occasion arise. My own uncanny sense of direction was equally helpful to me on my many hunting excursions enabling me to locate particular spots in which I was interested.

As we broke free of the dense foliage into the clearing, I had come abreast of Moga and picked up a conversation with him. So thick is the underbrush and foliage and narrow the paths through them that it is almost impossible to pass except in single file. Perhaps because of this, or perhaps because of the Bomunga's rather meager vocabulary, little conversation is enacted while upon the hunt or at any other time for that matter. No doubt my incessant need for talk, an inherited feature from my father, was a plague to the solemn Bomunga. I talked enough when I had the chance to make any man of Eire envious.

"Moga, my friend," I asked, "what would the Bomunga do if I were to take a journey by myself to the north country?"

He looked at me for a time. His expression was difficult to read, but I could tell he was perplexed by my question. Either he didn't understand why I should ask such a thing, or the answer was so simple and self-evident he felt no answer from him was needed.

"Why—nothing," he finally replied, after eyeing the surrounding foliage, awaiting the arrival of the *vruumtai* which the Bomunga warriors were now driving toward the clearing. "You are the *Yatahano!* You come and go as you please. There are none who can say where or when you should go or when you should return."

We stood in the clearing, back to back, awaiting the arrival of the small animals. The Bomunga split up into several groups, each taking a path leading to the clearing at a spot about a thousand yards into the forest. With small wood clubs which they used to create a terrible racket by beating them against hollow beanstalks some feet in diameter, they endeavored to drive whatever *vruumtai* there might be in the forest ahead of them toward the clearing. Only Moga and I stood in the way of the ferocious animals as they would race into the clearing looking for refuge. There could be two or three of the animals or there could be dozens. The sport was found in the anticipation of the danger of the hunt. Two men could easily handle a half dozen of the animals, but much more than that, the ferocious beasts could bring down and tear the warriors apart before help could arrive. Moga and I had stood like this in several other clearings over the past few weeks. At first he had been adamant about my not placing myself in so much danger, not being familiar with the unpredictable animals. But I finally imposed upon him as his chief to let me have a chance. In that first hunt, we had been overrun by no less then twelve of the wild beasts. Due to my amazing speed and lightness of movement on this planet, I was able to kill nine of the *vruumtai*, while Moga accounted for the other three. From that day on we looked forward to our sojourns into the forest on the hunt, never knowing if one day more than we could handle would come racing out of the foliage, eyes wild, hearts pounding, scared and mean from the fear of the racket the warriors were making behind them.

It was on one of these hunts that I decided to sound Moga out on the possibilities of my leaving the village.

"But if I leave, Moga, what will become of the leadership of the tribe while I am gone?"

Again he gave me that same, unreadable look.

"Nothing will happen. You are the *Yatahano*. You will always be the *Yatahano*. Only death or the tribe voting you out of power can change that! You are the one who gave us the law!"

Before I could answer, the screaming roar of the *vruumtai* assailed our ears. I could not tell, but it sounded like a frightful number of them were racing through the forest.

"*Yatahano*," Moga whispered, not taking his eyes off the forest to our left where the sound of the *vruumtai* was the loudest. "We stand together once again, yes?"

The twitching of his nose was more noticeable than I had ever seen it before. The Bomunga warrior was happy as a kid at Christmas time.

"We stand together, Moga. As always it should be," I replied honestly. The man was a repulsive creature to my earth senses, but a friend nonetheless. I was glad of the chance to experience the joy of the hunt with him and none other would I be willing to entrust my back to at such a dangerous time.

The animals exploded from the forest off to our left where we thought they would be. I counted over a dozen before they were upon us and I had no more time for such meaningless thoughts. Both Moga and I were nearly overrun in the first attack of the hairless beasts. Their pink eyes, blue tongues and yellow, inch-long fangs snapped at us from every quarter as Moga's and my blades swung right and left, decapitating heads on every side.

In case any of my readers might wonder at this needless carnage, let me explain. The *vruumtai* has the most succulent meat of any animal upon Ghandor. It is also one of the most ferocious and cunning. The Bomunga have found that there is only one way to kill the beast, and that is the fashion I have described. To try and hunt one down and kill it is a waste of time since none have been known to have been trapped in such a manner. Many attempts have resulted in the death of the tracker since the cunning animal seems to know exactly what the hunter has in mind and becomes himself the hunter and lies in wait to strike. Perhaps you have heard of the cannibal fish of Africa that can devour the flesh off a person in a matter of seconds. These *vruumtai* strike in much the same way; once they get their teeth into flesh, they won't let go, even if killed. They are ferocious animals, and it is only the extreme danger of the hunt that makes them an exciting quarry.

Moga was being hard pressed by several of the beasts. The fact that more than a dozen lay dead at our feet did not deter the remaining horde from pressing their attack, for they thought us the cause of their recent alarm.

Swinging my blade with all my might, I cut a path to the side of my friend and helped relieve him of a few of the *vruumtai* that threatened to break through his weaving blade.

"Ah, ha!" he called to me over the screams of the animals, "perhaps we have bitten off more than we can chew!"

"Nonsense, Moga, we shall prevail as we did the last time."

With that I believe he took courage for his blade became a living thing in his hand and though he wielded it without the skill of the master, he fought gallantly against the overwhelming odds. Perhaps we might not have survived the ordeal, except that our warriors emerged from the forest and fell to helping us out. And the *vruumtai* cannot be considered a dumb animal, for as soon as the others arrived, those who still could move made for the nearest path and safety!

"Well, we did prevail after all!" Moga exclaimed after he caught his breath.

"*Yatahano*," called one of the *howogi*, "I count twenty-seven *vruumtai*. Never have I seen so many before killed. You are the greatest warrior on all of Ghandor. The women will be singing of this to their grandchildren."

"Yes," added Moga loudly, "and the Taajom will hear of this and wonder at the greatness of the Bomunga and their *Yatahano!*"

The animals were quickly skinned and dressed. It was a joyful group of warriors that marched homeward that night. Already some of the *howogi* were beginning to make up words to a song depicting the battle. It seemed the Bomunga had a song depicting every act anyone ever did. I had once listened to them sing a few of them far into the night after a particularly important ceremony my first week in their village!

Three days later I was ready to leave on my journey to the north. I had convened the council and appointed Moga my chief lieutenant, he was to govern the Bomunga in my absence, or until they voted another into power. It was an eerie feeling I had as I left the village. All the Bomunga stood in the compound with right arms raised, fists shaking in tribute while I couldn't help but feel that Toogo was shedding a tear or two, even though I had never seen a Bomunga cry, nor did I even know if they could.

The animal upon which I rode, called a *thwod*, had an easy gait. Though terrible in appearance, the animal was really quite docile. It had taken me some time to get used to the two-legged movement of the *thwod*, but once I had mastered the unsteady gait, I felt it was more comfortable than riding the horses of my native Eire.

The Bomunga village is set in one of the periodic clearings that pinpoint the great forests of Ghandor. About five hundred yards across, it took me but a few moments to ride out of view of the village. It was with some sadness that I left the Bomunga behind, for they had become my friends and confidants. I had grown to respect them, despite their unseemly appearance. No better comrades in arms had it ever been my pleasure to serve.

I rode for several days to the north and east in the general direction of Toogo's map, which was etched in my mind before leaving the village. I spotted several weird-looking animals on my journey, many of which I had hunted with Moga over the past several weeks. I had come to really enjoy the meat of the small animal they called *Soo*, even more than the *vruumtai*, and it was upon these little rabbit-like creatures I made my meals. Another animal they called a *Yoo*, a boar-like creature as ferocious as the *vruumtai* though much less intelligent, I avoided whenever I could. This animal charged anything that moved and often stationary items, such as the trees and larger plants. Once while hunting with Moga I had seen a *Yoo* so enraged that it charged into a tree and split its head wide open!

The ever-present birds in the forest chirped as birds seem to do wherever they are found. I was always astonished by the vast numbers of these winged creatures. Literally millions of them were in the forest. I had never seen a single one in the clearings or upon the paths. Nor did any venture into the giant trees that were always present in the large clearings.

These huge trees had always been a puzzle to me. There were never more than one in any clearing. I had asked Toogo and Moga about them, but they had only shrugged their shoulders—a most disconcerting habit among the Bomunga—and stated their favorite saying to cover whatever they didn't understand. *"Buw mu gaa ithad,"* or, "that is the way it is." Curiosity was not one of the Bomunga traits.

On the sixth day out, I saw a very large object hanging in the trees off to the east. Changing my course in that direction at the first opportunity I made for this strange site. I couldn't tell what it was, but for some unknown reason I felt a deep apprehension within me as though I knew it to be something I feared to see.

As I traveled along a crooked but worn path through the dense foliage, I marveled at these frequent trails. For some unknown reason, the forest never grew up to choke off a path once it had been trampled or cut through the underbrush. It was as though the forest had given up on any additional growth. Perhaps at some time in the distant past nature had decided that not another single blade of grass, plant, or tree could survive so she shut down the growth cycles. In any event, when a path was cut it was there to stay. Nothing ever grew up to obliterate it, and passage along it was as wide or narrow as it had been when originally made.

The path I now traveled could have been cut three days ago or three million years ago ... they all looked the same. The uncanny directional senses of the Bomunga seemed to be aware of all the trails through the forest and they were always able to arrive at a point exactly where they wanted, irrespective of which path or the many branches from it they took in search of game or enemy.

During my many hunting expeditions, I had come to be able to do the same thing, thanks to my own sense of direction and a good memory.

Because of this I did not fear moving off the main trail heading in the direction of the glittering object in the distance. I was sure I could either find my way back to the original trail or keep going upon another toward the Thu country to the north.

As I traveled these several days, the picture of that beautiful face was ever before me. In fact, the girl I had saved in the clearing some weeks before was never far from my thoughts. There was no doubt she was the real reason I wanted to find the land of the Thu, though I kept telling myself it was merely to be among my own kind once again.

Finally I broke through a rather dense area of forest as the trail rounded a bend and I came upon the strange object I had seen some miles distant. As I looked upon it, my heart sank. It was a large, round airship which had crashed into the forest, though for what reason I could not tell.

The side of the ship was bent in a tangle of wreckage, and there were many holes torn in its hull. The four masts were severely distorted and looked like a giant had bent them at will. It was impossible to discern anything from the masts, as the flags or pendants had long since torn free and blown away in the high winds that sometime menace Ghandor.

With much trepidation I maneuvered my way under the hull of the airship. Again, my heart sank. I could see in the center of the hull was painted the same emblem as that on the airship that had taken the girl from the clearing ... the beautiful Princess Marjano. Was her beautiful form on board, a twisted, broken tangle of flesh? Had she met the same destruction as that of her airship? I shuddered at the thought as I made my way to the deck to see for myself.

CHAPTER NINE

Frantically, I climbed the overhanging branches up until I gained a foothold in the higher foliage. The Bomunga have a terrible aversity to heights, and to my knowledge, not one of them has ever climbed into the trees of the great forest. Whether this fear was due to the giant worms I had encountered some days ago or some other superstition I could not tell. In either event, though, I felt no such qualms about the heights, worms, or any other adversary. I enjoyed climbing among the trees and had done so much during my stay among the Bomunga, much to their consternation.

In fact, I had found a rather surprising phenomenon among the trees. About thirty yards up there exists a marvelous highway. This uncanny appearing opening in the dense foliage of the forest is totally free of all small limbs, flora, and even the fauna, as far as I had been able to determine. It was as though some race of people eons ago had cut out the entire forest at this height, except of course, for the boles of the giant trees. And the limbs had either grown, or been maneuvered by some powerful force, to form a network of intertwining branches with at times a rather smooth surface. You could usually see for some distance in any direction unless the boles of the trees were too tightly grown.

This opening among the trees was an even fifteen or so feet high and not a single twig, branch, or leaf existed below the roof of the opening, which was very tightly overgrown to such a density that one could not see into the trees that towered above.

While among the Bomunga I spent so much time traveling this avenue among the trees that they had given me the name: *Randa dumun twa,* which is to say, "He who flies through the trees."

Gaining the deck of the airship, I marveled at the work-

73

manship the craftsman had displayed upon the alloy used in the ship's construction. At close inspection I realized the alloy was not luminescent, as I had first thought. Instead, it had a high sheen to it, and from a distance appears to be luminescent while it is only reflections that cause the misconception. I also found that walking upon its surface was no easy feat, for it was slippery underfoot and I was continually losing my balance.

I searched throughout the airship looking for the Princess. The ship was constructed in three sections or decks. The lower two were used mainly for sleeping and eating quarters, though I also gathered from observing them that much cargo was carried below decks. From all appearances, the ship had no means of motivation. There were no sails, of course, nor any mechanical means which propelled it through the air. I saw no tanks, mechanisms, or anything that might appear to serve this purpose.

I also did not find a single soul aboard. Though the ship could be fitted out to carry perhaps a hundred warriors or more, this vehicle was completely devoid of people. Those who had been aboard when the airship crashed no doubt had survived the wreck and made their way down to the forest floor below. This lifted my spirits, for I had first thought I would find the girl aboard with those of her shipmates, broken in body as was the ship itself.

I tried to discern how long the ship had been pinioned in the trees. It evidently hit the branches above with enough impact to drive it well into the lower foliage, rendering it invisible to any rescue ship that might have flown over in search of it. This caused me more concern, for rather than Marjano being rescued by her own people, she no doubt had taken to the forest along with her warriors to find a way back to her land. Well aware of the dangers of the forest, I began to worry over her safety. Had she been captured by one of the rival Bomunga tribes? Was she now being marched through the forest to some far-off village? Had she already met her fate at the hands of some gruesome creature?

There was no question that her warriors would have protected her but their number might not have been sufficient to do so should they have run across one of the *Zumtai* tribes, for these warring creatures seldom traveled the forest except in overwhelming numbers!

This only added to my fear that Marjano had been captured by some barbaric tribe and that her life might even at this moment be in grave danger if, indeed, she were still alive. Descending from the airship I determined to find her at all cost.

I had spent a number of years in the woods of Eire and forests of the Continent, even in Africa, hunting and tracking. My woodcraft had been the envy of all my friends, yet when I first went into the forests with the Bomunga, I had to learn how to track all over again.

Tracking in my own world is based, in part, upon marks left upon the ground or brush. A bent twig, an upturned pebble, a patch of cloth caught by a twig. Time can be determined by the condition of the mark. For instance a footprint leaves a ridge around the impression. If the ridge is sharp and clear the print was recently made, but if the edges are crumbling and specks of dirt have fallen into the impression much time has elapsed since the print was made. Or a blade of grass takes so long to straighten itself after being stepped upon.

In a land where the foliage is never marked, where no new flora ever grows or older growth never dies, or where marks remain forever, the normal approaches to tracking become absolutely useless. An entirely different understanding and skill is required.

Though the multifarious forest does not grow up to obliterate passages cut through the foliage, there are other methods of tracking I learned to employ from Moga and other Bomunga warriors.

Though a broken twig or plant may look the same if it were broken two thousand years ago or just two minutes before, the dense foliage of the Ghandorian forests has other methods of marking the passage of animal or man in a matter of time. For some unknown reason, the plants in the forests are supersensitive to body temperature. Slight discolorations will appear upon the edges of foliage when a warm body passes within a few inches of them. Whether this is from the constant temperature on the forest floor despite the time of year, or the weather conditions in the upper trees, I cannot be sure. Perhaps the forest had grown so accustomed over millions of years of this constant temperature, which doesn't vary a single degree due to the denseness of the upper branches and foliage. The plants may well have lost all resistance to temperature variations they once had.

Were this the case, then it would be understandable why a person's body temperature as he passed by effects nearby vegetation. When I had asked Moga of this phenomenon, he merely shrugged his shoulders and said, *"Buw mu gaa ithad!"*

In any event, during my many hunting expeditions I came to learn the exact shade of color the different flora would turn due to this exposure to body temperature. I cannot to this day say exactly how you tell the difference between human passage and animals, but there is a distinct difference, though it may be more to the instinct of the tracker than to any exact marking.

The strangeness of the markings and the duration the flora is affected gives the tracker fair spoor to follow up to several weeks old. The *cwaiti* plant, for example, rather than discoloration, holds an image of what passes within sight of it. The *cwaiti* has a trifoliate leaf, much like a giant clover plant, with a high sheen on its underside. The leaf is slightly whorled, giving the underside good exposure in any direction. Much like a mirror, the leaf reflects an image, but the image doesn't disappear when the origin of the image passes by. Thus, a careful examination of the *cwaiti* will tell you what passed by within about a twenty-hour period.

There is also the *dachai*, a multifoled shrub with large, parrellel-veined clasping leaves. Within the sheafing of the leaf, a yellow, dust-like pollen precariously clings to the leaf stem. This pollen is easily shaken loose, and the mere wind created by someone passing quickly by causes it to fall to the ground. The pollen remains its yellow color for nearly two hours before it begins to turn a brownish color. The stages of the change in coloring is another method of determining the length of time that has passed since it was shaken loose from its sheath.

There are more, of course, but as any good tracker will tell you, it is not only the spoor that is followed, but the instincts of the person tracking that plays an important part in the successful pursuit of a quarry.

Though one would rarely venture from one of the paths that have been worn through the forest, there seem to be hundreds of thousands of these trails that intertwine to form a crazy maze to the untrained eye. I will always be indebted to Moga who showed me the method the Bomunga employ to always tell which are the main paths and which are not, and how to successfully track a very old trail, and how it varies from the tricks employed when tracking a fresh trail.

I cannot say that my mind dwelt upon all this as I raced through the forest. So keen was I in watching for the many telltale signs on the plants and vegetation, that it is doubtful my thoughts contained anything but the rapid interpretation of all that I saw in the flora.

It did not take long to realize the party from the airship, numbering only some thirty or so, had taken a trail almost due north from the crash site. It was easy to tell from the discoloration that still remained on certain of the wider leafed plants that the party had passed by more than four weeks before and perhaps as much as six. This served to emphasize the fact that Marjano had been aboard the airship, for that placed the time of the crash around the time that I threw Marjano onto the deck of the airship the first day of my arrival upon the planet.

Had I wanted to take the time, I could have easily determined the exact number of persons that had passed this way from certain discolorations upon an orbicular shaped leaf called a *zcotai* plant, but the number was not important to me . . . or so I thought.

Following the trail for more than a mile, I hurried to catch up with the Princess if I could. The trail was very cold, and it was only a matter of a few moments before I determined the direction in which they had traveled before I took to the trees to hasten my pursuit. This was not difficult to determine, since their route had passed many main trails that led away from the north. But always they had kept to a northern route, and it was a simple matter of deduction to realize this would be the shortest direction to their homeland. It would appear from this observation that the Thu people, for they were the ones who had been on the airship, either had the same uncanny ability to tell direction as the Bomunga or possessed some mechanical device to aid them for always they headed north.

As strange as it may seem, there are few trails in the forest that travel in a northerly direction. The *Zumtai* tribes have no love for the northern peoples and in consequence, have little to do with the northern areas of their forest home. Consequently, few trails have ever been blazed in that direction, for when a tribe had wanted to travel further north, they usually had done so in an easterly or westerly direction. Even though this might have taken them miles and days out of the way, they had a strong aversion to a direct trail to the north. Because of this it would not be difficult to track Marjano and her warriors from the trees above.

I sat in my mount for some time debating the merits of taking to the trees and gaining the highway above. There was no question that I could make much better time that way, but I didn't know how far I must travel. Should I leave the trail and do so, I would probably not return in this direction and therefore lose the value of my mount.

Finally, I decided it was more important to overtake Marjano's party. Untethering the *thwod*, I turned it loose to make its way home.

Jumping for the trees, I quickly gained access to the forest highway, as I had come to call it. From past experience, I knew I could travel as much in an hour as a person on foot along the paths below could cover in an entire day.

Descending only where paths merged or bisected each other from time to time, I continued my pursuit to the north. It was upon such descents that I determined that I was still traveling in the right direction, and this was more to salve my doubts rather than give me any additional information, for I had already determined that the warriors and Marjano would wind their way north as much as the paths would allow.

At the rate I was able to cover along the forest highway, I figured I would catch the Princess and the crew of the downed airship within a few days were they still traveling on foot. And that seemed a certainty, for only another airship would cut down the time it would take them to reach the northern extremity of the forest. Nor could an airship have spotted them had one flown over because of the denseness of the trees and foliage.

The thought of seeing the Princess in three or four days lifted my spirits and brought an old Irish courting song to my lips. I would be seeing her within a few days if nothing unforeseen happened and that was a mighty happy thought to me.

But as I was to learn, the unforeseen was indeed to happen, as it always seemed to happen upon Ghandor.

CHAPTER TEN

~~~~~~~~~~~~~~~~~~~~~~~~~~~~~~~~

Nights in the forest turned out to be most precarious. Large, predatory animals roamed the paths after dark and their passage below my perch was an awesome, fearful sound. One of the largest animals was the *mythai,* a four-legged, scaly brute with red, flaming eyes. Those flaming orbs were clearly visible in the stygian darkness and caused the hairs on the back of my neck to stand on end as I peered down through the occasional openings occurring where the branches were loosely entwined.

As darkness settles over the forest, a racket begins to develop which is a combination of screams and yells unheard of on Earth. Where the daylight hours are filled with the constant clamor of the millions of birds, their uproar is nothing compared to the shrill racket of the night-wandering predators.

Though the forest floor is alive with the fearful predators, there appeared to be none among the trees or other than the myriad species of birds. I had not encountered a single reptile on Ghandor and believed them to be nonexistent in this land filled with many other kinds of hideous creatures. Nor did I know of any type of living creatures in the trees except the birds and the giant worms, though Toogo often discussed some type of vague, ubiquitous creature that roamed the upper branches. When mentioning this unnamed creature, her comments were always in soft whispers, her eyes extended even larger than usual, her nose opening in quick, uncontrolled movements which is the equivalent of fear among the Bomunga, despite their not having a word to describe the sensation.

But I had always passed these off as superstitious ravings not unlike the many tales of little people, goblins and ghosts that were ever present in the stories of the older people in my native Eire.

The giant worms, though, were not superstitions. They had been real, their jaws capable of snapping a man in half as one had demonstrated to me not long ago. Yet other than on that one occasion, I had never encountered the slimy creatures again so I surmised they must frequent a specific area of the forest.

Being a strong man, well over six feet in height and much given to athletic games and contests, I found my first day of running along the forest highway somewhat less than taxing. In all, I figured I had covered some one hundred miles. This was mostly due to my increased strength and superior wind I possessed on this strange world, which never seemed to allow me to tire.

Even so, as darkness surrounded the forest, I settled down and quickly dropped off to sleep.

I dreamed of quieter days and romantic nights back on my native planet, of lasses and battles that had forged my very life. One pretty lass especially swam into my vision. A pert, bonny lass with freckles sprinkled over her nose and flowing along her cheeks. Soft lips that easily lifted into a devilish smile. As her face swam closer it began to change. The red hair turned yellow, and her stark white skin faded to a deep bronze. Her sharp features softened, and I caught the slightest hint of sweetness, and the face became that of the girl in the clearing, the Thuian Princess Marjano.

I reached out for her, but as I did so her features began to fade. A sharp odor assailed me, and the Death Wagon came into view. The odor became stronger and I felt as though a thousand fingers touched me.

The feeling was eerie, and I realized with a start I was no longer dreaming. The odor was overwhelming. I nearly gagged. I felt I was being suffocated by it.

I came fully awake and struggled under unseen hands that swarmed over my face and entire body. Hands? Why had I thought of them as hands?

Jabbing fingers—or tentacles—pinned me to the branches. I felt the very breath being crushed from me. Frantically I looked about me but couldn't see the faintest suggestion of a man or creature. The light trickling through the foliage from Ghandor's two moons was dim, to be sure, but I could clearly see my own person. I could see my hands, my legs, my chest, and nothing else.

What was it that was forcing me downward? What was crushing the breath from my lungs? Was I still dreaming? No. The pain was very real and I could feel the roughness of the tree limbs on my back. I knew I had little time left. With every ounce of strength I could muster, I pushed upward against the force that invisibly held me down. I could feel the sweat breaking out upon me as my strength began to wane, yet still I persisted.

Despite all my efforts I remained pinned, motionless, held to the branches by ... what? A terrible fear began to encompass me. Man or beast I did not fear, but this ... ! Had I traveled the thousands—millions—of miles through space to die here, alone, on a planet I knew not of? Would I come to my end at the hands of an invisible foe? Were I to die like this, without a sword in my hand?

Suddenly, the words welled up in me that Dowdalls had yelled at Canossa, Donia, upon the Salisbury Plain, and deep within the Inders Valley. The very same words a Dowdall had cried at the very gates of Paris with Rollo the Dane and another had sounded at Hastings with William as they turned the flank of the English.

The words welled up in me and burst out with the full force of my powerful voice: "I shall prevail."

Dowdalls had thrown that challenge at the Greeks, the Romans, the Celts, the English, and the Picts. And I threw it at my unseen antagonist.

"I shall prevail."

Despite my weakened condition, the words rang through the forest. The sounds of the night seemed to stop, and with added courage I shouted again with what little strength remained to me: "I shall prevail!"

The fingers probing me and pushing me downward relaxed and loosened. I could not tell if they had left me completely or still hovered about me, but I felt the breath return and I took heart. Again I tossed my challenge to the four winds, and with a mighty burst of renewed strength jumped to my feet, unsheathing my blade that still hung at my side.

I could still see nothing, but I sensed the fingers returning to touch and probe me. Angered by the frustration of this unseen antagonist, I spun about, swinging my sword in all directions.

"Get back!" I yelled, "who are you?"

No voice answered, but the odor I thought had been my dream came strong upon me. I felt, rather than heard, movement about me. It seemed to come from every direction at once. The hair on the back of my neck stood on end, and my skin crawled as I futilely searched for my unseen antagonists.

The blood of the Fian welled up within me. I swung my blade to right and left. With each stroke I could feel some resistance, as though I was cutting through something, though unseen, tangible. At first I doubted my sanity at this imperceptible tug upon the blade, but the stark, shrill scream that resounded all about me as I cut again to right and left restored my sanity.

"Ah hah, so you can be hurt," I yelled joyously, and took to swinging my blade with added vigor.

For fully ten minutes I fought the good fight. How odd that must have appeared beneath the thickly veiled twin moons of Ghandor. How strange the sight that met unseen eyes had they looked down upon this panorama of one man jumping about, laughing almost hysterically, swinging his sword in all directions, striking, as it would appear, empty space and all the time yelling taunts at an unseen enemy.

Toward the end, I began to realize I was alone upon the forest highway. Yet still I swung about, sword slashing, eyes flaming, lungs panting. But I was alone, and finally I stopped and stood spread-legged, eyes staring, sword outheld.

"Come, you heathens, come back and die. The son of old Fionn is not done yet! Come back, I say!"

How much time passed thus, I cannot say. It could have been minutes or hours. But eventually I realized what a ludicrous picture I must have presented, standing thus, my back to the thick bole of a tree, throwing taunts to the empty air.

Lowering the sword I relaxed my muscles and slid heavily down the bole to a sitting position. I vowed to stay awake, but before long I succumbed to the demanding master sleep and spent the rest of the night in fitful sleep, among slithering giant worms, slashing blades and unseen fingers that probed and poked much like a group of men checking an animal over for purchase. Not even the renewed clamor of the forest animals could break the great chain of sleep that claimed me.

As morning dawned and I struggled through half-sleep, my brain once again began to function, and I found myself beginning to doubt my sanity as I reviewed the events of the evening in my mind.

I had just about convinced myself that it had been but a dream when I chanced to touch my blade. My hands came away sticky. Instantly I was alert, and the first sight to assail my eyes as I opened them was a reddish-brown panorama spread all over the limbs, branches, and tree boles for some dozens of yards in every direction. My sword and my entire body were covered with the sticky blood.

Whatever the creature or creatures had been, they were not ghosts. They could bleed . . . and bleed a lot.

All that day I traveled north, stopping from time to time to check the trails below. I came across another one of the perfectly manicured clearings in the middle of the forest at midday. Grudgingly, I took time out to wash the sticky gore from me and fully cleanse my blade.

Throughout the day I continued to make my way north at a mile-eating pace. That night I again slept fitfully, this time dreaming of Marjano, first in the jaws of a giant worm and next in the grasp of a thousand unseen hands.

On the morning of the third day after seeing the airship, as soon as it was light enough to see, I again took up the trail. Descending after an hour to check a converging trail I noticed from the trees, I beheld a sight that made my heart stop.

I had just been about to drop from one of the lower branches to the path some twenty feet below when the light glittered off something metallic to my right. I could not make out in the dim light exactly what I had seen, but as I sat crouched there among the lower foliage of the tree, I could see many such areas where the dim light bounced and glittered off objects. Suddenly a stench filled my nostrils that was also new to me upon Ghandor, but not so new that I did not immediately place it from the many battlefields of my homeland.

Death was what I smelled, carrion! In the increasing light I dropped quickly to the ground and beheld what must have been a battle royal. At first glance it looked like some forty or more bodies lying at two converging trails. The battle had widened the two trails considerably so that a small clearing had been formed. Since the animals of Ghandor will not eat meat that is already dead, quite unlike the predators of my own land, all of the bodies were exactly as they had fallen in death. Nor, it was soon evident, had any of the bodies been carried off. And much to my delight, I could not see the body of the Princess among the dead. She must still be alive.

I quickly counted the dead. There were thirty-three warriors from the airship and eleven of some *Zumtai* tribe sprawled about in grotesque positions. There was no difficulty, of course, in telling the two types of warriors apart, but other than the fact that I knew there were thirty-odd warriors off the airship in this area, I could also tell they were from the ship as they all had the same insignia upon their shields and breastwork as was found on the underhull of the flying machine. It was the same magnificent insignia Marjano had worn upon her breast.

I cursed myself for not taking out the time earlier to have determined how many persons had alighted from the airship. It would have taken but a few moments to get an exact count from the many telltale signs the forest had offered. But I had been in such a hurry to catch up with the stranded party that I had not deemed it important. Now I did not know if all had perished or if, indeed, Marjano had been with them. I had taken it for granted that she had, but now I was not so sure. Would not she have fought beside them as she had wanted to beside me? And would not she have been killed in the battle?

It was evident from the signs in the forest that the *Zumtai* had lain in wait on both sides of the intersecting trail. The fight had taken place several days before. Tha black discoloration had all but disappeared from the edges of the vegetation around the battle area.

I searched along both trails for more than a hundred yards until I had definitely determined in which direction the conquering party had traveled. Following their path for several hours, it became evident they were traveling in a northeasterly direction, and though they had taken several intersecting trails, they always returned heading in that direction. I got the impression they were taking the different trails to sidetrack and confuse any would-be followers. Evidently they had expected pursuit. This might be to my advantage, for if they were expecting to be followed, they surely would travel more slowly in an attempt to cover up their trail as much as possible.

I took to the trees once again. Here I felt more at home, moving along the intertwining branches. Unlike the circling, crooked trails below, the branches offered me as straight a

path as I wanted to take. I could not fathom why the trees
seemed to have no foliage along their branches about fifty
feet above the lowest limbs. It was as though something or
somebody had willed it to be so. And the limbs were so thick
at this particular level that it was almost like walking upon
level ground. Yet every so often the limbs were sparse
enough to allow easy sight through to the ground. And the
areas of sparseness were always strategically located to afford
the maximum in observation below. It was almost, I believed,
as though someone had made it that way, but who or what I
could not imagine.

After several hours of steady pursuit I dropped to the
ground once again to get a closer look at the trail. Success
met my first attempt, for there, framed in the leaf of a *cwaiti*
plant, was the face of the beautiful Marjano. The image was
fuzzy and nearly faded from view, so I knew it had been
nearly a week since she had passed by. The image of several
Zumtai were also found among the leaves. Quickly I regained
the trees and took up my pursuit once again. I had been
about to stop for something to eat, but the sight of the
Princess on the leaf restored my vitality more than any nour-
ishment could have done.

Thoughts of the beautiful Marjano continually raced
through my mind. I couldn't help but think of the terrible
fate the *Zumtai* had in store for her. Had it been the
Bomunga, they would have cut off her head and presented it
to their enemies, the Taajom! It would not have mattered one
bit that she was a female or a Princess.

I spent that night impatiently awaiting daylight. The girl's
fate lay heavy on my mind. All night she seemed to be calling out for me to save her. Each time I saw her face clearly
before me I would reach out to touch her, only to awaken
quickly. And a good thing, so precarious was my perch in the
crotch of two branches. Though the upper limbs offered a
comparatively smooth and safe path through the trees, I had
not been able to bring myself to sleep upon it since that first
night. Instead, I had searched out a lonely spot where I felt
safer from stalking beasts and, especially, the unseen antagonists with whom I had done battle.

Morning light found me on the trail, once again making
sure of the spoor. Again I found the reflection of Marjano on
one of the *cwaiti* leaves. This image was far sharper than the
one I had seen the day before. I judged her passage to be no

more than three days . . . four at the outside. Exhilaration hit me as I could feel myself closing in on the girl and her captors. I had carefully counted the number as they left the battle area as nineteen. One of these was Marjano, which left only eighteen *Zumtai* warriors to kill in order to free the girl of my heart—a formidable task indeed.

No sooner was I back in the trees than I was racing across the limbs in the direction of the fleeing party. All morning I kept up the terrific pace that, due to my greater strength upon Ghandor, was faster than a man could have ridden a racing horse back in my native land. This, coupled with the slower pace men must travel along the circling, time-wasting paths below, I began easily to catch up to the party I chased. In a corner of my mind I was aware that the limbs upon which I raced were beginning to thin out some, and it was with greater difficulty that I was able to continue the breakneck speed with which I raced through the trees.

Off in the distance I became aware of a slight noise. At once I recognized it to be the noise made by a large body of warriors passing through the forest. My heart jumped! I had caught up with the girl. Looking off through one of the openings in the branches I saw the group of *Zumtai* warriors. They were walking single-file through the forest, and in their midst was the Princess Marjano.

She was wearing the same outfit she had on the first time I had seen her, strengthening my thought that the airship had crashed not long after I had thrown her upon its deck.

She walked with head high and, once again, I was aware of her strength and poise. Certainly, here was a regal being, every ounce the Princess of her birth. A rope encircled her neck and extended to the front and to the rear, held tightly by the warriors walking just in front and behind her. Despite this, she still looked every part the Princess. There was no mistaking her royal blood. Though a savage by earthly standards, she would have put all the ladies of all the courts on Earth to shame.

I didn't have time to further dwell upon her looks, for it was my intent to figure out a plan of attack. But, as I looked at the group, a sight caught my eye that stopped me cold. Off in the distance, perhaps a mile or so beyond the party, was the first city of major proportions I had ever seen anywhere upon Ghandor. This was not like the village of the Bomunga. It was of stone, with tall, tiered structures, ending in rounded tops. It was nothing like the castles of old Eire, for though built out of large square stone blocks, this city was built of a corbeled architecture that all outside structures were built so each successive stone projected beyond the one below it. This gave the city a perfect defense as no human could scale such a wall.

The city looked to be one single structure of gigantic proportions. There appeared no inner courtyard such as is found in the castles of my homeland. If there were courtyards within the city, they did not open to the sky.

Flags were flying from hundreds of masts spaced evenly around the city structure. I could not tell the markings on the pennants at this distance, but the coloring was nothing like the emblems of the airship that had rescued Marjano. I was certain this was not a Thuian city, just as I was certain it did not belong or at least had not been built by any *Zumtai* tribe.

The city was nestled amongst towering mountains, and I could see that the trees in which I moved were rapidly thinning out, ending at the edge of a clearing some five hundred yards from the city gate. And emerging from the gate were several warriors, coming directly for the party I was following.

These were not *Zumtai* warriors. Nor did they look exactly like the Thuian warriors I had found dead beside the trail. They were not deep pink in color as the *Zumtai*. Nor were they the bronze coloring of Marjano or her people. Their coloring, even at this great distance, was easily discernible as a yellowish brown, and they were more fully clothed than any people I had yet seen upon Ghandor, and more heavily armed.

There were fully fifty warriors emerging from the stone city, and each carried a long, pointed shaft, something like a short javelin, though much thicker. There was the ever-present sword at their hips, though not the large flatblades of the Bomunga but a smaller blade more like my own, only several inches longer. Also, each warrior had a bow about his shoulder with a quiver of oddly shaped arrows on his back. They wore garments that covered the body from neck to ankle, tapering along each leg like a pair of tight-fitting pants. They also wore the *kwait*, or skirt, of the warrior and the same belt harness as all warriors on Ghandor seemed to sport.

Their clothing was a solid coloring of the deepest purple

red I have ever seen, nearly matching the royal color of the English throne. This only served to heighten their odd yellowish brown complexions and gave me an eerie feeling as I spied them through the trees.

The city warriors were not traveling fast, and this made my next decision more applicable to success. For I had determined to attack the *Zumtai* along the path and rescue the Princess before they reached the city. The presence of another body of warriors approaching only heightened the need for speed.

All of this I observed and decided as I continued my pace through the upper branches. By the time I decided to attack, I was almost directly over the last warrior along the trail. Suddenly an idea came to me, and it was so simple I had no doubt that it might work. Dropping softly to the trail some twenty feet behind the last warrior, I followed stealthily along until a bend in the path appeared before them. Quickly I covered the distance separating me from the last warrior of the band, timing my approach so that I was upon him just as the others rounded the bend.

Because of the large mouth of the *Zumtai*, it would not be possible to shut off any yell with a hand. I decided against that normal method of securing silence in favor of using the heavy hilt of my sword like a bludgeon. Bringing down the heavy blunted weapon, the first warrior fell beneath my blow as silently as a ghost. Stepping over him, I advanced upon the next, once again bringing the sword hilt down upon his unsuspecting head. Since the Princess was halfway up the line of warriors, I had seven more creatures to fell before I could reach her and make for the trees.

I became concerned over the time it took me to fell five more of the ugly brutes, and I knew it was only a moment or two before the two warrior parties would meet. That would put an end to my rescue plans, I knew; for these warriors had been traveling through the forest for several weeks and they were tired. Being close to their destination they were languishing in their success and lulled to a partial relaxation, if it can ever be said that anyone on Ghandor ever relaxes from the dangers about him. But once the two parties joined, they would be ever more alert, the final destination but minutes away.

The next warrior fell below the hilt of my sword. I silently stepped over him and began to congratulate myself on the accomplishment of my goal. Only one warrior was left between me and the girl, and it would be but a moment before I reached the trees and safety with her. I could almost see her look of approval as I imagined it would be after I effected her second rescue. What words of praise would she use to acclaim my brave act? If only I had known . . .

Raising my hilt for the final blow, I saw my carefully laid plans go up in smoke—or come down in a scream, as it were. What fates were these working against me? Where the little people here on Ghandor, too, keeping me from my lady love? What evil thing was this that stalked me every time I came within grasp of my goal? Was I never to have the joy of seeing the Princess Marjano safe from harm?

CHAPTER ELEVEN

Steathily I crept forward, raising the sword hilt above my head. One swing and I would be able to catch up the girl and jump for the trees. Just as I began to congratulate myself on my achievement, a loud roar startled the quietness. Its shrillness nearly turned my blood cold. All else in the forest stopped, even the chirping of the birds.

So startled was I that I failed to continue my downward swing upon the head of the warrior before me for a split second, and that was my undoing, for had I dispatched him, I still could have claimed the girl in time to escape the ultimate fate that overcame me. But upon such split seconds are fortunes won and lost. For, as the shrill roar reached my ears, the warrior in front of me spun around and, seeing me, made the lightning-like draw of his four-foot sword from over his head. Before I had time to realize what had even caused this change of events, I was fighting for my life.

His sword swung downward in a graceful arc, and it was all I could do to turn it aside before it split me in two. The force of his blow knocked me to the ground, and as he raised the sword for another try, he saw past me for the first time and what he saw froze him in horror.

Though I did not know it at the time, the fallen bodies of the eight warriors I had dispatched had attracted the attention of one of the dreaded *mythai*, the cat-like beast of prey which is absolute King in the Ghandorian forests. This beast stands well over five feet at the shoulder, must weigh near a ton, and has a constantly antagonistic attitude. It is a formidable foe and possesses no weak spots that are known. Its hide is quite thick, and though its appearance is definitely feline, it more resembles the crocodiles of Africa than any other beast I had ever seen in its makeup.

In addition to its scaly hide and long, dangerous tail, it has the double-hinged jaw of the crocodile, with teeth more resembling those of man-eating shark, though somewhat longer. It has enormous eyes, bloodshot in appearance, and hideously protruding from the side of its head. It also has a thickly matted mane that hangs down at the side and underneath its huge head that tends to give it an even more awesome look as it charges down upon you with jaws open, ready to rip and tear.

It was this fearful sight that stayed the hand of my attacker long enough for me to run him through with my blade. It was also this fearful sight that turned Marjano's first look of grateful relief upon seeing me to one of horror as she saw the animal charging me.

In that short span of time between the roar of the beast and the look of the girl, I had not given any thought to what had caused the noise. Yanking my sword from the fallen warrior, I jumped to my feet and spun to see the great animal bounding up the path toward me, covering the distance between us in twenty-foot leaps. I barely had time to bring the blade to bear before the beast was flying through the air, full out toward me!

I knew I could not try and avoid the charge, for even if I were successful, the animal would continue on into the girl. And, as strong as I believed the girl to be, such a happening would crush the very life from her beautiful form.

All of this flew through my mind in but a fraction of a second, and even so, I was moving into action. For, as the beast leaped at me, I brought my sword up and braced it with both hands. No sooner had I done so than the beast landed upon it. A terrifying yell emitted from his large jaws, and down he came upon me.

I was struck with the repugnant hideousness of this strange beast. Much bigger than the tigers of Europe or the lions of Africa, it did not resemble any type of cat I had ever seen. Yet, there seemed no mistaking it for a member of the feline family. Perhaps it was the smooth way it moved that reminded me of the cat. I don't know, but in any event, it was an awesome creature that crushed me to the ground.

I stared into snapping jaws ringed with three rows of sharp teeth, each row slanted in a different direction. I felt sure that if those teeth ever closed about me, they would snap me in two, much as the giant worm had done to my companion weeks before. The creature's scales scraped the skin from my chest and thighs, while I struggled with its enormous weight.

As the brute struck me, the force of his leap carried me backward along the trail ten feet or more. The thought crossed my mind that the force should have carried us right into the girl, but I had no time to give it any thought, for the beast was rolling with me and I feared those gaping jaws.

I tried to roll free but the big beast's weight kept me pinned beneath him. He was adamantly trying to maneuver his ponderous head between his forepaws to get me between those rows of tightly packed and deadly teeth. Luckily, as the beast struck me and we went tumbling, I ended up with my face nearly even with the spot where my blade had entered his body. Grabbing the sword with both hands, I ripped it downward, along its underbelly, toward my feet. The fine steel cut downward and ripped the entire underside of the animal, as the beast let out another of its terrifying roars. Had I not possessed the overpowering strength that was mine in this strange world, I never could have managed this feat.

Realizing it was getting the worst of it lying on top of me, the animal sprung to its feet. I had a glimpse of the trail behind me as I jumped up and swung to meet another charge. Something about that trail bothered me, but I gave it no mind as I swung the blade, aiming at the beast's neck, hoping to sever the ugly appendage. Unfortunately, my hand must have slipped upon the hilt, so covered with the beast's blood it was, that as the blade struck, it turned in my hand and the flat of the sword gave the beast an ugly blow. Not enough to do any damage, but enough to deter its charge to the side of me. The blow knocked the animal off balance, and as it crashed into the foliage at the side of the trail, it was momentarily snagged in the undergrowth—just enough so that I could regain control of the sword and bring it down on the back of the great beast's neck. The metal sung as it smashed through the air but bounced harmlessly off the scaled neck, giving my arms a jarring repercussion. The scales that overlapped on the back of the animal had not even been dented by the keen edge of my sword.

Undaunted by my effort, I swung the blade back from the left with both hands and all the strength I could lay into the effort. In that split second before my blade struck home, the creature, struggling in the underbrush, trying to break free, swung its head up and away from me, thus exposing its neck.

The steel went through the scales at this point and into bone like a knife through butter. In that moment I thanked the great metalsmith who had carefully tooled that blade some several hundred years before. And I also gave thanks to the fates that had caused the creature to so move at that critical moment.

I looked down at my scratched and bleeding body. The animal, though only landing upon me for that brief moment, had taken its toll. Deep scratches were everywhere along my legs and arms. Quickly, I felt for the flaming pendant and was relieved to find it still about my neck. This was one thing, like my sword, I could not afford to lose, for it was the symbol of leadership of the Bomunga and I had sworn to protect it. I had tried to persuade Moga to let me leave it behind, but he had been insistent. "The great stone must always hang upon the *Yatahano*," he had said, "or there is no Bomunga!" Whether it was superstition or just tribal pride, I could not tell, but that they placed reverence upon the flaming stone there was no doubt.

Looking up the trail, I saw what had earlier bothered me. The path was clear. What had happened to Marjano and the other warriors, I wasn't sure. Most likely the warriors had snatched her up and beat a hasty retreat from the approaching *mythai*. The thought struck me that, undoubtedly, the last sight the girl had of me was my falling beneath the great animal. Perhaps she thought me now dead. What I would have given in that moment to know how she had taken that news.

Leaping for the lower branches, I made my way to the avenue through the trees. I did not have time to tend to my wounds at this moment, nor did they bother me greatly. I was so intent upon finding the girl that the pain was hardly noticed.

As I neared the end of the forest, overlooking the marvelous city I had spied earlier, I caught a glimpse of the *Zumtai* warriors and the stranger-looking warriors from the city. They had met and merged. For some time the *Zumtai* seemed intent upon the path from which they had emerged, but the city warriors apparently gave no concern to their fear. Perhaps the city warriors were used to the *Mythai* or knew some other creature even more formidable.

Slowly the two groups made their way back to the city gates, but here they stopped. Some squabbling or negotiating seemed to be taking place, but I was some five hundred yards distant and could make out little more than a few arm and hand movements. Whatever the problem, the city warriors had their way and evidently were not going to let the *Zumtai* into their city. Finally, they arrived at some agreement and escorted their captive rather roughly through the gate, which was nothing more than an elaborate breastwork built into the wall of the giant structure.

The *Zumtai* warriors stood around for a few moments shuffling their feet, and then headed back across the clearing. They did not, however, enter the same path they had been traveling. At first I was interested in this, then decided it was only because they feared the *Mythai* still within the maze of paths they had just left. As I watched them disappear into the tangle of vegetation, an idea came to me. Perhaps they were a little disgruntled at the city warriors, and maybe enough so as to be of help to me.

Moving swiftly through the trees along the perimeter of the clearing, I came to the path the warriors had entered. It was but a moment before I reached them and dropped to the ground a few yards before them.

I raised my right arm, bent at the elbow, hand doubled up in a fist. This was the Bomunga form of greeting that I hoped was recognized by all the *Zumtai*. Had I used only my left arm, it would not have been as significant, for the Bomunga warriors always keep their right hands free for a sword draw unless they are among their closest friends. Though this left me open to attack, I was counting on this sign of close friendship working in my favor.

"Toabe!" said the first warrior, rather hesitantly I noted.

"Toabe!" I replied loudly.

The warriors bunched together in the narrow trail and instantly they recognized me as the one who had been attacked by the *Mythai*. Astonishment crossed their faces ... that is, their audible intakes of breath noted their surprise!

"It is the *Mythaiumo!*" Since *mythai* means approximately "giant cat," *mythaiumo* literally means "giant cat killer." Actually, *mythaium* means killer of the giant cats, but by adding the "o" to the word, the entire meaning takes on new significance. They were not just telling me I was a killer of the giant cats. They were calling me the Giant Cat Killer, much like we might have named a fighting champion back home. It was a signal honor, and I knew instantly that I had both the respect and awe of these warriors. Now, if I could only gain their cooperation, I might yet rescue Princess Marjano. But I had not counted on their choleric nature, and before I could respond to their compliment I found myself staring at three swords which uncomfortably pricked my chest. This was my first encounter with a tribe that could both admire your prowess at the same time it was plotting your death. The Bomunga had been of a much different fiber than this.

How they had managed their lightning-like draw of those four-foot swords in that narrow path was and still is beyond me. I had never been able to master the quickness of that sword draw, much to the delight of the Bomunga, who found me a formidable warrior in every other aspect.

Exactly what provoked them or how they ever managed that draw in those cramped quarters, I will never know, but that they meant to do me in right there on the spot, I had no doubt.

CHAPTER TWELVE

Strike me down they would have done had not one of their fellows to the rear pushed himself forward and stayed their hands with a sharp command.

"Who are you?" he asked.

"My name is Robert Dowdall."

"From where do you come?" he asked, not even blinking at my strange-sounding name.

"A faroff land called Eire."

Nor did he try that word, either.

"Where did you get that?" he asked, pointing at the flaming stone I wore about my neck.

"It was given to me by Moga, of the Bomunga people," I replied honestly, not sure what significance he would place upon the stone or upon the manner in which I received it.

"The Bomunga would not have given that to you," he replied, and I could almost detect a smugness in his tone as though he had caught me in a lie, though the *Zumtai* races do not understand lying or ever employ the distasteful practice. Probably he thought I was ridiculing its purpose and the high esteem in which the Bomunga hold this prized jewel.

"You are correct, the Bomunga do not just give this stone to anyone. But to me they gave it for I won the right to wear it and rule over the Bomunga people. I defeated Portoona, the wicked ruler of the Bomunga with one single blow from my fist ..." as I spoke this I once again raised my right fist and this time shook it in his face, but much to my surprise and his credit, he didn't move a muscle ... "that killed him on the spot. Moga passed the stone to me as symbol of my reign. However, I did not take it until all of the Bomunga made it clear in council that I was to be their leader. And that is what I am."

The chief of these warriors still had not moved but continued to gaze at the stone. Finally he reached out and touched it. This he did with great reverence.

"You killed Portoona? With one blow? He was a mighty warrior, a *Yatahan!*"

It was evident he did not think me capable of besting the Bomunga, so I decided to show him my great strength. Looking around, I noticed a small tree by the edge of the path in which we stood. These small trees that line the paths are of a different species than the big trees of the forest. Though sizable in some respects, standing some hundred feet or so in the air and about two to three feet through the bole, they are an extremely weak tree at the base. I was surprised the first time I was forced to test the strength of one while trying to avoid the charge of a Soo that Moga and I had cornered upon a path while hunting. The tree held firm, but I was astonished to see that the bole was crushed by my weight about three or four feet off the ground. After that I made much sport crushing the trees with blows of my fist, much to the merriment of the Bomunga warriors.

As I spied one nearby, I decided to give the *Zumtai* before me the shock of their lives and at the same time add emphasis to my story, for I was in hopes that these warriors might be able to help me rescue Marjano from the city, if I could but get them to side with me.

"Watch," I said loudly, so all the warriors could hear me. "I will crush this tree with a single blow."

For some reason the *Zumtai*, with their triple jointed arms could not muster enough strength with a short blow to damage the tree in any way, or so I had learned from several Bomunga warriors trying to match my feat. I hoped these warriors before me had never been able to master it either.

Spinning to my right, I struck the bole of the tree a terrific blow with my fist. It sank into the yielding fiber to the wrist, and the bole split in several directions at the same time. The tree toppled as though it had been felled with an ax, though the wood was not separated by my blow.

"*Ooaab!*" exclaimed the warriors as though with one voice. I had never been able to place a proper translation upon this word; let it suffice to say that it is an exclamation meaning "great surprise."

"You say you did not wear the stone until after all of the

Bomunga agreed that you should rule?" Only the leader had maintained his calm during my demonstration.

"I set down many new laws for the Bomunga. One was that no one should rule by right of arms or strength alone—only through acceptance of all the warriors!"

"And the *bamo* agreed?"

"Not just the *bamo*, but all of the *bamato* and even the *bamoto*. The rules and laws pertain to all of the Bomunga, not just a few!"

"A wise thing you have done, *Yatahano*!" With that, all of the warriors before me nodded at the waist, a sort of short bow the *Zumtai* profer to their ruler.

"We are of the Togaoa. The Bomunga are our cousins* to the south. Our boundaries lie next to each other and we are not at war with them. We will honor you, *Yatahano*, when we return to our village, since it is much closer than that of the Bomunga."

"Thank you for the honor, my friends, but I cannot return to your village, nor mine. I have come north on a special mission which may take me many months. A part of that mission lies there in the stone city."

The leader raised his shoulders in the Bomunga emotion of displeasure. "That city is filled with *yuda*. Nothing there can be of any value!"

A *yuda* is equivalent in Bomungese to calling a person a swine back home. It was evident that the city warriors had insulted these creatures before me.

"I need to know of the girl you took to the city and what is to become of her."

His expression did not change, but I could tell that my question was not what he had expected.

"The girl we found in the forest? The one whose guards we killed? She is of interest to the Bomunga!"

---

* The *Zumtai* are all interrelated in such ways as to make ancestry among them hard to determine. They do not use such words as father, mother, son, aunt, uncle, etc. Nor is the word cousin part of their understanding. They have a phrase *"ooda yai"* which there seems no English equivalent. Suffice it to say that in this case cousin is as close a translation as one could find, though you would never hear Bomunga referring to any of the other *Zumtai* tribes with what they would consider as such an incriminating statement.—DD

"She escaped from the Taajom and the Bomunga would like to capture her to show up these *yuda* from the south."

Though this was the truth, it certainly was not why I wanted information about the girl. I hoped the Togaoa leader would not pursue this line much further.

"Ah, I see. A good quest, *Yatahano*. The girl is of the Thu race as you know. The people in the stone city beyond the clearing are Meoathai. They hate the Thu even worse than we do, though why I cannot tell, for except the color, I cannot tell them apart!"

With that his companions all roared with laughter, but immediately stopped when they realized I was more of the Thu race than their people.

"My apologies, *Yatahano*. It is but the habit of centuries."

"I understand, my friend. Do not be bothered. Tell me more about the girl."

"The Meoathai have a standing offer to reward the Togaoa handsomely for every person of the Thu race we bring to them. Frequently, the Thuian flying birds crash and we capture them, though this time the warriors put up a stronger battle than I have ever seen them do. I still do not understand why they fought to the last man. It was much to my dismay that they did, and we had to kill all of them. The girl we were able to save for she did not carry a weapon and was instantly felled with a blow to the head from the *thwarpa*."

I cursed under my breath at the thought that one of the heavy missiles from the warriors' sling had struck the beautiful Princess, but since I had seen her walking through the forest, the blow could not have injured her severely.

As we talked, I learned that the Meoathai kept any Thu captives in a central compound at one of the lower levels of the city, probably in a jail or dungeon. There, they worked as slaves, making powder that the Meoathai use in one of their weapons. Since the Meoathai have been at peace with the Togaoa for many years, the warriors before me saw no reason why they shouldn't benefit from the Meoathai needs.

Marjano were merely one of scores of captives the Togaoa had turned over to the city people. Almost all had been warriors. Marjano was only the third female they had ever found in the forests. Evidently, the Togaoa did not know that Marjano was a Thuian Princess, and this was probably the reason why the Thuian warriors from the airship had fought so gallantly in her defense.

I gained an understanding from the warrior as to how the city was laid out, at least the part he had been in during his infrequent trips there with prisoners for sale. It seemed a complicated structure, but the Togaoa's uncanny sense of direction, like that of the Bomunga, served to help me visualize the structure in precise terms and routes.

I tried to enlist their aid, but they would have nothing to do with the city. The warriors had been told that if any of them were ever again seen at the gates they would be killed. Usually this would warrant an all-out war between the two races, but the Togaoa informed me that these city warriors had weapons that could kill from great distances and they would not stand a chance in any battle. For the Meoathaians seldom, if ever, left the confines of their great city and never traveled in the forest, as their weapons were not effective except in the open spaces of the clearings.

It was this that had inspired the shaky truce that existed between the Meoathai and the Togaoa. Since the latter had no interest in the city, and the Meoathai never traveled in the forest, it became evident to both races that a truce would serve them both. The Meoathai, so they would not have to be concerned with attack from the south, and could spend their energies developing their weapons for what the Togaoa informed me would be a great attack on the northern peoples. And the Togaoa were glad for the truce, as they had their hands full with their natural enemies on the east and west boundaries of their kingdom. It is always nice to know that you are secure from attack on at least one front, and if on two, then so much the better. A shaky truce, for no other type exists on all of Ghandor, is better than no truce at all, I learned.

But the Togaoa had been badly mistreated at the gates a few moments before, which led me to believe that the truce had come to an end, though I'm not sure the warriors standing before me had yet reached that conclusion. Old ways are hard to break on Ghandor, and most of the races I was to learn about were slow to change their thinking. It would probably take a full-scale attack by the Meoathaians for the Togaoa warriors to realize that they no longer could feel safe along their northern border. However, that didn't keep these warriors from offering me their assistance in the forest for to return the insult of their treatment at the city gates was foremost in their mind. And I learned that such incidents were not infrequent between the two races. Though safe from a large attack, the two races often made a game of small skirmishes when the opportunity afforded itself. This was usually when the Meoathaians strayed too close to the edges of clearings where the Togaoa warriors could jump them with little fear of their terrifying weapons.

I asked Poaha, the warrior leader before me, if he would send back one of his men to bring up additional help should we need it later, for I expected all sorts of problems and it was always better to be prepared. As he agreed to do this I bade them farewell and swung to the trees. I was eager to be off on my quest for the Princess Marjano's rescue. And I was to set into one of the most bizarre adventures I have ever experienced.

CHAPTER THIRTEEN

By dark, I had determined how I could enter the city, though my plans once I was inside the city were quite nebulous. It had been evident from my observation of the great fortress that several races lived within the stone structure. I saw some of the deep pink *Zumtai* tribes, there were even several of the bronze-skinned people from Thu, but I got the impression these were servants or possibly slaves. I also saw a couple of other races I had not seen before. One was of a silvery white skin, almost brilliant in color, and the other was a very comely race of high-cheekboned, deep-chested warriors of a tan, almost cocoa-brown coloring. It was impossible to distinguish features any clearer at the great distance I was forced to stay in order to remain concealed among the trees. I had, however, learned several things about the city.

It was built of great stones as I had first imagined, and upon close inspection I found it to be more like the ancient castles of Europe than I had first believed. It didn't have a moat filled with water about it, but the ground had been dug away for nearly fifty yards in a great depression which had been filled with large, jagged rocks, making passage in that direction most difficult, if not impossible. There were several gates into the city. Two I had already seen, on each of the three sides that were visible from the forest. The fourth side of the city was nestled up against the mountain, though I could not tell if there were any space between the two.

I had also climbed to one of the uppermost limbs of the great trees near the edge of the clearing and learned that, indeed, the city did have openings to the sky, but in a most ingenious fashion. The roofs, though joined, were of varying levels. Spaced evenly at about fifty-yard intervals was an open courtyard covered with a clear material much like glass. This material, or glass, was slightly yellow in color which, I later found, was an effective means of filtering out the sun's burning rays. I could distinguish foliage beneath the glass, and this is where I caught sight of the many peoples of the city.

I also had seen many doorways that opened onto the different roofs of the city, and this is where I intended to make my entrance.

Before I had left the Togaoa warriors, Poaha informed me that he had a friend within the city. Her name was Droaih, and she was Meoathaian. How Poaha had made her his friend I never learned, but that she was loyal he had no doubt. Many times she had sought him out on his trips to the village with captives and given him information. These helped the Togaoan to better understand the yellowish brown people with whom they did business. It also gave him a better understanding of the purpose of the truce and why they needed the Thuian captives. On his last visit there, some weeks earlier, he had learned for the first time of the powder being made as a necessary part of a new weapon by which the Meoathaian ruler, Euoaithia, hoped to conquer the races to the north and become ruler of Ghandor.

That seemed like a tall order, but not so when you understand the psychology of the beings of this planet. For some unknown reason, each race I encountered seemed to feel they were all-powerful and supreme. Even though the Togaoa realized that the Meoathaians had superior weapons, this did not deter them from considering themselves superior in every other way. Only the Thu seemed to have a place of eminent authority in the minds of the Meoathaians, and they no doubt felt that to destroy their northern enemies would give them full rule of the planet. I learned much later that there was far more to it than this simple explanation.

From all that I had been able to determine, the *Zumtai* races knew absolutely nothing of what might exist in other areas of the planet. There were wandering tribes and peoples known far and wide, but what existed outside the forest area, which covered several thousand square miles, was mostly known to me by bits and pieces as I had heard it relayed by Toogo and Moga.

Euoaithia's boast to become ruler of Ghandor was probably more accurately stated as wanting to become ruler among the peoples he knew. Euoaithia sounded a great deal to me like another man I had sworn to stop by the name of Cromwell.

I asked Poaha what he thought of this venture of the Meoathai, and he shrugged and expressed the only philosophical view I had ever heard among these creatures: "*buw mu gaa ithad*," "that is the way it is." He also informed me that none of the *Zumtai* had any interest in the quarrels of the northern kingdoms. If this conflict took the Meoathai farther to the north to settle, so much the better. If not, well, *buw mu gaa ithad*!

Poaha also told me of several of the Meoathaian ventures to control the southern, or lesser kingdoms, in ages past, which had met with little success. At first, he told me, these yellowish brown people had tried to convert the *Zumtai* tribes to their way of life. But it proved most disastrous to the lesser tribes, and they overthrew the Meoathai, who beat a hasty retreat to their stone city.

The more Poaha told me of these people who had built such a magnificent city, the more they seemed to resemble the hated English of my own world. Thus, they became my natural enemy.

I listened to more of the Togaoan's words, for though I was impatient to be off, I also realized it was to my best advantage to learn all I could of these people whose city I was determined to penetrate and from whom I intended to rescue the Princess Marjano. Poaha told me how to find the girl Droaih, once I made my way into the city. Since he, nor any of the *Zumtai*, had never been in the trees, none of his people knew of the doors and openings in the city's layered roof. Because of this, he had shown grave doubt as to my ability to find egress through one of the many gates, since they were heavily guarded and passwords were needed to enter. The girl had tried to tell him the system that was used to change the passwords every hour, but he had not been able to fathom their intricacies.

When I told him I would have to find another way, though I could not tell then what that might be, he replied:

"You are the *Yatahano. Buw mu gaa ithad.*" or, more accurately, if it is to be, the Mighty One can do it. I only hoped he was right!

Both moons were visible in the heavens, but due to their lack of reflective light, I found myself in almost total darkness. It was with this advantage I dropped from the trees and made my way carefully across the clearing. I had noticed earlier that, as dusk settled, the guards had withdrawn into the city and closed the massive gates behind them, no doubt not to be opened again until daylight save for someone calling out the proper password. I felt sure watches were posted within the outer walls of the city, but since no one travels the forest at night, I was hoping the guards would not be too diligent in their watch. Thus it was that I made my way across the clearing and over one of the several bridges, or elevated crossings of the rocky moat.

Reaching the wall of the city, I worked my way around to a low roof I had spotted earlier from the trees. This roof extended to the edge of the city and dipped below the corbeled wall some three or four feet. Since the roof was still some thirty feet above the ground, the city builders, no doubt, felt safe in extending it below the wall, though for what reason it had thus been built I could not guess. I had noted several architectural oddities from my perch in the trees, none of which seemed to offer the slightest suggestion of their purpose. It was at this low roof point I had decided to make my assault on the stone city that imprisoned the Princess Marjano.

Gathering my legs beneath me, I exerted all my power as I jumped to the roof. I expected the wall to present some difficulty to me as it was corbeled to extend nearly ten feet farther out than its base. This, coupled with the ground that quickly fell away toward the moat area, meant that I had to jump nearly forty feet to reach the roof. Thus, it was with much delight and satisfaction that I reached the roof with ease. I made my way across the loose stone shingling to one of the doors in the many promontories of the roof I had seen from the trees.

Based upon Poaha's description of where the entrance to the dungeons might be, I made my way across the roof to a door in that general vicinity. I was surprised to find that it opened easily to my touch. No doubt, the Meoathaians did not expect anyone to be entering their city from the roof. I later learned that none of the doors on the roof of the city were ever latched. All led merely to hallways or corridors and were there for the inhabitants of the city to reach the roof should there be a need or desire. Due to the corbeled construction of the outer walls and their great height, none felt, and rightfully so, that anyone could gain access to the roof. Certainly, I would not have been able to without my additional strength.

The door opened into a long hallway rather than a private room, as I first had feared. Using the inner map of the city, as Poaha had been able to relay it to me, as well as my own uncanny ability to determine direction, I wound my way through intersecting corridors to the lower levels. When I had gained the level I thought was right, I made my way carefully through the deserted inner passageways toward where I understood the Togaoan's friend to be.

As I passed through the corridors and passageways, I was struck with the architecture of this strange city. Nothing like it had I ever seen. Each corridor was fully twenty feet wide and beautifully decorated with works of art and carvings cut directly into the stone of the walls. Crystal in great abundance hung from the ceilings, though it did not appear they served as anything other than decoration. The floors were covered from wall to wall with rich, thick carpeting with beautiful designs worked into the weave.

Though beautiful in design, most of the artworks, including the carpeting, boasted figures in battle. I did not take time to scrutinize the pictures displayed, but it appeared from my brief perusal that several races from Ghandor were all lined up in battle against the yellowish brown Meoathaians. And in every case that I noted where a warrior had fallen, it was one of the other races that were cut down, never one of the Meoathaians.

The passageways, and I refer to them as different from the corridors since they were slightly narrower, about twelve to fourteen feet wide, were more sparsely decorated and of totally different construction, nor were they carpeted. However, their appearance was altered more by the structure of the walls than by the lack of ornamentation. Instead of the walls sloping outward from the base as did the corridor walls, these passageway walls curved from the base to the ceiling, forming almost a cylindrical tunnel. I wondered at the strange purpose of the odd shaped walls, but had little time to dwell upon the matter. For as I rounded a bend in the main corridor I was traversing, I came face to face with a group of Meoathaians. At first, I believed them to be a group traveling down the corridor, but as my moment of surprise left me, I saw they were involved in a heated argument. One, a girl, and the only one facing in my direction, was evidently frightened by her companions, and as soon as she saw me, called for aid.

"Oh, thank Nazu!" she shouted. "Please help us!"

As thus she spoke, three of the other four drew their swords and began pressing the fourth, who had also drawn his blade. I noticed quickly that these were not the big flat swords of the *Zumtai* warriors, but a blade much like my own but slightly longer.

Without thought of consequence, I drew my own blade and leaped to the side of the girl's companion. He was being hard-pressed by the three antagonists. As I did so, I passed very close to the girl and saw that she was quite attractive, having the yellow hair and the bronzed skin of the Thu, and I immediately recognized her for being from that distant kingdom rather than being a Meoathaian. Her eyes were large and held me for a moment, and gratitude crossed her face before she turned back to see what was transpiring with her companion. As I joined him, I was amazed to see that he was of the yellowish brown Meoathaian race, as were the three attackers, and wondered at this strange alliance, if, indeed, that was what it was.

"It would appear you could use some help, stranger," I remarked as I came to his side.

"Never have I needed it more," he replied, his words incongruous with his stoic expression.

And then I was into the thick of the fight and had no time for more words.

The three pressing us were excellent swordsmen and quite tenacious. No doubt, had they been equipped with blades of steel like my own, the fight might have been drawn out, but instead their blades were made of the alloy called *oluhn*, and no match for the biting edge of my blade. I made three quick passes, and in much less time than it takes to tell the tale, I had cut through two of the blades and rammed my own point through the heart of one of the attackers.

The second Meoathaian, whose blade I had severed, turned to run, but the third had the girl's protector in a precarious spot, and before I could come to his aid, had run the poor fellow through. He turned to me, a deep smile slitting his otherwise handsome face, and brought up his sword, still dripping with blood.

"And you," he said boastfully, "are next!"

"Oh, ho! You boast before the deed? Tis not a wise thing to do, my friend," I replied, blade dipped slightly, awaiting his advance. Like his companions, he wore a scarlet cloak

lined in bright yellow. His head was fitted with a sallet, or
skullcap, and the cowl of his cloak hung loosely at the back
of his neck. He wore a deep purple tunic that was tight-fitting
at the neck and flowed loosely to the waist, where it was
bound tight by the lower belt of his harness. The tunic was
tight-fitting below the waist and divided upon each leg, continuing to the ankle where it disappeared in short boots on either foot. He wore twin scabbards at either hip and was
advancing toward me with one of his drawn sabers. He had
narrow-set black eyes, a long pointed nose, and a prominent,
square chin. His flaccid skin was yellowish brown and gave
him a sallow, unhealthy appearance in the brightness of the
corridor.

"But there is nothing of which to boast," he said sarcasti-
cally. "You are no match for Uthalai!"

"And who is Uthalai that he thinks to best Robert of
Eire?" I taunted, for I could tell he was an egotistical man
and unused to being on the receiving end of his boasting.

"Oh, so now it is you who adulate your own prowess. Well,
we shall see."

"There will be little for you to see, my friend, except your
blood upon your tunic, for even if you use both your blades
you will not survive this meeting."

Evidently, he prided himself on using just one blade,
though I had little doubt that the wearing of two sabers de-
noted that these Meoathaians wielded both to gain the advantage over the average warrior. He said, "Perhaps you had
best concern yourself with the one I am holding, for that is
the one that will end your useless life."

Ever since first seeing these guards in the corridor I had
wondered about the two blades they wore. I had never known
a man to wear two before and had wondered if both could be
brought into play at the same time. As I awaited his attack, I
stood as I'm wont to do when facing a possible antagonist. I
was in the preparatory position with arms extended out from
my body, obliquely downward, my blade in prolongation with
my right arm and body turned to expose only my side to attack. I stood with legs slightly bent, a habit that caused my
European *maître d'armes* much consternation, but one of
best balance to me and one which allows me the quickest
movements if suddenly attacked.

Uthalai, done with his talking, came to a guard position as
did I, then we both saluted each other. I was somewhat sur-

prised, under the circumstances, that the strict code of the fence was observed here in this strange world. When life and death hangs in the balance, warriors often commence an attack without warning trying to gain an advantage. Except for sport or serious duel, I have not known many swordsmen to bother with such formalities.

"You salute very nicely," he jeered. "Now, let's see if your *phrase d'armes* is as good."

With that, he engaged my blade in *tierce*. He feinted with palm down, a rather unorthodox maneuver, and began a one-two compound attack. His maneuver was perfectly executed, and had we both had the same gravitational limitations, it would have been an interesting duel. But with my quicker speed I parried in *quarte* and executed a compound riposte that was deftly avoided, but my redoubling of the riposte sliced him neatly along the upper arm.

Uthalai recovered well in *tierce* but I could tell he was greatly surprised. Palm down once again, he passed his blade under mine and delivered a beat with the back of his blade on the inside of mine. His intention, I am sure, was to follow up with another beat, reversing his palm and sliding through for a serious cut. But, I diverted his blade, feinted to the outside, followed with an expulsion in low *tierce* and attacked in compound riposte once again, this time to the low side. I scored again and he quickly retreated in the guard position. He was hurt and we both knew it.

Without giving him a chance to recover, I moved forward in *balestra* and ended with a powerful lunge. His parries became weaker and his opposition failed to deter my blade as I struck him again in low *quarte*. But, I have to give him credit, for he immediately came on guard, disengaged in *tierce*, and lunged himself. As I parried he redoubled gamely, but his movements were not quick enough, and I think he began to realize that he was overmatched.

Gasping for breath, he jumped back, eyeing me carefully. I didn't follow, letting him catch his breath, which was coming in ragged lungfuls.

"You are very adroit with the saber. My compliments!" He saluted and came back on guard.

"You are no slouch yourself, my friend. A shame we must continue this, for I do not wish to kill so fine a swordsman."

"Do not concern yourself with such trifles, for you will be merely bait for the dogs tonight."

I returned his salute and awaited his next attack. It was not long in coming and I marveled at his courage, for he had lost a lot of blood and was much weakened. But he nonetheless pressed on, which was quite unexpected, for it requires good wind and much agility to complete the complicated run he chose; it was only my heightened reflexes on this world that saved my life.

Reacting in the high guard position, I blunted his attack and back jumped to the side as I circled with his movement. Opening up enough space between us, I recovered my guard as he approached again, though more wearily.

There was no doubt the Meoaithaian intended the fight to end in no way but death for one of us. But, I had no desire to kill such an excellent swordsman. Yet, unless I could wear him down sufficiently to disarm him, it was doubtful I could manage to end the duel harmlessly.

I parried his next attack and disengaged, feinted twice, and lunged. My maneuver, which had always startled my European tutors, for it is not an attack usually accomplished with the wider saber, was meant to surprise him and offer me an opening whereby I might deliver a disabling rather than killing blow. In such combat situations I have always found this maneuver, often referred to as the "Bind," created such an opening and usually brought about a quick end to the fight. It was several such attacks that had been so successful against the Bomunga warriors in my first fracas upon Ghandor. But my present antagonist was certainly a superior swordsman, and he managed somehow to deflect my blade enough that I only nicked him on the cheek. Quickly, I followed my advantage with two more unusual maneuvers. The first was a cross which, though failing to deliver a cut, surprised him further. I followed with an *evelopment*, another difficult and unusual saber attack, and the combination coming so quickly of the three unexpected attacks completely unnerved him.

Jumping back and then retreating as fast as he could while still keeping his balance, he valiantly attempted to regain his composure. Bleeding from several wounds, he eyed me dispassionately. The bright yellow lining of the scarlet cloak was covered with blood, as was much of the purple tunic. It was difficult to believe he could still sustain his strength.

"You do not kill! Why?" he hissed.

"I have no wish to kill the only skilled swordsman I have

encountered on all Ghandor," I replied honestly, for the man was deft with the blade and I felt no animosity toward him.

"Then stand and die, for there can be no peace as long as both of us live."

"And why is that?" I asked. "Is there no room in the city for two master swordsmen?"

"No," he almost yelled. "I am the *Yatazu* and there is only one among all the Meoaithai!"

Yatazu is to say "King's Sword," much like I supposed a royal *maître d'armes* in a king's court of my own world and, indeed, I could see his point. The Meoaithaians have for centuries been a warring people. Their ancient kings created the myth of invincibility centuries ago. According to their logic, they were the original race and would someday be masters of all Ghandor. Such was the conditioning of the people and such a psychology must inevitably create the pride and prestige of being the master at the trade of death. Neither as a race nor as an individual, could Uthalai allow me to live, for I was his superior with the sword and he knew it.

"It is a strange world in which you live," I replied sadly.

"Perhaps, but one in which only one of us will long remain," he replied heatedly, still catching his breath. No doubt some of his strength was returning to him as I allowed him to rest.

"Kill him quickly," the girl interjected hotly. "If you wait much longer, his companion will return with more guards."

I could see that she was correct in her summation, for Uthalai's tactic now was most certainly delay. He was waiting for help so that he could make sure of my death and thus salve his standing as the top swordsman in the city.

"Do not think that help will save you," I replied quickly. "Nor that another blade will enable you to best me. I am Robert of Eire, the best swordsman on three continents. Whether we fight now or later when you have your help, I shall prevail."

My remark angered him, as I had intended, and he lunged at me, disengaging twice, looking for a possible opening. I counterparried his attack and, when I didn't follow with a riposte, he redoubled. I easily parried, disengaged and lunged in high *quarte*. He parried and attacked, but I renewed my own attack with the *remise*. Only a brilliant counterparry saved him and he closed, no doubt trying to conserve time till help arrived. Jumping back, I opened space between us then with a *balesta* that ended in a powerful lunge, I attacked.

He retreated steadily along the corridor, trying to buy more time, for he realized that he could not stop my weaving blade. I relentlessly pursued, engaging him all the way with dazzling maneuvers of wrist and blade that had won me much acclaim on the continents of my own world. I knew from past experience my blade was merely a blur to him as he backpedaled, trying to counter each rapid movement that threatened to run him through. I finally went into a triple feint that threw him off balance and left his point in a poor position to counter a crippling thrust, but I could not bring myself to take his life. Instead, I engaged his blade in my own patented swirl of movement and, spinning it out of his grasp, sent it flying through the air.

He shot me a hateful look, then turned and fled, tossing over his shoulder as he turned into a bisecting passageway, "We shall meet again, but the end will be different, I'll make sure of that!"

I turned to the girl as he disappeared from view, surprised that such a fine swordsman would turn coward in the end. She was kneeling beside her fallen companion. At first I thought she was concerned for him, but I quickly realized that she was looking for something in one of the pockets of the heavy cloak he had worn.

"Your skill with the sword is beyond belief. Never have I seen such deftness, but you should have killed him for he surely would have run you through had he the chance." She had spoken to me without looking up, still trying to find something within the fallen man's pockets. Finally, locating the object, she slipped it into the folds of her own cloak.

"It is enough that he is gone and you are safe," I replied. "I'm sorry about your companion, though."

"You would do better to be less concerned about the dead and more concerned about the living! Uthalai does not boast in jest. He is the *Yata's* chief killer," she spat vehemently. "His venality is below contempt. You would do well to be aware!"

"Hopefully, I will not be in the city long enough for a vendetta to develop between us."

At no time did she look directly at me, she was so engrossed in what she had taken from her fallen companion. Then, standing, she stared off down the corridor after the departing Uthalai. Finally, breaking her reverie, she started up the corridor from the direction in which I had come.

"We must leave this spot, for there is no telling who might venture here or if Uthalai or his companion is even now heading back with reinforcements."

I quickly followed her as she headed down a bisecting passageway, and in a few moments we had wound in and out of several connecting halls so that I was sure no one would have been able to catch up to us. As we negotiated the passageways, I tried to ask her some questions, but she only shook her head and bade me be quiet until we reached our destination.

Some time later we passed through another corridor, the first I had seen since we left the one in which the battle had taken place. This emptied into a large courtyard. No doubt, this was one of those I had seen from the tree tops. Or at least one just like those I had seen, for I now believed we were on the far western edge of the city, and I had not been able to see much of this sector from my forest perch.

The courtyard was more like a park than anything else. It had finely manicured trees and shrubbery in vestibules that were evenly spaced across the grassy slopes. Benches were everywhere. No light emanated from the glass above, yet the courtyard was fully illuminated. Pots of varying sizes hung just out of reach and formed a ceiling over nearly half the courtyard. The outer walls of the courtyard were finely decorated with carvings and paintings that would have made the builders of the Egyptian tombs envious. But, like the artwork I had observed throughout the city, these, too, showed battle scenes between the Meoathaians and other races. And, as in the other works, the Meoathaians were always the victors.

Yellow-orange grass covered the ground. Paths of inlaid gold wound through the rolling lawns. Bright jewels studded the sides of the paths. Emeralds, diamonds, rubies, jade and many other precious stones, varying in size from that of a bird's egg to my fist, were inset along the edges of the paths. The display of wealth was staggering. As I stopped to gawk at the abundance of gold and precious jewels, the girl grabbed my arm and pulled me through the courtyard and into a corridor.

"Come, we haven't much time. It is almost the *yehde* of *zynth*."*

I didn't have a chance to question her what a *yehde* of *zynth* might be as she dragged me after her.

We passed into another passageway only to quickly turn down still another. About fifty yards from the courtyard she stopped in front of one of the many square inlaid areas I had noted all along the several passageways and corridors. Intricately carved, I had at first believed them to be merely decoration, but as the girl touched one of the carved panels and a doorway mysteriously appeared, I realized my error. I passed into a large and beautifully appointed apartment as the panel closed behind me. The girl turned and slid a heavy bolt into place, effectively sealing off the entrance from unwanted visitors.

The room was about thirty feet square with several couches made of a smooth satin cloth. Here, as elsewhere, were finely carved and painted figurines on the walls, all depicting the same battle scenes. Reds and oranges, greens and blues shone throughout the room in a brilliant, yet pleasing manner of decoration. I could see no method of illumination, yet the room was bathed with light that had a soft, iridescent glow. Potted plants hung from the ceiling, which was about fifteen feet in height. Fingers of vegetation spilled over the side of the pots and tumbled down in a profusion of bright colors. It looked much like the courtyard we had passed through, except for the soft-looking couches and chairs and the lack of grass or precious stones.

Along the far wall were three openings. The doors were closed, but I guessed they led into other rooms of the apart-

---

* Though Ghandor is on the same orbital path as Earth and possessing the exact same 365 day rotation period around the sun, it rotates on its own axis slower than that of Earth. A Ghandorian day is approximately twenty-one hours and fifteen minutes Earth time. A Ghandorian hour, or *yehde*, of which there are twenty in a single rotation, is about sixty-eight Earth minutes long. Darkness falls at about the fifteenth hour (*yehde* of *pyoth*). The twentieth hour is referred to as *zynth* and had two significances. *Zynth* is the figure twenty in the Ghandorian language. It is also the word used to describe witches and goblins; thus the *yehde* of *zynth* not only means the twentieth hour, but also the bewitching hour. A complete breakdown of the Ghandorian time sequence is shown at the rear of this writing, as was found in the original manuscript.—DD

ment. Along the near wall was a long table filled with what appeared to be a banquet set for a king.

The girl, whose name was Senmai, had crossed the room to one of the doors and passed through into a room that must have served as sleeping quarters. I could barely see a large bed with canopied top and thin veil-like curtains.

While the girl was thus occupied, I crossed to the banquet table and chose some food and refreshment. It had been some time since I had eaten a good meal. The food was delicious. There was a type of fowl that had a delectable taste.

Slabs of meat adorned several platters, and there was a dull red liquid that appeared to be a light wine, but tasted more like thinned honey as I drank it. You might think me rather ungallant for taking her food before it had been offered me, but it was the custom of Ghandor, I had been informed by the Bomunga, to eat whenever entering a person's abode. Nor will your host offer it to you, but expect you to dig right in. It is considered a rudeness of the worst order not to do so. But it had not been the custom that had turned me toward the food, but my empty stomach.

The girl was gone for nearly fifteen minutes before she returned. As she passed through the doorway back into the large living room, a startled intake of breath escaped her.

"*Ooaab!*" she exclaimed. "You are not a Thuian!" It was almost an accusation.

"No, I don't believe I said I was."

"No, no, of course not. But I thought you were. That is why I rushed you to my apartment. Any Thuian caught out after *zynth* is hauled before the magistrate. In all such occurrences the result is imprisonment and slavery. Thinking you were one of them, I couldn't let you stay there and be caught, for surely the two who escaped would have reported the incident." She crossed the room and sat down upon one of the couches.

She was quite a pretty girl with smooth, bronze skin, yellow hair, and animated green eyes, though not as deep in color as those of Marjano. She had a full, generous mouth. A pointed chin was the only detracting feature in an otherwise attractive face.

Her throat was long and femininely curved, tapering to strong shoulders. An ample bosom was distinctly noticeable beneath her harness and tight-fitting tunic.

She was an attractive woman and no doubt desirable, but a

garrulous nature and tendency toward masculinity cooled any interest in her I might have had. Besides, her coloring so reminded me of Marjano that the princess was ever on my mind during my stay in Senmai's apartment.

"What started the argument between you?" I asked.

"It was no argument. Those three guards had stopped Jainha and me. They wanted to know where we were heading. It is not permitted for a Meoathai man to be found in the company of a Thuian female. Those three were trying to take my companion to his quarters and were going to report me for being out so late in the corridors. That Uthalai is a hateful man and is always looking for some way to plague me."

"Why can't you be out late in the corridors?"

"Where are you from that you do not know of the laws of Meoathai?" she asked quizzically.

"From a far off land called Eire which you no doubt have never heard."

"It must be on the other side of the world from me never to have heard of it. For the Thu are familiar with all the known races and countries on Ghandor. But, you don't look like one of the lesser races. You look as intelligent as any Thu I have ever seen."

"Are there no people on Ghandor more intelligent than the Thu?"

She eyed me for a long moment before answering. "I suppose there could be, but outside the northern kingdoms, there are not any known. It was to the entire northern kingdoms which I was referring more than my own people, for you do not resemble any of the peoples I have ever seen. That red hair is unknown on all of Ghandor, I would have thought. Is this Eire, from which you come, not found in the lesser kingdom's region?"

I tried to explain to her that I was from another world, but the concept was lost in the translation. No one on Ghandor had any knowledge of other worlds in the universe. They do not possess telescopes and believe the many stars to be merely pinpoints of light to gaze upon, serving no other purpose. I did explain to her my mission, passing off that though I was not a Thuian I was indeed upon their side in any fight. I told her of my discovering the downed airship and following it to where the Togaoans had massacred the inhabitants, except for a maiden whom I had followed to the city. I did not elaborate upon my battle with Poaha's warriors on the trail and my near miss at saving the girl before the Meoathaians arrived on the scene. Nor did I mention my fight with the *mythai*. At her inquiry as to where I had met the girl, I merely stated that I had once before saved her life and grown very fond of her.

For some reason, I could not bring myself to mention to this girl who the Thuian maiden was that I was hoping to rescue. Perhaps it was because I was not sure of her deep loyalties, or maybe it was that everyone on Ghandor seemed to be everyone else's enemy, and I simply did not trust anyone. In any event, I passed the princess off as one I loved, and Senmai accepted that without question. Evidently chivalry among the Thuians is a practiced art.

I played the role of a thwarted lover in his quest to save his lady love and enlisted the girl's aid. However, as she explained, there would be no way to accomplish anything until first light, for the corridors and passageways were heavily guarded after the midnight hour and it would be foolhardy to even step out her front door.

While we waited for dawn, I learned a great deal more about Ghandor and the Meoathaian city which they called Meoat, which means "purist dwelling place." Meoathai, in the odd, paradoxical method of all the races on Ghandor of changing meanings by adding or removing letters from another word, means "Race of the pure," or "the first people." I never was quite sure of the literal translation. I was quickly learning one thing, though, about the language on Ghandor, it was not as Toogo had indicated. The Thu and all the other northern kingdoms speak the same language as the Bomunga; however, the Bomunga language is so archaic, so limited in vocabulary compared to the higher races' speech that it is no wonder that the Bomungaese thought they spoke a different tongue.

As we talked I learned that though all of the races within the city, with the exception of the Meoathaians, had to be in their apartments before the midnight hour, none were allowed along the corridors after dark. It seemed the corridors were reserved for the elite within the city and these, of course, were Meoathaians. It was hard to imagine, looking about me, that any apartment could be more plushly decorated, but I held my tongue and listened as she told me more of the city.

The Meoathaians had not built the city originally. It had once been part of the Cluvian empire. The Cluvia had been the common predecessor of all the northern races and had once been part of the Cluvian empire. The Cluvia had been the known world. They had even been the masters of the *Zumtai* races, though a benevolent one. Evidently, a great plague struck Ghandor, at least in the northern hemisphere, some centuries ago, wiping out most of the Cluvians. The survivors scattered in all directions in their haste to get away from the deadly effects. Different pockets of Cluvians settled throughout the lower regions of the northern hemisphere, and from these sprung the modern races of the northern kingdoms.

The Cluvians had not understood the plague that had swept through them, killing nine out of every ten inhabitants. They had attributed it to their great god Nazu as a punishment for the many advanced experiments in which the intellectuals of their society had been meddling. The only one experiment to survive was the power by which the airships were transported about the planet, and this only the Thu understood.

So deep was their superstition about the cause of the plague that all such modern technology as they had acquired was forbidden, and eventually, the several scattered settlements lost contact with one another, sinking to tribal, barbaric customs and laws. Over the centuries only the Thuians kept their ancestral ties, and though they call themselves by a different name, they are aware of the history of the Cluvians, if not their inventions.

The Meoathaians were not descended from the Cluvians, a fact which branded them of the lesser kingdoms. Over the centuries they developed an obsession to prove they were as good as the northern kingdoms. Finally, they decided they were better, and a desire to rule the planet overcame them. For hundreds of years they had been attempting to develop some advantage by which they could become masters of the Cluvian descendants. The power of the airships had long been a deterring force, and it was only recently that they had developed what they considered to be a weapon with the potential they needed. They were, Senmai believed, nearly ready to launch an attack on the northern kingdoms. All they evidently lacked was the manufacturing of enough of this new weapon to outfit their army.

So strong was the hatred of the Meoathaians, they reveled in the capture and slavery of any of the northern races, especially the Thuians, since they were the most advanced with their airships and direct ties with the past. Only members of other races who came into their city willingly were free from this persecution, though they are carefully watched and not afforded any of the advantages of the city.

"How is it then, that you are not a slave?"

"My mother was a Thu and from her I have gained my looks and coloring. However, my father was a Meoathaian, and it is because of this that I am tolerated here. I have no rights, but have been granted this apartment out of respect for my Meoathaian heritage."

I learned her father, who had been a great warrior and general in the army, had been put to death, for intermarriage between a Meoathaian and another race was strictly forbidden. It had always been the belief in the Meoathaian kingdom that they, not the Cluvia, had been the first race upon Ghandor. And though they had not advanced to the degree of the Cluvians—a fact the Meoathai blamed upon the region from which they sprang, a windy, cold region to the extreme south called Gonzuma—they were the master race. And it had ever been a law to keep the master race pure and unsoiled from the interbreeding of other races.

It was this law of endogamy that made the guards accost the girl's companion. I learned from her that he had not been her lover but a member of a faction within Meoathai that did not want a war with the northern kingdoms. In fact, I learned there were many such Meoathaians within the city. Mention of this conspiracy brought my mind back to Poaha's friend, and now I understood why he had thought her loyal. Unaware of any conspiracy, as would be any *Zumtai*, since lying and cheating were not known to them, Poaha had taken Droaih's actions as a befriending gesture, though I doubt if the Toagaoan would have put it in such words since there is no understanding of friend or friendship within their ranks. Thinking of the girl, I asked my host, if she knew of Droaih.

"Yes, I know who she is. Her apartment is on the third level, not far from here. We can leave for there at first light, if you wish. But, how is it you know her?"

"The warrior I met in the jungle, the Togaoan told me of

her. He said she was his friend* and that I could count on
her help in any venture I might seek within the stone city."

"That's strange," she mused, almost to herself. "The girl of
whom you speak is also of the conspiracy I have mentioned.
It is strange to me that she would have told the Togaoan,
since they have been on friendly terms with Meoathaians."

"I don't think Poaha realizes there is any conspiracy or
that Droaih is antagonistic toward the present regime. The
Zumtai are too simple a people to delve into the inner work-
ings of politics and conspiracies. To him, the girl is merely
someone who seemed loyal to him. Consequently, because of
his attitude toward me, he suggested that she might be of
help in my adventure within the city."

"A *Zumtai* is friendly toward you? That is even stranger! I
can understand why they might be friendly to the city since
bringing captive Thuians here is profitable for them. But to
you, a stranger in this land? Why is that?"

I briefly told her of my standing within the Bomunga tribe.
I explained in brief detail the events that led to my receiving
the flaming stone that hung around my neck. I did not, however, go into any detail about the princess, only that I wanted
to find her.

"And you are the *Yata* of the Bomunga?" she asked incredulously. "Never have I heard of such a miracle, for the
zumta tribes are obsessed with their dislike for the human
races on Ghandor. Ever since the ancient Cluvians dominated
them centuries ago, they have been at war with the higher
races. It is a strange tale you tell!"

"Yes, but one that is nevertheless true." I was not too interested in proving to the girl the truth of my story, nor was I
unduly interested in the conspiracy or political atmosphere of
the city. What I was interested in was finding a successful
way of saving the Princess Marjano.

"Do you think the girl, Droaih, will help me?" I asked finally.

"Oh, of a certainty. Anytime a Thuian can be wrestled

---

* The word for friend among the higher races is *"togu,"* and
though it is used sparingly, it nonetheless means exactly the same
as it does in English. It is a word, though, that is not found
among any *Zumtai* tongue. They neither understand the word or
its meaning. When a *Zumtai* refers to someone in such a manner
he calls them a *"boaimu,"* which is somewhat equivalent to saying
"someone who is not my enemy."—DD

from the grasp of the Meoathaian clutches, any member of the conspiracy will lend you aid. That is, so long as it doesn't threaten the movement. Of that, you can be sure. But, what effect this might have on our plans I cannot imagine. You will have to wait to ask Droaih of that."

Waiting for the dawn in Senmai's apartment that night, I learned the northern kingdoms were rejecting an alliance the ruler of Thu, Than Tan, was offering as the only defense against the expected aggression of the Meoathaians. It seemed so little trust existed on the entire planet that it was difficult for any of the kingdoms outside Thu to grasp the meaning of cooperation. The kingdoms had been ruled by war lords bent upon the lining of their own pockets for so many centuries that by the time Than Tan, which means Mighty Ruler, came to power there seemed no possibility that the other northern kingdoms would pay any attention to forming an alliance.

War to the other lords had always meant to hit and run, looting all that could be handled in the time it took to decimate a town, a city or a caravan. There had never been an all out war upon Ghandor as long as anyone could remember and it was with great difficulty that Than Tan had even been able to get the concept over to his neighbors. Once he did, he was only met with laughter. A new name was given him, but only behind his back, for none would have dared say this to his face such a ferocious warrior was he. He began to be called in the halls of his neighboring kingdoms as Than Tanai, which is to say Mighty Coward, the gravest of insults. Had Than Tan known of this, Senmai told me, he would have raided his rival kingdoms rather than trying to save them!

As Senmai told me more of this eminent northern ruler, an admiration built up within me, for ever had it been my nature to admire great fighting men. Even the English had a few, and to these I gave my grudging respect; however, the hated Cromwell was not among this number, being a butcher and killer of women and children.

I could almost picture the great Than Tan as the girl told me of his attempts to reconcile the northern kingdoms and prepare them for the invasion that he knew was sure to come. Senmai learned of this from the several captives of the Thu and other northern kingdoms that had been brought into the stone city. Yet, despite the knowledge that would undoubtedly have aided the great Thuian ruler in his attempts to bring the northern kingdoms under one alliance, I learned that the conspiracy felt it impossible to get the message of Euoaithia's despicable plans out of the city, so well was it guarded. Consequently, they had devoted all their energies to trying to stop the king's plans from within before they could be accomplished. But, even the conspirators, I learned, had realized just recently that this was an impossible task so far along was the work on the new weapon. Had they known of the weapon in time, they well might have been able to prevent its manufacture.

Still, despite all this information, my thoughts kept coming back to Marjano and her eminent father, the great Than Tan. I wondered if I would ever see this princess again or her famous father.

How little did I know of the fates that would bring us all together. Nor could I then imagine all that would transpire before I met this erstwhile ruler.

CHAPTER FOURTEEN

At first light, after a fitful sleep on the cushions in the outer room of the girl's apartment, she led me down a maze of intertwining corridors. There were few people out at this early hour and, with the help of the full-length, cowled cloak that Senmai had lent me, no one paid me any mind. We reached Droaih's apartment without incident, but as we turned into the passageway Senmai became anxious, though at what I could not tell.

As we approached the doorway, we found it ajar. It was the first such open door I had seen in the numerous passageways I had traveled within the city.

"Something is wrong," she whispered.

Drawing my sword, I carefully pushed the door aside with the toe of my boot and surveyed the room. It was a replica of Senmai's spacious apartment. Only the room had suffered greatly for cushions were strewn about, furniture overturned, and general disarray was evident.

I moved into the room with Senmai at my heels. I noticed from a quick look in her direction that she had drawn both long knives that hung at her waist. The women on this planet did not seem in the least in need of male protection as they did on my own.

An inspection of the room proved for naught. It was empty and we could not ascertain what result had been accomplished in the struggle that had taken place here. My only guess was that this city had burglars and assassins as those that frequented the royal courts of Europe. Though I found this later to be true, it was not the cause of the disarray of the apartment nor the mystery of the girl's disappearance.

"Look, here!" Senmai exclaimed as we reentered the living room chamber from the bedroom. "She has left the sign."

As hard as I looked, I could not distinguish a single sign of which Senmai indicated.

"Where? What is it?" I asked.

"Over here. It is the danger sign of the conspiracy."

I noted a small marking on the wall that joined the two apartments to my right. It was a small squiggly, vertical line with two horizontal crosses drawn through its middle. It, of course, meant nothing to me, as, no doubt, it had meant nothing to the apartment's looters.

"It is the sign we use to warn others of immediate danger. Come, we must leave at once. Droaih has left a warning that the guards will be back."

No sooner had she spoken than in through the apartment door sprang a half dozen of the city's guards. Dressed like those I fought the night before, these wore scarlet cloaks that came to the knee, the narrow rapiers at their hips and a deep purple tunic that clothed them from neck to ankle. On their heads were round skullcaps that covered the entire head, like a large, overturned bowl. Other than my own tam, which I was wearing beneath the cloak's cowl, these were the only other headgear I was ever to see upon Ghandor.

I noted with some amusement that all of the guards' swords were sheathed, and no doubt they expected little trouble from us. And as though reading my very thoughts, one spoke:

"Come with us, you are under arrest. The *Yata* wishes to see who all his enemies are before he puts them to death!"

I have already explained the language of the Bomunga covering such terms as leader and ruler. The Tojoga races have added another word to indicate "king" or "head of state," as it is literally translated. *Yata* would be none other than Euoaithia, king of the Meoathai.

It has always been my habit to fight when cornered and ask questions later. I have found this to be the best road to follow, for usually your antagonist is not prepared to fight when he has you vastly outnumbered, and by the time he becomes aware of your motives, you may have cut his number down to a more workable force. This was my intent as I drew my sword. Six antagonists had not proven to be my match in the past upon this planet, and I had no reason to believe that they would be now! But, before I could bring my sword into play, one of the guards had seized the girl, Senmai, and held a dagger at her throat.

"We have heard of your prowess with a sword, my friend, and are not about to take any chances. Continue this fight and the girl will die immediately, for it is you that the *Yata* desires to see!"

I cursed the chivalrous nature that bound me to my battle code and sheathed my sword. We were led down several corridors to another part of the city. As we traveled, I again noted the fine workmanship that had gone into the artworks that adorned the walls, carpet, and the many courtyards through which we passed. There were still few people up at this hour, and I got the impression that the city was, perhaps, not as populated as its size would warrant.

My sword had been taken from me, as well as the long knife I carried at my hip. The girl's two knives had also been confiscated, and it was a depressed Senmai who made the long trek at my side. While we traveled, I used my sense of direction to pinpoint where we were and add to my knowledge of the stone city.

We were ushered into a large room that was even more beautifully adorned than what I had already seen. The walls were covered with works in gold and bronze. Jewels were everywhere. One entire wall was a mosaic of huge precious inlaid stones. The carpeting on which we walked was plush and we sank to our ankles as we crossed it to stand before a raised dais in the center of the room. I was struck with the similitude of this room and the one in the Bomunga village that had been my throne room. But the Bomunga had none of the craftsmanship that had gone into the decoration of this great chamber. Even the ceiling had been painstakingly carved with the ever present figures in battle. Paintings, rather than being hung on the walls as in my own world, had been worked directly upon the walls and ceilings with intricate care. Whatever else the Meoathaians might be, they were excellent craftsmen and artisans.

The room was full of some twenty to thirty nobles, arrayed in fine apparel. Silks and satins adorned both men and women from neck to ankle. The only difference was that where the men's garments covered each leg individually, the women's apparel was a long, tight-fitting skirt that hung to the floor. The ladies' garments were trimmed in beautiful fur, mostly from the prized anator, an animal found only in the regions of the far north, I have been told. It was a highly prized animal because of the unbelievable softness of its fur.

No swords or weapons of any kind could be found upon the nobles or their women, but I was certain they were there, hidden within the folds of their clothing, for I had never seen an unarmed person upon this planet other than a prisoner or slave.

A great hush fell across the room, and I looked up to see a giant of a man entering the great hall from behind the dais and make his way toward it. He was attended by four heavily armed guards, two on either side of him and I could see a fifth guard station himself at the entrance through which they had entered.

This, no doubt, was Euoaithia, a wicked and vengeful man I had gathered from Senmai during our long conversation the night before. He was dressed in long flowing robes rather than the tight-fitting tunics of his subjects. He had a short sword on either hip and the scabbards were a riot of jewels and inlaid gold. It seemed to me the weight of the swords would have stooped an ordinary man, but, as I said, he was a giant. Not so much in height, for I doubt if he was as tall as I, but fully twice my weight.

His face was finely chiseled and, though turning somewhat to fat around the jowls, it still bespoke his strength. His eyes were dark pools of hatred and dark circles had been etched beneath the heavy lidded orbs. His nose was flat and crooked as though it had been broken many times in his youth. A wide, cruel mouth was set above a chin that jutted out to meet a square jaw. His robes were of the purest white, as was the full-length robe he wore that had a stand-up collar reaching almost to the top of his head. He presented a pompous appearance, and its effect was not entirely lost on his subjects. His eyes were alive and, from the moment he entered the room, they never left mine.

He moved with a grace belying his great weight. His swords clanged about his knees as he moved across the floor and took his place upon the dais. He dismissed the greetings of his nobles as though they were not there, and pointed a well-manicured, painted nail at me.

"Who are you?"

"I am Robert Dowdall, my grace, and who might you be?"

Insolence was not usually my habit, but his mawkish arrogance bothered me. He had everything in his favor, at least for the moment, but I didn't want him to feel he had me beaten, such is my nature.

His reaction to my question took him back for a moment, and a great fire leapt into his eyes. He was, without reservation, the most irascible man I had ever met.

"Hold your tongue or I will have it cut from your head. Now, from where do you come?"

"I come from the proudest country on Earth, Eire. County Armaugh, to be exact!"

If the unfamiliar terms surprised him, he made no show of it. I realized immediately that, though the man was powerful, I did not feel he was very knowledgeable, and rulers upon Ghandor were expected to know all things. It was because of this, not wishing to be shown up in front of his nobles and servants, that I believed he responded in the way he did.

"Ah, yes, Eire. I have heard of it often. We have others of your race within our dungeons. Tell me, what is your connection with the half girl, Senmai, and with Droaih? They are conspirators to the crown and will soon die. Are you one of them?"

"No, I am not," I answered truthfully, but the look in the eyes of Senmai made me continue with words that salved my injured pride if not my better judgment. "But, that is only because I just arrived in the city this morning and knew nothing of such a conspiracy. Had I known of it and your tyrannical rule, I surely would have joined it in order to free the Meoathaians of a cruel, vicious *Yata!*"

"And who are you that you could succeed against the mighty ruler of Meoathai, the greatest people on Ghandor?"

"I am also the *Yatahano* of Bomunga, the ruler of all the *Zumtai*; the great Mythaiumo; and Ran Dumun Twa. By these names I am also known. My sword is invincible and at my beck and call I can bring twenty thousand warriors down upon you!" Perhaps, I had laid it on a bit thick, but the dander of my homeland was within me at that moment and I didn't feel like kowtowing to this *Yata*, the expressed enemy of the Thu and captor of Marjano.

I wasn't sure what part of my speech had shocked the *Yata* or his nobles, but the look upon his face and the whispers that raced around the room told me I had hit a weak spot. But the knowledge of that weak spot was not at all what I expected it to be.

"You go among the trees?" Euoaithia asked me in a hushed voice.

"Of course I do! Don't you?" My haughty tone did not have the effect I had thought it would. It wasn't that the Meoathaian ruler was afraid of heights, as I had supposed; he was afraid, as were all the people in the stone city, of supposed beings that traveled the trees.

"You are of the *Blou Tou*? I had never supposed I would ever see one up close!" he said candidly.

The *Blou Tou* is the name given a type of creature that supposedly haunts the upper areas of the forest trees. Literally translated, it means Ghost People. They are mightily feared throughout Ghandor. Though no one had ever seen one, there was no doubt to the races of this planet they existed, for who else had cut the avenues through the trees? Who else had taken off with animals, possessions and other items during the nights in the forest. No party was safe in the forests at night, especially in the northern regions of the trees. Toogo had mentioned something of this to me, but I had passed it off as the superstition of the unintelligent Bomunga. I was surprised to find the superstition among the more educated Meoathai, and in such great strength. But then, who am I to say what is real and what is not? What was it that had attacked me that first night in the forest along the avenue of the trees? What had shrieked and bled in profusion throughout that long battle? Had that been the *Blou Tou*?

Readily, I had an advantage here, but I wasn't sure how to proceed with it. I knew nothing of the Ghost People, or that is, of what the superstitions of the Meoathai had attached to the Ghost People. Could they disappear at will? Were they indestructible? Did they eat people? All I knew is they ... if that is who had attacked me ... could bleed. I decided to play out my hand.

"Yes, *Yata*, I am of the *Blou Tou*! Not only that, but I am the *Yata* of the *Blou Tou*," I equivocated. As I was the only *Blou Tou* of which I for sure knew that also meant I was the ruler of the *Blou Tou*. "I have fought many battles with your people in the forest and never once have I been defeated, or even seen. I am indestructible and can annihilate all of you in this room if I choose to do so."

A strange look came over the face of the *Yata*. I couldn't discern for the moment what it meant. Was he buying my tale? I decided to press on for definitely the nobles believed my words and were slowly inching their way back from me on all sides.

I slowly looked about me, catching as many of the nobles' eyes as I could. My gaze was as contemptible as I could make it, and the effect I had upon them was as I had hoped. Yet, I was unable to fathom Euoaithia's feeling as I turned back to him.

"It is best that you return my sword and possessions to me, *Yata*, before I do something drastic, like making everyone in the room vanish!"

An intake of breath from the nobles about me was an audible sound that hung heavy in the room. A small smile touched the lips of the Meoathaian ruler as he sat on his throne looking down at me.

"Yes, yes, of course. But, first, I would like to have a few words with you in my private chambers. Would you join me for some refreshment and meat?" The words were not exactly a question, more like a subtle command. But it seemed a way out of my dilemma, for if he called my hand, what could I have done to back my threat? I could have shouted "Boo!" or its Ghandorian equivalent, but, I doubt if that would have worked for long. Euoaithia's look told me he completely understood my thoughts and again he offered me a way out.

"I'm sure the *Yata* of the *Blou Tou* would like some soft wine before returning to the forest?"

"Most certainly, my friend. Lead the way."

As we passed through the doorway at the end of the great chamber, the several guards fell in behind us. I was a little apprehensive of my predicament, but at least the odds were now but six to one instead of the forty or fifty arms that could have been raised against me in the great chamber.

We passed through a long corridor as immaculately carved as the others I had seen, though this one had an abundance of gold and jewels worked into the walls and ceiling carvings. Running along the base of both walls, where the carpeting connected to the walls, a base flashing of gold framed the entire corridor. There were also several of the square inlaid areas that were like the doorway entrances along the corridors and passageways of the stone city. Again, the difference in appearance was that the inlaid areas were of solid gold instead of the wood carvings of the other doors I had observed.

At one of these doorways, the *Yata* stopped and pressed it open with a touch to a secret device. He motioned me into the apartment, then followed, ordering the guards to remain outside. As the door swung closed, we were completely alone. At least, there were no others in the room. I was sure there were guards at each of the half-dozen doors that I could see along the four walls of the apartment.

"Now, my friend, just who are you? You are, of course, not *Blou Tou*, for there are no such creatures. Nor is there any place upon Ghandor where there are white-skinned, red haired people. And upon all of Ghandor I have never heard of anyone equaling your height, for I am the tallest of all about whom I have ever heard. Nor can there be a place called Eire, for such a name is cumbersome to the tongue and difficult to pronounce."

"You seem to have heard of it when I confronted you in the great chamber. Are you a liar, too?" Now that the odds were down to just the two of us, my normal bravado had returned. I was determined to play out my hand and not let him know the situation seemed lost to me. The Dowdalls have a saying, one that they had carried with Rollo the Dane when he invaded Paris, with William when he conquered the English, and throughout their years of battle in Eire. It is "I shall prevail!" It is the motto inscribed beneath our coat of arms and has been carried into more battles than can be counted.

I stood in the well-guarded apartments of the Meoathaian *Yata*, my fate completely at the mercy of his whimsical nature. That he was cruel and unfeeling I had no doubt, but that he had something in mind that he wanted to confront me with was also a surety. Despite the fact that I could see no way out of my present predicament, I was determined to uphold the Clan's name and go out with as much blood on my blade as I could. Unknown to the Meoathaians, I still had the Bomunga long blade strapped to my back, hidden beneath the long cape Senmai had furnished me to disguise my light skin and red hair.

"Come, come, my friend, just who are you?"

"What makes you think I am not the *Yata* of the Ghost People?" I asked, somewhat circumspect.

"Because there are no such creatures on Ghandor. And to bring this conversation to a head, for I have something to discuss with you, let me tell you why I know that you are not of the *Blou Tou*. One of my ancestors, Cloaithai, the first to implant the idea among the Meoathai that we are the chosen people, also decided that he wanted to become *Yata* of all Ghandor. In order to do this, he knew that he needed much power and many warriors. He instituted a movement among the *Zumtai* to enlist their aid through a benevolent imperialistic control over them. To accomplish this design, the Meoathai sent many stories into the *Zumtai* lands to conquer them. To subdue the *Zumtai*, they told a tale of a strange people that lived among the trees to the north of their boundaries. So scary were the tales, and so ferocious were these strange people made to be, they effectively cut off any warring parties of the *Zumtai* traveling back to our city. Thus, we were safe from attack and free to carry the battle to them whenever we wanted."

"The plan would, no doubt, have worked," the Meoathaian continued, "but for Cloaithai's untimely death. It was many years before his son, and my grandfather's grandfather, Zoiathia, was bitten with the same dream to rule the world. He built up stories of the strange, vicious people of the trees, not so much to frighten the *Zumtai*, though it effectively kept them from this part of the forest and Meoathai free from attack. His main purpose in the stories of the Ghost People as they became known, was to keep his own people imprisoned within the stone city. For decades many of the warriors had been leaving the city to sell their fighting skills to other tribes, so great is the Meoathai's desire to fight. Keeping the warriors at home and building up their interest in banding together into one army was all part of the plan for, until then, though living within the same city walls, each family owed fealty to no one. There was no central government nor any accepted leader. Each family leader had been a *Yotahan* in his own right and unwilling to relinquish any of his rights to another."

The *Zumtai* had given the name of *Blou Tou* to the strange people said to frequent the trees, for no one had ever seen any of these strange creatures. But their exploits were well known, not only from the stories the Meoathai had spread around, but they had also left evidence of great carnage in the forests and blamed it upon the Ghost People.

At Cloaithai's death, the idea died out among the Meoathai so that by the time Zoiathia revived the tales over a century later, none among the Meoathai who had been with Cloaithai spreading the tales were still alive. And outside this small circle of Meoathaians, it had been a well kept secret.

Cloaithai was a cunning man, and he had deemed that any advantage might well work in his favor, thus the secrecy of the origination of the tales.

By the time Zoiathia's son came along, Bouaithai by name, the father of the present Yata, the plan had been developed to a regular strategy. The *Zumtai* warriors were not needed for the Meoathaian scientists were developing a weapon they thought would offset their smaller number when attacking the northern kingdoms. The weapon, which Euoaithia did not describe to me was apparently of some long range variety that would give one man the power of a legion of men.

With this, the Meoathaian scientists also discovered what made the mighty and greatly feared Thuian airships operate. They had great difficulty in putting this discovery into action, but were finally close to its perfection by the time Euoaithia came to power. They were almost ready to attack now, thanks to the many Thuian slaves who had been manufacturing the powder needed in the mechanism of the airship controls.

The airships operated by a means of negating gravity. In the center of the underside of the hull, the airships contained a device that could upset the balance of the gravitational pull of the planet. The powder the Thuians were forced to develop in the dungeon workshops was instrumental in negating this force. In some way that Euoaithia did not understand, the device operated on a principle of drawing its lateral movement by pulling itself along by means of any of millions of gravitational fields of which the planet was evidently made. Unfortunately, for the Thuians, as well as the Meoathaian scientists, these gravitational fields collapsed from time to time and when one did so that was being utilized by an airship for lateral movement, the ship might lose a great deal of altitude before it could pick up another gravitational field to continue its lateral movement. If the airship happened to be at a low altitude when the field collapsed, there was little chance it would survive a crash. No doubt that had been the fate of Marjano's airship. This also might be the reason why the airship had not landed on the ground. This defect no one seemed able to overcome, yet it happened so seldom that neither race considered it a deterrent to air travel. But for this strange, rare malfunction within the planet's crust, I would still be on my way to Thu, and Marjano would be safe at home with her people! I have often contemplated on the strange circumstances of chance that change and mold our lives.

So effective had been the tales of the *Blou Tou* over the span of several generations, it seemed everyone upon this western hemisphere of Ghandor believed in the Ghost People. Evidently, Euoaithia was the only one alive that felt there were no such people. As for me, I was no longer sure. I had often scoffed at Toogo's tales, but something had bled all over my sword.

"What is it you wish to discuss with me?" I finally asked, after telling him as much about myself as I felt inclined to do. He accepted me as the *Yatahano* of the Bomunga and a visitor to his part of the world from one of the lesser races to the east. So unknown is the vast expanse of land to the east surrounded by the great sea that he was in no position to deny there could possibly be a race of light-skinned, red-haired people, though he had never heard of them.

"I needed to know that you were not aligned with the Thu or any of the other northern kingdoms. As you unfolded your story in the great chamber I deemed a plan that would greatly benefit me in whipping the Meoathaians into line and, thus, enabling me to step up my plans for attack. Unfortunately, there are many people in this conspiracy against me who do not want us to rule the world. I cannot understand their unwillingness to be a part of my great plan, but do fully comprehend their danger to me."

"Just how can I help you, *Yata*?" I had decided to follow along with him until I could find some way out of the dangerous situation in which I found myself. I was certain that I would be dead before the day ended if I refused the Meoathaian ruler his plan, for he could not afford to let me live as I knew his secret of the Ghost People.

"As the *Blou Tou Yata*, you will bring added strength to my plans. When it is known that the *Blou Tou* have joined us in our plans to attack the northern kingdoms, many of the nobles who are opposing me will be forced to join forces and that will completely crush the conspiracy, for it is by the strength of the many nobles who oppose me that this conspiracy remains hidden."

"I will make a plan with you, *Yata*. You have in your dungeons a Thuian girl who was brought to you this day by the Togaoan warrior, Poaha. She is the reason I came to the stone city in the first place. My Bomunga tribe lost much face to their enemies the Taajom when the girl escaped from us a few weeks ago. To prove my good stead with them, I must send her back. If you will do this for me, I will join your forces as the *Yata* of the *Blou Tou*." Once the Princess was safe, I decided, I could deal with this pompous ruler, but until then it was better to have him on my side.

"I know of the girl about whom you speak. She is, indeed, in my dungeons, and if that is all it will take for you to join me and thus crush this infernal rebellion confronting me, it is done. I will give orders that you are to claim her whenever you wish. But, how will you return her to the Bomunga tribe, for my plans make it necessary that you are not absent from the city?"

"I have several of my warriors awaiting me outside the city," I replied, hoping Poaha was still there. "They are concealed within the forest. A call will bring them to me and they can have the girl. I will not need to leave for I do not wish to return to the village after seeing your beautiful city. Better to be a servant here than a king among the Bomunga." I had no intention of turning the girl over to anyone, nor to become a servant of the Meoathai, but that story sounded good and played well upon the Meoathaian's vanity.

"Good, good. It will be done as you say. Come, let us rejoin my nobles so that they may hear from your lips that the *Blou Tou* are about to join forces with Meoathai. I daresay the conspiracy will be a thing of the past by dawn." As he opened the door and we passed down through the corridor, his laughter rang out in great peals. Indeed, the *Yata* was in high spirits and, until I had the Princess Marjano at my side, I was intent upon keeping him in this same mood.

When we were settled back in the great chamber, the *Yata* on his throne and me at his right hand, he explained how he had talked me into joining forces and bringing my *Blou Tou* into the Meoathaian camp. The news met a variety of reactions, for evidently many of the nobles who opposed Euoaithia were present in the great chamber. Indeed, when we returned to the great hall, there were fully a hundred or more Meoathaians, three times the original number present. Evidently, the word of the *Blou Tou Yata* being in council with Euoaithia brought them at the run.

Senmai was still under guard, not ten feet from the throne,

and the look she gave me as I took Euoaithia's cue to speak and confirm his startling statement told me she would have liked to cut out my heart and throw it to the dogs, or whatever the Ghandorian equivalent might be.

"Yes, my friends, what your *Yata* says is true," I began, trying to ignore the hateful look Senmai was giving me. "The *Blou Tou* have long admired you and your great city as we have your illustrious leader, Euoaithia. As you well know, the *Blou Tou* are invincible. What you don't know is that we have as much hate for the northern kingdoms as you do. Centuries ago the Cluvians exiled us from their empire and forced us into the forest. While there are some among us content with our plight, others of us want revenge! For this reason, I am willing to join Euoaithia in his quest to defeat the Cluvian descendants to the north!" Looking around, I could tell my ingratiating words were having great effect. Though I had spoken solely for Euoaithia's benefit, many of the nobles in the room were, no doubt, seeing their carefully laid plans going awry, while others were ecstatic over the possibilities of an easy victory in the north.

"I have at my beck and call," I continued, fully enjoying my audience hanging on my every word, "twenty thousand warriors among the trees. Though we have never fought for anyone, I am now prepared to commit the *Blou Tou* whenever your army moves for the north."

The hatred in Senmai's eyes was so great it was hard for me to look in her direction. I could well imagine that running through her mind were many ways she would like to see me die. All of them, no doubt, slow and painful. That death might come at her hands immediately I was ill-prepared to acknowledge, nor did I believe her capable of it, for though I had found the women of Ghandor stronger than those of my own planet, I am afraid I still judged them in terms of their femininity. It was because of this I came face to face with a naked blade that looked as though it would end all my chivalrous plans to rescue the beautiful Princess Marjano.

As I finished talking, I turned toward Euoaithia to see the look upon his face, so much was I counting on appeasing him until I got Marjano away from the city. As I turned, I caught a slight movement out of the corner of my eye and quickly swung back to see Senmai rushing toward me. At first I believed this to be just a female reaction of rage that I had seen so often among the lasses of my native land. I was not at first aware of her raised hand. Nor did I immediately note the naked blade of a curved long knife arching down at my breast.

CHAPTER FIFTEEN

I was once again thankful for the lesser gravity on this planet, for had it not been so, I would not now be alive to tell the tale. As the knife descended, involuntarily my muscles bunched and reacted. The normal action would not have taken me far enough backward and clear of the blade, but the lesser gravity gave added strength to my movement and caused me to jerk back far enough to cause the blade to miss me in its downward plunge.

So close was the call, that the fine edge of the blade cut cleanly through the upper belt of my harness. Both large belts are connected with a double belt that runs vertically upon which are hung many fascinating objects of a warrior's battle tools. The smaller belts hold the upper one from falling to the floor, but not so for the hidden long sword that had been strapped at my back. For as the belt separated, the sudden looseness disconnected the thongs holding the long sword and it clanged to the floor at my feet.

The girl, in her hatred, had acted so swiftly, snatching a knife from one of her guards and lunging at me, it took everyone in the great chamber by surprise. Because of the commotion of the guards quickly grabbing her and wresting the knife from her grasp, it seemed doubtful that any of the nobles had noticed my long sword falling to the floor.

Euoaithia had come off his chair at the sudden attack of Senmai, and as the sword fell between us, he quickly stooped down to scoop it up, He and I seemed to be the only ones that noticed the sword so intent was everyone upon Senmai and her struggle with the guards.

"Take her away to the dungeons!" the *Yata* demanded angrily.

"Yes, Mighty Leader," an aide answered, and motioned the two guards now holding the girl to follow him. As they

137

dragged her from the chamber, her eyes never left mine even though it must have caused her great pain to twist her body around against the guards' restraining grasp. The look in her eyes was a study in pure hatred.

As for the sword, Euoaithia never mentioned the incident. I don't know if he placed any significance to my hidden sword. If he did, he never allowed any indication to cross his facial expressions. In fact, everything appeared to be running smoothly as we traveled about the city letting everyone know Euoaithia and the *Yata* of the *Blou Tou* were in good stead and had joined forces. I couldn't help noticing, though, an odd look in his eyes everytime I unexpectedly caught him looking in my direction. At first I paid little attention to it, thinking it but one of the many odd characteristics about this fanatically cruel leader, but after many hours I began to feel he had little trust in me. It was this enigma about the man that bothered me. I made it a point to remember his distrust lest I fall prey to one of his maddening schemes once he was through with me. However, I did not expect the danger to come so quickly, or exactly in the way it did.

It was sometime after *Praithyehde** that I finally persuaded my host that it would be well for me to gather up the Thuian girl. I told him I wanted to hand her over to the members of my tribe that awaited within the jungle before it got any later. The *Zumtai* did not like to be this far north at nightfall and seldom liked to be in the jungle at all during *zynthyehde*, or witching hour.

We had just concluded a large feast in my honor. Or, I should say, in the honor of the *Yata* of the *Blou Tou*. Euoaithia had made much over our alliance during the long feast, frequently jumping to his feet to offer me a toast or make some wild, unbelievable remark about the *Blou Tou* and their power.

The feast had been a lively affair with fully a thousand in attendance. I never did learn the number of inhabitants of the stone city, but that there were several thousands I had no doubt. I had heard there were more than three thousand slaves in the dungeons alone.

Vast quantities of food and wine had been served. Gallons

---

* *Praithyehde* is the fourteenth hour. *Praith* stands for fourteen and *yehde* is hour. This would be approximately twelve minutes to five in the afternoon.—DD

of *cloa*, a strong, nectarian drink, had also been served. This latter drink is unique among the Meoathaians, for nowhere else in all my travels upon Ghandor did I ever see anything stronger than wine except in the stone city. There had been dancing girls, sword swallowers, men doing acrobatic dances with flaming swords and an exceptionally exciting display of what is called the *cu duo*, or slap dance. This was performed by three short, almost black natives from a faroff region to the south known as the *Gonzuma*. Ghandor is a strange planet, for while the north pole region is ice-packed, as is Earth's, the south pole is far more equatorial in climate.

The inhabitants from that far southern region are an extremely dark purplish-black race with wide foreheads, small eyes squeezed together on either side of a narrow but very long nose and shiny, bald pates. They are square-jowled, large-eared and powerfully built. I saw none of them taller than five feet among the many within the stone city. Most of these wore the kilt-type *kwai* rather than the ankle length clothing of the Meoathaians.

While none had hair that I had seen within the city, the three performing the slap dance all supported short-cropped wigs, or so I took them for. This hair was gray in color with a slight maroon tint to it and flew about despite its shortness as they performed their energetic dance.

The dance began with the three running into the great hall from opposite sides, slapping their forearms in rhythmic unison. They performed in an area that had been cleared before a raised banquet table where the privileged few sat. This was where most of the entertainment had taken place, though there had been several dancers and artisans performing in other cleared spots throughout the great hall. No doubt this had been due to the *Yata*'s interest in wooing all the important nobles and their ladies within the city. He didn't want anyone made to feel they were being left out of the festivities.

The three black men joined in a triangle, facing outward from each of the three points. They began a uniform dance that was perfect in its timing, denoting long hours of practice. Legs raised, bodies jerked, heads swung from side to side, all the while, with each movement, the hands were struck against the body in perfect timing creating a distinct slap that echoed throughout the hall. Because of the dark skin, it was not possible to tell if the blows were punishing or not, but I well believed that had the three performers been of a much lighter skin, welts and bruises would have been visible by the time they finished their entertainment.

It was at the conclusion of this act that I had leaned over to my host and suggested I see to the business of the girl.

"Yes, yes, of course," he replied between overtures he was making toward an attractive young girl sitting on his other side. "I have been a slothful host for not seeing that you had taken care of your business before this." He dropped the girl's arm which he had been casually caressing and turned toward me. "It will take but a few minutes till she will be yours," he added with an expressive wink.

"It is not that I am in any particular hurry for the girl," I whispered, "it is only that my warriors in the jungle prefer to be gone from this area before *zynth* arrives. I'm sure you can well understand why."

"Ah, but of course," he replied, giving me another of his clandestine winks. "When you have secured her and she is in the hands of your tribe, return and I will see that you have your choice of our fair maidens."

He discussed in some detail the many delights of the Meoaithaian women, and finally concluded, "And now, Zynthmai, one of my aides, will take you to the Thuian girl and you can succor her from her dungeon prison yourself. I'm sure that will impress upon her what you have planned. I certainly have no love for the Thuians, and any additional terror that I can arrange for one is most pleasing. 'Tis a shame I cannot be present to witness her demise at the hands of your people."

I nodded, hardly able to hide my anger, and stood to follow Zynthmai, Euoaithia's aide, out of the banquet hall. The name of the *Yata*'s aide puzzled me, despite my annoyance at the depravity of the Meoaithaian king.

The language of Ghandor often has no rhyme or reason to it, nor can one define a word just because it is the conjunction of two or more other words. Still, it seemed odd that the aide carried the two words *zynth*, meaning midnight, and *mai*, which is usually attached to a word to give it a female or feminine meaning.

As we made our way out of the hall, I chanced to look back at Euoaithia. The *Yata* was giving orders to another of his aides. I would not have placed much importance upon this clandestine huddle, for the head of state of a large people must have many things being brought to his attention throughout the day and evening that require his immediate attention. But just as I passed through into the corridor, the person to whom he was speaking chanced to look in my direction. It was none other than Uthalai, the guard with whom I had dueled upon first entering the stone city. Whether the glance he shot me was due to something the *Yata* was saying to him, or just that he still carried the wounds of his defeat, I could not tell, but that there was hatred in that look there could be no doubt.

Uthalai would be a worthwhile enemy, and I made a mental note to be on the lookout for him, yet at the same time I knew I would be outside the city before the dawning of a new day with the Princess at my side and quickly cast aside any concern over the Meoaithaian swordsman. And upon such thoughtless decisions are the fortunes of men won or lost.

We wound through several corridors, staying clear of the passageways, as the Meoathaians are wont to do since the smaller avenues are usually left to the other races within the city. We came to one of the many courtyards spaced throughout the city, but this one was quite different. It had the same decorations of gold walkways, hanging plants, and beautiful ornamentation, but unlike the many other courtyards I had seen, this one boasted a dozen guards, most of whom were stationed beside or near a large, intricately carved wooden door. And, too, the courtyard was fully three times as large as the others.

Zynthmai was saluted by the guards and passed through the doorway as was I, though I received some strange looks. We entered into a long hallway devoid of any decoration. It was made from the same stone work I had seen from outside the city and it was the first such exposed stone I had seen inside the great structure. Evidently, the Meoathaians had plastered over all of the stone surfaces within the city structure but this hallway which led downward at a slight angle, had been left exposed. A narrow strip of plaster had been applied to the ceiling and ran along the full length of the hallway. From this plaster a mysterious light emanated. This, then, was how the entire city was lighted. Some compound or element within the plaster was the mysterious source of light within the giant structure.

Although I did not understand the principle, the compound

gave off a soft yet penetrating light. Every corner of the hallway was bathed in its brilliance.

While we descended into the labyrinth beneath the city, I asked Zynthmai of his unusual name.

"No wonder you might be surprised, my friend for it is a strange name with which I am unfortunately stuck. It was given me because my mother gave me birth at the midnight hour rather than at the culmination of the normal gestation period. From all I know, I am the only person of all Meoathai and perhaps even on all Ghandor that was born out of time cycle. It is a heavy punishment to bear."

As we descended into the lower dungeons, which were upon at least four levels, I learned that the physiological makeup of the humans on Ghandor was unsuspectingly different from my own race upon Earth. Unlike the random births of my own planet, the bearing of children on Ghandor follows a very strict cycle of gestation.* Though the duration is about the same, there is no deviation. Full term is exactly 269 days. The cycle always ends within a couple of hours either side of *Toaiyehde*, or noon hour, and always on the two hundred and sixty-ninth day. This time period from about *Kreyehde*, or the eighth hour, until *Taithyehde*, or the twelfth hour, is commonly referred to as the *maion woun*, or fulfillment time!†

A child being born out of cycle, or at some time other than the *maion woun*, is looked upon much like we might think of a mongoloid or retarded child on Earth. As a matter of fact, Zynthmai was one of the sons of a royal house

---

* There is some discussion among medical men on Earth at the present time about the human gestation cycle. There apparently are many medical men who feel the female pregnancy period does not vary a single day when the child is carried full term. Delivering early or late is nothing more or less than an incorrect determination of when pregnancy commenced. Since the doctor usually makes such determination from the mother's calculations, it is easy to see where such variances could occur.—DD

† At first this might seem a rather odd phenomenon, but the more it is considered the more one might take into account the strange oddities that have always surrounded the birth cycle. For instance, ask any nurse in a maternity ward and she will tell you that during any month, more babies are born during the full moon than at any other time. Odd? Yes. But records will bear this and many other oddities out should the reader care to research the subject.—DD

of the Meoathai. Under normal circumstances he would have been one of the nobles being wined and dined this night, but as it was, he was only an aide to the *Yata*. A signal honor, to be sure, but not the usual fare for a person of royal birth upon Ghandor.

In the short time it took us to traverse the city and wind our way down to the lowest level of the dungeons, I had grown to like this Meoathaian. He was a pleasant fellow with a wry wit and an easy manner of speech. Except for Moga, this was only the second person on Ghandor with whom I had made friends. He told me where his apartments were and any time I would like I was welcome to stop by and take meat with him.

The lower we dropped, the more dankish and foul smelling the dungeon became. The odor assailed my nostrils, reminding me of the pungent aroma of sweat and blood I had witnessed in many places of incarceration upon my travels in Europe. The walls glistened with moisture and a green moss-type plant grew where many of the huge slabs of rock had been joined. The smell was intensely repugnant on this, the fourth level, and I could tell that my guide couldn't wait to return to the upper levels of the city. Indeed, I was anxious to be gone from the foul smell, moaning voices and depressed state of affairs that exist in such places as that in which I found myself at the moment.

Zynthmai motioned to the jailer to open a gate solidly wedged in the corridor leading to the cells directly before us. As the gate swung open on rusty hinges, we made our way along dozens, perhaps hundreds of heavy oaken doors set into the wall on either side of the corridor. Small peepholes appeared at eye level in each door, and for all the world I would have believed I was in the dungeons of one of the old European castles I had seen.

The guard finally stopped before one of the heavy wood doors and fumbled with a large key on a ring that was nearly two feet through the middle, which supported hundreds of keys. As we thus waited for the door to be swung open, I noticed another figure coming down the corridor toward us, but paid it little mind as we had seen several cloaked figures in the halls of the lower dungeons. Something about him struck me as slightly familiar, but the anticipation of once again seeing the Princess Marjano pushed the thought from mind. The expectancy of seeing her again was almost more than I could stand, and it took some iron control of my emotions to keep my guide and the guard from seeing that the girl was more to me than just a captive.

As the door swung open I caught a glimpse of a beautiful face framed in golden hair. It took but a second for those big, green eyes to fall upon me and I again wondered at what words of wonderment might fall from the girl's lips once she recognized me. But, alas, I was not to know, for no sooner had her eyes widened in recognition than something struck me over the head from the rear. As the blow landed, two distinct impressions passed through my mind before darkness overcame me. The first was that the blow was not delivered from the side where Zynthmai was standing, but from the rear. The second impression was that the girl had uttered one word upon recognizing me: "*Yatahn.*" But before I could puzzle out its meaning, the side of my head struck the straw covering the floor just inside Marjano's cell. As I felt myself falling into a whirlpool of darkness, I thought I heard a scuffle behind me but the light went out before I could grasp its meaning.

CHAPTER SIXTEEN

I awoke to a throbbing within my head and a stiffness throughout my body. It took all my will power just to get my eyelids open, not that it did me much good, for from my position on the floor all I could see was a thick mat of scattered straw. It seemed like an eternity before I could gather the strength to drag myself into a sitting position. I felt like a mule had kicked me ... no, several mules. My cloak was gone as was my tam and harness. The only thing I wore was the *kwai* of plaid I had made before leaving the Bomunga village. It took me several moments of puzzled thought, as I sat upon the straw-covered floor, to determine where I was. Slowly the puzzle took shape and I could remember the events that led me to this dismal place.

The cubicle in which I was incarcerated was about eight feet square. A thick bundle of straw in a corner evidently served as a pallet for sleeping. No other object shared my prison. A little light filtered in through the peephole in the door, but other than that, the room was dark and dank. I had often wondered as a boy playing in the ruins of castles in Eire, where only the dungeons were left intact after the centuries of wind and weather, what one of the inhabitants of such a prison had felt. Unfortunately, I now had the answer to that and it looked like I would have a lot of opportunity to learn more of the condemned for surely there was no way out of these stone walls.

Futilely I searched the entire cubicle looking for some flaw in the stonework. Some forgotten weakness, trap door, or weakly covered opening. But there were none. No window or bars bound me. Only solid stone. The walls, roof, and flooring were all of stone and from what I had seen earlier walking through the dungeons, the stone was several feet thick and as durable as time itself.

145

Never before in my entire life had I felt such depression as I then did. Yet, for some unknown reason, the Dowdall words came easy to my ears. "I shall prevail!"

Here I was without adequate clothing in the dampness of a subterranean dungeon, no arms with which to defend myself, no real understanding of what my captors had in mind for me, nor the slightest idea of how I was to escape this invincible prison, but my spirits rose with every repeating of the words that had staid the Dowdalls from one conquest after another in Scandinavia, Europe, England, and Eire. And here upon Ghandor it would serve still.

I was literally shouting the words before I realized it, so strong was my feeling for freedom and need for action. When I finally quieted down, I heard a faint stirring to my left and I carefully made my way in that direction.

"Hello, my friend," a familiar voice reached me.

"Who calls me? Is it you, Zynthmai?"

"Yes, it is I, Zynthmai. I heard you yelling and knew no other would brave the punishment of the guards in such a manner."

"How can it be you talking to me, Zynthmai? I have circled the cell and found no one sharing my prison with me. And the walls, they are so thick that no voice could penetrate them."

"I am in the next cell, my friend. There is a metal grate set in the wall at the very base of the stone between our cells. It is only a few inches square, but enough for us to talk if we both lay upon the floor and place our faces toward the grating."

As I moved toward the sound of his voice, I could barely make out a darker spot along the base of the stone wall. As he had said, the grating was only a few inches square and no doubt served to add cross-ventilation to the small cells within the underground dungeons, for as I later learned, each cell had such a grating on each side wall.

"Yes, I see the grating now," I replied, as I knelt down beside it and positioned my face next to it as Zynthmai had suggested. In such a manner we would be able to talk more softly and there would be no chance that we could be overheard from the corridors beyond the cells.

"How come you to share such a fate with me?" I asked of him.

"It is a short tale. When Uthalai hit you over the head I attacked him. I did not know at the time that Euoaithia had sent him down to do just that, though why he did I cannot say."

"So it was Uthalai that I saw in the corridor outside Marjano's cell," I mused, more to myself than my companion.

"Yes, and all Meoathai knows how you defeated him in an encounter with the sword. His comments on how he would get even with you have been well voiced. When I saw that it was he who had struck you, I immediately attacked him, thinking he had chosen this instance to make good his threats. In any event, I was overpowered, for he quickly told the guard it was Euoaithia's wish that the both of us be thrown in prison. At the point of a blade we were both dragged to these cells and deposited here."

So the clandestine meeting between the *Yata* and Uthalai was more than some matter of state. Uthalai had been well chosen as the one to carry out Euoaithia's desire to have me out of the way. No doubt the *Yata* had such a plan in mind from the beginning. Looking back, it was easy to see how my gullibility had led me to this place. Euoaithia had only wanted to use me as a wedge to make all his nobles subservient to his plan for war. With the mighty *Blou Tou* in his camp, Euoaithia would be invincible. The *Yata* had played the deception to the hilt, and no doubt his feast of the night before had been successful in wooing the opposing nobles to his side. With that being the case, Euoaithia no longer had any need of me, since he well knew I did not have twenty thousand ghost warriors at my beck and call.

"Your efforts were most meritorious, my friend, and I appreciate your act, but surely the *Yata* will have you freed once he knows of the tale since you did not know what was afoot but only protecting your charge."

"I do not think so, for the *Yata* has been trying to find some way to get me out of his hair for some time," he replied casually. There was no question in his mind that he was here to stay. "You see, being a *luumai* I have always been an embarrassment to him. The only reason I belonged to the courier staff is the position of my father as one of the nobles that pose a threat to Euoaithia's plans. It was a sop to my father for the *Yata* to place me in his personal courtiere. I think this is just the excuse for which he was looking, for my father will not be able to raise a voice against my imprisonment when it is learned I struck the guards of the dungeon in the performance of their duties. No, my friend, I think I am here to stay, or until such time as the *Yata* can quietly do away with me."

His voice trailed off and I left him to his thoughts which, no doubt, were dark and gloomy at the moment. Finally he shook off his apathy and asked, "But tell me, my friend, why be you here? I thought you and the *Yata* had just formed a powerful alliance. It seems to me he is endangering the entire city by placing you in prison. Won't your Ghost People come to your rescue?"

"The alliance was short-lived. I think I have served the *Yata*'s purpose and my work is done," I replied with a smile, for surely Euoaithia had no more plans for me other than a secret death.

"But what of your legions? Surely they will not follow Euoaithia without your presence to lead them," he persisted.

"Euoaithia has no fear of the *Blou Tou*, for as far as I know, I am the only *Blou Tou*."

"What do you mean?" Zynthmai asked in a puzzled tone. "You said there were twenty thousand warriors of your tree kingdom."

"Yes. But it was only a tale to serve the *Yata*'s and my own individual plans." It took but a few moments to tell him the tale of my being within the stone city, up to and including the secret conversation with the *Yata*.

"It would seem," I concluded, "that your *Yata* wants to have me killed because I know too much and I have served him well. Probably he will tell his nobles that I have returned to the forest to prepare my legions and only await his call. He no doubt will pass your absence off as having returned with me to the trees, perhaps as an assurance that our alliance is protected, or something like that."

"Yes, I can see that such would make sense and give him the upper hand he needs with running the risk of your telling the truth and upsetting his plans."

We passed some time in silence, both no doubt lost in our private thoughts. It was somewhat comforting to know there was a friend close at hand but I longed to be out of my cell and rescuing Marjano. It seemed almost diabolical the way fate was staying my hand every time I got within sight of the princess of Thu. What was it that was keeping us apart? Who was guiding my affairs to such constant failure? Was there a force over which I had no control affecting my life?

Thus my thoughts ran until Zynthmai broke my reverie by saying, "Do you know, I have not the slightest idea of your name"

"My name is Robert. Robert Dowdall, though you will have trouble pronouncing it. I am from a country called Eire, a small, beautiful island off the coast of Britain. Oh, how I long to see my homeland once again."

"Robert," he said hesitantly, though he didn't quite pronounce it correctly. "Eire? Britain? Island? Coast? What are these names of which you speak?"

Most of the people upon Ghandor of which I had met knew nothing of oceans or islands. Their land to them is all that exists, and the thought or concept of great seas is beyond comprehension. It took many hours for me to sketch in words the great concepts of which I spoke. Hampered as I was by the darkness and not being able to see his face, I was not sure if he entirely believed me or even understood me. Eventually, I gave up on trying to explain the concept of the solar system and other planets, but felt I had somewhat succeeded in getting the idea across of great bodies of water and what an island would be.

"I would sometime like to see this island of which you speak," he finally said, something akin to awe in his voice.

"So would I, my friend, but I have often felt in recent weeks I would never have that chance again. I believe the fates are working against me and perhaps I am stuck here in your world."

"Well, at least you have the Thuian girl. Me I have no one." There was a note of sadness in his voice.

"Why is that" I asked.

"I am a *luumai*. Who is there that would marry such as I?" The sadness deepened for a moment, and I felt somewhat depressed myself for I did not have an answer. But his next words seemed cheery enough, "But, let us not dwell upon such things. Tell me, who is the Thuian girl whom you came to rescue?"

I told him of Marjano, not divulging her identity for fear of placing her in further danger, only that she meant much to me personally.

"Yes, I could tell that from your look as the cell door was swung open. No doubt had you not been so intent upon seeing her, you might have seen Uthalai in time to avoid such a fate as this. But one look at the girl and I can well understand your preoccupation, for never have I seen such beauty. If she were not Thuian, she would have been in the *Yata*'s household long ago, for he has a weakness for beautiful women."

The thought of Marjano brought quick memory of the last time I saw her. Despite her ordeal through the forest and her two days in the underground dungeon cell, she had appeared as fresh and alive as she no doubt did on royal occasions in her homeland. I longed to be with her. Though I had not seen many women on Ghandor, it was apparent to me that her beauty was outstanding by any Earthly or Ghandorian standards.

The stone walls that were keeping me from her weighed heavy on my mind. I said as much to Zynthmai.

"I have a plan. It is a shaky one at best, but I think with any luck we might be able to pull it off."

I pressed my ear against the grate as he lowered his voice. He told me that during the several hours I had been unconscious there had been two changes of the guard. The first change brought a man to our section of the dungeon who Zynthmai had befriended in the past. It seems that Zynthmai's duties on the courier staff had brought him into the dungeons many times, and though he had gotten to know many of the lower level guards, none had ever shown an interest in him or his duties other than what regulations demanded. Only one guard, Roolai by name, had overlooked Zynthmai's chance of birth and paid him any mind. It wasn't exactly that a friendship developed, but a bond of respect grew between them. On several occasions Zynthmai was able to arrange extra leave and lighter duties for the man and it was to this my companion now felt he would be able to draw upon.

"While we were talking at the hole in the door, Roolai seemed most despondent," Zynthmai continued. "When I asked him why he felt so, he replied that he had just lost in the *Naijkoomb* lottery and thus would have to spend the year end on duty."

"*Naijkoomb*," I interjected. "That means five days of festival, doesn't it?"

"Not just five days of festival, my friend, but *the* five-day festival."

On Ghandor, I learned, there are five days left over every

year outside the regular months of the calendar.* These days are celebrated as the *Naijkoomb*, a festival that lasts five days. During that time, no business is conducted of any kind upon the planet. Most debts to state or individuals are forgiven and life begins anew. It is a time of great merriment and little restraint. Within the stone city, at least, many acts are committed, with the exception of murder and robbery, that go without punishment. Besides being a time for pleasant devilry, it is also a time of great inner contemplation to the more religious in nature. Not only are temporal debts forgiven, but to these the debts of spiritual transgressions are also forgiven.

To be on duty at such a time is most distasteful, since one would not only miss out in the more temporal pursuits of life but would also miss the opportunities of gaining absolution from both spiritual and legal debts as well. Though I felt certain the guard to whom Zynthmai referred was not interested in the spiritual pursuits of life, he nonetheless would be downcast over the prospect of missing out on the fun and advantages offered during the festival. I could well imagine his unhappiness, though how it was of interest to us I could not fathom until Zynthmai went on to explain.

"Roolai owes me many favors and I mentioned this to him during our conversation," Zynthmai added with a laugh. "He wasn't too happy about the idea, but at least is enough of a man to realize that what I said was true. Of course, while he was thinking of such mere things as increased food rations, extra drink and other such items of personal comfort, I was suggesting escape."

At the mention of the word escape, my heart began to

---

* Though in an identical orbit with Earth and therefore on the same 365 day rotation around the Sun, the Ghandorian calendar is somewhat different from that of Earth, having evolved in a different manner. The year is divided into ten months, each with thirty-six days. At the end of the year, the extra five days are celebrated by festivities and once every ten years the festival is increased to eight days and referred to as the *Krejkoomb*. This is done, of course, to keep the Ghandorian calendar even with the planet's rotation around the sun, in the same manner as our own leap years on Earth keep the earthly calendar in line with the sun. A complete explanation of the Ghandorian calendar may be found at the conclusion of the book.—DD

race. Perhaps here was a way to get out of my prison and free the Princess after all.

"What was his reaction to that?" I asked.

"He didn't like the idea, but said if I could think of a way to accomplish such a feat without any blame being placed upon him, he might consider it."

"Did you think of anything?"

"Yes, I think so. After Roolai was relieved, I sat here thinking of a plan. It is not the best perhaps, but it should work if Roolai will agree to it."

Briefly he outlined the plan he had developed. We lay for hours with our lips to the grate discussing the merits of the plan and our course of action in it. Like Zynthmai had said, it wasn't the most foolproof plan one might adopt, but when one is without hope, one will grab at straws.

As Zynthmai pointed out, during the *Naijkoomb* even the guards are granted much wine and all regulations and inspections are relaxed. In fact, I learned, the number of guards is reduced to a bare minimum, usually only one per dungeon level.

I asked if he thought we could get a key to the Princess' cell, and Zynthmai suggested that once we are free we merely force the guard to accompany us there and open her cell.

"How long before the *Naijkoomb*?" I asked.

"It will be upon us within a few days," he replied hesitantly, and I could well understand why, for the waiting would be the most difficult part. And, too, the longer we waited the more chance of failure there would be. I asked if there was no way in his mind we might induce the guard to aid us before the festival, and he told me that even if we could get Roolai to do that, which he seriously doubted, we would still be faced with the problem of passing through two other dungeon districts to get Marjano and then up three flights of prison guards and into the heavily guarded courtyard outside the only entrance.

"To try and escape at any other time than the *Naijkoomb* would be folly," Zynthmai concluded. "It must be on the fifth day of the festival, for that is the night when the wine and *cloa* flow the heaviest and even the guards will be well into their cups."

We spent more hours discussing the possibilities once we had managed our escape. Zynthmai brought me up to date on the routines of the guards within the dungeon and up in the city levels. He was quite concerned about getting safely out of the city, for that is what I confessed to him was my intent once I freed the girl.

"I'm not so sure that will be easy, my friend," he said, after I persisted with the idea of leaving the city. "Better that you come with me to my father's household that we might hide out from the *Yata*'s men."

"Leaving the city will be no problem for me," I replied, "and I would think you would want to come with us, for surely the *Yata* will search the city over at your escape for he is sure to feel that you know all about me by now and he cannot allow you to live and pass the word of his treachery."

"Perhaps you are right," he replied, a note of sadness in his voice, "but I cannot leave the city without offering my blade to the conspiracy that is trying to put a stop to Euoaithia."

"Yes, I learned about the movement from the girl who was hauled into the great chamber with me. Although I must confess I am not interested in the internal politics of your city, I am nonetheless against the tyranny with which Euoaithia rules. If you will accompany me to Thu while I see the girl home safely in her household, I will return to your city and help you in overthrowing the *Yata*'s power. Surely if you stay, Zynthmai, you will be discovered and put to death by Euoaithia's men."

"What you say, my friend, makes good sense. I'll have to give it some thought, but an adventure to the north does sound intriguing, and what you say about it being foolish for me to stay in the city is probably true."

Later that evening, around the eighteenth hour the guard, Roolai, came back on duty. I could hear muffled conversation coming from Zynthmai's cell through the grate, but could not distinguish any words, nor even the mood of the guard. It was with mounting impatience that I awaited my companion's return and report, for much hinged upon Roolai's willingness to take part in our escape.

It seemed like an eternity before I heard a rustle near the grate and Zynthmai's hushed voice.

"The guard has agreed," he said, his voice full of jubilation. "We will effect our escape at the *zynthyehde!*"

My spirits jumped, and it was all I could do to contain myself. As Zynthmai outlined the plan, it was really quite simple. By the end of the twentieth hour on the fifth day of the festival, there is hardly a person within the city that isn't full of the wine. Being the last hour of the holiday, everyone is trying to cram all they can into a moment of living. As Zynthmai put it, an army could walk through the city at that hour and not a single citizen would know it.

As for the guard, he would claim he had been steeped in drink and didn't see a thing. We were to damage the door of one cell, once outside, to make it look like we had forced a weak panel. The guard would be found bound and gagged to insure that his superiors agreed that he had not been at fault.

The days dragged by slowly. It seemed an eternity had passed when Zynthmai let me know that there was only one more week until the festival was to begin. An entire week, I thought. And upon Ghandor a week is nine days long. Nine more days plus five during the festival made it fourteen days in all ... two full weeks, Earth time. My spirits, which had picked up some at Zynthmai's words, now dropped noticeably when I figured the time by Earth reckoning.

We ate twice a day. Once about the tenth hour and again just after dark, about the sixteenth hour. The meal generally consisted of a thick soup that was tasty and surprisingly hot. We also received a chunk of leavened dough, not unlike bread but with a stronger taste, more heavily salted and almost black in color. A small pot made from crockery was placed in my cell each morning full of water, and if used sparingly, would last the entire day. Once every three or four days we received a real bonus. This consisted of a three-inch square of a cake-like substance that was extremely sweet to the taste.

This was surely not like I had thought prisoners had eaten in the old dungeons of my homeland and no doubt they had not. But Meoathaian slaves are expected to do a day's hard labor perfecting the materials for the secret weapons and the airship drive. For this reason they are well fed, and Zynthmai's friend, Roolai, saw to it that we received the same fare at meal time despite the fact that we were never allowed out of our cells.

At first I thought this strange, but then I quickly realized that Euoaithia did not want us around the other slaves, or indeed, around any of the guards other than the four who stood shifts in our specific cell area. These, no doubt, had been briefed in such a way that seeing the *Yata* of the *Blou*

Tou in prison did not bother them in the slightest. Perhaps they knew nothing of their prisoner at all.

Zynthmai told me about the twelfth day that he had been able to get word out to Marjano that we would be freeing her and make our escape on the fifth day of the festival around the twentieth hour. But as the days wore on we did not hear any word and did not know if she got the message or not. In fact, we did not really know if she was still in the same cell or not. What if she had been moved? Or what if Euoaithia, defying law, had taken her into his household? The thought of this turned my blood to boiling, and my impatience nearly got the better of me. I was all for effecting my escape that very moment, and it took Zynthmai quite a while to talk me out of it. Finally his good sense got through my thick skull and I relaxed a little, but the time wore heavy on my hands.

The night planned for the escape finally arrived. The previous four days had seen a noticeable change in the atmosphere within the prison, for even the slaves had been released from the duties, and all of us had been given generous portions of food and wine each day. There was much singing and loud talking, and though distinct words could not be heard through the thick walls, the hubbub of noise was like distant thunder and seemed to continually rumble through the dungeon.

If I thought it had been difficult waiting before, I was in for a shock, for the last few hours before the Witching Hour arrived seemed to drag without end. As the hour approached I began to wonder for the first time at the task before us. Not only did we need to get to Marjano's cell and free her, but then make our way up three flights of stairs to the courtyard above. Even though Zynthmai had assured me the guards would pose no problem because of the festival toasting and merrymaking, it still seemed no easy task upon which we were about to embark. And even were we to make it into the city, reaching the roofs, for that is how I deemed we would make our escape, it would be no simple matter. But I felt once out of the dungeons we would stand a much better chance to make good our plans.

A scraping at my door broke through my thoughts. The heavy wooden door swung open and Zynthmai stood in the doorway. He looked a little more the worse for wear than the last time I had seen him, but his eyes were alive and eager. I jumped to my feet and took the sword he proferred me. I was disappointed that it was not my own trusty blade but was glad to see my cloak, tam, and harness that he also carried. Quickly shrugging into the leather belts and tossing my cloak about me, I hurried out of the cell that had been my prison these past twenty-four days.

The guard stood behind him, a wizened old man with rough beard and cruel eyes. His cloak had long since needed washing, and from the looks of his harness and sword, I was sure it had not been used for many years. His bent figure bespoke the years of hard labor under which he had once been subjected and no doubt his assignment to the dungeon was the last job he could find.

While Zynthmai bound and gagged him, I bent to the task of springing the door. With my added strength on this planet, it was no difficulty and within a moment several planks of the door stood loosely in my grasp and for all intents and purposes looked like someone had broken through from the inside.

A few moments more and we were rushing down the corridor, Zynthmai with the guard's keyring and me with my thoughts upon seeing Marjano once again making my steps light and my spirits high.

Turning at several points, we followed the passageways that led us to the same cell we had traversed to upon our first journey together into the dungeon. At every turn I tensed, expecting trouble, but as Zynthmai had predicted, we encountered not a single guard.

As we hurried along, a low rumble ran through the stone flooring. I had felt these often in the last few days of my imprisonment and wondered at their origin. I had asked Zynthmai about them, but he had merely passed it off as the moving of the heavy city structure settling into the bowels of the planet.

In a moment we were once again before Marjano's cell door and when Zynthmai slid the key into the lock and loosened the door I put my shoulder to it like a young buck on his first courtship. As the door swung open Marjano flew into my arms. Evidently the word had reached her, and she had been waiting hours for our arrival.

"*Yatahn*, you have come!" she said breathlessly. Zynthmai shot me a surprised look but said nothing as he politely waited for us to be done with our reunion.

She was as beautiful as last I saw her. For all the days she had spent in her prison cell, she seemed as fresh as the morning sun. I wondered how a girl, spending the same length of time in the dirty, dank cell as we had, could emerge looking so fresh and lovely when Zynthmai and I looked so bedraggled. I wondered if there weren't some guardian angel that looked after fair maidens while leaving us warriors to shift for our own.

We were just inside the doorway to her cell. She felt soft and wonderful in my arms, and I was reluctant to let her go. But Zynthmai stirred restlessly beside me and I knew we had to be on our way. I started to remove her strong arms from about my neck when I heard a shuffling in the corridor outside the cell. Turning, I saw two dozen warriors converging upon the door.

"We've been betrayed," Zynthmai yelled. "Roolai sold us out! If ever I see that vile man again, I'll run him through and feed his heart to the dogs!"

As the guards converged upon the open door and Zynthmai cursed his oath, the entire picture zoomed into focus for me. Euoaithia, needing a reason to kill off the noble's son, had concocted this elaborate scheme to present Zynthmai's father with a perfect cause for the son's death. For who could expect foul play in a death resulting from an attempted escape? That the slain should have weapons and kill some of the guards in the process, so much the better. And in such an easy way, the *Yata* of the *Blou Tou* would quietly meet his Maker and whoever he was, be permanently out of the way! It was very neat. And if conducted in secrecy, it would still satisfy the Yata's plans of conquest.

All this swam before my eyes as I pushed the girl behind me and into the far reaches of the cell. With drawn swords, Zynthmai and I backed up to give ourselves fighting room yet still protect the girl from flying blades. Our plight did not seem envious, for there appeared little chance at escape as surely another hundred guards could be brought to the aid of those before us were they to be needed.

But there was little time to concern myself with such trifles. The first guard emerged into the cell and I easily ran him through. Three more rushed in on his heels and Zynthmai and I dispatched them quickly. I was somewhat surprised at the ease with which we had bested them when I realized that Euoaithia, in his need to show some dead guards to Zynthmai's father, had probably not warned some of the warriors that we would be armed.

Zynthmai and I exchanged a quick glance before more guards flowed into the room. These we both realized would be aware of our armament and more cautious.

"Well, if it isn't the great swordsman," a familiar voice called out. Looking up I recognized Uthalai, the guard who I had dueled in the corridor when I first entered the city. He was the same that had bashed in my skull in front of the Princess' cell several days ago. I surely had a grudge against this man, and this time I wasn't about to let him get away with it.

"So chance has it that we meet again, my friend," I replied coolly.

"Chance had nothing to do with it, braggart. I asked Euoaithia for this opportunity. Only this time I do not come alone, as you can see."

"Do you intend to stand and fight today, or run and hide like the last time we met?" I taunted. I could tell the remark stung him, for he shot a quick glance to the side to see if his companions had heard me.

He cursed me violently and wagged his blade back and forth before him. Had it not been such a serious occasion, the gesture would have been comical. As it was, he looked much like a spoiled child who has not been given his way.

"Well, let's have at it, Uthalai, or do you plan to stand there and try to scare me to death with your vile looks?"

With that he lunged for me without pretense at a salute or coming on guard. He wanted done with me and was counting on more than one blade occupying my attention in order to accomplish his task. But the cell was small and difficult to maneuver in, so it was that seldom during our encounter I was bothered by more than one foe. Nor was Zynthmai hard-pressed, for he was a good swordsman and able to hold his own against the guards who tried unsuccessfully to press in between us.

I was not interested in a duel with the Meoaithaian this time, nor did I intend to withhold a crippling blow as I had done the last time we crossed blades. I knew Marjano, Zynthmai and I had little chance at escape, but if such a chance were to be realized, it would be due to Zynthmai and I dispatching our antagonists as quickly as possible before the numbers wore us down.

So as Uthalai lunged at me, I parried his thrust easily and with a special sidestep attack I developed in the European courts, slid his blade down my own and wedged past his guard and ran him through. It happened so quickly that even I was surprised, for Uthalai was an expert swordsman and well gifted in the art. Evidently he had been overconfident in his suit and, no doubt, wanting to win back some of the respect he had lost among his peers from our last encounter. "Pride doth goeth before the fall," I thought to myself, then had no time to consider Uthalai or the quickness with which I had dispatched him.

Though Uthalai's death must have shocked his companions, they took heart in their superior numbers and pressed forward into the cell.

Another of the awesome rumblings shook the dungeon, and I saw several of the guards' eyes go wide in amazement and fear, but so hard pressed were they by mine and Zynthmai's blades there was little time to give the phenomenon further thought.

As more of the guards worked their way into the cell, we were pushed back to the far corner of the tiny chamber. I could feel Marjano's hands lightly upon my back, giving me advance warning there was little room left in which to retreat. The end was surely near, for I could not see any mercy in the eyes of our foemen.

I regretted the lack of opportunity to tell the girl of myself and my homeland. I had not really had a chance to learn anything about her other than that she was a princess. My love was so great for her, I realized I could not bear the thought of having my life snuffed out on the eve of our first real moment together. I suddenly realized that for this single reason I had braved the terrors of the forest, the Ghost People legend of the trees, the Togaoan warriors upon the trail, and finally the rigors of the stone city and its dungeons. For a love I had not known existed until this very moment which would probably be the last of my mortal life. Oh, if I could but hear the profession of her love for me before I left this cruel world, all would not have been in vain. Yet it seemed I would never have the chance as a dozen blades pressed me back and back until I could feel Marjano's body pressed tightly against mine, knowing hers in turn was pressed tightly against the wall.

Suddenly I became enraged that all my plans and efforts

had come to naught. The call of the Clan came easily to my throat. The yell no doubt had an eerie effect within the confines of the cell, and as I shouted the age-old call, I lunged forward, cutting down two of the guards in my first move.

"I shall prevail!" rose from my lips as I fully deemed I would not go out without taking every blasted guard in Euoaithia's command with me!

Taking the girl by the hand with my own free one, I slid across the wall to try and join Zynthmai, all the while keeping Marjano safely behind me. To my great delight he was still alive and holding his own, though like me, he could not hope to hold out for long.

I let out another eerie yell, echoing the heavy brogue off the walls and ceiling. Zynthmai retaliated with a call of his own that was music to my ears.

The remaining guards, some ten in number within the cell, let up on the fighting and backed to the far end of the chamber. Only about five feet separated us. But it was evident from their expressions that they did not find the prospect of further battle much to their liking. The small cubicle was strewn with the dead and dying. Many others, wounded, had crawled out of the cell to see to their wounds. How many more were converging on the doorway in the hall I could not guess, but knowing Euoaithia's desire to have us killed was indeed strong, I fully believed that his entire soldiery would be called up if needed.

Whether the guards inside the cell had broken off because they were taking a breather or whether it was because they were having second thoughts about carrying out their *Yata*'s wishes I did not know, but the respite gave me an opportunity to think of the girl for a moment or two. Turning slightly, I looked at her for the briefest of moments.

"Are you all right?" I asked quietly.

"Yes," she whispered, "I am fine now that you are here with me." Her coolness and poise reminded me of the first time I had seen her. Then she had been running from a dozen Bomunga warriors out to kill her and with no chance at escape, she had still retained her coolness and presence of mind.

"We cannot hope to survive, I'm sorry to say," I said, not really wanting to voice such negative thoughts but also not wanting to build up false hopes within her. "I had much better plans for you, but all my efforts have only brought you doom, for they will surely kill you as well."

"It is enough that you are here with me. From the first moment I saw you on the plains of *ghorai* in that strange costume, you have been ever on my mind. Then on the trail in the forest I could not believe my eyes to see you once again for I had surely thought the *Zumtai* had killed you when you fell from my airship. And how in the name of Turai did you manage to escape from the *mythai*? But it is of no moment, you are here. You must truly be invincible, *Yatahn*. Surely you . . . we . . . will prevail as you say, even here."

I could not figure out the title she had now thrice given me, but it seemed of little importance at the moment. Her undying faith in my ability touched me deeply. How I wanted to find a way out of this predicament from which there seemed no possible avenue of escape.

Either the guards were being pressed from behind to renew their efforts in the cell or they worked up enough courage to try once again for they lunged almost as a body upon us. I parried the first blade cast in my direction, saying over my shoulder to the girl, "I wish we could have had some time together, Princess!"

"As do I, *Yatahn*," she replied softly, her hands lightly upon my shoulder.

There was another of the giant rumblings, this one greater in volume than the others, and the earth heaved and pitched in erratic convulsions. The eyes of the guards were frantic. Another giant shock wave hit upon the heels of the first. One entire wall of the cell collapsed outward. The thought of escape burst upon me.

Still another shock wave shook the dungeon and the guards were thrown backward as the flooring under them buckled and cracked, giant slabs of stone pushing up beneath their feet.

The sound was deafening!

"Quick! Zynthmai!" I yelled above the roar. "Make for the opening. We might escape yet!"

I grabbed Marjano's hand and took a step toward what appeared to be freedom beckoning at us when a fourth shock wave hit. The stones beneath our very feet convulsed like a churning, angry sea. Before I had time to even brace myself, they crumbled beneath us and gave way.

Once again, just when it looked like there might be a way open to us, fate took a fickle turn.

Still holding tightly to the girl's hand, I fell into a black, seemingly bottomless void.

CHAPTER SEVENTEEN

The fall was endless. Throughout the perilous descent I continued to grasp the Princess' hand. I did not know if Zynthmai had met the same fate as we or if he had managed to escape through the collapsed wall.

I fully expected to be crushed to death when we struck the bottom of this cavernous opening into which we had fallen. We lit, however, in a deep pool of water that saved us a terrible end. Nevertheless we hit with terrific force. The shock broke my hold on the girl's hand, and for a few moments I was too concerned about stopping my downward plunge into the depths of the water to have thought of her. But only for a moment, for as soon as I realized we had survived the fall I reached about me in the inky blackness of the water until I grasped hold of the girl once again. Then with every ounce of energy I possessed, I fought my way to the surface, dragging her behind me. Breaking water I sucked in lungfuls of air, all the while holding her above the waterline, not knowing if she was unconscious or not.

"Are you all right?" I asked between gulps of air.

"Y-yes, I think so," she replied raggedly. "At least I seem to be all in one piece, though I never expected to find myself thus once the floor gave way beneath us."

"Can you swim?"

"I don't know," she replied hesitantly, "I have never before been in water such as this. There is no water in the northern lands, or anywhere upon the planet of which I know."

"Then relax and I will hold you up while we swim to shore." I'm sure I sounded much more confident than I felt, for I had no idea in which direction there might be land, or even if there was anything other than straight up and down walls clear to the water.

I felt her immediately relax as I slid my arm across her

breast and under her arm and struck off in the direction in which I hoped was a shelf or some other formation that would offer us egress from the water.

It was difficult to tell in what type of place or area we were. There was complete darkness. I could not see my arm in front of my eyes. If I did not have my arm about the girl I could not have told that she was near me.

The blackness tended to depress me, and had I not had the girl to think of, I am sure it would have gotten the best of me. I could see no way out of this predicament. I did not know if there was any way out of the water, let alone out of the cavern or hole or whatever it was. But we were alive and the thought of this made my spirits soar. I was with Marjano and she was safe and for the moment that was enough.

Within a few seconds my feet touched bottom and my already elated spirits rose even higher.

"We must be near the edge of the water now, for I can feel the bottom," I said to reassure her.

I could tell that the bottom sloped slowly upward, and felt more confident that there would be a shelf or land before us. Had the bottom curved upward rapidly I would have feared that it ended in a steep embankment, but as it was, I was sure there would be a place from which we could climb from the water. And I was right!

Lying upon the hard flooring of the underground cavern beside the girl to catch my breath, I took stock of our surroundings. I could see nothing, but I tried to picture in my mind what might be before us. A slight sound caught my attention. It came from the direction of the water behind us.

"Robert, Marjano, are you here?"

It was Zynthmai! He had not escaped from the guards as I had hoped but had fallen through the cell flooring with us.

"Over here, Zynthmai," I yelled. Then, with our calling to him, he slowly made for our location. In a moment he was on the bank beside us, though we knew this from sound rather than sight.

"I am sorry that you did not escape before the flooring gave way," I said as he settled down beside us.

"Do you mean that you have changed your mind and no longer want me to journey to Thu with you and Marjano?" he chided me good-naturedly.

"I can think of no one I would rather have join us," I replied honestly. "But at the moment there seems little likelihood that we will get out of this underground cavern, let alone make it to Thu!"

"I must admit," he laughed, "that were I here by myself I would be greatly concerned. But I have found in my short acquaintance with you that where you go great adventure follows. And as unbelievable as it seems, you always manage to come out on top, despite the harrowing odds that confront you! No, I think my chances for survival are greater down here with you than up there in the city."

"As do I," Marjano added solemnly.

We discussed the prospects for finding our way out of the cavern while we caught our breath. The only sensible thing to do, we agreed, was to join hands and cover every square inch of the bank before us until we found a passageway or natural tunnel that led from the cavern. With Zynthmai and I on either side of the Princess we started off. We moved cautiously in order not to fall into an opening or run into a wall. I must admit that I did not have much hope of finding a way out, for I feared that we were in an underground cave that had been carved out by moving water over millennia of time and in which we would be forever entombed.

We continued walking for quite some distance. The bottom of the tunnel or cave was quite smooth and made for surprisingly easy travel. At first I thought it had been man-made, but then I realized it could have been worn smooth by some underground waterway. This realization only led to a reinforcement of my earlier opinion that this was a huge underground cavern carved out by subterranean water seepage in some distant eon of time.

After what seemed an hour, we stopped to rest. I felt fairly certain that we had been walking in a direct line and not circling about. If such were the case, it seemed likely that this was not just an underground cavern, but perhaps a waterway that had run underground for some length. Thinking upon that I decided that our chances for escape might be good, for if this were an underground waterway then it might well terminate on the surface of the planet if we were to follow it far enough.

"What is your name, *Yatahn*? It is strange, but I do not even know by what you are called," she asked me as we sat resting. Her hand had never left mine, and I was continually amazed at the great strength of this lass. Never once in our entire ordeal, either in the dungeon or this underground blackness, had she voiced a dissenting word. Here indeed was a woman. One, if we ever got out of here, I would never want away from my side. What a race these Thuians must be!

"It is Robert," I replied. "Robert Dowdall the Fifth, of Eire, to be exact."

I could tell the strange-sounding name puzzled her, though when she voiced my name she did so in such a way as to give dignity and importance beyond anything I had ever before heard.

"That is a strange name upon Ghandor. Where is this Eire of which you speak?"

"It is in a faroff land, Princess. Very far indeed. But I think you would like it."

I told her the story of my arrival on their planet. I made it brief, leaving many gaps, thinking to fill them in later. For though we needed a rest, I was eager to see if my hunch about this being an underground waterway was correct.

As I talked I began to notice that I could make out the faint outline of both my companions. At first this didn't mean anything to me, for it is very natural for the eyes to adjust to darkness to the point where you can see someone next to you. But after a time I realized that the reason I could begin to make out my companions was due to the fact that there was some light in the cavern; in total darkness the eyes cannot ever adjust, for it takes some amount of light to see anything.

Looking about I finally pinpointed the source. It was just barely discernible. Quickly, I told my companions of my thoughts, and we made for the light source. I surely hoped that it would prove to be a way out of our predicament.

Drawing near to the spot, I realized that Marjano had not been startled to learn that I was from another planet. Whether this was because she did not believe me or simply accepted the statement as commonplace, I did not know, but her reaction puzzled me. However, I had no time to think further about it for as we neared the light we could see that it was emanating from around a giant outcropping of rock. Upon closer inspection we found a tunnel leading off from the cavern in which we had been walking.

At first I had hoped the light was from the sun, and my hopes were a little dashed as I saw that the light was coming from the very walls of the tunnel rather than some outside source.

The light came from the walls just as it came from the walls of the city above, though this was far more brilliant. In fact it was almost overpowering as we first entered the tunnel but after our eyes adjusted to the glare we found it not unbearable.

The light didn't cover the entire walls or ceiling. Instead, it came from veins of rock interwoven into the entire stone about us, much like a vein of gold or silver might appear in a mine on Earth. Only this ore gave out a brilliant light.

"This is a *yaama* mine," Zynthmai exclaimed in awe.

"Since we are under the ancient Cluvian city," Marjano added reverently, "this must be the original mother lode of *yaama* our ancestors discovered thousands of years ago!"

"What is *yaama*?" I asked stupidly.

"This rock is *yaama*," Marjano explained excitedly, pointing to one of the light-emanating veins. "It is the most precious ore on all Ghandor. Centuries ago the Cluvia discovered it. When it is melted down, a liquid is formed which can be painted upon any substance. The liquid paint retains the light and thus we have light in dark places. Unfortunately, all our scientists believed the supply on the planet was exhausted centuries ago."

"Many wars have been fought over *yaama* stockpiles," Zynthmai added. "My people have plundered entire kingdoms just to add to their supply."

"Just because it gives light?" I asked. It seemed insane that people would kill for such a simple thing. Then, as suddenly as that thought struck me, I realized that upon my own planet, entire kingdoms had been destroyed for nothing more than gold and other precious ores that on this planet were so plentiful they held no monetary value whatsoever.

"It is not just because it gives light, *Yatahn*," Marjano replied quickly. Then, realizing what she was about to say, she shot a quick glance in Zynthmai's direction. As she did so I could tell she was sorry she had. Color leaped into her face, and both Zynthmai and I could tell she was embarrassed.

"What is it, Princess?" I asked.

"I was about to say something that my people have held as absolute secret for thousands of years. I stopped because my mind told me Zynthmai was an enemy. But he, of course, is not. My thoughts betray my weakness, for Zynthmai is far more a friend to me than many a Thuian. I apologize for such an ignoble thought, my friend."

"Think nothing of it, Princess. It is difficult to break a life-time of training in one day. And do not feel compelled to tell me anything that is sacred to your people," he replied gallantly, and without guile.

"If I cannot trust the two of you," Marjano replied quickly, "there is no one on this entire world whom I can trust, for not even my very own father has braved what you two have done to save me. Come, let us continue along the tunnel and I shall tell you of the real importance of this ore."

I learned that besides the *yaama* ore being used as a means of trade between nations, it was the sole source of power for the Thuian airships. When the ore was melted down and applied to a special substance-coated sheeting, it dried to a hard finish that could be stripped from the surface and crumpled into powder. In this structural arrangement of its elements it is mixed into a specially but easily prepared liquid mixture of oxygenized gases. Molecules are rearranged and an entirely new structure formed. It is then hardened to a solid mass. In such a state it has the property to defy gravity. Not only that, it can be quickly liquefied and refrozen at will. In this manner its gravity-defying effects can easily be negated or enhanced.

A giant ball of the frozen element is placed in a specially prepared cylindrical structure that runs from the deck of the airship all the way to the bottom of the hull. Its slight protrusion on the bottom of the airship is what I had seen painted with a special insignia.

Several levers are attached to the cylindrical structure that operate the heating and freezing of the element. Though it can be changed from liquid to solid mass in less than a second, it is so fragile and the process must be so exact that many times the changeover fails at a critical moment. Not only did this *yaama*, when perfected, become the equalizer of gravity, it also was the source to keep the airships from plummeting to the ground when the gravitational fields collapsed. Usually, this is why the airships did not crash at such a time; however, if those at the controls are not constantly vigilant, they can be too slow to compensate and disaster strikes. Such had been the case with Marjano's airship after I had tossed her to the deck. When I had fallen after being struck, she had let out such a shriek and made such a fuss that the tenders of the element had been distracted. Unfortunately for Marjano, and ultimately for her crew, the gravitational field upon which their airship had been drawing power chose that very moment to collapse. Before the tenders knew what had happened they were passing over the trees and out of control. The reason the Bomunga had not seen the crash was because the airship had passed over the edge of the clearing and thus out of sight.

Despite this apparent danger, such instances are infrequent, and flying is considered by the Thuians to be the safest means of travel.

"We have over a thousand such airships," Marjano continued, "all equipped with the *yaama* drive, as it is called. The element lasts forever once it is so altered, or at least it is believed. There has never been an instance of it deteriorating; however, we do not have enough left in our kingdom to build any more airships. Our air navy is at maximum strength. If the Meoaithaians were to discover this tremendous store of *yaama*, they could rule the world."

"I thought only the Thuians understood the principle of the flying airships," Zynthmai remarked.

"As did I, until I ended up in the dungeons. There I learned that your people are at this moment working on the perfecting of the elemental transfer. Within a year I suspect they will have it perfected. The only thing that holds them back is enough of the ore to mount a sizable navy. Were they to discover this stockpile, they could build a million airships."

"Would they know how to fly them?" I asked.

"Yes. They have already repaired two of our crashed ships. It is a guarded secret in the stone city, but when I was traveling with the *Zumtai* warriors that captured me after our airship crashed I heard them talking of it. The chief of the little band felt they would gain a sizable reward when they told the Meoaithaians of the whereabouts of the downed ship."

I also learned that what little stockpile the Thuians had of the *yaama* had been turned over to several of the northern kingdoms to firm up shaky alliances. For Than Tan, her father and *Yata* of the Thu kingdom, suspected an attack from the Meoaithaians and realized his kingdom was in no shape to withstand an overall aggression from the warlike people of the south. Although war between kingdoms of any size is relatively unknown on Ghandor, Than Tan, thanks to his informants within the stone city, had learned that Euoaithia's plan was to one by one attack and conquer each of the smaller northern kingdoms until he had half the world behind him when he confronted the powerful Thuians.

Than Tan had spent the better part of the last two years trying to convince the northern kingdoms of this danger but had only been laughed at for none of the northern *Yatas* believed such a thing was possible. The tactics that had served Ghengis Khan and Alexander the Great so well were completely unknown on this world. None except Than Tan and Euoaithia understood the significance of such strategy.

Marjano told us that her kingdom was suffering from near-bankruptcy, so much of their *yaama* wealth had been used in trying to save Ghandor from the Meoaithaians. Even so, the alliance was shaky at best, she explained, and could crumble in a moment. If that happened, Urvia, the Thuians' largest city and seat of Than Tan, would surely fall into disrepute and the Thu people would be subjugated to the ridicule of their neighbors.

"I think I understand all that you have said, and though it seems to make sense," I said, "I am curious as to how the magnetic fields were discovered in the first place and how the captain of an airship knows how to use them since they cannot be seen."

While we continued to traverse the lighted tunnel, Marjano answered, "I do not really have an answer for your first question. The science has been lost among the Thu. Our ancient ancestors, the Cluvians, with their advanced technology, discovered and harnessed the power. Some of their knowledge survived them. The process by which the airship moves is really quite simple to explain . . . to a point. Evidently the planet is made up of many different, overlapping magnetic fields. While there are levers that freeze the ore to defy gravity and raise the ship and melt it to lower the ship vertically, there are other levers to move the ship horizontally. These levers are switched and others placed into motion. This movement causes the power of the *yaama* drive to reach outward from the ship and search out a magnetic center. Once a magnetic field is thus located, the drive is connected and the force of the gravity pulls or repels the airship in whichever direction the field is located. This movement continues until you begin to lose altitude. Usually this is a gradual change as the magnetic field fades and begins to collapse. At such a time you know you need to switch over to still another, more distant, field. It is a simple matter for earlier Cluvian scientists had mapped the billions* of gravity fields on the planet and we possess their ancient charts. All airship captains have committed to memory the location of each field's magnetic center."

As we progressed further into the tunnel we came across many small fissures that had been caused by this last, or perhaps, earlier earthquakes. I learned from Zynthmai that the rumblings in the earth were common enough in the Meoathaian city, but none to his knowledge had ever struck with such force. While he explained that the portion of the dungeon in which we had found Marjano had been built many centuries after the original city was constructed, I began to understand what might have happened. Centuries before when the Cluvians ruled the hemisphere and built their stone city, they hadn't just chanced to build it here.

They had discovered a great quantity of the *yaama* ore from which their newly discovered light source allowed them to build such a mighty structure with inside rooms that normally would have been as black as the bowels of the planet except for the precious ore. They built their city close so they could mine and stockpile the *yaama* without having to cart it great distances.

At some time in their construction, they found the ore was not into the mountain as they had first supposed, but dipped down into the depths of the earth. Since the city was already well under construction, they no doubt decided to tunnel under it. Several large air vents had to be dug vertically into the mines to allow for the miners to breathe. One of these air vents must have filled with rocks and dirt to some depth over the years, as no doubt all of the openings that led into the subterranean mines must have done after the great plague that wiped out the entire city.

---

* As far as I could tell from the manuscript there is no such word as *billion* in the Ghandorian language. The word my ancestor used was *zitbotuhj. Zit* meaning "beyond" and *botuh* meaning "number." The "j" added to the end of the word, as with all Ghandorian words, makes the word plural; thus, "beyond numbers." *Zy* is the Ghandorian word for "ten." *Zytoai* stands for "ten tens" or one hundred. *Zitzyzy* is to say "beyond ten tens, ten times," or ten thousand. *Zitbotuh,* meaning "beyond number" might be akin to saying a million. Thus, *Zitbotuhj* is beyond that number. It might stand for several million, a billion, or several billion. An explanation of the Ghandorian numbering system will be found at the end of the book.—DD

When the Meoathaians moved into the city centuries later there was no indication that the mines existed anywhere in the vicinity. But the Cluvian stockpile of precious ore was no doubt the means by which the first rulers of the stone city decided they might conquer the world.

When it came time to increase the size of the city's dungeons centuries later, the Meoathaians extended in the direction that took them over the closed-off air vent. Perhaps the many rumblings or tremors that shook the mine area loosened the rubble in the air vent, or perhaps it was only the last, large quake that finally did the job. In any event, the shaking of the earth's core cleared the air vent and further shakes dislodged the stone flooring in Marjano's cell and down we fell. It was only a stroke of luck that the pit into which we tumbled was a water seep, though not so miraculous for most old mines will fill with water at certain levels unless they are constantly pumped out.

I voiced my thoughts to my companions as we traversed the tunnel and they agreed it was as good an answer as any to the incidents leading up to our escape from the prison above.

While moving along the underground tunnel Marjano and I talked of many things. At one point she asked me about the flaming stone that still hung about my neck. The fact that it had not been taken from me during my incarceration greatly surprised her, for the Meoathaians have a great love for precious stones.

"That is strange," I agreed. "Perhaps they realized it was valuable only to the *Zumtai* and therefore of no value to them."

"In what way is it valuable to the *Zumtai*?" she asked.

"Among the Bomunga tribe it is the symbol of leadership. All the *Zumtai* have some similar tribal stone denoting the authority of their *Yatahano*."

"How come you to have it, Robert?"

Quickly I told her the story of what transpired after I fell from the airship that took her away from the Bomunga in the clearing.

"You mean you killed Portoona with one blow?" she asked incredulously. "No wonder you became the Mightiest One among them. I personally saw Portoona kill three of his enemies at one time. He was a mighty warrior. But then, I should not be surprised by anything the killer of the *Mythai* does. Your exploits, *Yatahn*, have been truly magnificent, if nonetheless puzzling!"

"In what way have they been puzzling?" I asked, stopping to look at the first of many fissures that obstructed our progress. This was the first one that my two companions would not be able to jump, so taking Marjano about the waist, I prepared to jump the fissure with her, thinking to leave her on the other side and go back for Zynthmai. As she recognized what I had in mind, she began to struggle in my grasp, but then shutting her eyes and clenching her teeth, she relaxed her struggles, trusting her soul to me.

"In many ways," she said, forcing the words between her teeth as, eyes tightly shut, she clung to me as I swung her up and jumped the fissure with ease. "And this is one of them," she finished, after I had placed her down on the other side.

"How do you mean?" I asked, preparing to jump back for Zynthmai.

"How is it that you can jump so far? That fissure is fully thirty feet across. No man can jump that far. Or so I had thought."

Leaping across the cavernous opening, I encircled Zynthmai's waist, and much to his chagrin, recrossed the fissure. To his relief we landed beside Marjano and began to continue our journey along the tunnel.

"I am not sure of the exact reason or all that might be involved," I finally said, "but the world from which I came evidently has a much larger mass and thus its gravity is much stronger. My muscles are as accustomed to my planet's gravity as yours are to Ghandor. And because Ghandor's gravity is less than my planet's, my limitations are less here, and thus my strength is greater."

She thought about that for a time, but her puzzlement still persisted.

"You are still puzzling, Robert. Perhaps your explanation covers your miraculous feats, but it does not explain your words or the way you sometimes act."

"What is so strange about that?" Zynthmai prodded, a slight smile touching the corners of his mouth. "Men have been puzzled by women for centuries. Shouldn't a woman be puzzled by a man once in a while?"

"No, no, I don't mean in that way, Zynthmai," Marjano chided, chuckling despite the seriousness of her concern. "It is just that the first time I saw Robert he was defending me against a dozen *Zumtai!* He was magnificent. In less time than it takes to tell of it, he dispatched the entire party that threatened my life. Then, in the next instant he runs from a fight when I have committed myself to stand beside him though it surely meant our death. Don't you find that strange, Zynthmai?"

"Before you answer that one, my friend, I should point out that there were five hundred Bomunga warriors, all armed to the teeth, descending upon us, screaming for our blood."

Zynthmai's laugh was boistrous in the confines of the tunnel. "Don't ask me, Princess, for I would have run from the first dozen. But I have heard of the strange fighting ideas among the Thu! Perhaps you are judging our friend before you understand his code. After all, he comes from another world. He certainly cannot be expected to know the peculiar oddities of the Thuians."

"I think I resent that last remark," Marjano laughed. "Were it to come from anyone but either of you, I am afraid I would have to take action. However, I would recommend that you not make any such accusation, Zynthmai, once we reach Thu for my people take their ancestry quite seriously."

"Come, come, my friend," I replied quickly. "Do not take offense. All races have peculiar habits and customs. Did you know the *Zumtai* show affection, the male to the female, by rubbing the appendages upon their knees against each other?"

"No!" Marjano exclaimed. Then, blushing slightly, she changed the subject. "I'm sorry that I struck you, *Yatahn,* when you were trying to lift me up to my airship," she said demurely.

"Those love taps?" I asked jokingly. "Why I hardly realized I was being struck. But tell me, Princess, why were you objecting to my saving your life? Did you really want to stand and fight? You certainly couldn't expect us to defeat that horde."

"Of course not. It is just the Thu code. When a comrade wants to fight, you simply must assist him. You didn't run for the airship and I thought you wanted to stand and fight. It was demanded of me to stay and fight with you."

"See," interjected Zynthmai, "I told you they have peculiar ways." He gave me a big wink which Marjano could not see, then laughed uproariously when she shot him a reproachful glance.

"But when I tried to get you to run for the airship with

me, why did you refuse?" I asked, genuinely puzzled over the nature of this racial oddity.

"Why, once I had decided to fight I could not then run," she replied simply. Her tone told me that for her to have even considered running after once deciding to stand and fight would have been paramount to cowardice. Which meant, of course, that for me to run away with her was a cowardly act and reproachful in the eyes of the warriors on board the airship. And to Marjano. I shook my head at the unusual nature of the Thuian mind.

"At first I thought you a coward," she added apologetically. "It wasn't until we were flying off over the *Blou Tresai* and I thought you dead from the blow on your head from the *thwarpa* stone that I realized no coward would have defended me against the *Zumtai* as you had done. I really hated myself for what I had thought of you, and thinking you dead, there was no way I could rectify my rudeness!"

She gave my hand a squeeze and I felt the situation more than rectified.

As we continued along the tunnel, I puzzled over the odd customs of the Thuian race. Zynthmai was certainly correct, they were peculiar in some ways. But then, my own customs of Eire would no doubt seem odd to both my companions were they to be spirited to that far off world.

We had been traveling for some hours by my reckoning when we reached a particularly large fissure. It wasn't any wider than many others we had jumped, but this one extended up the walls on either side and across the ceiling. It looked as though some great giant had severed the tunnel with a huge knife, much like a person might cut through a loaf of bread.

I had just jumped the chasm with Marjano in my arms when I heard a terrible, high-pitched yell coming from the tunnel in front of us. Before I could jump back across the fissure with the Princess, a huge animal broke from a bisecting tunnel. It lumbered into view with an ungainly stride, emitting another yell that curdled my blood.

Standing well over nine feet in height, it advanced on two stumps that served as legs. It was fully as wide as the tunnel, and though the going was slow because of the cramped space, the distance between us quickly diminished. I could have easily jumped back across the chasm myself, but there was no time to grab hold of the girl once again and carry her to safety. Instead, the only course of action was to dismember the beast before it could tear us apart.

Not wanting the creature to come any closer to Marjano, I drew my sword and ran directly at him. Whether it was this action or for some other reason, the animal stopped its forward charge and rose to its full height to eye me.

The beast was awesome in its size and gruesome in appearance. It looked like a giant insect, though of no species I had ever before seen. Its head was the size of a boulder and rested upon the upper thorax, which was covered with a decaying, mottled fur, though how it was attached to the exoskeletal structure I could not tell. A strange, triangular spot of bright yellow was noticeable under portions of the decaying fur upon the upper thorax.

Mauve in color, the creature was a frightening sight!

It had two thorax segments, each with a pair of arms. A third segment, or abdomen, ended in several circular parts that tapered off into a tail about ten feet in length and extremely thick at the base, tapering to only a few inches at its tip. The yellow spot upon the upper thorax was the only bright coloring upon the creature.

The two eyes which held my gaze were large, flaming orbs. They did not appear to be many segmented as those of a fly, but similar to a human's, except that there was no white around the iris. Red in color and giving the appearance of fire, the eye had two dark pupil spots that were quite noticeable. The upper jaw extended from either side of the eyes and curved down and out from the head. Several layers of yellowish teeth could be seen below large oversized lips. Its lower jaw was uncinate, hooking down from the upper lip creating a weird, mirthless smile. It appeared to be without a nose, though having two pairs of antenna which sprouted up from the top of the eye sockets and curving downward to the side, one set almost reaching its shoulders. Its overall appearance was gruesome, and I did not enjoy the prospect of engaging the slimy creature.

It was definitely an invertebrate hexapod, or six-legged insect, but the upper two pair of legs had evolved into arms. These ended in many-jointed fingers, while the two lower legs ended in flat, bony structures that served the beast as supporting pads. No doubt the tail also served for balance, though I got the feeling it would make a formidable weapon as well.

The insect watched me furtively but made no effort to attack. For this reason, I held my blade at the last moment. It seemed to be considering its predicament; then, letting out one of its ear-splitting screams, it turned and bounded off down the tunnel. I watched it until it was out of sight before turning my back toward my companions.

"That, that was a *gloaid*," breathed Marjano. "They have been extinct for millions of years, or so I've been told. They used to rule the planet long before man evolved. Ancient cave paintings show that thing as man's worst enemy. Legends have it that it would attack anything that moved, be it animal, man, or plant life. I can't believe there are any still living, or that it didn't attack us!"

"Well, let's thank whatever providence that changed its mind and get out of here before it decides we'd make a tasty meal!" I replied.

After jumping back to get Zynthmai, we pressed on. Throughout our entire trek I had been trying to puzzle out our whereabouts under the city. I believed we were running on a parallel course with the mountain, perhaps around the stone city. If this were true, the entrance, if it were indeed open to the surface, should not be far off. I felt the ancient Cluvians would not have had their tunnels run far from the city proper. What I feared was this tunnel was not the main digging, but rather an arm that would end where the miners had left off, perhaps directly under or into the mountain core itself. However, I did not deem it worthwhile to voice such doubts to my companions, for they were trusting in my leadership.

Perhaps an hour later we came to a fork in the tunnel. This was not one of the smaller bisecting tunnels that we had passed before, but an equally large tunnel that forked off before us. To the right the tunnel continued in a straight line as far the eye could see, disappearing out of sight due only to the perspective of its great length. The left fork traveled only a short distance before it curved rapidly to the extreme left and out of sight. I was tempted to take the left fork, for if my senses had not deceived me, this seemed to lead back around the city to where I felt the tunnel opening would be found. The other tunnel seemed to lead off away from the city and I felt for sure the Cluvians had kept their egress to the underground diggings near to the city structure.

We had just entered the left fork when another ear-splitting scream broke the Stygian gloom of the tunnel. It was the yell of the fearsome creature which had appeared earlier, and I didn't cherish another confrontation with it. Not able to tell from which direction the sound emanated, I didn't know whether to advance or retreat from this tunnel fork. Turning I saw the creature bounding down the tunnel up which we had been traveling. It came toward us in long, bounding strides.

"Quickly," I yelled, "this way."

Up the left fork we ran, hoping to make the bend in the tunnel before the animal overtook us. Perhaps we might find safety around this curve of the tunnel. But we had not taken a dozen steps when around the bend before us appeared not one but two more of the awesome creatures. Without breaking stride, I turned on my heels and half-carried, half-dragged the Princess back along the tunnel, hoping to make the right fork before the two groups of creatures reached us.

Luckily the right fork was empty, and as I saw this avenue of escape, a plan of action formed in my mind. It wasn't much of a plan, but it was all we had. At least it would buy Zynthmai time to get the Princess to safety.

"Zynthmai, take the Princess and go on ahead. I'll slow the creatures down some and then follow right along behind."

"No, *Yatahn*, let us all stand and fight together," she called, but both Zynthmai and I realized that one stood a better chance in the narrow tunnel than two or three. In fact a second blade would more than likely be in the way, since only one animal could attack at a time due to their great size and the confines of the narrow tunnel.

"Hurry, both of you. See if you can't find some means of escape up this tunnel. I will be along in a few moments," I called back. Before Marjano could reply, I added, "Princess, don't let me down. Find somewhere that we may escape this maze of tunnels and these fearsome creatures."

She tossed me a worried look over her shoulder as Zynthmai guided her along the tunnel, her mouth forming words. But I had no time to notice or hear for backing into the tunnel mouth for as much protection as I could manage, I made ready to meet the charge of the foremost rushing creature, which was emitting a terrible screaming roar.

I recognized the one in the vanguard as the same one I had encountered earlier from the triangular-shaped yellow spot high on the upper thorax. None of the others were so marked. I wondered at the oddity behind this one bright color on all of the creatures that I could see. This time, however, he was backed by fully a dozen of his companions, and he didn't seem inclined to turn tail and run.

Rage shook the yellow-spotted hexapod, and the bilious creature let out another of his ear-splitting screams as he closed with me.

He reached down to grab me with one of his greasy arms, but I jumped above his grasp and swung my blade toward his neck. The terrific blow severed his prodigious head and a nauseous, bluish slime gushed forth, splattering me, the walls and ceiling of the tunnel. I did not have a chance to notice the creature's death throes as the second hexapod clambered over the fallen body of his comrade and made to clamp his thirty-inch-wide jaws around me.

Another swing of the blade and this creature fell at the feet of his companion, the bluish slime gushing out upon the surrounding *yaama* ore, dimming its brightness. Yet the quick dispatching of two beasts did not seem to lessen the ardent pursuit of the others, for still a third creature made his way over the slain carcasses of his fallen comrades to crush me with his great bulk. Jumping back with one of my mighty leaps in the lesser gravity, I escaped the creature's enormous body and incapacitated his head with still another sweeping blow of my sword.

Footing was getting difficult in the narrow tunnel with the bluish slime now entirely coating the walls and floors, necessitating more caution on my part lest I lose my balance and find myself overrun by the creatures.

The brightness was all but gone from this small section in which we fought and I knew that retreat here would be the better part of valor. I saw another pair of the flaming eyes coming at me and jumped upon the back of one of the downed hexapods for a better position from which to defend myself. Perhaps if I could kill another one and have it fall on the bodies of its comrades, it would effectively block off further pursuit, at least for a time.

Swinging the blade with both hands much after the fashion of the European long sword carried by knights of previous eras, I kept the beast at bay. Either their bodies were boneless and connected by a type of chitinous membrane, or the sword with which I worked was as sharp as the one I had brought with me from my own world. For in two of the swipes I severed one of the beast's arms and nearly sliced him in half near the bottom of the first thorax joint. I pressed my advantage in the midst of terrible cries from not one, but several of the great beasts. The sound was almost deafening.

One of his three remaining hands reached out and closed around my leg, but a downward swing sliced through that appendage and left me free once more. If the cries of rage the beast had already been emanating could have increased, they did in that moment as it lost another of its arms. Quickly reversing my thrust, I swung upward with the blade and sank into the center of the upper thorax. I didn't know if these creatures even had a heart, but if they did, I was hoping that it was centrally located, as it is in all of the animals and humans I had ever previously fought.

The point must have struck true, for the animal emitted a final cry and fell forward, almost on top of me. It was only by a stroke of luck that I avoided being pinned beneath it, for as I jerked my blade out in retrieval, my strength threw me off balance. Teetering on the edge of the piled hexapods, which I had previously dispatched, my foot slipped on the blue slime and gore of the felled creatures and I toppled backward onto the tunnel floor. An outstretched, many-jointed hand fell within inches of my head as the beast tumbled upon his fallen comrades.

Jumping to my feet I retreated down the tunnel as fast as I could go. I didn't know how long those bodies would cut off pursuit, and I wanted to be gone from there before they succeeded in clearing the way. Nor did I take time to look back in my flight so when I finally came upon Zynthmai and Marjano, I didn't know how much time we would have before the hexapods caught up with us again.

"Oh, thank *Nazu*, you are safe, *Yatahn*," the princess exclaimed as she saw me approaching. "What happened?"

Briefly I told them as we continued our flight down the tunnel. Surely there must be an end to it soon, or perhaps another fissure would present itself that would cut off pursuit. This I was thinking while telling them in cryptic terms of the fight with the beasts.

"It is a miraculous feat you have accomplished," Marjano exclaimed when I finished. "For centuries the *gloaid* has been considered the most ferocious animal ever to have lived upon Ghandor. It is believed they were invincible."

"They were probably thought to be so only because there

were no weapons such as the sword to withstand them for the creatures have bodies susceptible to the blade."

"Perhaps so," Marjano replied, "yet you are the only man to ever kill one so far as any ancient writings and signs portray!"

We ran a little while longer before I asked, "If they were so invincible, why did they become extinct ... at least upon the surface?"

"No one knows for sure, but it is believed that the entire *gloaid* kingdom existed only here in this area of the western hemisphere. Geologists claim that sometime in our dim past there was a tremendous upheaval and the entire face of the planet was changed. At that time this entire area, it is believed, opened up and was swallowed into the bowels of the earth. Many of the first Cluvians were destroyed as a result, and only those in the northern and southern parts of the planet survived. The entire Ghost Forest now covers the area that the upheaval is believed to have taken place. In fact, the entire forest sits in a sunken bowl, and it is quite a climb to the surface when you emerge from the trees."

Knowing the extreme distances of the forest, I could well imagine the cataclysm that must have taken place. It would have had to have been gigantic in proportions. Indeed, if anything had lived in that area, it would have perished.

As we ran I tried to pierce the brightness ahead of us, hoping to see a different type of light, such as the sun shining through an opening. But this was to no avail. There was nothing before us but the same intensity of light emanating from the *yaama* ore.

"I still can't get over the fact that you killed four of the creatures," Zynthmai said after a time. We were becoming winded by now and in need of rest. Perhaps, just perhaps, I thought, the beasts had had enough. Maybe they weren't following after all. With that thought and the need of a breather, I signaled for a halt.

Leaning against the wall, catching my breath, I looked at my fighting companion.

"Yes, there were four that fell beneath my blade, but despite the fact that they have tender skins and can be easily severed, they are a persistent lot. Completely free from fear, at least in a pack," I added, remembering how the first one had run. "But I'm sure the battle would have turned out differently had we been fighting in larger quarters. The beasts could not bring their tails into action in the confines of the tunnel, and I do believe that is their greatest fighting strength."

"Are the *gloaid* following, *Yatahn?*" Marjano asked, gasping for breath. She was propped along the wall with her back facing in the direction we had come, evidently too tired to turn around and look for herself.

"I don't know, Princess, for I didn't wait around to find out and I cannot see them now. But they are such persistent creatures that it would seem inconsistent to me if they didn't follow!"

As though my words had been a signal, the yell of one of the hexapods shattered the otherwise stillness of the tunnel. Looking back, I could barely make out several of the creatures coming up the tunnel some two or three hundred yards away. They were moving quickly, and with their great strides it seemed as though they would be upon us in a matter of moments. Indeed, our chances seemed mighty slim. Yet hope springs eternal in a human breast, and I made ready to move my companions on along the tunnel, hoping against hope for some exit from the underground mine.

Another blood-curdling scream penetrated the tunnel, but unlike the other, it did not come from behind us.

Looking up ahead, about the same distance away as the *gloaids* behind us, was another group of the creatures bearing down upon us.

If our chances had seemed slim a moment before, they now appeared impossible. The two groups of hexapods would be upon us from either side in a matter of moments.

CHAPTER EIGHTEEN

As the creatures closed in upon us from both sides, I could think of nothing but the awful fate into which I had cast my beautiful princess. I said as much to her, adding, "For you it would have been better had I never found you in the dungeons. At least you might not have been dashed into this subterranean world and now facing the jaws of these fearful creatures."

"*Yatahn*, we shall prevail!" she replied enthusiastically.

Her words sent shivers of excitement through me, and my love for her increased, if that were possible. Here indeed was a woman! Clasping her hand I swung her between Zynthmai and myself. Facing outward, the Meoaithaian and I formed a protective shield for the girl and offered the only defense we could mount. All seemed lost, but the girl's unfailing faith caused me to face the coming onslaught with some degree of hope.

"They are not overly bright, Zynthmai," I called to him over the yells of the approaching animals, "and quite irrational. The heads are easily severed as are the limbs. Their heart seems to be in the middle of the upper thorax."

"Luck to you, Robert of Eire. May we all three see tomorrow's sun," he called back.

The creatures were less than a hundred yards distant and we lapsed into silence, each with his own thoughts of what the next few minutes would bring. Our chances did indeed seem slim, but the touch of the girl's hands lightly upon my arm and her faith buoyed up my spirits as nothing else could have done. Casting my eyes about for another answer as I am wont to do, I saw something at my feet that puzzled me.

Set into the smooth flooring were two notches about the size of my fist, though they were rectangular in shape. They were about two feet apart. Looking further I could see no other marks upon the tunnel floor. These two indentations appeared to be quite old and confounded my understanding of what purpose they had served. It was as though they had been placed there to brace something. Like a ladder, I thought.

Recognition flooded across me. Looking up I saw another of the air vents like the one through which we must have fallen. Its sides appeared smooth as though it had been bored with an instrument. I could not see any markings or footholds upon the circular surface of the vent. But due to the dim light within it I hoped that indeed there were for it was our only chance of escape. Certainly there must be some way to climb upward in the vent or why had the ancient Cluvians cut the braces in the floor, if they were not to support a ladder? Of course there was only one way to find out.

In less time than it takes to tell, I saw the markings, discovered the vent, and was lifting Marjano up into its cavity, explaining as I did that there should be foot or handholds by which she could climb to safety. She weighed less than a feather in my hands, and in seconds she was almost completely within the air vent, the ceiling being only about ten feet above the tunnel floor.

"Do you see anything?" I yelled.

"Yes, yes! There are metal supports extending from the rock. They seem to go upward as far as I can see." As she said this, I could feel her climbing free from my grasp and quickly she disappeared out of sight.

"Quick, Zynthmai, time is short."

He shot a hurried look over his shoulder at the creatures bearing down upon us. They were less than fifty yards distant. He took my offered boost and in a moment, he, too, had disappeared up the shaft.

The screaming cries were overpowering. No doubt the beasts were enraged at seeing their quarry slipping from their grasp. I fancied I could feel their hot, fetid breaths as I sheathed my sword. I had but one chance and that would be to jump as high as I could into the vent opening, hoping to be able to grasp one of the handholds that Marjano had spied. If they were set on either side and I chanced to reach to the appropriate sides, I would be able to save myself. But if I chanced to reach in the wrong directions, I would not have a second chance and would fall down into the clutches of these horrible beasts that were even now within reach.

Bracing myself, and calling upon all the saints that were holy, I leaped with all the additional strength this world seemed to give me.

My leap took me well up into the shaft as I had intended it should, for I was not sure if the supports began right at the bottom or further into the opening. At the apex of my jump, I reached out on both sides of me for a handhold . . . and found nothing!

Frantically, I flayed about as I began to fall back down into the tunnel. A sharp sense of despair pierced through me as I visualized falling back into the midst of the *gloaids* below. At that moment as I lost hope, a strong hand closed over mine.

"Quickly, Robert, take hold of the support. It is directly in front of you." Zynthmai spoke with urgency for he could see what I could not, one of the beasts beneath the shaft was readying itself for a leap to snare one of us.

The supports turned out to be before and behind me . . . not to the sides as I had supposed. Grasping hold, I began to clamber up the shaft behind my scurrying companions when a hand closed upon my ankle and began dragging me back toward the tunnel below! The hexapods evidently had great leaping ability, for I must have been twenty feet up into the shaft when one of them grabbed me. How it managed to wedge its way up the narrow opening I could not guess.

Drawing my sword I hacked at the arm I could barely see in the dark, narrow vent. As my eyes became more accustomed to the darkness, I could see the beast was wedged into the shaft and could not move. Had he another arm free, he could have surely finished me, but as it were, I was able to sever his one arm that lay hold on me and climb away from the slavering jaws. His screams of rage shook the walls of the shaft.

"Greed will get you every time," I yelled as I resheathed my blade and once again started up the air vent.

I climbed for some time before I reached my companions. They had halted in their ascent.

"It's blocked," I heard Marjano say.

"Is there no opening at all?" Zynthmai asked.

"No, none that I can see," she replied quickly.

"Princess," I said as I came upon them, "can you see any light through the rocks above? We must be near the surface for we have certainly climbed the distance we fell earlier."

There was a pause, then: "Yes, yes there is. I see several small pinpoints of light directly above me."

As I climbed, the thought came to me that these had been more than air vents to the ancient Cluvians. Surely, they would not have placed hand and footholds in the vertical shafts if they were only to let in air. But if they had served also as escape hatches in case of emergency, that would explain the existence of the supports. It also occurred to me there must have been numerous such apertures in the ceiling of the tunnel through which we had come since first finding the lighted tunnel; however, because of my stupidity, we had not discovered them for I had been looking down at the flooring and walls rather than up.

It had been Marjano's words that shook me out of my self-incriminating thoughts. If the passage were blocked above, we were doomed, for we could not descend to the tunnel below. The hexapods would not give up easily, and how long could we hang suspended in the air?

An idea occurred to me. If the earthquake had loosened the debris in the other shaft, surely it must have loosened some of the rock and dirt blocking this one. Perhaps if we worked at it, such debris would fall free. I said as much to my companions and suggested they lower themselves a few feet upon the supports while I climbed to the blockage to see what I could do. The entire effort depended upon how far below the surface we were. If it were more than a few feet, it seemed doubtful we could succeed.

Reaching the end of the shaft directly over Marjano, I looked at the blockage. After a few moments I could see the pinpoints of light to which the princess had referred. They were very small, but I believed them to be openings to the surface through which the sun was shining.

"Flatten yourselves out against the shaft wall directly below me," I called to them. "If I can loosen any of these rocks, I don't want them to fall upon you. It would be wise, in fact, to strap yourself to the support should one of the boulders strike you."

I loosened my top harness belt and handed it to Marjano, instructing her to place it around her body just below the shoulders and strap it close about the support. When Zynthmai had done likewise, I began wedging my sword up into the debris above me. No sooner had I done so than fine dirt shifted down, covering my face and falling into my eyes, making it difficult to see. But I kept at it, for it was our only means of escape from the underground mine.

Two hours later I had succeeded in only covering myself and my companions with dirt that had worked free from the debris above. The rocks seemed tightly wedged and nothing I could do to free them seemed effective. My arms were tiring rapidly from constantly holding them above my head. I suggested to Zynthmai that he take a try at it while I rested. Carefully we traded positions, moving past Marjano and each other by climbing the supports upon the opposite side of the shaft. Since the shaft was about five feet across, this proved to be no problem, and in a matter of a couple minutes, we had successfully changed positions.

For nearly an hour more Zynthmai struggled with the rocks, but to no avail. Finally we changed positions again, and I attacked the blockage with renewed vigor.

"When we get out of here, have you given any thought as to how we will get back to Thu, *Yatahn?*" Marjano asked simply as I struggled with my blade and the rocks.

I marveled at her faith. Never had she doubted that we would manage our escape.

"Yes," I replied casually, not sure at all I would be able to free the air vent of the solidly wedged rocks. "We will take the avenue through the trees north until we are free of the forest, then it will be easier going. Surely we will spot one of your flying airships somewhere along the way."

"The avenue through the trees? You must be joking!" she replied in astonishment.

I could not believe that she was afraid of heights as are the *Zumtai,* for she had scampered up the shaft like she was born to it. Nor had she voiced any concern about hanging hundreds of feet high in the shaft. I voiced my feelings to her on the subject.

"It is not the heights, it is the *Blou Tou* in the forest. They are pledged to kill anyone they find in the trees," she replied quietly.

"That is merely superstitious ravings of the madman, Euoaithia of Meoathai. For it was his ancestors that began the rumor some generations ago," I replied.

Quickly I told her the same story I had received at the lips of the cruel Meoathaian *Yata* that I had related to Zynthmai during our days of imprisonment beneath the city. When I covered the part about posing as the *Yata* of the Ghost

People myself, Marjano's intake of breath was followed by a low chuckle.

"You are a rash *Yatahan*," she laughed, referring to me as a great warrior, but a reckless one at that.

"It has always been the curse of the Dowdalls, my fair lady," I replied jokingly.

"But I am surprised that anyone believed you for it is said the *Blou Tou* are invisible and cannot be seen."

"Perhaps that is just a feeling of the north kingdoms, for among the Meoathaians no such attitude exists. It also seems strange to me Princess, that such a rumor would have traveled to the north kingdoms and been believed."

"Not really. You see the north kingdoms are very religious races, dating back to the ancient Cluvians. It was due to the strong religious beliefs that such blame was placed upon the ancient scientists because of the plague. That attitude is still shared by many of the kingdoms outside of Thu and is one of the reasons why it has been so difficult for my father, Than Tan, to effect any permanent alliance as we have revived some of the old Cluvian knowledge. And besides, none of the north kingdoms venture into the forests. The Thu fly over them and the others give the Ghost Forest a wide berth in their travels. As a matter of fact, I doubt if any of the north kingdoms outside the Thu really are sure the Meoathaians even exist for they have never seen their great stone city."

As Marjano had been talking I was earnestly working upon the rocks above with my sword. So intent upon her words had I been that I did not at first notice one of the rocks working free. It was only at the last moment I was able to stay its fall until I had warned my companions below. Letting it fall into the vent, I fancied I could hear it striking one of the hexapods below. Whether it might have been the one still wedged in the shaft opening, if indeed he still was, or another I could not tell nor in fact was I even sure I heard anything at all so great was the distance. However, the intermittent screams of the enraged hexapods assured us that they were still there. Because of this knowledge that we could not descend, the loosening of the rock served to excite me and I began to work upon the rocks blocking the shaft and safety with renewed effort. Several more rocks worked free and it was but a few moments later that the three of us stood upon the surface of the planet once again.

"That was a narrow escape, Robert of Eire," Zynthmai said sighing in relief as he stood, dusting the rocks and dirt from himself that had fallen atop us all as we wedged the debris in the shaft free but moments before.

"Yes, it was, my friend," I replied, "but I have the feeling it will not be my last, for on this world of yours I have found nothing but impending danger throughout my entire stay here."

"Wait until we get to Thu," Marjano interjected. "My land of happiness and joy. While danger is always possible, there is much to relax and enjoy there."

"Thu," Zynthmai said slowly. I could tell he was still struggling with his concern over leaving his family and the intrigue of his city.

"Come, my friend," I said, breaking into his thoughts. "The trip to Thu will prove to be another venture and I am not sure I would like to tackle it without your faithful sword at my back."

As Zynthmai's eyes began to brighten, I added, "and as I promised, my friend, I will return with you to the stone city to overthrow your vicious *Yata* as soon as I have seen my Princess safely home."

Several days later found us traveling the avenue among the trees far to the north. Zynthmai had agreed to accompany us to Thu though he had vowed he would return to Meoathai to quell the evil forces that controlled his people.

Our mood was light from our recent escape, and though Marjano and Zynthmai had been hesitant to join me in the trees when we first entered the Ghost Forest, three days of travel without incident had served to remove their inbred fears.

While I had been quick to remind them that there was no *Blou Tou,* for it was but the propaganda of the Meoathaian *Yatas,* I still found myself wondering about the strange creature or creatures that had attacked me that night. Surely I had not dreamed the adventure, for blood had been spilled that night in profusion as the light of day revealed. But for that one incident, my many travels through the trees had met without incident save the giant worms of the southern region.

I couldn't shake the uneasiness that prevailed over me as I swung my Princess into the branches and led the way to the avenue among the trees, but three days of travel without incident had served to remove my fears and those of my companions.

"This is really beautiful," Marjano had simply said on the fourth day when our feelings began to become light once again. The first few days in the trees had tended to dampen our spirits so full of concern were my companions.

"Yes, it is," I replied. "I have spent much time here and often wondered what or who could have created such a marvelous and exotic pathway so high among the trees."

"Perhaps they simply grew this way by some quirk of nature," Zynthmai suggested, though I doubted that even he believed in the possibility.

"Or, perhaps there really are *Blou Tou* and it was only by accident that the ancient Meoathaian *Yatas* hit upon the unknown truth of the Ghost People." Marjano's eyes were bright, and the thought fell heavy upon me for a moment, but I quickly threw it off.

"Perhaps, my Princess, but whatever prevailed here among the trees in times past must surely have perished in the long ago of the ancient past of which you have spoken. For surely, if these Ghost People still existed, they would have made themselves known before now."

"Or perhaps they made themselves known to you once," Zynthmai interjected, "and you beat them off so severely that they fear attacking you again."

Zynthmai was referring to the adventure in the trees some days ago when I had shed the blood of some unknown and perhaps invisible foe. I quickly related the story to Marjano for I had neglected to mention it to her previously.

"Yes," she said when I finished, "perhaps that is so. For you are a brave warrior and one to be greatly feared as all who have crossed blades with you have quickly learned. Perhaps we can rightfully call you the *Yata* of the *Blou Tou*, Robert."

On that light note we continued through the trees. We discussed many things and joked as young people are wont to do, but every so often I found myself looking back over my shoulder to see where we had been. Was it because I was beginning to believe in the *Blou Tou*? Of course not, I told myself. I was only looking back to see what our back trail looked like should I have to retrace my steps at some future time. This is often a habit of mine since a trail looks much different when viewing it from a different direction. Or was it really because of something else? Some unseen enemy that stalked us?

It was near evening of the eighth day that we stopped to rest when calamity overtook us. We had been discussing the length of time it would take to reach the Thuian city of Urvia where Marjano's family resided. It seemed from the Princess' calculations, we would be in the forest for another two or three days before reaching the highlands which marked the beginning of the northern lands. According to Marjano, the highlands completely surrounded the forest and according to theory, had been the level of ground of the forest itself before the age-old upheaval. Thus, the entire Ghost Forest was settled in a large, almost round bowl of land some hundred feet or so below the level of the surrounding countryside.

"If we don't chance to see one of our airships," Marjano stated, "we can always find some *thwods*."

The uncomfortable gait of the two-legged riding animal of Ghandor wasn't a happy thought to me, and I hoped one of the Thuian airships would be traveling close by when we cleared the forest.

We were moving quite easily along the avenue of the trees, running a tireless gait, sometimes walking, occasionally resting, but usually, as now, running along, making light of our past experiences and looking toward our future with much interest and jovial comment. I judged we were more than two hundred miles from the Meoathaian city when we stopped to rest.

We had killed many of the birds that frequented the trees as some smaller game found along the trails below in great abundance in this part of the forest. It was while after one of these small animals, which slightly resembled a rabbit though without the long ears or lightning-fast movements, that I felt a premonition of danger quickly approaching. I was further from my companions than I cared to be, yet knew they were in good stead. The avenue was so open that it would be difficult for anything or anybody to creep unobserved upon them. And Zynthmai was a brave and excellent swordsman.

Just as I caught a glimpse of the animal I was seeking, I had the feeling to turn back and see that my companions were safe. But I knew they would think me foolish should I return without meat and find them well. So working my way above the animal, which Marjano had told me was called a *muplu,* or tiny rodent, I dropped to the trail below and speared him with my sword before it knew I was near.

Marjano's yell pierced the quiet of the forest, and without waiting to secure the animal, I sprang into the trees and made my way quickly back to where I had left them. To my great consternation and puzzlement, they were nowhere to be seen. For as far as I could see, the avenue among the trees and the trails below were completely empty. Nor could I raise them with my repeated calls.

I cursed my foolish pride at not wanting to appear before my friends empty handed when I had felt that something was amiss. For more years than I could remember my premonitions had served many times to win battles or save my life. Had I responded to it along the trail and returned sooner I may well have been in time to save the Princess from whatever fate had befallen her. A fate about which I knew not, nor did there seem any way in which I might rescue her from it for though I spent the hour of light left to me, I could find no indication anywhere in which direction Marjano and Zynthmai had been taken. That they were captives somewhere I had no doubt, for surely they would not have left of their own accord. But captives of whom or where I could not guess.

I spent a fruitless night combing the avenue among the trees, I was in hopes that whoever might have taken them captive would hear me and try to take me as well. In that way, at least, I might know who it was that had taken my beloved Princess.

As I moved noisily among the trees, yelling for my companions and cursing their abductors, the creatures of the forest fell silent. It was as though they felt some kinship to me for at no time did a single animal raise its voice to drown out my own intermittent pleading and cursing.

But the effort proved to no avail and by daylight I had returned to the spot where I had last seen Marjano and Zynthmai. I had left the Princess sitting upon the intertwined limbs with her back against the bole of a particularly large tree. Zynthmai had been standing nearby. He had offered to go for food himself but I could tell he was quite winded from our days of running through the trees. As I had moved off, he had settled himself also against the bole of the tree, some few feet from the Princess. One glance told me that neither could have fallen through the limbs to the forest some hundred feet below, for the limbs were of a particularly thick composition at this point, almost like a solid flooring that someone had carefully laid. But, however impossible it might seem, I decided to leave nothing unchecked so I carefully made my way into the lower branches and moved back to the spot beneath where Marjano had sat to see if some type of trap door or opening could have been effected.

Despite my careful scrutiny, there appeared to be nothing out of place beneath where either had sat. Still, I checked the limbs and forest beneath, all to no avail. It was as though the tree had opened up and swallowed her.

Making my way back to the spot, I studied the tree for any type of opening or mechanism. Nothing could be found. Climbing into the tree above the spot, I made my way fifty feet into the upper branches, yet I could still find nothing out of place. As I started my descent I noticed a strange thing. Looking straight down upon the spot where Marjano had sat, there was an opening formed through the dense foliage of the tree. It was as though someone had wanted to see that exact spot and had created this opening for that purpose. I had not noticed it as I climbed upward, but looking down upon it, the opening was unmistakable.

Looking above I could see that the opening continued for several hundred feet so I continued to ascend the tree. Footing was not difficult as the branches of the close packed trees form numerous hand and footholds. Except for the shaft or opening up which I was climbing, the rest of the forest was so dense at this point that only patches of light could filter through.

In less time than it takes to tell, I reached the end of the opening in the leaves and found a tightly entwined mass of limbs blocking my path. Working my way around I finally found access above the limbs and emerged upon another of the wonderous avenues among the trees. I had not suspected another of these unusual openings, or avenues as I called them, existed in the forest. I had not before been this high in the trees and wondered if still more avenues might exist in the upper reaches which still towered over me by some four or five hundred feet.

I had little time to wonder, though, for as I looked about me I could see several man-made openings in the boles of the trees. In fact, in places there were structures wedged between the boles to form a continuous solid mass of bark all along the avenue to the left. And it stretched upward into the foliage above as far as I could see.

I started toward the nearest opening, thinking this was where Marjano and Zynthmai were being held captive. Drawing my sword, I approached the dark cavity before me.

I entered into the tree and found myself in a long corridor that wound off to my left. Following the corridor, I found a labyrinth of passageways circling in among the trees, connected to the boles that had been hollowed out. A cleverly constructed network of limbs had been caulked with a rough but solid substance to keep out the weather.

As I wound through the corridors I continually thought of the *Blou Tou*. Was there really a Ghost People on Ghandor? The thought left me with an uncanny feeling. At first when I saw no one, I wondered if Marjano and the Thuians were right. The Ghost People were invisible! However, after more than an hour of seeing nothing that indicated the passageways had been inhabited recently, my hopes of finding Marjano dimmed.

It seemed as if the passageways hadn't seen a person for centuries. Yet something about the interior of the tree kingdom bothered me! I couldn't put my finger on it right away, but it gave me added reason to keep looking. After a while of going from one passageway into another, I realized what had been bothering me. The passageway didn't lead into a single room or chamber—only into more passageways. Something was wrong.

It dawned on me that I had been going around in circles.

Calming my keyed-up nerves, so distraught was I over not being able to find my Princess, I commenced to once again follow the network of passageways through the trees. It took me only a few moments to realize that my last thought had been correct. My senses easily told me what I had feared. I was going around in a circle inside the tree kingdom! Perhaps this structure in the trees was not empty of life after all. I began to feel that I was being deliberately led from one blindfall to another by someone opening and then closing off behind me one passageway after another. Then, too, I began to feel that someone was watching me. I could feel their eyes upon my back but no matter how often I looked about, I could see nothing in the dim light within the corridors.

"Marjano!" I called out in desperation. "Can you hear me?

Zynthmai! Marjano!" I listened to my voice echo through the passages.

"All right," I finally called out, anger mounting within me, "whoever you are! I know you are here and I am not leaving until I find you and rescue my friends!" I was speaking to no one in particular, but I felt certain that someone was near. "I know you are somewhere just out of my reach. You can save a lot of time if you will stop this game and show yourself."

My sword was extended and I was circling slowly in order to keep a lookout in all directions. Were there, after all, Ghost People? The thought kept coming back to me for I could feel a presence close to me, but could see nothing.

Suddenly a part of the wall disappeared beside me and I nearly fell into a large, spacious room. It was well lit, and beautifully appointed with furniture and draperies. If I had thought the apartments that I had seen within the Meoaithaian city of impressive appointment, this made those seem like dungeon cells. There was gold and jewels everywhere. The precious ore and stones were worked into the flooring, walls and ceiling. Beautiful crystals hung in profusion from the ceiling and I noticed that this room, too, had been coated with the melted down *yaama* ore to give it light. Furniture seemed to be suspended in air, while large beautiful paintings appeared to be hanging along the walls, several inches out from the partitions, without benefit of any wires or support. There were likewise many objects of art seemingly hanging in midair all about the apartment.

So great was the mystery of the objects defying gravity that I at first did not notice the person standing in the center of the room. He was tall, nearly my height, though of less weight. He appeared to be older, though not showing any specific signs of aging. It was just that as I first saw him, I thought of him being older.

His hair was strikingly white and long, hanging to his shoulders. His skin was of a washed-out bronze coloring and seemed to hang upon him as though he had once weighed considerably more but over the years had lost most of it. He was dressed in a silver gray tunic that covered him from neck to ankle covering each leg individually, but not tightly like the clothing the Meoaithaians wore. He did not wear a cloak and in my recollection was the only person I had seen without one, other than the *Zumtai*.

"I perceive that nothing we might have done would have

deterred you from remaining within our city," said the man in a soft, rather musical voice.

"That is absolutely correct, nor do I intend to leave until I have the girl whom you stole from me restored to my side, as well as my friend, Zynthmai. Where are they?" I demanded.

"They are not here. They were not taken by us but rather by the *Ooda Yai* to the north. Unfortunately, your foolish persistence must go unrewarded." Who he was referring to I knew not, but he had used the term denoting relative, but in a rather caustic manner. "They took the girl and your friend," he continued, "through the opening at the base of the tree below while you were hunting."

"You lie!" I yelled, slipping into earthly habit. He flinched slightly but made no comment. "I have searched the trees below in extreme detail and have found no opening whatever. I think they are here. Release them or I'll run you through," I said, pointing my sword menacingly at him.

The man before me smiled slightly. "You would have disappointed me had you not done just that. You remind me of another time, another world."

"Look Old One," I began, referring to his age in an effort to get through to him that he was in danger lest he conform to my wishes, "I am in no mood for games. Free the girl and my friend or I'll cut you in two."

"Ah, but you are persistent! Too bad it must be in vain."

"Last chance," I said, moving my blade slightly to lend emphasis to my words.

"Ah, but to be young once again," he said, almost to himself. "But the two you speak of are many miles from here on their way to the kingdom fortress of the *Abdaith*. They are the ones who captured your two friends upon the limbs below. And," he added in a kind, but firm voice, "you would best look behind you before advancing any further."

No wonder he had been so cool in the face of my blade. For standing just inside the room were five heavily armed warriors and many more could be seen over their shoulders in the corridor beyond.

"I am afraid," the Old Man added sadly, "you will never see them again, for all who enter our secret city may never again leave."

CHAPTER NINETEEN

The warriors escorted me out of the Old Man's apartment and along a network of corridors deep into the Tree City. Emerging from the apartment I immediately began to entertain the thought of escape. My captors, after disarming me, sheathed their own weapons and were loosely guarding me. Perhaps they did not expect any trouble from me or perhaps they were so confident in their numbers or ability they felt fully capable of handling me.

As we progressed along the corridors, I was singularly impressed with the beauty of what little I could see of the Tree City. The abundance of large jewels showed that the tree dwellers either placed little value upon the stones because of an overabundant supply or they were extremely ostentatious in their social makeup. In any event, many of the passageways we traversed were solidly bedecked with these precious stones, being inset over excessive amounts of *yaama* ore coating which shone through the jewels causing a riot of color that was both distracting and beautiful.

I also noticed that the *yaama* ore coating on the walls was somehow treated or affected to cause it to brighten as we walked along and immediately dim as we passed. In the Meoathaian city the lighting had been constant. If they had wanted areas dimmer than others, they merely placed less coating on the walls. Here in the Tree City the builders possessed some advanced knowledge and were able to use the valuable ore more to their advantage. This perhaps explained why the passageways were so dim when I first entered the Tree City. They no doubt had not wanted me to feel that the Tree City was inhabited and therefore had affected the control of the lighting in some manner as to keep it darkened even though I passed along the corridors. Their evident abil-

ity to control the lighting by some unseen or perhaps tele-
pathic ability intrigued me.

We were walking along a particularly bejeweled area when
a portion of the wall on my right disappeared and a beautiful
young woman stood framed in a doorway. I had been mar-
veling at the lack of doorways and even bisecting passageways in the Tree City as we had been traversing this main
corridor. Evidently, much like the stone city of the
Meoathaians, panels were so cleverly inset into the passageways that it was difficult to know where they might be. My
first impression of the girl was one of beauty, but as I saw
her more clearly, I noticed a dimness in her eyes that seemed
to exist with all the tree dwellers that I had met so far. Even
so, her wide mouth, large eyes, and small tilted nose gave her
a startlingly beautiful face framed by an over abundance of
black, shiny hair. She wore the same type of dress as the rest
of the tree dwellers, covering her from neck to ankle, hers
being a very bright, almost shocking shade of pink. So startling was her appearance that before I could do more than
register these impressions of her looks, we were past the
opening and continuing on down the passageway.

While the opening startled me, both my captors and the
young woman seemed to not even notice one another. So un-
concerned about the occurrence were the warriors that the
start of an idea began to form in my mind. Slowly, I edged
my way closer to the wall on my right, hoping another person
would open their "door" as we passed by as had the young
woman.

The eight warriors were stationed before, behind, and at either side of me. They wore the same type of clothing as had
the Old Man and the woman of a moment ago. They were
covered from neck to ankle, though the warriors had
leather harnesses upon them from which their swords hung.
Also, upon their harnesses hung twelve-inch curved knives,
pouches, and one or two other items that were beyond my
ability to describe.

Where the Old Man had been dressed totally in black,
these warriors were dressed in a riot of colors, all bright
shades, as had been the girl.

One of the warriors wore a scarlet outfit, another bright
blue, two wore shades of green, and the other's clothing was
a mixture of bright yellows and oranges.

They looked nothing like warriors. Not only was their

dress unnatural for a warrior to wear, they seemed lacking in build and strength as well. Their mannerisms reminded me more of the courtiers at court in England and the Continent of my own world than the fighting men with whom I had been familiar.

Suddenly another opening appeared on my left and a man and woman appeared. I cursed my luck that caused someone on the far wall opening their "door" and not on the closer wall on my right.

Just as I was cursing my luck, a panel opened on my right, framing another attractive young woman. She wore the same type of clothing as my escort, her hair was a shining black and her coloring was a pale brown as I had found all the tree dwellers to be.

She was, I suppose, a beautiful woman except for her eyes. Like the other girl, they were distant, faded, almost empty. I wondered for a moment that perhaps these tree dwellers were blind, but her eyes moved lazily over me and I saw a slight flicker of awareness which quickly disappeared. Her breast lifted noticeably as she sighed deeply and waited motionless for us to pass.

All this took place in less time than it takes to tell. The panel opened, I saw the girl and I leaped toward the opening, pushing the guard nearest me into the girl and both into the apartment.

The three of us sprawled atop one another and in but a moment I had the warrior's sword free of its scabbard and sprang to my feet ready for the expected onslaught of my escort.

I was aware of the girl regaining her feet and the warrior pushing to his, reaching for his knife after realizing his sword was gone.

I brought the hilt of the sword down upon his head, grabbed the girl and pulled her close and swung my blade to intercept the warriors that were just now reaching the doorway.

"How does this panel close?" I said tightly, almost into her ear.

"Just move back away from the opening," she replied quickly.

"Can you lock it?"

She indicated a small aperture to the left of the opening. I backed away from the doorway but nothing happened.

"The opening must be clear," she said in response to my look.

Before I could respond the warriors pushed on into the apartment and I was hard-pressed to keep them at bay. Retreating before their drawn swords, the girl whispered in my ear, "Here, follow me."

Turning, she led me deeper into the apartment, through another opening that materialized in a rear wall and out into a corridor. We quickly traversed several bisecting passageways that opened as we neared the panels that closed them off.

"Where are you taking me?" I asked her as we fled along unfamiliar passageways.

"To a friend," she replied simply. For the first time I noticed something in her eyes ... it was spirit. Her eyes had been dead, as had been those of the warriors. Even the Old Man's had been devoid of life. It was as though everyone I'd seen in the Tree City were without hope. Now, though, this girl showed some excitement.

"Who are you?" she asked. "Are you from the outside?"

"Do you know how to get out of this city?" I countered.

"There is no way to get out," she said sadly, "only the *Mantai* can do that."

"Can do what?"

"Can unlock our prison walls."

Before I could learn more, we turned into one of the bisecting passageways and ran right into another group of warriors. I didn't wait to see if they were looking for me or not, but drew my sword and hacked my way through their midst, pulling the girl along behind. As the warriors saw me, a flood of light seemed to flicker into their eyes, almost like a visible wave of excitement flooding over them. Perhaps this was the very thing that saved me, for recognition of what was happening came to them only after I had burst into them, pulling the girl behind me.

We were through the warriors' ranks before they knew it and on down the passageway by the time they could recover and give chase. Turning a bend in the passageway we came upon another group of warriors. A third corridor branched away to our left, but it seemed certain we could not continue to outrun a dozen warriors forever.

"Quickly, escape down this other passageway," I yelled to the girl. "I'll follow along."

"But what of you?" she called back.

"I'm tired of running," I said simply and turned to face the approaching warriors. And indeed, I was tired of running through this complicated network of passageways I could not fathom, running from an enemy that didn't seem to be able to fight and faced with the task of finding Marjano and Zynthmai in a city a thousand feet high in the thickly foliaged trees upon a strange planet.

I was totally frustrated and as angry as I had ever been. Swinging my blade high over my head I advanced toward the warriors who had slowed their approach. We were not more than ten yards apart by now, and their pale brown faces showed the pallor of not seeing the sun for some time, perhaps years.

Something else was apparent. Their eyes shone with life. Evidently I was a welcome diversion for them. Over their heads I could see scores of reinforcements converging upon us. Turning I could see another dozen fighting men with swords drawn running toward us down the third corridor. We were completely surrounded and there seemed little chance of escape, but despite the evident failure of my aspiration, the age-old call came to my lips.

"I shall prevail!"

Pledging to sell my life dearly, I started to jump forward to engage those nearest me when the world came crashing down upon my head.

A paralysis swept over me and I felt the sword fall from my numbed fingers as I slumped to the floor. Just before I lost consciousness, the thought occurred to me that nobody had been behind me but the girl, who had not made any attempt to escape as I had suggested. Before I could pursue that thought further, blackness engulfed me and I didn't even feel hitting the floor.

CHAPTER TWENTY

I awoke hours later with the Old Man staring down at me. We were in the same apartment in which I had first seen him that morning.

"The girl saved your life," he informed me. "She acted wisely when she saw your plight was hopeless."

"I thought she had betrayed me," I replied slowly. My head felt like it weighed a ton and was being hammered upon by dozens of angry men, swinging broadaxes.

I was lying on the floor in the Old Man's apartment. The rug upon which I reposed was thick and soft, and I found the position most comfortable, though awkward in carrying on a conversation. Why I was not in a dungeon or cell, I could not say.

"She acted very foolishly in trying to help you get away," he replied calmly, almost as though he were discussing the time of day. "But it is understandable. The young of our city are impatient and restless. Any diversion is a welcome event. You supplied quite a diversion for many of my people this day."

I drew a ragged breath and moved carefully onto my side and attempted to climb to my feet. The Old Man watched me carefully, as though he were dissecting an insect in a laboratory. Gaining my feet was no easy matter since I felt my head were going to topple off with each new movement I made. All I could think of at the moment was the tremendous wallop that lady had.

"Just who are you?" he asked, after I had regained my feet and taken a proffered chair that seemed to hang suspended in midair. "I know much of my world, and never have I seen your red hair, blue eyes, and white skin anywhere upon Ghandor."

"I am not of your world," I replied, feeling it best to be honest with this man who seemed to have the ability to see

202

right through me. His eyes gave the appearance of great age and wisdom. I could not imagine him being responsible for Marjano's capture, though I determined to find out right here and now what had happened to her.

"Of what world do you hail?" He had not used the term meaning extraterrestrial, and when I told him I was from another planet, his eyes lightened for the first time and I could feel a sense of urgency as he continued to question me. I told him I was from a planet called Earth and that I had surmised that, according to the star constellations I had observed here upon Ghandor, not to be too much further away from the sun than his own world, though occupying an extremely different part of the solar system from Ghandor.

We talked about the heavens and the universe for some time, all the while I could feel his interest mounting. After he had pumped from me all that I could tell him about my own world and my understanding of the solar system, he seemed to relax, evidently realizing that I knew far less than he, but as I tried to pry information from him on this subject, he became quite evasive. It wasn't until I began asking him about his own world that he became amenable once again and loquacious.

"We are of the ancient Clu," he mentioned at one point. "Our ancestors were the First Man and our heritage dates back more than fifty thousand years. The ancients ruled the planet and fathered most of the races that are advanced enough today to be called Men. And we here in Clu are the direct descendants of the old Holy Order of the Ancients. We possess the Knowledge of the Ages as Pitinai and Gylcota knew it. Even the Jeddidites and the Klootites paid homage to our ancestors. We conquered the skies, defied gravity and found the warp windows. You are among the most advanced peoples in all the universe and here standing before you is the last and greatest of the Caji of my people."

His declamation pointed out his rather pompous attitude and I almost laughed at his brag of being the King of the greatest people in the universe. In his way, he was more bombastic than had been Euoaithia of the stone city, though the Old Man was far more sophisticated and suave in his eloquence. And, from the appearance of the tree dwellers' technology, far more intelligent.

As the Old Man had said, the city was simply called Clu, meaning beginning or start. Its very existence and all the marvels within it were attributable to the precious *yaama* ore that the tree dwellers had brought to the dizzying heights of the forest a thousand years before in great profusion.

What they had learned to do with this ore far surpassed any of the uses the Thuians had developed from all that Marjano had told me. The pictures and art works suspended in midair, as well as furniture and heavier objects, were the result of being coated with the melted down ore in such a way as to not only render them free of gravity, but freeze them into a specific spot in midair. They had carried the flying ship principle to its ultimate in even small objects, and the Old Man bragged that had they desired to do so, they could suspend the entire city above the forest.

Being direct descendants of the ancient Cluvians, the tree dwellers called themselves by that name, and I pressed the Old Man for the story since it seemed to differ from what I had heard of the Cluvians and their ancient culture from Marjano. I was especially curious since I had been led to believe that only the Thuians still used any of the advanced Cluvian technology.

As the story unfolded from the Old Man's lips, many other bits of Ghandorian knowledge fit into place, filling the gaps in my understanding of this strange world. The Cluvian culture extended back in time more than fifty thousand years according to all that the ancients knew.

As the Cluvians advanced their culture they branched out in many areas. They passed through the Bronze Age quickly and into an age of far advanced weaponry and metals. They were the first to develop the plasticized alloy from which the airships and swords were made. Though inferior to steel in biting strength, its light weight made flight possible when combined with a special coating of the *yaama* ore. Ghandor, it seemed, did not possess iron ore and it became necessary to find a way to mold elements together to form the *zoain* alloy that was the planet's principle element of strength. The Cluvians developed the ability to combine the elemental structure of hydrocarbons, protein, bronze and another ore they called *syaamo*. It proved to be quite a breakthrough and immediately made them the dominant race upon Ghandor. Their weapons were superior to the bronze swords and tools of the other races and their culture spread out throughout the entire western hemisphere. Their caravans carried back from other lands the riches of Ghandor. They brought with them slaves to handle the menial tasks of living, and in a few thousand years the Cluvians began solely turning to the arts and pleasure of life. No longer were they interested in conquest, rule, or scientific achievements.

This evidently gave rise to a different breed of Cluvians that slowly came into being within the Empire. These new Cluvians felt the relaxed life and easy living was ruining the Empire. An Empire that by now stretched over almost a million square miles with consuls in every land of the western hemisphere, receiving tribute from local tribes. They had conquered every foe that had stood in their way and even the great Meoaithaians of the south paid homage to the Cluvians. Only the Jeddidites of the eastern hemisphere and the hated Klootites of the southern regions rivaled the Cluvian Empire.

As the Cluvians turned to the arts and pleasures in their Empire stronghold, outlander regions were still conquering for the homeland and Xylords, or generals, carried the banners of the Clu to the east and south until the great Jeddidites and Klootites fell beneath the heel of the Empire. But after continued centuries of homeland apathy to the efforts of the Cluvian Legions, and with no more foes opposing the Empire, the enthusiastic thrust of the military juggernaut lost its drive and even the far flung outposts of the Empire began to deteriorate into the depths of personal pleasure and greed.

The new breed of Cluvian called themselves the *mantai*, or Rediscoverers. Their purpose in life was to restore the Empire to its former height of inventive genius and discovery that had made the Cluvians strong. They feared the Empire was beginning to disintegrate due to the lack of interest the people had in anything other than their pursuit of leisure and easy living. They also feared the modern technology that had made tremendous inroads to discovery would fall into disuse and finally oblivion. Even then only about a hundred men and women were familiar enough with the sciences as to understand the past inventions and discoveries of their ancestors. Although almost any of the thousands of officers in the Empire could fly the airships by which they then traveled over the entire planet, only a hundred or so scientists understood the principles of the gravity negating force.

Another growing menace was the active rebellious attitude of the Meoaithaians to the south. This race had surrendered to earlier Cluvian Xylords without even a struggle, but the bonds of servitude weighed heavy upon the heads of the younger generations and they were growing stronger than the Cluvians.

Another group within the Cluvian Empire also struggled into the *Kagia*, or the Elite. As the people grew weaker and less interested in their empire and the politics which ran it, ruthless leaders fought an internal struggle for power. Much in the manner of ancient Rome, a small group of powerful men designed to control the Empire. They took control slowly through legislative means and within a few hundred years ... the life span of the Cluvians was nearly a thousand years ... they had absolute power. But even so, these *Kagia* worked their secret plans without the populace ever becoming aware of their imperialistic intentions.

At first the *mantai* bound themselves over the *Kagia* for both had a single purpose in mind. Crush the Meoaithaians before they became too strong. In addition, the descendants of the Jeddidite and Klootite kingdoms in the east and south were beginning to flex their muscles, following the lead of the Meoaithaians.

The *mantai* developed bolder, more advanced weapons and the *Kagia* strengthened the Empire's armies. Rather than taking the normal step of attacking the smaller kingdoms and putting down their rebellions, the *Kagia* struck right at the heart of their problem, at the Meoaithaians. The struggle lasted nearly fifty years, but in the end the rebels fell and were nearly wiped out as a result of the ruthless leadership of the *Kagia*.

The armies of the Xylords, which were by now entirely run by the *Kagia*, had annihilated the Meoaithaians on three fronts, and the only thing that saved the race was their bold escape into the Ghost Forest. The *Kagia* may well have followed them into the forest kingdoms, but the *mantai* prevailed upon the *Kagia's* good senses by reminding them that an all-out expedition on the *Zumtai* nations would not add to the stable peace the Cluvians had enjoyed with these vicious fighters for several hundred years.

Turned away from their desire to wipe the Meoaithaians off the face of the planet, the *Kagia* turned their efforts to the Jeddidites and Klootites, the only other races that had supported the Meoaithaians. So great was their anger and power, the Xylords crushed what little defense the two defeated races could bring to bear and were exposed to the carnage and total destruction that was wrought upon them.

The carnage wrought by the *Kagia* woke the *mantai* up to the kind of beast they were serving. But too late, for the *Kagia* were now well seated in government and power and the scientists found themselves at the mercy of the cruel cadre they had helped put in power.

Steeped in this extreme power, the *Kagia* forced the scientists to develop more weapons and bolder, more devastating means of killing the enemies of the Empire.

At first the *mantai* agreed to help, knowing that no other enemies could be found and feeling that the *Kagia* might be appeased by this show of cooperation. However, the scientists did not realize the scope of the *Kagia's* thirst for power, for the maddened imperialists were now bent on conquering the stars.

They pressed the scientists to develop the gravity-negating force so that it would be strong enough to fly an airship between planets. Secretly, an interplanetary vehicle was developed and fitted with the beefed-up power drive of the *yaama* ore. A first flight successfully reached the nearer moon, *Tho.* Soon another voyage successfully reached *Plo,* the farther moon. But when a third voyage tried to reach *Dlo* which at that time was a third moon of Ghandor, even more distant than the present far moon, *Plo,* the vehicle exploded as it tried to negotiate that moon's gravity.

The *Kagia* were maddened by this failure and began pressing the scientists even harder to straighten out the problem and design a spaceship that could take them to other planets and the stars. By now the *Kagia* were drunk with power. They envisioned themselves as conquerors of the universe and reveled in the treasures and added power this would bring them. But as the scientists unravelled the mystery they found the vehicle had exploded from one of the elements of the *yaama* ore used for the drive. In fact, the ship hadn't exploded, but imploded, for the *yaama* ore in the drive, when combining with a certain element in space, reversed its elemental structure and began to fall in upon itself. An implosion was the result.

Tireless years of research turned up an answer, but the result was so terrifying that the scientists refused to turn it over to the *Kagia.* They had discovered a ray or beam as a result of trying to eliminate the reversal of the *yaama* ore. It was a fantastic, powerful force no larger than a pinpoint of light, but strong enough to be shot into space and strike an object millions of miles away.

As scientists are wont to do, they experimented with the ray before they fully understood it. They pointed the beam at what was then the furthest moon, *Dlo,* meaning "far orb." They wanted to see if the light would travel that great distance. The ray had previously been bounced off the nearer two moons without any effect whatever. However, when the ray struck *Dlo,* the satellite began to break up. Quickly the scientists shut down the ray, but too late. A reversal of the molecules was already in effect and within hours the moon had imploded and space was filled with dust and debris. These particles were attracted to the two nearest heavenly bodies, the other two moons, and now surrounded each moon causing the dimness of light I had often noticed during the Ghandorian nights.

The effect of the ray was impossible to keep hidden as the scientists had hoped to do and the *Kagia* became excited about the power that could destroy an entire moon, even a planet, perhaps. These menacing leaders forced the scientists to turn over the awful secret of the ray, but not until the *Kagia* had killed nearly half of the scientists who had risen up to rebel against the use of the weapon. Knowing full well how the weapon would be used, the scientists swore to find a way to eradicate the *Kagia* from the Empire.

Numbering some twenty thousand strong by this time, the *Kagia* controlled the capital city of *Glounmai.* They had been so devious in their plans that the entire Cluvian populace were still unaware of their sinister plots. This is not surprising when you consider that the *Kagia* strengthened their political position by creating laws and organizations that completely relieved the populace from worry or want; thus the Cluvians were left free to pursue their interests in the arts and their own luxurious way of life, completely satisfied with their leaders.

Several plans were formulated by the scientists but all met with failure for they were developed in the two areas that could never bring them success. First, they tried to find ways to overpower the *Kagia* and since their numbers were so few, plan after plan proved futile. Secondly, they tried to formulate plots that would expose the *Kagia* to the populace for what they were—war-mongering politicians drunk with power. These plans also proved unworkable since the populace felt their present government was most beneficial to them. Then, too, it was doubtful if the Cluvians would have raised up against the *Kagia* even had they been fully aware of the plots and counterplots of their government, for they had spent thousands of years in luxury by this time and were most apathetic toward anything outside their individual interests.

The scientists then began working on a hidden weapon—germ warfare, to eradicate the *Kagia* from the Empire once and for all. It was an ingenious plan, its only weakness being that a few thousand Cluvians would also die in the capital city when the malignant virus was exposed. The scientific community voted to go ahead with the plan despite this unfortunate result and a virus strain was finally developed. The strain was so potent that all felt certain not one person in the city would be left alive. Plans were laid for the *mantai* to be well away from the city when the strain was unleashed. All was progressing well until the *Kagia* got wind of a plot to destroy them being fostered by the scientists. A wave of maniacal killings swept the *mantai*, and the virus strain was unleashed in retaliation before all the scientists were wiped out and none were left to check the evil control of the *Kagia*.

Unfortunately, the scientists had not had time to think far enough ahead to foresee the terrible results their act would cause. The virus, unchecked, spread over the entire western hemisphere. For some unexplainable reason, the virus only affected the Cluvians and nine out of every ten who came in contact with the strain died. The scientists themselves appeared at first to be immune to the virus, and all twenty-three that remained from the *Kagia* purge escaped its terrible fate. It was later learned that their experiments in developing the strain had exposed them to just enough over a long period of time that an immunity developed within their systems.

It was partially because of this immunity and partly due to the *Kagia* rumors that had been spread over the Empire about the scientists to keep them in check that the surviving Cluvians set about to kill the *mantai* and their followers. A rash of killings followed, but none of the scientists were put to death. Warned of their pending doom, the twenty-three escaped into the Ghost Forest to the south and eventually built the treetop city.

As a result of the terrible catastrophe brought down upon them, though they didn't understand it, the surviving Cluvians outlawed all scientific research and created laws making the use of any such inventions punishable by immediate death. Like the Inquisition of the thirteenth century in Europe, bands of Cluvians set themselves up to judge their fellow man and thousands died as a result of these witch trials. About this time two men came upon the scene named Hitherbaun and Clo Thu. Both were scientists, but had never been aligned with the *mantai*. Both saw the need to organize the remaining few Cluvians and set down some laws by which the survivors could live. It took years and a supreme effort on the part of these two Wise Men to stop the flow of blood and overcome the strong fear of governing forces that the Cluvians had built up as a result of the disaster that had struck their once-powerful Empire.

The great armies and Xylords were called home by Hitherbaun. The Empire faded into history as the outposts were abandoned. And the Cluvians set about to build up their homeland. Clo Thu, perhaps the wiser of the two, developed a strong following and he traveled extensively throughout the northern regions trying to restore order while Hitherbaun concentrated on the formation of a government that the Cluvians would accept. He finally hit upon the idea of a religious base rather than a political base for his government, and over the years the movement took hold until his philosophies controlled the thinking of the Cluvians.

Clo Thu differed greatly with Hitherbaun's philosophy, especially when it came to the banishment of all scientific research, knowledge and inventions. So great was this difference, that Clo Thu eventually removed himself and his followers to the north country where he established his own nation. Than Tan and the Thuians became his descendants, Clo Thu being the forefather of my own Marjano.

With this rebellious movement, the remaining Cluvians began to be split by inner dissension and eventually over the centuries split off into numerous groups or nations making up today what is referred to as the countries of the North, of which Thu is the largest and strongest.

Clo Thu had doggedly held to the belief that science was not all bad and preserved many of the inventions and much of the knowledge of the *mantai* until Than Tan's grandfather, the fifteenth great grandson of Clo Thu, revived the ancient knowledge of the airships. Much of the other knowledge and inventions seemed beyond the present Thuians to understand

and master. While there had always been a natural division between the Thuians and the other nations of the North, this revival of the forbidden ancient practices served only to drive a deeper wedge between the cultures of the northern kingdoms.

In the forest the remaining scientists created a comfortable city high in the trees using many of the inventions they had discovered. Fearful at first of discovery, they safeguarded their city by placing it high in the trees and free from casual observance. They set up space windows throughout the western hemisphere so they could step from their treetop city into almost any point within the western hemisphere. In this way they hoped to keep an eye on their enemies. These windows had been discovered by the scientists much earlier and were what the *mantai* had been working on when the *Kagia* forced them into the development of weapons and interplanetary travel.

These first windows were temporary in nature, not being able to be maintained for more than a few minutes at a time. They were utilized in the manner of spying for when the field collapsed instant death would occur for any person traveling through it had he not quickly returned. In the years to follow, the scientists learned the secret of setting up permanent windows through the use of the temporary ones and these they scattered about among the major areas of habitation to see what their fellow Cluvians were up to.

As these scattered Cluvian nations reverted back to the Bronze Age from lack of leadership and knowledge, the scientists in their tree top city began to feel safe for the first time and turn their thoughts to the future. They could not shake their feelings of extreme guilt over the deaths of a billion of their fellow beings nor forgive themselves for the creation of the powerful ray and other weapons that had been their downfall. They vowed that none of them would ever leave the tree top city of Clu, nor divulge their knowledge or use their inventive genius for war again.

As their children began to grow, marry and have children of their own, the scientists set up a commission or board of governors to rule over the city in order to insure their pledge. These became known as the Old Guard to the younger generations that were born and lived their lives of imprisonment in the trees.

"But how did they keep the younger ones from leaving this

tree city?" I asked when the Old Man had arrived at that point in his story. We were standing just outside a large, heavily guarded door up in the fifth level of the city. He had taken me on a tour of his tree top city during the course of his discussion.

"The answer is quite simple and lies just behind these doors," he replied casually. "Come and I will show you."

Inside, the room was completely bare of furniture or ornamentation. This was the only area within the entire city that I had seen free from the display of wealth and works of art other than the first passageways I had entered.

The room was round, about two hundred feet through the middle. The ceiling rose to form a giant dome and the floor was perfectly smooth. More than a thousand doors could be seen evenly spaced around the perimeter of the room. Upon closer inspection, though, I found these not to be doors at all, but the space windows like the one through which I had stepped onto this world.

Each space window was clearly marked with a narrow outline of gold upon the wall. Filling the square formed by the gold outline was the same swirling, barely discernible mist I had first seen upon the hills overlooking Drogheda. Each doorway was approximately nine feet in heighth and about four feet in width. Above the doorway was lettered, no doubt, the location at which the doorway emptied. But it was lettered in the Ghandorian language and I had not yet learned how to read and write in this new tongue; mostly because the *Zumtai* tribes do not have a written language.

The room was completely bare of any furnishings or controls. It was simply a large room with hundreds of openings marked along the wall. The only ingress or egress of the room was the doorway through which we had entered. Nor was there anyone in the room, neither guard nor workman.

To the left of the entrance door was an opening that led into a narrow corridor, so small was this corridor and doorway I had at first overlooked it in the immensity of the room. It was through this short corridor that the Old Man led me. We emerged in a small room that had a single table placed in its middle and upon the wall at the far end of the room the mist of a space window swirled about. Upon the table were two strange devices, and on the wall over the space window were several round circles, one of which glowed profusely.

The Old Man pointed to one of the two devices upon the table with an extravagant gesture.

"This was one of the last inventions. It is a type of force field, for want of a better term by which to explain it to your limited understanding."

I bristled at the insult, but immediately realized he was absolutely correct. I did not have the technology to understand even the simplest things the Cluvians took for granted.

"It completely protects the outer perimeter of the city," the Old Man continued. "It was first developed out of fear of attack and annihilation. But as it became evident the city was free from discovery and attack, and as younger generations grew to challenge the need for continued imprisonment in the city, the force was turned to a different use. It now keeps people in, rather than out. It is operated at all times and only I or one of the Old Guard can cancel its force."

"How do you do that?"

"With this," he replied, opening his left hand. A piece of metal had been surgically worked into his palm. How it had been performed or what had kept it from causing infection or discomfort I could not guess, nor did he bother to explain. "When it became necessary to use the power of this device to keep the young bucks from leaving the city, it was realized that a foolproof method of control was necessary. Prior to that it had been connected by a simple switch, but that would never do. We of the Old Guard realized that the field had to operate permanently, yet cancellable by an external means that could be absolutely controlled by a select few. An element had to be found that could be inserted into the field at its connection between two points within the device. This would give control to the select few only if the element was not obtainable within the city. Through our space windows, we searched the planet for some element or metal that was not known in the city. It had to be of a substance to break the field, yet external to Clu. A difficult assignment since the original Cluvians had brought with them about everything that had been of value in the Empire. Eventually, the search proved futile!"

I could imagine the Old Guard's plight. Afraid the young bucks would leave the city and use their natural inherited intelligence to develop scientific devices to once again bring ruin down upon the planet. A dangerous plan was developed to use the space windows to travel to another planet to see if something usable could be found. Several windows were set up that would be used to travel to neighboring planets within the solar system. It seemed strange to me that the very thing the ancient *Kagia* wanted, interplanetary travel, would have been theirs had they let the *mantai* continue with their normal scientific pursuits. They had been on the very verge of space window discovery; however, the *Kagia* had forced them away from the endeavor into developing a space drive that eventually spelled their doom.

Through giant telescopes before the virus was unleashed, the scientists had become aware of five other planets in their solar system. Theses windows were set up and five of the scientists volunteered for the perilous journeys. The five stepped through the space windows never to return. Not knowing what had happened, five more volunteered.

The windows were checked and recalibrated. The volunteers stepped through and were also lost. This led, somewhat belatedly, to the realization that the other planets to which they traveled did not support a breathable atmosphere such as Ghandor possessed. This was difficult for many to accept for it was not consistent with the general knowledge of extraterrestrial bodies developed by the sciences centuries before.

Quite by accident, while bending a space window around the sun, they stumbled on the presence of an unknown planet in their solar system. Lots were drawn and a shaky loser stepped through the space window onto this heretofore unknown planet. He emerged moments later to tell of a beautiful, though colder more sluggish, world which he had found. A permanent window was set up and a quick investigation led to the discovery of certain metals unknown upon Ghandor. The scientists had time to transport only a very small quantity of the ore back to the tree city as a revolt broke out among the younger generations that cut all further discovery and investigation short.

Once the rebellion was crushed, the ore was mined and a hard, powerful metal resulted. It was found sufficient to break the beam and they had their answer. Small pieces of metal about three inches by two inches were cut and surgically implanted into the hands of the thirteen remaining scientists. These were the only means of shutting down the force field in all the city since the left over metal was disposed of through an open window into space.

"But what prevents others from cutting off your arm or forcing you to hold it between the points of the device to shut down the field?" I asked.

"First of all, it takes two of us to do so, since the beam can be negated only when it strikes this metal from both points. And secondly, we have set up such a guard about us, that to capture two would be almost impossible. Besides, no one wishes to be free from the city any longer. You see after the last rebellion, we decided to eliminate that possibility in future generations so a law was passed against future births. It has been so strictly enforced that we no longer have any new generations to indoctrinate to their fate. The effect has been the desired one: escape from Clu is no longer a problem for us."

"You spoke of yourself as being among those who put down the rebellion. I thought that was several thousand years ago."

"Yes, it was. But you see, I am one of the original Cluvian scientists," he replied, a slight smile touching the corners of his lips.

"But you couldn't be," I blurted. "They lived, according to your own account, more than ten thousand years ago. You have also stated that the Cluvians had a life span of between nine hundred and eleven hundred years. So how could you be one of the original *mantai*?"

"It is really a simple matter, though I can understand your consternation. You see, after settling in this tree city we realized that we would have younger generations with which to deal. Since many of us were young and married at the time, we voted against regulating births, so we decided a longevity serum had to be invented. Much work had already transpired on this subject and it was finally perfected several centuries after the plague. Just in time, I might add, for as you can see, I am quite old. I was, like my companions of the Old Guard, nearing the end of my life cycle when the serum was finally developed. Another hundred years and I doubt if any of the original *mantai* would have survived. That thought often comes to me in my sleep and I still shudder to think of the consequences of our descendants free to continue our experiments; no the thought is too ghastly for there will always be people like the *Kagia* and given enough power, they could have destroyed the world—perhaps the universe." He paused for a few moments, lost in his thoughts. Being young myself,

I could not share in his defeatist attitude. Certainly there are always the *Kagia* present in any civilization. England and Europe had seen their share. And, no doubt, would see more throughout the history of Earth. Ghandor, no doubt, would also. But the difference, to me, was that those who develop the inventions can do more to keep the other balances of power in line. Perhaps the original *mantai* were too weak, or too concerned about their own interests to be concerned about the interests of their people until it was too late. In either case, it was not necessarily true that their descendants would make the same mistake.

"We knew," the Old Man continued as suddenly as he had fallen silent, "that by expanding the length of our life cycles we could control the city and its laws for as long as necessary. Of course none of us expected to live this long, as it is really a dreadful curse. But our plans for future generations to ultimately lose the knowledge and understanding of our inventions were not realized. Undoubtedly because of our love for luxury and constant usage of the powers which we developed."

He told me many more things about the old Cluvians and I marveled at their wisdom and genius in the areas of their advancements, but was appalled at their inability to handle their fantastic rise to power and affluence.

That night as we sat in the Old Man's apartment, after touring the twelve levels of the treetop city, I asked him about Marjano and what had become of her. I had been dying to do so all during his discourse, but every time I was about to, his conversation would take a new turn and the moment never seemed right to broach the subject. Now, however, I could wait no longer.

"Ah, yes," he replied, after I asked him, "the girl. I had almost forgotten about her, so pleasant has been our talk. It is seldom I get a chance to discuss the past with anyone. It has been so pleasant. It is a shame to bring up such disagreeable thoughts."

"Is she in danger?" I asked apprehensively, fear building within me.

"Not at the moment. But let me explain. As I said earlier, there are several space windows throughout the western hemisphere. By chance a group of *Abdaith*, a kingdom of fierce pirates in the extreme north, direct descendants of Hitherbaun, stumbled into one of these space windows to the west.

This was about a century ago if I remember correctly. When you get as old as I am, you tend to forget some of the more recent history in favor of youthful memories," he apologized.

"Yes, of course. But the girl?"

"I'm getting to her and your friend. But first, you must understand the circumstances." He shot me a disdainful look, then continued, "The *Abdaith* in accidentally discovering this space window, which leads across the forest to a point eastward, was, for them, a miracle of chance. Now they would not only have a quick route to the rich caravan trails in the east, but could bypass the fearful forest of the Ghost People. A legend, I might add, that we have always tried to encourage among the other races to help ensure our privacy here in the trees."

"I thought the Meoaithaian *Yata* had created that superstition," I said, recalling Euoaithia's tale.

"Oh, we are aware that the Meoaithaians built the tale of the Ghost People into giant proportions for their own purposes; however, it served our needs at the same time so we helped them along with 'incidents' that made the stories all the more real. Yet, in the beginning we started the stories and the Meoaithaians, a people less caught up in superstition than the Cluvian descendants, were slow to believe them until their *Yatas* took to embroiling the tales in fantastic lies."

"I see," I replied, "the story is becoming clearer by the moment. But what has this to do with the girl?"

"I am getting to that, my impatient guest." He stood up and moved across the room. There was no doubt that the impatience and vigor of a much younger person disturbed his otherwise stoic nature. I suppose if I had lived as long as he, impatience would be rather unsettling since time itself would have no meaning.

As he continued, he explained that the space windows on either side of the forest had an intermediate stopover in the forest, directly below the tree city. The tree against which Marjano had been leaning was the exact spot where the window opened. No doubt if she had sat down a few inches from where she had, she would have fallen through the window. And so dim is the light along the avenue of the trees I could not discern its presence. How I had been able to move about as I had in search of her without stumbling through the window I could not guess.

For a century the *Abdaithians* had used the windows from

which to attack the riches of eastern caravans and escape back to safety. They were pirates in the true sense of the word, though not using ships or Jolly Rogers.

The Old Man also explained that it was not possible to collapse the windows so the avenue was always open to the *Abdaithians*, though he did not explain why the Cluvians were not able to accomplish what seemed to me to be a simple task. Instead, they set up a watch in the city above to see what would transpire from the pirates using this method to transport across the fearful forest. Several years of study through the carefully cut shaft above the spot on the avenue below convinced them the pirates had no inkling there might be other such phenomena in existence. This, to them, was a miracle of chance. A blessing from the gods that watched over pirates!

While I had been gone for meat, a half dozen pirates appeared through the window at Marjano's feet. So startled were the Princess and Zynthmai, they were made prisoners by the always cautious pirates before my companions knew what was upon them. The pirates had then stepped back through the window from whence they had arrived. And they had taken Marjano and Zynthmai with them.

"No doubt they are even now riding like the wind for their northern kingdom," the Old Man concluded. "For *Aptao Mahn, Yata* of the *Abdaith*, has a voracious appetite for the ladies. And if you don't mind my saying so, the girl was quite a looker from what I saw of her—even to these tired, old eyes."

"You saw the whole affair?" I asked, astonished.

"Oh, yes, we keep a constant eye on the space window below. It so happens that I was looking down upon the spot when the three of you stopped to rest."

"Then why didn't you do something when you saw the pirates making off with my friends?"

"We do not involve ourselves with the affairs of the other races upon Ghandor so long as they do not endanger us," he replied matter-of-factly.

"But you could have saved the girl, or at least let me know immediately what became of her and I could have gone to her rescue. Isn't there any chivalry within you Old Man?" I spat out.

"Unfortunately, we have laws. They may not be chivalrous, as you call it, but they were set up to safeguard thousands of lives and billions of people. Our life, or even a hundred, do not count in the long run, for there will always be *Kagia* who will want to rule but if there is no genius around to invent the scientific tools, they must content themselves with their own kingdoms and petty problems. To let the world know who we are and where we are would be courting planetary disaster."

"But a people who throw away human life deliberately in order to preserve a philosophy are not civilized. A people exist because of the rights of the individual, not the other way around."

"*Buw mu gaa ithad!*" he replied. "You are very young. When you have lived as long as I, you will see the folly of that statement."

"You have lived too long, Old Man," I replied heatedly. "When a person lives so long that his values of life and what life is all about become warped, he would better serve his people by committing suicide."

"Ah, the rashness of youth," he replied, more to himself than to me. I could see that further argument in this direction would prove futile. Nor would it tell me the whereabouts of my beloved Princess. For until I knew exactly where she was and how I could get to her, I was unable to effect her rescue.

"But of the girl?" I inquired.

"Yes, yes, of course, the girl! Well, *Aptao Mahn's* interest in a girl does not last very long. Because of this his pirates are always on the lookout for comely maidens wherever they travel. We have seen numerous young maidens transported through the windows below over the years. No doubt when those pirates return with your friends they will be rewarded, for the girl is very fair. So, for the moment, she will be treated kindly. Her captors will not dare harm her in any way, lest they lose their reward from *Aptao Mahn*, and most likely, their heads."

"And when she gets to the city and *Aptao Mahn*?" I asked, my voice flat, for I already knew the answer.

"Ah, but that is another matter. One, unfortunately for you, that cannot be altered. I understand the *Abdaithian Yata*, with his great appetite for the ladies will take her as his own because of her great beauty. But, he will tire of her quickly and no doubt turn her over to his nobles. She will finally end up as the plaything for the royal guards. It is a shame, but that is the way of life upon Ghandor."

My anger got the best of me. His callousness was beyond my patience to endure. No doubt I would have hurled myself upon him and wrung his bony neck had not he anticipated my temperament and called for the warriors that seemed to protect him every second.

"We will talk again when you are calmer," he said politely as I was led away.

"Old Man," I yelled over my shoulder as I was dragged from the room, "if anything happens to my friends, I will kill you."

CHAPTER TWENTY-ONE

I spent almost a month within the treetop city. I thought at first the Old Man would have me put to death because of my threat, and perhaps he had decided to do so, but at least for several weeks I was free to wander the city. In all that time Marjano's fate was heavy on my mind. Time and again I had rescued her from terrible circumstances only to have her whisked away again to some new, hideous doom. Each time I had been able to grasp her from the very clutches of death. But it was with a heavy heart that I viewed her present calamity. There seemed no possible way I could escape from the treetop city. For more than four weeks I had secretly covered every square inch of the city. At one point I had cut through an outer wall high up in the trees hoping to find a place where the protective force field might not have penetrated, but to no avail. The field was everywhere.

After nearly two weeks of unsuccessful attempts to find a weakness in the field I realized that only through negating the field could I find a way out of the city. But that was easier said than done! Without the metal used to break the beam at the control center, the field could not be shut down. And since the beam had to strike two metal surfaces instantaneously I would need the metal from two of the Old Guard. And I didn't even know who any of the others were, let alone how I was going to get two together in the room.

In my wanderings about the city I met many interesting Cluvians. They were nice and quite polite, almost to the point of being solicitous. Whether this was by order of the Old Man or their normal nature I wasn't sure but felt the latter to be the case.

One custom among the Cluvians much impressed me. Rather than allowing themselves to become bored with a conversation while having to appear interested as people of my own world do, the tree dwellers have a remedy much to my liking. When a conversation steers around to a subject about which one or more in the group are not interested, they merely say, *"dun mai tia,"* which roughly means, "I am absent." This, then, allows the person to remain in the group but to pay no attention to what is being said around him. He can meditate, observe others in the area or anything he likes. When the discussion veers back to something in which he is interested he rejoins the conversation.

After learning of this custom I often thought how much an improvement it would make in the royal courts of Europe.

The city was simplistic in nature but extravagant in wealth. Everywhere, except for the first corridors I had entered and the space window room, there was a profusion of jewels, gold, and precious metals and stones. Their works of art were beyond description. Unlike the works I had seen on the Continent of my world, these paintings made you feel you were seeing real life. Rather than the flat, two-dimensional paintings I had been used to seeing, both on my world and in the stone city of the Meoaithaians, these paintings had a three-dimensional quality. You felt like you were really there. Paintings that showed carnivorous animals seemed like they were readying to spring right out of the picture at you. War scenes, of which there were mighty few, made you feel like you needed to draw your sword to defend yourself. Scenes of intimacy between lovers gave you the distinct impression you were right there with them and you wanted to slip away, unnoticed.

Despite all the joyous scenes of wealth and beauty, though, most of the tree dwellers seemed extremely unhappy and nowhere did I find any industry, activity or works of art in progress. It was as though everyone was sitting around waiting to die. Nothing but simple conversation seemed to interest them.

I learned many things during those weeks in the city. The most important of which was that not everyone who swore fealty to the Old Guard were in favor of the stringent laws of the past. But they evidently felt it was better to be a live prisoner than a dead dissenter. Perhaps this was a result of thousands of years of subjugation. The will to rebel had been successfully rooted out of them in their younger years. All appeared to have accepted their fate.

Just how many there were I did not know, but I had made

friends with a man by the name of Jaanta who filled me in on several points of culture and invention among the Cluvians. It was to this same Jaanta that the first Cluvian girl I met, whose name was Athad, had been leading me when we had run afoul of the Old Guard's warriors and she had hit me over the head in order to save my life.

The space windows to which the Old Man had referred were all housed in the large room he had shown me. Nowhere else in the treetop city was another space window located. Astonished that previous dissenters hadn't used the space windows to escape I learned that they were operated only when the outside force field was shut down.

The Old Man was called Gaonthai, though I never learned the name from him. He had not bothered to ask me mine nor tell me his. Jaanta also told me that Gaonthai, or the Old Man, was not exactly the Caji or *Yata* of the tree dwellers, though he served in that capacity. Actually the city was run by the thirteen original *mantai* scientists that had survived. They used Gaonthai as their spokesman and figurehead, though he actually possessed no more power than the other twelve members. They were called simply, the Old Guard. But despite these other twelve men being the rulers of the city, no one knew exactly who they were! Only Gaonthai was known to everyone. It was he who meted out the decisions of the Old Guard and held the councils with the people.

News of this depressed me greatly for I had been in hopes that I could find out more of the Old Guard in order to find the two pieces of metal I needed. And since every male in Clu wore a type of glove or hand covering, the other members of the Old Guard could not be recognized in that way. No doubt their anonymity had made it even harder for any rebel leaders to plan a way out of the city, a fact the Old Man had neglected to tell me.

I also learned that a temporary space window could be opened anywhere on the planet. If a permanent window was desired, an elaborate compilation was needed and the elemental structure of the window worked out from both ends of the area the window would serve. If a window was to be collapsed, the same elaborate elemental structure had to be reversed at both ends through another temporary window. Since this involved as much effort and danger as when setting up a window, many that were no longer in use were left unreversed. This, to the Cluvians, was a simpler answer. Also, a window could be set up from the spot of origination without utilizing a temporary window if one didn't care where the window's opening at the other end was to be. In cases where the scientists had opened space windows on other planets, this was the means they employed. However, to dismantle the window it was always necessary to do so at both ends, no doubt the reason why the window open to my own planet was still operating when I stepped through it for the Cluvians are not too interested in facing the possible dangers inherent in using a window that opens into an unknown area.

Jaanta explained that since the *Abdaith* guarded the two ends of the space window on either side of the forest it was impossible for the tree dwellers to collapse either one without endangering themselves and risking being discovered. Thus the window had always remained open, even after the pirates had discovered it.

The fact that no *Abdaith* stood guard at the intermediate window in the forest below bespoke of their genuine fear of the forest and its creatures. They, too, probably had their own superstitions about the *Blou Tou*.

"But why are there windows that originate elsewhere than in the great room here in the city?" I asked him. "When I stepped through the space window that brought me from my own world to this one, it delivered me into a meadow completely surrounded by the forest, many miles to the south."

"Like the window below through which your friends were abducted," Jaanta replied, "as well as the one through which you stepped into our world, many were originally set up by the Old Guard long before the force field was perfected. They feared the younger ones would escape from the city if the whereabouts of the windows were known. So they hid many of them in diverse places. Now, however, they no longer need to fear the younger ones, so all the windows are housed in one central location."

Jaanta also explained that he had worked in the space window chamber from time to time though for what reason I could not imagine nor did he elaborate upon. He told me of traveling to several points upon the planet through temporary windows he set up and all the sights he had seen. He even found a girl in the Thuian city of Urvia with whom he had fallen in love but could do nothing about it.

"Why not?" I asked.

"Because the space window can be set up for only a few

minutes at a time. About *zynthyehj*,* to be exact. Then the window collapses automatically. . ."

"But if you are on the other side what does it matter? You could then remain with your lady love. Or is it the law you fear so much that you dare not stay?" I taunted, then felt guilty for Jaanta had been very friendly to me and did not deserve such a barb. It was just that the apathy of these people had begun to wear upon me.

"No, it is not the law," he replied, oblivious to my sarcasm. "I have no love for that!" This was the first indication that he was not in favor of total destruction of any dissenters among the Tree Dwellers.

"It is the elemental structure of the space window," he continued, "that keeps me from staying with Urthea. When the window collapses, the elemental structure dissolves all elements that are foreign to it and the area in which it exists."

"But you could be far gone from the area when it collapses, couldn't you? Twenty minutes seems long enough," I persisted, for I was thinking of Marjano and her rescue rather than Jaanta and his Thuian love.

"No, no, you do not understand," he said patiently, like a schoolmarm trying to get her message through to the class dunce. "The elemental structure through which you pass is connected directly to the entire mechanism. On a permanent window, you pass through as a separate entity, but with the temporary window you pass through as part of the elemental structure. I do not understand any more of the scientific principle involved than that, but suffice it to say that when the window collapses, if you are still part of it, no matter how far beyond the window you might be, you collapse with it. Your elements burn and dissipate. You just—disappear."

"Do you know this to be a fact?" I asked, suspicious that it was just more of the Old Guard's propaganda.

"Yes," he replied. "Many years ago a close friend of mine talked me into letting her take a journey to a faroff place through a temporary window. We had been told many times never to do so and the results of such a venture, but being young and reckless, she wanted to go. I went with her more for her protection than anything else, for I had already been on several such trips and by then they had lost much of their

---

* Twenty minutes in the Ghandorian time cycle. About thirty-five minutes Earth time.

appeal to me. But I went along to watch out for her," he added quietly. As his voice trailed off, he paused for a time. I was aware that the girl had been more than just a friend and became interested in the outcome of his tale.

"We saw some sights that we had never believed to exist. She had picked a spot on the planet to which I had never before journeyed and it was strikingly beautiful. Numerous waterfalls, luscious flowers and flowing rivers were evident everywhere. I had never before seen anything like it for there are no waterways in our part of the world. After the twenty minutes were up and we returned, Dairlmai, my friend, wanted to go somewhere else. She persisted until I finally gave in and we traveled to another beautiful land. We kept coming back and popping through to some other, strange, often exotic place. But after awhile it became harder and harder to get her to return. We kept pressing closer to the twenty-minute deadline each journey, so much so that I greatly feared for our safety. Then, on one trip, she said she didn't believe in the law nor the myth of the temporary window's collapse. She thought it was just something the Old Guard had made up to keep us from escaping. I tried to persuade her to return but she wouldn't. I—I was going to stay, but as the minute arrived I—jumped through the window back to the city. I was afraid." He paused again, no doubt recalling in every detail the event.

"By my measurement," he finally continued, "the window existed for another minute beyond the expressed time, but then it collapsed. And Dairlmai along with it. I actually saw her burning alive. Her screams still haunt me in my dreams." His voice trailed off again, and then he looked straight at me, as if seeing me for the first time. He added, "Oh, yes, my friend, it is all very true!"

"But the girl in Thu. Why not bring her here through the space window? Or does it work in reverse too?"

"There are two reasons. First, it is against the law to bring anyone into the city. If one is brought in, they are immediately put to death, as I am afraid you will soon be. The second reason is I wouldn't want to force this imprisonment upon someone I loved!"

I had not thought of that, of course. To imprison a free soul was seldom the intention of a person in love. But something he said bothered me greatly.

"Why do you say I will be put to death?"

"Because it is the way with the Old Guard. Only three have ever come into the city in the past to my knowledge, and all were killed after a few days."

"But I have been here for several weeks. Why haven't I been killed before this?"

"I don't know, except none of the others came into the city as you did, from the forest. The others, all women, were brought here through the space windows. As soon as they were discovered, they died. Perhaps you are still alive because the Old Guard hasn't met since you arrived and they need to talk over your special case before a decision can be made. They are very democratic when they condemn someone." The last he spat out quite bitterly.

That night a plan of desperation began to unfold in my mind. It required a bit of manipulating of the Old Man's benevolence toward me, an extremely large amount of luck and Jaanta's deep underlying attitudes about his imprisonment. I decided I had no more than two days in which to carry it off before Marjano's captors were due to reach their northern city. And, too, I didn't know how soon the Old Guard were to meet to decide my fate.

The plan was well established in my mind by morning, but even to my normal optimistic nature it seemed rather futile, so shaky were many of its contingencies. If I could find a way to get Jaanta and myself into the window room, I would at least have a chance; however, the plan was based a lot upon the Old Guard's technology, of which I knew nothing.

I met with Jaanta that day and briefed him on my plan to leave the city. He was eager to help me. When he learned just how I was going to accomplish this his interest was really piqued, for in my plan he found a way for him and those like him to overthrow the Old Guard and gain control of the city. When he told me there were many others that would help once we had carried out the first steps of my plan, I became eager to help him and his friends in their quest. But I made it perfectly clear that the rescue of my two friends from the northern city was my first concern. He, of course, agreed to help me and we sat far into the night planning our rebellion.

But as such things go, it was not as a result of our planning but by a sheer stroke of luck, or so I thought, that made the first step of my scheme possible.

It was the morning of the day I had calculated Marjano would arrive in the *Abdaithian* city that the Old Man summoned me to his chambers. I had not seen him since my aborted attack upon his life the night he had so callously condemned Marjano to a fate worse than death. I had been trying to see him since Jaanta and I had worked out our plans, but until his summons, had not been successful. Panic had begun to seize me as those last two days slipped away for I could not in my mind's eye get Marjano out of the evil clutches of *Aptao Mahn.* So it was with a great deal of relief that I accepted the Old Man's summons.

"Well, well, my young friend, how is life treating you these days? I trust you are well and enjoying your stay within our pleasant city?"

I was surprised at his outright friendliness. This had been one of my concerns for my plan depended largely upon his attitude toward me. As he spoke I became more confident that my plan would succeed.

"Why, certainly I am enjoying my stay. If one must be a captive, one certainly couldn't choose a more luxurious or beautiful place in which to enjoy his captivity. You have been most propitious."

"Ah, I am glad to see your rancor of our previous meeting completely dissipated."

"Yes, as you say, *'buw mu gaa ithad!'*"

"I compliment you on your comprehension of the facts. No matter how unpleasant the situation with your friends might be, it is unresolvable by you. I am so glad that you have come to realize this."

I waited patiently for him to come to the point of his summons. I wasn't sure what he had in mind but was hoping that if any decision reached by the Old Guard was to take my life, that it would be postponed long enough for me to effect Marjano's rescue and bring mine and Jaanta's plans to fruition.

"I asked you here to see if there wasn't something I could do for you," he continued after a long pause. "After all, we have interferred with your normal pursuits in life and I would like in some way to make that up to you. Perhaps there is something within Clu that might interest you. Someone?" He placed heavy emphasis on the last statement and his meaning was clear. I vowed then and there if I ever rescued Marjano and we were successful in our planned coup of the city, I was going to make the Old Man pay for his callousness when it came to dealing with other people's lives.

"Perhaps there is some place within the city you would like to enjoy? Learn more of or explore?" he offered once again.

I couldn't believe my ears. All the way down to his apartment I was wondering how I could work the conversation around to this very point. Curiously I wondered if mind-reading was one of the advanced technologies of the scientists. I certainly hoped not, for my plan was based solely upon the element of surprise.

"No, I can't think of anything that you have I haven't already been furnished. Unless, of course," I added cautiously, not wanting to be too eager, "you have some more marvelous inventions of which I am not aware?"

The conversation took a turn in another direction for a few moments and I mentally kicked myself for not pressing my advantage while I had one. Now it seemed I was going to have to bring up the subject and I wasn't sure how I could do it without appearing too eager after turning him down a moment before. My fears were quickly erased, for the Old Man broached the subject a few minutes later.

"You earlier mentioned inventions. I do have something with which I think you might be interested. It is a device by which you can observe and even take part in circumstances some distance from here. However, there are dangers to it, but if I've sized you up correctly, I don't think you will object to that."

I almost fell off the chair. He was offering me that which I wanted more than anything else in the city. Entrance into the space window chamber.

"Of course not," I replied slowly, not wanting to tip my extreme interest. "In fact, I'd even welcome some adventure after my four weeks of inactivity."

"Yes, I thought you might. Do you remember the room in which I showed you the device that controls the force field about our city?"

"Yes."

"Well I never did tell you the purpose of the other device. It is, as you might have guessed from the space windows in the larger chamber, the controls of the temporary windows that can be set up. I thought you might enjoy seeing a bit of the rest of the planet, since you told me you had seen little of it since arriving here."

I tried to keep my voice steady and unemotional as I replied. "Why, thank you. That would be very interesting. When can we begin?"

"Today, if you like. Right now. I will summon Jaanta and have him join you in the space window chamber. I've noticed that you and Jaanta have become good friends so I'm sure you wouldn't mind his company?"

"Of course not. I'd be delighted."

"Fine. Jaanta has worked in the room before and is familiar with the temporary window technology. He will help you visit anywhere you wish."

As I left the Old Man's chambers, I nearly ran up the flights to the control room. Everything was working out better than I had hoped. I had every reason to rejoice, but a nagging feeling haunted me all the way. I couldn't help feeling the whole thing had been too easy. Like granting the last wish before an execution.

Joining Jaanta in the control room off the space window chamber, I brought him up-to-date on the discussion I just had with the Old Man. Jaanta was not pleased.

"It is not like the Old Guard to make such allowances," he said firmly.

"Why not, you have told me you and others have used the windows for the same purpose."

"Yes, but never with direct permission. Oh, I'm not saying they didn't know what we were doing, but officially the windows have always been forbidden!"

"Well, it won't matter, Jaanta, once I get into Euoaithia's apartment. When I get my hands on my steel blade, I believe we can put an end to the imprisonment of you and your fellows."

Neither of us felt too good about the circumstances surrounding our adventure but it didn't matter to me what the Old Man had in mind, for once I got my blade, I felt certain I could rescue Marjano and Zynthmai. I would willingly give my life if I could but rescue my Princess from the evil clutches of *Aptao Mahn*.

It was with buoyed spirits that I stepped through the temporary space window into the Meaoithaian city. Jaanta had made the calculations based upon principles I couldn't fathom, nor with which I concerned myself. My only interest was getting my blade and returning inside twenty minutes.

The *Yata*'s apartment was as I had remembered it. And to my good fortune, it was empty when I stepped through the window into it. I had been forced to step through unarmed for the Old Man had not, of course, deemed it wise to give me a weapon.

My first visit to this room had shown me much of its master's habits. One of which was his hoarding nature. One wall was decorated with hundreds of weapons, instruments and items that I believed the huge ruler had confiscated or robbed from his enemies over the years. It was upon this belief that hung the success of my venture. But much to my dismay, the weapon which I sought was not upon the wall.

Quickly I tore the apartment apart. All three rooms fell to my frenzied search. In less time than it takes to tell about it, the apartment was a shambles. But still I had not found my sword, that grand old blade made of Earth steel.

All the time I had been working I had been counting the time to myself. I judged there were less than five minutes left before I must step back through the window or die in flaming dissolvement within the royal chambers of Euoaithia.

As I was passing the wall of weapons the door to the outer room swung open and I heard voices approaching. Quickly, I yanked one of the decorative swords off the wall and turned just in time to see Euoaithia enter with two of his nobles. And praise to all the saints, upon the harness of the Meoathaian ruler hung my sword. With time running out, I jumped forward and downed one of his companions before they realized I was in the room. Another thrust disabled the second companion, and as the *Yata* yelled for succor, I slammed the hilt of the sword down upon his head, knocking him to the floor. I cut the belt with my own sword which I unsheathed and yanked the scabbard free from the ponderous body. Grasping the blade of my homeland in one hand and the scabbard in the other, I jumped for the window, hoping against hope I wasn't too late.

As I stepped back into the control room, I was met by five guards with drawn swords. Jaanta was upon the floor with blood seeping from a shoulder wound. There seemed little doubt what the Old Man had arranged for the conclusion of my adventure.

As I stepped into the room, the five rushed me.

CHAPTER TWENTY-TWO

To my advantage was the fact they did not expect me to be armed, nor with such a powerful weapon. The steel of my blade had since proven itself on this planet as being the strongest metal available. And no sooner had I stepped through the space window than I was in a fight for my life.

The first warrior lunged at me, but a quick sidestep, aided by the lesser gravity, took me away from the point of his blade. Stumbling, he went on through the space window, to be met, I hoped, by the guards coming to Euoaithia's rescue. If the window's collapse didn't burn him immediately, certainly the Meoaithaian blades would.

Though hard-pressed, I rejoiced at having my blade in my hands once again. Using the swordsmanship I learned from master swordsmen on three continents, I drove the four remaining guards back across the room. A double feint and thrust dispatched another, and one of the trio disengaged and ran, no doubt, for help, for the Cluvians had not before seen me fight nor understood my extreme power on this lesser gravity planet. Had the Old Man known of this, he surely would have sent more than five guards to dispatch me.

The remaining two stood little chance against my superior sword and skill. In less time than it takes to tell, they lay dead beneath my feet.

Turning to the force field device, I inserted the blade of my sword into the beam emanating from both sides of the green-colored box. If this didn't work, I knew, not only would my blade possibly be destroyed, but all chance of escape and effecting Marjano's rescue would be forfeited. Yet I fully believed it would work, for surely the planet to which the Old Man had referred had been my own Earth of prehistoric times. And surely the metal of which he talked was steel, for what other metal was there on Earth that Ghandor did not possess?

As the light struck my blade, it sputtered and died. It had worked! All around the city the field was collapsing. How it could be started up again I did not know but I wasn't giving anyone the chance to reenact the power. Twirling dials and levers upon the other devices as I had seen Jaanta do, I set up a space window into some unknown place. Then ripping the force field power unit from the table upon which it had been bolted, I threw it through the space window opening. Where the device came out I did not know nor did I care, for it would take forever for anyone to discover even if it were not destroyed when the window collapsed, for I redialed the controls, leaving no clue as to where I had sent the mechanism.

I feared for the return of the guards before I could enact the rest of my plans but to my great surprise, none arrived. Quickly, my thoughts turned to Jaanta, both because he had become my close friend and also because the success of my mission to rescue my princess depended upon his knowledge in dialing the correct location for the space window to take me to the northern kingdom of the *Abdaithians*.

Leaning over my friend, I found him to be not too seriously injured. The blade of one of the guards had sliced through the skin to the bone, but no artery had been severed. As I staunched the flow of blood, a wave of Cluvians entered the chamber.

Jaanta, who by now had regained consciousness, quickly told me they were his friends. They had been waiting outside the room to see what would happen. If we had been unsuccessful in negating the force field, they would not have come to our rescue. Not the most courageous men I have known, but as it was, they had joined forces with us as soon as our success was realized. They were milling about us as though they had won a great victory. It took me but a moment to convince them that the war was just begun.

"Quickly, block the door," I yelled at them, "for the guards will be upon us in a few more moments. Some of you grab the weapons of these dead warriors, and if any of the guards should break through and gain the chamber, kill them."

Turning to Jaanta who was by now being cared for by two of the women who had entered the room, I said, "Come, my friend, I must have the window set for *Abdaith*. Can you manage it?"

"Of course," he replied weakly, but gamely. I was surprised to see his strength as he slowly got to his feet and made his way to the control dials, for he had lost much blood. With his bandaged shoulder showing signs of red and his face almost white from the loss of the precious fluid, it seemed remarkable that he was able to hold himself upright. But his efforts were enough to place the dials in proper position and indicate to me that the window was ready. As I prepared to step through, he spoke with a strong voice and a smile upon his pallid face.

"Remember, my friend, only twenty minutes. Any longer and our cause is lost."

Not to mention my life, I thought, but I merely replied, "Thank you, my friend. I shall not forget. I will return shortly with my friends."

I stepped through into a room of enormous size. It was well appointed with paintings and art treasures. The interests of the room's owner were expressly shown for the paintings, sculpture and other works of art were all descriptive of baseness to which he had fallen. Illicit and erotic works were displayed throughout the entire room. A large, round canopied bed stood upon a raised platform in the center of the room. And moving toward the bed was a giant of a man, richly robed, gone to fat of face and belly. He was scuffling with another person. Jaanta had opened the window right into none other than *Aptao Mahn's* bedchamber, and he was at this very moment trying to entice a young maiden to his bed and in no gentlemanly manner.

As he twisted and turned under the violent attack of the girl, her face came into full view and it was none other than my princess Marjano. At the sight of her in his clutches, my blood ran cold and I jumped forward to save her from his nefarious plans.

"We shall prevail!" I yelled, and the princess turned to stare into my eyes as I leaped for them. In that fraction of a second her face bespoke all that she felt for me. It was enough to double my strength and I had in mind to cut the *Abdaithian Yata* in two until I chanced to remember Jaanta's last words "Twenty minutes, my friend, or our cause is lost."

Leaping to her side, I pointed my blade at the quickly retreating pirate *Yata*. His face was purple with rage and a study in hate. The years of depravity had wreaked their toll on what might at one time have been a handsome countenance. He spat out several vile phrases I could not hear, but that he was sealing my doom I had no doubt.

The door burst open and several guards streamed into the room. The *Yata* pointed a bejeweled finger in my direction and screamed uncontrollably. All I could really make out was that he didn't want the girl hurt. As they charged in our direction his words were unmistakable: "Kill him, kill him, kill him—"

Not wanting the guards to cut us off from the space window, I scooped Marjano up in my arms and jumped for the swirling mist. Before *Aptao Mahn* or his guards could comprehend what was happening, we disappeared from their sight. I was laughing at what must be going through the cruel pirate's mind as he saw us, especially the beautiful princess, disappear into empty air. I'm sure my princess thought me mad at that moment as my laughter rang in her ears.

Stepping back into the control chamber in the treetop city, Marjano's eyes were ablaze with questions. But rather than ask any, she made a curious statement.

"Though I have called you *Yatahn* many times and you have not responded, I still must feel that you love me. For I can wait no longer." With that she circled her arms about my neck and pressed her soft lips against mine as I held her cradled in my arms.

"Of course I love you," I finally managed after a lengthy respite of tenderness. "I thought you understood that." I was beginning to think my father correct, women are a hard lot to understand.

"How could I?" she replied, "you never told me, nor have you still." A slight pout was playing at the corners of her mouth.

"What else can I say but 'I love you'?" I asked desperately.

It was at this point that Jaanta came to my rescue. He was still in the control room when we had stepped back through the temporary window, no doubt waiting anxiously for my return.

"My friend," he began amid chuckles, "on Ghandor when a maiden calls a man *Yatahn*, she is telling him that he is The Mighty One of Her Life—Her Love! The only way to react, if you feel the same way, is to call her *Maitahn*. I believe she is trying to tell you this is what she would like to hear." His laughter mocked me good-naturedly.

Oh, the strange customs of peoples and, yes, worlds. Marjano had repeatedly used the endearing term and never once had I reacted. No wonder she had not understood how I truly felt about her. For though I had tried to express my love to her in many earthly ways, none had served to convey my message correctly to this Ghandorian princess.

"*Maitahn*, love of my life," I said softly, so only she could hear me, "I have searched half a world for you just to tell you how deep is my love for you."

Her arms tightened about me and she whispered words in my ear that are too private to mention here. It was pleasant that moment of peaceful, endearing love. A moment I have since cherished often. But only a moment it was for a loud commotion broke out in the chamber and we could hear the guards banging at the door.

"Quick, my princess, we must act. We are under siege here and are greatly outnumbered. Is it possible for you to summon your royal guard to our aid?"

"Certainly I will summon them, Robert, my love. But are we in Urvia? I do not recognize this place."

"No," I replied quickly, "we are in the Ghost Forest in a secret hidden treetop city. I will explain all that later. But now we need the help of your Palace Guard."

"But if we are in the Ghost Forest, we are weeks from Thu. How can I summon help for us in time with your enemies assailing the door?"

"Your Palace is but a foot or two away," I quickly replied, hastening to explain the space windows and the one Jaanta had told me was positioned within the palace walls of Urvia, the capital of Thu, and Marjano's home.

"Quickly, then *Yatahn*, show me the way," she responded as she grasped the significance of the space window and how she could help. "Let us go to Urvia and bring back aid."

"No, my love, I cannot go. I am needed here, but you must go," I called back as I led her across the large chamber that housed the scores of space windows. "Hurry, my princess, for we cannot hold out very long here."

Jaanta, who by now was looking much better and able to move upon his own, followed us across the chamber. "Do you want me to accompany your princess?" he asked as we neared the window.

"No, Jaanta, for you must reset the dials on the temporary window so I can return to save my friend, Zynthmai. Also, you must strengthen the resolve and courage of your friends until I can return."

"Go with *Nazu*," Marjano called back over her shoulder as she stepped through the window. Turning, Jaanta and I ran back across the chamber and while I stood impatiently he reset the dials for me to have access into the dungeons of the northern kingdom city of *Abdaith* where Zynthmai lay incarcerated.

Jaanta's friends were still milling about the large chamber, not knowing what to do and needing direction. They had no experience in rebellion. As Jaanta finished with the dials, I spoke to him in hurried tones, "Have the biggest of your friends press against the door. Try to keep the guards out until the princess can return from Thu with aid. I will be but a few moments."

As he nodded I stepped through the window and into a dank, dirty passageway strewn with filth and smelling for all the world like a manure heap.

There were several heavy wooden doors flanking both sides of the passage way. I could not tell in which one Zynthmai was being held, but made a quick search of the doors nearest me. Luckily the dungeon was not very big. No doubt the *Abdaithians* did not keep prisoners very long! I hoped that Zynthmai had not met some foul end before I could effect his rescue.

"Zynthmai, are you here? Do you hear me?" I called out after receiving no response from him at the few doors I had tried.

"Robert?" he called back, some distance away, "Is that you, Robert?"

"Yes, my friend, it is I. Keep calling so I can locate you."

"I can't believe my ears! I had given up all hope that you would know of our whereabouts after crossing that great desert for many weeks."

His voice was strong and I assumed he was no worse for wear and was glad of it for he would be sorely needed when we stepped back through the window. I hurried down the corridor toward his voice. As I located the cell door and tried to wedge the lock open with my sword, I found the rusty hinges unyielding to my efforts. As I continued to pry, I quickly brought him up to date as to what had befallen me since I had left them in the trees that evening in search of meat. As I hurriedly looked around for something to break the persistent lock, Zynthmai told me briefly of what had happened to them on the avenue of the trees and their long journey to the north kingdom of the *Abdaithians*. It had not been an easy journey, he told me, but it was uneventful. In answer to my question, he told me that Marjano had been respectfully treated. To that, at least, I was grateful.

While I still toiled at the lock, well aware of the time slipping away from me, a guard came running down the passageway. No doubt he had been drawn in this direction by my calling Zynthmai but moments earlier.

"Here, here, what are you doing?" he called as he ran. "Who are you?"

I swung upon him, yelling, "I am the *Yata* of the *Blou Tou*, and if you don't shut up that yammering, I'm going to eat you alive." And thus saying this, I sprang for him as I had seen dangling from his harness a large ring of keys. I heard Zynthmai calling behind me: "If he is a tall, lanky man of extreme ugliness, he is the guard with my key and one who has not been too pleasant in his dealings with me."

Half a dozen giant leaps took me to the startled guard's side. So surprised was he at my being able to cover the great distance so quickly, the thought of bringing his sword into play never apparently occurred to him. In fact, as I approached, he shrank back from me and quickly cowered before my blade. I did not know whether he was more afraid from seeing me thus approach him, or that I had called myself the *Yata* of the *Blou Tou*. In any event, he was of no consequence to the moment, and I picked him up bodily and carried him back to the cell door of my friend.

"The key, where is it?" I demanded, depositing him at the cell door.

"Here it is," he weakly managed. "Please be careful with the point of that blade, won't you?" he continued whining.

"I'll be careful with this blade only if you open my friend's cell and be quick about it! Otherwise, I'll run you through and feed your remains to my ghostly friends."

He managed to find the key with shaking hands and somehow insert it into the lock. The simple tumblers moved and I swung the cell door open. Zynthmai jumped out and we pushed the jailkeeper in and swung back the door, turning the key.

"Quick, Zynthmai, we have no time to lose," I said, turning and running down the passageway. Scooping up the guard's sword, Zynthmai followed closely behind.

I ran toward the window and as I approached I could barely make out the swirling mist in the dark dungeon corridor. I was hoping against hope that we still had a few seconds before the window collapsed. As Zynthmai caught up with me, I motioned him through the window. He asked no questions though I am sure he thought me somewhat mad, for the window was beside a stone wall and for all appearances he must have thought I was asking him to jump into the wall itself. But stout heart that he was, he took no heed to appearances and jumped into the mist at my urging.

We reappeared in the control room of the treetop city to the clang of swords. A quick glance told me the door had been forced and the Old Guard's warriors were pushing through. We had returned in the proverbial nick of time.

The half-dozen of Jaanta's friends who were armed were putting up a fight, but didn't stand a chance against the warriors and in but a few moments they would have easily been dispatched. Lifting my sword, I jumped to the aid of Jaanta and his friends.

"Come Zynthmai," I tossed over my shoulder as I entered the melee, "our blades are yet needed once again."

"Ah, another fight. You are a good friend, Robert," he jovially called to me, "to share your merriment with me."

" 'Tis the least I could do for a friend," I replied as he gleefully joined the fracas beside me. I had started to say more, but several warriors pushed through the door and we were too busily engaged for more conversation.

Zynthmai and I moved to the front of the fight for the defenders in the room were both poorly armed and lacking in skill with the sword. At least thirty warriors were now in the room and though Zynthmai and I held our ground, it was doubtful we could last long against such overwhelming odds, if Marjano and her Palace Guard did not reach us quickly. And there seemed no way we could whittle down the odds against us for each time one of their number fell before our blades two more entered the chamber to take his place. Evidently the Old Guard were calling in all their forces, realizing this was to be a fight to the finish with ultimate power and control of the treetop city hanging in the balance.

There was now only one other defender in the chamber with a blade beside Jaanta, Zynthmai, and myself.

"Quick," I called to them, "escape through the space window to Thu. Save yourselves for we cannot last long at this rate."

"It is not escape we want," Jaanta called back, dodging a deadly swipe of a blade meant to separate him from his head. "We want the freedom of our city. We can accomplish this only through defeating the Old Guard. We must stand and fight if we are to call ourselves men."

With Jaanta's heroic words, others of his friends, who had not before had the courage to fight with a sword, scurried about looking for weapons on downed comrades or enemies.

Zynthmai and I carried the brunt of the attack despite the fact that most of the defenders of the chamber were now armed. It was too bad they did not have even a rudimentary knowledge of the weapon which they held, for if they had, we certainly could have put an end to the battle in short order.

Back and forth across the large room we fought. No matter how many of the warriors fell, there were dozens more to enter the room and take their place. It seemed as if we were trying to stop a tidal wave with our puny swords.

" 'Tis a sorry fate I saved you for," I called Zynthmai as we fought side by side at one point.

"Ah, but it's better to die with a sword in hand beside a friend than rot away in a foul dungeon cell," he replied with gusto. A quick glance told me he was thoroughly enjoying himself. Never before had I seen a man more cut out for battle. The Meoaithaian blood coursing through his veins had long ago taken its effect. Nor had the propaganda of centuries been lost upon him. He was a fighting man for that is what all Meoaithaians were at heart.

"You fight well, my friend," I said, smiling as he cut down another of the guards.

"Not as well as you, my earthly companion, but well enough to dispatch these poorly trained warriors. In fact, I even hesitate to call them warriors. Old Women would be more accurate," he spat vehemently as one got in past his guard and nicked him slightly.

"Surely their only refuge is in their overwhelming numbers," I agreed, having the same opinion of the Old Guard's warriors.

A new charge separated us for a moment but renewed efforts brought us together again, for in this way we both realized lay our only hope. I had long since lost track of Jaanta and those of his friends who still fought. For all I knew at that moment, they had all been struck down and only we two still stood.

"What of the girl, Robert?" Zynthmai asked as we backed together for mutual protection. "Can you get back to the pirate city through that hole in the wall and save her? Perhaps I can cover your retreat, for surely you must rescue her from that evil pirate's grasp."

"She is safe enough at the moment," I replied, not wanting to waste my breath explaining to him that Marjano was even at this moment in Thu trying to effect our rescue.

"But you do not know of her fate. She is not in the dungeons as was I," he yelled over the din of battle so as to be heard. "She is imprisoned in the *Yata's* chambers for the vile *Abdaithian* has an unspeakable fate in mind for her."

Another charge of the guards pressed about us and it was next to impossible to continue our conversation. I lost sight of Zynthmai in the course of the perilous fighting that ensued. I was backed into a corner on the far side of the chamber and I could feel the blood upon me from a dozen wounds. My strength, though beyond anything with which I had ever fought on Earth, was nonetheless beginning to wane due to the loss of blood.

I caught a glimpse of Zynthmai across the chamber and noticed he was being hard-pressed by dozens of warriors. I could not see another pocket of fighting anywhere in the chamber and believed Jaanta and his friends to all be dead by now, or at least seriously wounded and out of the fight.

Anger mounted within me as I thought of Zynthmai and, no doubt, myself falling beneath the never-ending flood of warriors the Old Guard kept throwing at us. Was there no end to them? I marveled at their number but scoffed, as had Zynthmai, at their poor ability with the sword. Give me a dozen good fighting men of the Old Sod and we would have dispatched the entire treetop city long before now!

These warriors were not too much better than Jaanta's friends, but there sheer weight of numbers might yet be our downfall if Marjano did not arrive soon. At least she would wreak havoc upon the treetop city in avenging my death should I not still be standing when she arrived. This thought, though, seemed to anger me even more. Was I, Robert or Eire, swordsman *extraordinaire* of three continents and now two worlds, to die here beneath such novices? No!

I gathered my legs beneath me and sprang to the side of my friend. As I jumped over the heads of our antagonists they stared up at me in disbelief, as did those encircling Zynthmai when I dropped to his side. They had never before seen such a feat and its effect was successful in aiding my friend from his very dangerous position long enough for me to render him succor.

"I perceived you might need some help, my friend," I called as I landed at his side.

"Someday you will have to teach me that jump of yours," he replied jauntily, "I can see where it might come in handy from time to time."

Together again, we beat back a renewed attack, guards falling everywhere beneath our never-still blades.

"The girl, Robert. You must save her," Zynthmai finally managed between thrusts.

"Don't worry about Marjano," I called back, lunging forward and sinking my blade into a warrior's shoulder and neatly withdrawing it in time to ward off an attack by his neighbor. "She is safe for I rescued her before I saw to your needs. When we returned here, I sent her on to Thu to implore her Palace Guard to come to our rescue."

"They will never arrive in time to help us," he said dubiously. "Thu is a long way away. Even by airship it would take several days."

"But you forget the space windows," I replied between thrusts, beating back an urgent charge by three warriors. "Through the windows anywhere on the planet is merely a step away. They will be here shortly, and we must hold out till then."

But this appeared easier said than accomplished for still more guards poured into the chamber, making fully a hundred that besieged us! And the chamber was already full of the dead and dying, and their gore and blood strewn about the chamber made footing most precarious.

Several more daring thrusts by Zynthmai and myself kept them at bay for a few more moments, but the pressing of their number in the rear forced those in the front ranks in upon us. While this was a difficult movement to stop, it was also the very thing that saved us from being run through, for the warriors in the front ranks were unable to bring their swords to effective use because of the pushing and shoving that they received at their backs.

Sheer numbers propelled us back to the far wall. I dared not be pushed too far for were I to step through one of the space windows at my back, I had no idea where I might emerge or how I might return to the treetop city or Urvia.

I saw Zynthmai fall beside me and all seemed lost as I was heavily pressed upon all sides and my strength was slipping from me fast. Blood was all about me, running down my right arm from the many warriors I had slain until even the hilt of my sword was beginning to slip beneath my tiring grasp. My prospects seemed dim to say the least, but the loss of my friend served to renew my vigor and caused my anger to boil over. A brave warrior he had been. A rare fighting man of skill, hardened by years of combat only to fall beneath the numbers of unskilled hordes that besieged us. In that moment, with the blood of a thousand fighting men coursing through my own veins, I vowed not to fall to these worthless fighters. I called upon all the strength I could muster.

"I shall prevail!" I yelled as loudly as I could, lunging forward and driving the warriors before me back several feet. Though I was tired and using the last ebb of my strength, my blade was a blur before me, dipping in and out, cutting here and there, blocking this thrust and that and finding its way home into the hearts of my enemies. The warriors fell before me and the eyes of those who yet lived were round with fear and fright, yet they could not escape for my blade covered them from the front and to the rear they were pressed by the weight of their fellows.

"I shall prevail!" I yelled out again.

"We shall prevail!" called a feminine voice from across the room. "Hold on. *Yatahn*, we are here!"

Looking in that direction between thrusts of my blade, I spotted Marjano stepping through the space window from Thu. And on her heels flowed a seemingly endless parade of her Palace Guard. And in the lead was a handsome, well-muscled man of great breeding. He wore the same double harness as do all warriors on Ghandor that I had ever seen, but his was magnificently studded with rare jewels and gold tooling. He was perhaps not as tall as I, for I stand well over six and a half feet, but he certainly outweighed me and the breadth of his chest was something to see. He was all muscle and the bronze skin of his smoothly rippling skin shone brightly. His eyes were alert, blonde hair flowing behind him, and in but a twinkling of an eye he quickly took charge of the warrior legion that followed him into the massive chamber. In a matter of a second or two he had correctly sized up his enemies' strength and deployed his legion with sharp commands in a low, base voice that commanded much strength and could be heard across the breadth of the chamber.

This could be none other than Than Tan, *Yata* of the Thuians and Marjano's erstwhile father.

"Come, men," he called, "we have work to do!" His voice, though I am sure he had not used much force, carried above the screams and yells and the clanking of blades. His countenance was stately as he swung into action and a devilish look spread across his face. Here was a man born of the sword, and one born to command.

In a matter of minutes the warriors of the Old Guard were completely surrounded and being cut to ribbons. They didn't have the stomach for the fight any longer, and many threw down their swords, though pockets of holdouts were still found in the great chamber and Than Tan's men quickly made short shrift of them.

It appeared Jaanta's friends were all dead or critically wounded, and as the battle raged about us, I could see one or two rising to their feet to join in the melee. Though bloodied and, no doubt, in poor condition, they wanted in on the final victory. While thus sweeping the chamber with my glance while I had a moment free from interference, I saw Jaanta regain his feet, a hand held to the side of his head and blood seeping from between the fingers. I also saw Marjano jump to his side and help stop the flow of blood, but otherwise, he appeared to be no worse for wear as I had previously feared.

As the fighting died down, I ran to Zynthmai, who by now was propped in a sitting position against one of the Thuian warriors. He had been wounded in several spots, but none seemed serious. Another Thuian warrior was bandaging his wounds.

"Are you all right, my friend?" I asked earnestly.

"As good as a pin cushion has a right to expect to feel," he jokingly replied, referring to an Earthly object he had never seen but of which I had once referred.

"I am relieved to find you alive, and in such good spirits. I had thought you done for when you fell beneath that torrent of unskilled swords."

"I was only stunned. I believe the flat of a blade struck me across the head. But once I went down, I could not regain my feet so thickly were they pressed about you. I am sorry I could not be of more help to you."

"If ever I must fight again," I replied honestly, "it is my hope that you will be at my side."

"And you beside me," he replied quietly, a bond of friendship and respect building between us as only it can between two men who have fought and nearly died together. Before I could say more, a voice spoke at my shoulder.

"You must be Robert," the deep, base voice said. Turning I saw the leader of the Thu standing beside me. He was splattered with blood, though none of his own, and that devilish smile still played at the corners of his full mouth. He stood straight and tall and through it all had not even worked up a sweat. His breath was even and controlled, as compared to my gulping large lungfuls of air.

"And you would be none other than Than Tan, mighty *Yata* of Thu, who themselves are mighty warriors. My extreme appreciation for your help this day for surely it was needed." I was shaking his hand, Earth-fashion, as I spoke to him.

"I had always thought the Thu were truly the greatest with the sword anywhere upon Ghandor before today," he replied seriously, "but you are a swordsman of which I have never seen an equal. When you fight you are like a blur to the eyes. One cannot follow the swift movements of your wrist and blade. The two are as one. I would like you to teach me the moves with which you felled so many this day." His arm was circling the chamber, indicating the scores of warriors that lay dead or wounded about the large room.

"Gladly, great *Yata*," I replied, "Anything you can ask of me will I surely do. For had you not arrived, the battle would have been lost."

"Perhaps," he replied skeptically, "but you dispatched far more before we arrived than any one man has ever before done. I doubt if these would have fought longer against such ferocity as that which you displayed. Come, Marjano awaits us."

"Gladly, Than Tan, but first there is something more I must do here."

Leaping from the room, with Than Tan and Jaanta on my heels, I quickly made my way to the Old Man's apartments. All through the corridors warriors lay slain and the citizens of the treetop city whom I had before thought so unemotional and lethargic, were jubilant. They were free at last!

As we arrived at the Old Man's apartments, we found him and the rest of the Old Guard also slain. The room was a shambles. There seemed no doubt the Cluvians had wreaked their vengeance upon the original *mantai* despite their being the Old Guard's descendants.

Somehow I felt the Old Man was finally at peace with himself, irrespective of his manner of death. He had lived too long and seen too much. He had been partly responsible for more deaths than, perhaps, any other man had ever before seen. He had lived with that tragedy every day of his thousands of years of life and now it was finally over.

"So this is how it all ends," Jaanta breathed beside me. "It is a shame my fallen comrades could not have seen this glorious thing. The Old Ones had not the faith to trust the younger generations with the secret of their power and thus it ends, here, for them."

"What is this all about?" Than Tan inquired softly of me, as I turned to go, leaving Jaanta there in the middle of the apartment to stare at the remains of those who had held he and his friends imprisoned for so many long years.

"I will tell you later, for it is a long story and I am much too tired to begin it now," I replied quietly. "Come, didn't you say Marjano awaited?"

"I surely did, Robert of Eire. Let us go seek out the fair maiden," he added with a wink.

CHAPTER TWENTY-THREE

≈≈≈≈≈≈≈≈≈

It is now more than a month since the battle in the treetop city of Clu that I sit upon the grassy slopes of my native Eire, writing down in this journal all that overtook me upon Ghandor.

When the Old Guard of the tree dwellers were killed, the last bastion of resistance ended and Jaanta and his friends took over. They offered a great banquet that night in our honor with Than Tan and his Palace Guard as the proferred guests. It was a splendid affair with Marjano the life of the celebration. Her wit and charm swept the Cluvians off their feet, and they gave her the title of First Lady of the city. Much to my surprise Jaanta and his people elected me their *Yata*, for it had been my plan and unequaled fighting ability that saved them from their imprisonment. But I turned down the signal honor, claiming that Jaanta deserved the post more than I for he was of their blood and well schooled in the Cluvian knowledge of the ancients.

"I will indeed act for my people in your absence," he called to me as we readied ourselves for the passage through the space window to Thu. "But you are the *Yata* of Clu and whenever you return, you may claim your rightful throne. Until then, my friend, go with the wind and unsheath your sword only in the defense of yourself or others."

So I had risen to become the ruler of two distinctly different races upon a world as strange and beautiful as it is dangerous. When we stepped through to the royal palace of Thu in Urvia, it was to the great relief of the *Yata*'s wife and household that he was back safe among his people. The remainder of the Palace Guard and the legions of the Thuian army had been summoned by Dortonja, Than Tan's beautiful wife, should the *Yata* need them, though none knew how to go to his aid since to the great consternation of his household servants he had seemed to vanish with his warriors and daughter into midair.

I spent a glorious week among the Thuians. A happy, jovial race of bronze-skinned, yellow-haired people. They paid me the greatest of courtesies and I was welcome in all the royal houses of their kingdom.

And such a kingdom. It far surpassed anything in outward appearance that I had yet seen upon Ghandor. Unlike the stone city of the Meoaithaians, Urvia was a sprawling metropolis of towering spires, multistoried buildings, and numerous single dwellings. While the jewels and gold of the Meoaithaian city and that of the treetop city was noticeably missing in Urvia, it was spotlessly clean, with paved roads, sidewalks, and business districts that seemed to be the centers of teeming masses of Thuians at all hours of the day and night. Perhaps the most imposing sight in the entire city were the numerous walkways high among the buildings that connected living and working centers throughout the city.

The city was, for the most part, colored a bright chartreuse with some mixtures of other shades of green noticeable among some of the lesser buildings. Nestled among the northern jungle lands, the city blended into the background majestically, and from the air, I was told, was not immediately discernible. It was a far cry from the cities of my homeland— dirty, sprawling in no apparent pattern, and a sore thumb sticking out in the surrounding countryside.

Marjano and I spent much time together, and she was eager to set the date of our union, but I kept begging off. Finally one evening she asked me why I was so hesitant about the event.

"Is it because you don't truly love me, after all, *Yatahn*?"

"No, no, nothing like that, Marjano. For you are my *Maitahn* and shall always be so!"

"Then why, Robert of Eire, do you postpone our union? Do you not wish to be united with me, even though you love me?"

"Because I am Robert of Eire. Because I must return to the land of my birth. I must learn the outcome of the battle that was to be fought on the morrow of the day I stepped upon your planet. Surely there is something I can do for my people. I should have returned long before now, but I have not been able to tear myself away from you."

"Must you go?" she asked, though knowing full well the

answer, for once I had explained to her the circumstances surrounding the fight my countrymen waged and its purpose, she knew I could do no less.

"Yes, I must, my princess. But as soon as I have accomplished the thing, I shall return and then we will be united with all the pageantry that a princess of Thu deserves."

That was over a month ago. Jaanta had located the space window to Earth where it originated in the meadow of *Ghorai.* And it was with great difficulty that I made the decision to return. I was not happy about leaving my friends, but it was Marjano I thought about the most as I made preparations to leave.

Nor have I seen my love, Marjano since. For after discovering the carnage and upheaval the tyrant Cromwell wrought upon my people, I was loath to return at once. I sought to reconcile the Clans that had once vowed to stand behind me at Drogheda, but they were now scattered in foreign lands, exiled and now in the service of various Continental armies. Nor would they rally to my call, for they thought me a traitor to the Old Sod. For why else had I disappeared on the eve of battle? Why had I not lived up to my word to lead the thirty thousand that were ready to stand at my back?

My own family disowned me when word came to them that I yet lived. For in death they thought me a hero, having helped to combine the forces of the clans that had been divided after the Ulster Rebellion. Though our lads had been defeated, I had still been considered a hero until they found I was alive. Now, realizing I was alive, they felt I had turned tail and ran on the eve of Cromwell's landing. To my family and the Clans I was a traitor. I was unworthy to bear the name Dowdall. My name was stricken from all the family's records, and I was forbidden asylum in any of the settlements of Eire.

When my efforts failed to right the terrible wrong that had been done me, I gave up and returned to the grassy slopes outside Drogheda. I couldn't blame them. Who could believe I had spent the past year on a foreign planet, fighting for the cause of an alien princess? I couldn't blame them. So it was that I had retraced my steps to Drogheda, taking in a last long, look at my island home because I was going back to Ghandor, never to return again. I was returning to where the most beautiful girl on two worlds awaited me with open arms.

But the space window had disappeared! And I could not get back!

And so it is that night after night I wander the lonely hills and sloping fields, looking for a triangular, swirling mist to show me the way back to Marjano's side. But for the past forty-three consecutive nights I have wandered the hills in vain. And for forty-four consecutive days I have sat in the hills overlooking Drogheda, or what is now left of it, even a year after Cromwell sacked it.

I relive each day that terrible massacre the beast Cromwell wrought upon my people. His success was due, at least in part, to the strange circumstance that propelled me millions of miles away on the very eve of the battle. What more terrible fate could a person suffer than to be but a step from his love, though millions of miles away, while faced with the torture of knowing he had, even though unwillingly, allowed the massacre of more than four thousand of his fellow countrymen—men, women and children. It is a fate I can hardly stand to bear.

But I write this down upon these pages that some future generation might more fairly judge me. Whether I will ever find my way back to Ghandor, I cannot say, for the space window has disappeared since my return and whether it should stabilize again, I know not.

Perhaps Jaanta and the Cluvians dismantled them all thinking I had already returned to Thu. Perhaps the elemental structure of the window cannot last forever when projected through space as was this one. Perhaps the window is still there, trying to reestablish itself, having disappeared due to the movement of the two planets through their orbits. With the window wrapped around the sun, perhaps it has appeared and disappeared many times over the past several thousand years. Whatever the reason, the window is gone and I cannot relocate it.

Jaanta had been very fearful of this happening and had tried to dissuade me from returning through the window three months ago.

"I fear for you, Robert of Eire," he had said upon that occasion. "For though you be the *Yatahano* of the Bomunga and *Yata* of the Clu and surely the bravest man upon two worlds and definitely the meanest with a sword, the elemental structure between planets is totally outside my knowledge and that of all the Cluvian survivors and I know not of the possible dangers that may befall you."

"Fear not, my friend," I replied, "my fate be in the hands of the saints and ancient *Sochrea* of the Old Sod. I shall return as soon as I can look to my countrymen and make sure of the outcome of their battle with the hated English." I looked at my princess and saw her trying to mask her concern. "And, my friend, I shall return for there is nothing on Earth that could sway me from returning to Ghandor and my princess, the beautiful Marjano." She squeezed my arm to her breast and snuggled even closer to me.

"I know not of this Cromwell or the English of whom you speak," interjected Zynthmai, "but wherever you go I choose to follow for your life is a charmed one and full of wonderous adventure. 'Till I met you I was a lowly servant, feared by some, hated by most. But now I am full of life and have realized my undying need for battle. I shall join you upon your return to your world for I desire to once again stand at your side with arms. For surely the enemies of Robert of Eire are the enemies of Zynthmai, too."

I was nearly overwhelmed by his intense desire to follow me into what must appear to him as the strangest and perhaps the most fearful of adventures—that of traveling through space to another world. But before I could answer, another voice added his request, "And I, Than Tan, will join you, too, Robert of Eire. For where you go the needs of justice must be strong, and I desire to add my sword to your cause."

"Thank you for your offers, my friends," I replied somewhat reluctantly, for I would dearly have loved to have them accompany me. "But while I can think of none other than the two of you that I would desire to have at my side in any battle, I must go alone for I need you both to remain here in Thu." I paused and looked at them fondly. I had fought through much with Zynthmai at my side and in the past few days had developed a strong friendship with Than Tan, a man among men.

"I think your two blades and mine might be all that's needed to hammer Cromwell back into the sea, but as important as that would be, I now realize there are endeavors even more important to me, Than Tan," I said, placing my right hand upon his brawny shoulder, "you must stay and prepare Thu for the coming war with the Meoaithaians. I plan to return soon to be united with your beautiful daughter and I want to find Thu and Urvia free from Meoaithaian rule. Only you can weld the northern kingdoms together for that battle with what we have learned of Euoaithia's plans."

I could read in his eyes that he knew what I said was true, and he reluctantly acknowledged the fact.

"And for you, my friend," I added, turning and placing my other hand upon Zynthmai's shoulder, "you can do me the greatest of service by looking after Marjano in my absence for she is more important to me than life itself. I cannot bear to think of the princess in danger while I'm off to my homeland."

Zynthmai looked deep into my eyes, and we both knew he would die before allowing any harm to come to Marjano.

The princess placed her hand upon Zynthmai's other shoulder showing her acceptance of his protection. Thus we four stood with hands upon each others shoulders in the Ghandorian custom of swearing an honor pledge. The closest Earthly practice I can think of that might explain this deeply moving Ghandorian practice would be the Blood Oath of the Berbers of northern Africa.

Jaanta interrupted our Meathi, as it is called in Ghandorian, and the moving moment was past. "But a man should not enter the house of his enemies alone. Here am I, let me join you."

"And thank you, too, my Cluvian friend," I replied, "but you have a city to rebuild and a people to lead. Besides, I need you here to watch the space window so I can return."

We talked on, but finally I made ready to leave. Marjano clung to me fiercely for a time then pulled away.

"Do what you must, my *Yatahn*. I shall be here awaiting your return. I will not move from the spot from which you depart until once again you set foot on Ghandorian soil," she said fervently.

Before I could comment, Jaanta interrupted us, "Robert, I still fear the window to another planet. Who is to say what might happen as the planets speed through space. Perhaps the window can move or shift. Or even disappear. I wish you would change your mind."

"Thank you, my friend, for your interest and concern. But the saints will see me through, and I shall return to my princess' side if I have to fight my way through hell itself."

Now as I stand upon the grassy slopes overlooking

Drogheda, I sadly recalled Jaanta's warning. Whatever the reason of the disappearance of the window, I cannot say, but that I remain here day after day, contemplating my fate and wandering the hills at night looking for the strange swirling mist, have no doubt! For it is my burning desire to return to Ghandor, my Princess Marjano and my many friends. Should I be lucky enough to pass through the space window back to Ghandor, I will never again leave her side, of that you can be sure.

Lin Carter's bestselling series!

☐ **UNDER THE GREEN STAR.** A marvel adventure in the grand tradition of Burroughs and Merritt. Book I.
(#UY1185—$1.25)

☐ **WHEN THE GREEN STAR CALLS.** Beyond Mars shines the beacon of exotic adventure. Book II. (#UY1267—$1.25)

☐ **BY THE LIGHT OF THE GREEN STAR.** Lost amid the giant trees, nothing daunted his search for his princess and her crown. Book III. (#UY1268—$1.25)

☐ **AS THE GREEN STAR RISES.** Adrift on the uncharted sea of a nameless world, hope still burned bright. Book IV.
(#UY1156—$1.25)

☐ **IN THE GREEN STAR'S GLOW.** The grand climax of an adventure amid monsters and marvels of a far-off world. Book V. (#UY1216—$1.25)

DAW BOOKS are represented by the publishers of Signet and Mentor Books, THE NEW AMERICAN LIBRARY, INC.

THE NEW AMERICAN LIBRARY, INC.,
P.O. Box 999, Bergenfield, New Jersey 07621

Please send me the DAW BOOKS I have checked above. I am enclosing
$_____(check or money order—no currency or C.O.D.'s).
Please include the list price plus 35¢ a copy to cover mailing costs.

Name_____

Address_____

City_____State_____Zip Code_____
Please allow at least 4 weeks for delivery

ALAN BURT AKERS

Six terrific novels compose the second great series of adventure of Dray Prescot: The Havilfar Cycle.

☐ **MANHOUNDS OF ANTARES.** Dray Prescot on the unknown continent of Havilfar seeks the secret of the airboats. Book VI. (#UY1124—$1.25)

☐ **ARENA OF ANTARES.** Prescot confronts strange beasts and fiercer men on that enemy continent. Book VII. (#UY1145—$1.25)

☐ **FLIERS OF ANTARES.** In the very heart of his enemies, Prescot roots out the secrets of flying. Book VIII. (#UY1165—$1.25)

☐ **BLADESMAN OF ANTARES.** King or slave? Savior or betrayer? Prescot confronts his choices. Book IX. (#UY1188—$1.25)

☐ **AVENGER OF ANTARES.** Prescot must fight for his enemies in order to save his friends! Book X. (#UY1208—$1.25)

☐ **ARMADA OF ANTARES.** All the force of two continents mass for the final showdown with Havilfar's ambitious queen. Book XI. (#UY1227—$1.25)

DAW BOOKS are represented by the publishers of Signet and Mentor Books, THE NEW AMERICAN LIBRARY, INC.